What Happened to Billy Shears?

Steve Goddard is a public relations consultant, working mainly on exhibitions and films. He has been a sub-editor on the sports pages of the *Liverpool Daily Post* and *Liverpool Echo*, and is currently co-editor of www.shipoffools.com, the theological comedy magazine and online community. His first novel, *Rattles and Rosettes*, was a work of social history charting the lives and loves of two young football fans in 1914 and 2010.

Whatever Happened to *Billy Shears?*

STEVE GODDARD

Marylebone House

First published in Great Britain in 2017

Marylebone House
36 Causton Street
London SW1P 4ST
www.marylebonehousebooks.co.uk

British Library Cataloguing-in-Publication Data
A catalogue record for this book is available from the British Library

ISBN 978–1–910674–42–0
eBook ISBN 978–1–910674–43–7

Typeset by Lapiz Digital Services, India
Manufacture managed by Jellyfish
First printed in Great Britain by CPI
Subsequently digitally printed in Great Britain

eBook by Lapiz Digital Services, India

Produced on paper from sustainable forests

For Allison

Prelude

James Winston has never needed a newspaper report to bring him up to date on the potholes of Blackburn. He has been in and out of most of them, with bruises for proof. Friends and family badger him to swap pedals for petrol but they'll never understand. He enjoys cycling from one client's house to the next, tool case strapped firmly behind the saddle. It's a hard push up the hills these days but it keeps him fit. What's more, he has become a bit of a local institution. People wave at him from street corners and the tops of buses. He moved here in 1996, some twenty years ago, and carried on doing what he loves most: tuning pianos.

As a child he watched and listened with fascination as two men in succession, both blind, went to work on his family's out-of-tune Bechstein. With a child's logic he presumed all blind people were born to be tuners and that he would have to lose his sight to become one himself. In fact, only three fellow students at the London College of Furniture were sight impaired. Tuning, he tells friends, is like having an argument with a child that won't behave. It isn't necessarily about listening to the pitch of the note itself but to the beats, the interference or distortion when two strings of different intervals are struck together. For James Winston, one hour spent fixing a piano stops the mind from wandering where it will but shouldn't go, towards the darker side of the soul.

On nights like this, however, when sudden heavy showers make roads greasy and treacherous, he wonders how long he can keep going. He is returning home much later than normal, after receiving an urgent request from a client in the village of Brockhall. She needed her 1929 Broadwood baby grand tuned to concert pitch in time for a soirée tomorrow. A former opera singer, she is inclined to hum with vibrato as he tunes. While the habit is disconcerting she does at least have a fine piano to work on. These new digital affairs offer an inferior sound and, worst of all, never go out of tune.

1

James's friends have been of little help, suggesting he retrain as a repairer of these ghastly instruments (so called). He scoffs at the idea. He is just one year from pensionable age and in any case, if he had wanted to be an electrician he would have become an electrician. Plenty of people are handy at mending a fuse or two. No, the skill is in the ear: the ability to hear that underwater, wiggly wavering sound. And that wavering is what you learn to count.

He pushes gamely up another steep hill. He is not far from home. A Tautliner lorry throws up spray that soaks him to the skin. He swears with passion but recovers his composure in time to remember two potholes ahead. He looks behind and pulls out wider to avoid them. A cream-and-green sports car, a classic by the looks of it, rushes past, the turbulence almost brushing him into the gutter. It is surely travelling too fast to respond to any change in the lights at the crossroads ahead. He glances through the rear window of the car. He cannot make out much in the gloom but the passengers are gesticulating to the driver. One of them leans forward. The traffic lights change to amber, then red. The car slews to the left but keeps on going, straight through the lights. A truck is approaching the junction on the green light. Horn blaring, it cannot avoid the car. Tyres squeal, followed by the sickening thud of colliding metal. Windscreen glass bursts and shatters over the road. The sports car flips on to its side, screeching as it slides across the road.

Trembling with shock, James phones 999 on his mobile, then abandons his bike to join a small crowd gathered round the vehicles. A woman, probably in her forties, is helped out of the car, blood pouring from her head. She explains that there are two more people in the car, before collapsing on the side of the road. One of the men is trapped in the back of the vehicle. The other is visible, head turned at a sickening angle to his neck. He is not moving.

'Bloody hell, what a mess,' says a man in the crowd.

'Is there anything we can do?' says a woman.

The man shakes his head. 'They'll have to be cut out with the proper gear.'

'The one at the front,' says the woman, 'I've seen his face before, in the papers. He's some bigwig, I think.'

Sirens wailing, the police arrive, swiftly followed by an ambulance and a team of firefighters. They close off the road and a rescue team pull the two men clear. A policeman asks for names and addresses, reminding everyone who saw the accident they have a legal obligation to give an account. James tells him of the argument in the car. The policeman takes his name and address and says he will be contacted in the event of an inquest.

Still shaking, James gets on his bike and slowly heads for home. Seeing those men laid out on the road has reminded him of his own mortality. He pushes his bike up the garden path, removes the clips from his ankles, parks the bike in the garage and enters the house by the back door.

'You've been a while, love.' Mrs Winston is busy knitting a sweater.

'Nasty accident at the crossroads,' he says.

'I thought I heard sirens.' Mrs Winston doesn't look up. 'You know I don't like you being out so late on your bike. You're not as young as you used to be.'

Before she says it, James has mouthed his wife's last sentence but, still trembling, wonders if he should take more notice of her. They've been renting a cottage every summer on the Isle of Wight for years and the owners have put it up for sale. All the grandchildren look forward to holidays there and he's saved just about enough to be able to retire.

Maybe there is a reason why he witnessed the accident. Maybe it's a warning. Maybe he is getting nearer to his own end than he thinks. Maybe it really is time to hang up the tuning fork for good.

Chapter 1

Six months earlier

Forgive me, Father, for I have wind . . . now if I wait a few moments . . . wow . . . look at that. It works . . . I talk to the screen and the words appear just seconds after I've said them . . . although . . . hang on. I said *sinned* . . . I have *sinned* . . . Slow down, Billy . . . you need to articulate . . . clearly. That's better. Bound to be a few teething problems using voice . . . recognition . . . software . . . for the first time. The Read Me notes say the application takes a while getting to know your accent. It's picking up my Surrey infection reasonably well. In*flection*, that is . . . I say Surrey because I can't and never will accept this London Borough of Croydon bollocks. Good, no profanity filter. Croydon is a city in all but name but we're too close to the smoke . . . so close that in the old days we were the horses' first watering hole on the way to a small town on the south coast. Now then, according to the instructions . . . let me see . . . I have to say two words to create another paragraph.

Clever. I said the words new paragraph.

Ha! It's done it again. I'll get the hang soon enough. What a brilliant Christmas present. The truth is I've been far too long getting round to this dictation lark. The family complain about the hollow thud, thud, thud that resounds from my study late at night. They say there's no need to attack a computer keyboard like I do but they don't understand. I learned to type years ago on a manual typewriter, one of those big black Imperial sit-up-and-beg affairs. Just looked one up on Google Images . . . truly monstrous. You had to slap those keys hard, tell 'em who's boss. Old habits and all that. For a nostalgia trip, I downloaded an app for the iPad that recreates the sounds of a typewriter. There's a delicious ding at the end of each line. If I was a few years younger I'd say it was awesome.

I never learned to type properly, mind, the way women were

4

taught in the 1960s. If you were a young girl, with one of those foot-high beehives, your destination was the typing pool. I can see those women now, sitting in rows, all Mary Whitehouse specs and black headphones, cigarettes dangling from the corner of their mouths, gazing into the distance, correct fingers instinctively hitting the right keys. You'd never catch a lad typing at a desk back then. I was too embarrassed to tell my friends I even owned that old Imperial. It was like a bloke pushing a pram round the park, totally *infra dig*. Now we're all at it.

Seems to me the human male has been demolished and reconstructed, not just through social and political pressure. Women consume contraceptives containing sky-high amounts of synthetic female sex hormones. When they relieve themselves, all that oestrogen gets recycled into the water supply for men to imbibe. Fertilizers and insecticides are full of the stuff, too. We're not just discovering our feminine side, soon we'll *be* women. Our sperm counts are down as well. Come to think of it, that would have been a positive advantage all those years ago . . . which reminds me.

Forgive me, Father, for I have sinned . . . you are reading my first-ever confession at sixty-three years of age. You might well argue that an iMac with a 3.06 Intel Core i3 processor is a piss-poor substitute for a saintly man behind a glass visor. It suits me, though.

With all this in mind I ought to lock the study door . . . just a minute . . . there . . . I have to talk quietly. If the family hears me conversing with a screen they'll regard it as the next logical step in my burgeoning relationship with this computer. Last Valentine's Day I received an e-card signed 'Your loving Mac xxx'. I found out who sent it soon enough. Beth, my daughter, was stifling giggles in the corner of the room. Emms . . . that's what everyone calls my wife, Emma . . . reckons it's only a question of time before all computers are equipped with a discreet orifice alongside the USB ports. She may be right. I have to admit I miss the old iMac, the one with an adjustable screen on a pivotal arm . . . motherboard, CD drive, printed circuits and whatever else housed inside a dome-like case that curved seductively, like the top of Emms's backside.

This isn't sounding very much like a confession. The date is 25 December 2015. It's 2.45 a.m. and I can't sleep, not because of the imminent arrival of a man in red but because of a heady cocktail of alcohol, euphoria and guilt.

A few hours ago, I turned up scuttered for Carols at Candlelight. I wasn't the only one, of course. Nothing like getting Christmas off to a traditional start – tumbling into church, fresh from the Prince Albert, shouting, laughing, stifling giggles, singing 'O come, let us adore him' before running out and heaving up on top of Edmund Tinsley, born 9 October 1878 died 8 December 1937, sorely missed. Lots of people do it and, by and large, it's pretty harmless. However, there was a subtle difference tonight. I was leading the service.

Believe me, you have to have your wits about you in that state. Slurring or rushing your way through the liturgy is a dead giveaway, so it's vital to take your time. However … deliberately … slowing … things … down is even worse – like going fifteen miles per hour behind the wheel of a car when you've had too many at the pub. Exactly what the cops are looking for. However, and without wishing to sound too much like Basil Fawlty, I think I got away with it.

The truth is, I was in a buoyant mood first thing this morning and had every reason to be. The iconic events of Christmas 1914, when an unofficial truce was declared between British and German soldiers in the trenches, were commemorated with great emotion last year, particularly the carol singing and football match in no man's land. I gave a talk on BBC national radio that was well received. Because of that I was invited to give a speech today, at a Christmas Eve lunch reception at Wembley Stadium. Some big names in the worlds of sport and politics were there, so I spent several days in preparation.

Being honest, and this *is* a confession after all, most people have never heard of me. In my time I've been a cub reporter on a local paper, a minor radio sports commentator, a part-time priest and chaplain and, latterly, a media consultant; as Beth has remarked more than once, a jerk of all trades. To use a football analogy, I've spent my life warming the bench. Every now and then I've stripped off, run up and down the touchline, before being told to sit back on the bench again. Or think of Troy McClure from the Simpsons. Forget his jutting chin and rugged good looks and you've got me, William Shearwater. I'll bet there's a compilation of McClure's greatest moments on YouTube . . . yep, thought so . . . here you go:

'You may remember me from such videos as *Mummy, What's Wrong With That Man's Face?*, *Smoke Yourself Thin*, *Here Comes the Metric System* and *Dig Your Own Grave and Save*.'

Similarly, you won't remember me updating the score from Crawley Town's Broadfield Stadium on BBC Radio Sussex or doing *Pause for Thought* at some ungodly hour on Radio 2. I'm Mr Reliable, a safe pair of hands. As a unit, Emms and I even pre-date the coming to power of Mrs Thatcher. In a world of busted vows and broken homes, we're a safe pair of glands. But the truth is, I'm too dull to be dangerous, too polite to be provocative, too careful to be compelling.

So how did Troy McClure find himself addressing such august company at the home of English football? Well, if nothing more, the commemorations of *that* Christmas in no man's land nudged a national conscience. Inflated leather and lung-bursting song on a battered, bruised turnip field in Flanders: it's an incredible story. But I've gone back even further than that. For years I've researched the history of William McGregor and gang, founding fathers of the Football League in 1888. I've written articles and the odd book or two on the subject, all to a thunderous lack of applause – until now. It seems my time might have come. A high-up at the FA read one of my articles and likes how I link the two worlds of professional football and local community. Would I be interested in giving a seven-minute address on my views of the game, past and present?

So at lunchtime today I headed for the Bobby Moore Room – dubbed by Wembley its 'grandest space' and 'the jewel in the crown' – to be met by a chatty young intern with sparkling bluey-grey eyes, a series of ever-lengthening necklaces and a discreet nose stud. As we walked towards the room she asked me if I had ever been to the venue before. Many times, I told her. In fact, the first time I saw 'Sir' Bobby play (his lack of a knighthood is a national disgrace), was against Uruguay in the 1966 World Cup.

'That was well before my time,' she said. 'In fact my *parents* hadn't even been born then.' The insensitivity of youth. I was tempted to tell her she looked a lot like Lucy Pitcher who moved into our road that same week in 1966 but she would have had no idea who Lucy was. Lucy is my memory. My indulgence. My problem.

I have to say, the Bobby Moore Room does justice to the eponymous legend. It is immaculate, unruffled and as spotless as the great man's hands when, after giving them a discreet wipe on the velvet tablecloth, he received the Jules Rimet Trophy from Her Majesty. Through one window you can gaze over the deep green Wembley pitch and dream impossible dreams; through the other, look out over the grey, urban sprawl of north London and embrace dismal reality. Today, more than two hundred lords, ladies, MPs, journalists, former players and foreign emissaries tucked into a festive four-course meal in a room on two levels. The lower and mezzanine floors are connected by sweeping staircases – elegance redolent of the man himself. Which is why eyebrows moved northwards as I stood up to speak.

'My lords, ladies and gentlemen, fellow fans, it's an honour to be in a room that celebrates a legend of the game, but let's be honest about Bobby Moore. He was slow, heavy-legged, not a good runner, couldn't head a ball or make a tackle.'

I'd gone in hard. Nobby Stiles would be proud.

'They're not my words but those of a former teammate, Eddie Lewis and his manager at West Ham, Ron Greenwood.' I paused and silently counted to five. 'Bobby Moore was the best defender I ever played against and a gentleman of honour. Not my words, either, but those of arguably the best player of all time, one Edson Arantes do Nascimento, better known as Pelé. So ... how could people have such conflicting views of the same player?'

I did a one-eighty-degree sweep. Four hundred attentive eyes gazed back.

'Of course, what I haven't told you is when the comments were made. Moore was a raw junior when Lewis and Greenwood first saw him at Upton Park; Pelé made his famous remark when Moore was captain of England, at the peak of his career. So how did a blond, curly-haired kid from Barking with limited natural ability make it to the very top of the game? The answer is simple. He listened to everybody around who knew how to play the game. For hours every day he listened and learned, listened and learned, soaking it all up like a sponge that never gets saturated. Years later, the kid who was slow, couldn't head a ball or make a tackle came up with arguably the finest interception ever, against Jairzinho at the World Cup in 1970. The last time I looked, that tackle had been watched 197,000 times on YouTube.'

Yes, Moore was good. I was good, too. In fact, I was *so* good I wanted to listen to myself. And take notes.

'All of us here today could learn a lot from Robert Frederick Chelsea Moore. Football, the sport we love, the game that engages more people round the planet than any other – male and female, rich and poor, black and white – needs to take a serious rain check. It has to do a Bobby Moore and start listening again: to the housebound pensioner who can't afford to watch his local club live on TV because the monthly fee busts his budget; to the divorced father who, every fortnight, took his two young sons to a game but had to stop when it cost almost £200 for the privilege; to the thousands who have turned their backs on international football because of the corruption rife throughout the game; to the sound of a pin dropping here at Wembley, when England are playing a World Cup qualifier. Something's wrong and we have to fix it. Fast.'

Now I was Alan Ball on the wing, running himself daft.

'Bobby Moore wasn't the quickest, or the most skilful, but he developed something few could match – an immaculate sense of timing, and not just in the tackle. Take that free kick for England's first goal in the World Cup Final, for example. He waited just long enough before delivering a perfect ball for an unmarked Geoff Hurst to nod home.'

I paused again. We were deep in extra time. I took a long pass out of defence and hit the ball hard. Out of the ground would do.

'Ladies and gentlemen, fellow fans, the commemorations of that football match in no man's land in 1914 remind us that the game has the power to unite the bitterest of enemies. Can we take hold of that spirit and harness it for the common good?

That is the challenge before us. If we are to recover the soul of football, we need to be honest, transparent and beyond reproach. A window of opportunity has opened which may not stay open for long. As Bobby Moore learned, timing is everything. Let's make a goal-saving tackle on corruption and exploitation. We *can* recover the soul of this great game. Let's do it, for the sake of our children and their children's children.'

I sat down to, though I say it myself, thunderous applause. 'Nice, one, Shears.' It would be name-dropping to say who leaned over and made that comment from the side of his mouth. The speech seemed to cut it with the media, too. I did a bunch of interviews for radio and TV, pressed some influential flesh, got pleasantly mashed on a smooth French brandy and, on the way home in the taxi, nodded off in a warm stupor.

'Well?' said Emms, when I ambled through the front door. She was busy wrapping presents on the kitchen table.

'Couldn't have gone better,' I said, closing the front door behind me. 'After I'd finished speaking several people said how—'

'That's great. Perhaps you can help me put name tags on these presents.' Emms is always the first to prick whatever bubble I have inflated.

With the last present tucked under the tree, I lay down on the sofa to try and sober up before Carols by Candlelight. I dozed off and now my mind was wandering: back to the late 1960s and those swirly art deco shops with black and gold interiors and subdued lighting, pumping out loud psychedelic sounds and strange-smelling incense; giggling girls trying on feather boas, wild plum-coloured hats with huge brims and floaty garments for drifting around in at home or looking groovy at the latest happening. And Lucy, cute in a red woollen mini-skirt, so short it must have taken only one ball of wool to knit.

Forgive me, Father, for I have sinned . . .

Chapter 2

Friday 25 December 2015

Before and since I lost Daggert (most people called my husband by his surname) to the little c, it has fallen to me to bring some measure of calm to our grandson David's heart on Christmas Eve. Each year it threatens to burst out of his chest.

'Read him one of those long Christmas classics,' said Helen, last night. 'They always sent me off to sleep.' I *think* there was an ironic smile on my daughter's face. So before bedtime I poured the usual glass of sherry for Santa. David put it by the fireplace, along with a carrot or two for the reindeer. My son-in-law Matt, the king of fads, has a nature and environment thing going on at the moment. Next to the carrots, he left three extra-large Tesco shopping bags, reusable ones, with a note saying Poop Here – 'just in case the reindeer are caught short'. The notion that Rudolph might choose to empty his sizeable bowels chez Daggert sent young David into emotional orbit. Sleep was impossible. When he wasn't bouncing around on the bed, I tried to sit him on my knee and read a story or two. No matter what Helen says, to my mind it's never too early to start them on a classic. I tried *Papa Panov's Special Christmas* by Tolstoy and *The Burglar's Christmas* by Willa Cather. He wriggled, squirmed and changed the subject by asking me why I had a plaster on my arm.

'I gave some of my blood to the hospital this morning,' I explained.

He looked alarmed. 'Did it hurt?'

I shook my head. 'And if it saves someone's life, it's well worth it.'

'Mark says that if you have a blood test and fail, you die.'

I laughed. 'You can't fail a blood test.'

'Did Grandagg die because he ran out of blood?' Grandagg was his own name for Daggert.

'Not exactly. Grandagg ran out of good blood.'

11

'I still miss him.'

'So do I.'

'Mark has four grandads.'

'That's very fortunate.' I explained that his friend Mark has four grandads because both Mark's grandparents have divorced and remarried. Only two were 'real' grandads and that quality was more important than quantity. Too much explanation: his eyes glazed over.

'I've only got one now and I hardly ever see him,' he said.

'He lives a long way away,' I explained. 'It doesn't mean he loves you any less.'

It was my turn to change the subject. 'Pick any book from the bookcase with my name written on the inside cover.'

'What, Nan?'

'No, look for Sophie. I had some of these books when I was your age. I wasn't a nan then.'

In a matter of moments, the contents of an entire shelf lay strewn across the floor.

'Nah . . . nah . . . boring . . . nah . . . this one looks good.' In David's hands was *Mr Pink-Whistle Interferes* by Enid Blyton, priced 2s 6d. I inherited the book from my own grandmother.

'No, no. You won't like that one,' I said. The cover illustration features a chubby, middle-aged man in a top hat and red tailcoat. Stubby hands outstretched and eyes open wide (too wide), he is grinning at a little blonde girl sitting up sweetly in bed. She has been playing with her toys but as Mr Pink-Whistle (seriously, Enid, what were you thinking?) approaches, the soldier, sailor and twin teddy bears are running for their lives. Pink-Whistle has form – or so it seems to twenty-first-century eyes.

'He's a paedo,' said David.

'How do you know what a—?'

'Everyone knows what a paedo is.'

'But you're only . . . seven.'

'They warn us at school.'

'Well, I'm glad you're listening, but—'

'What's this?' A handwritten poem, wedged for several years between *Mr Pink-Whistle* and Roald Dahl's *Matilda* (now *that* would be an interesting relationship) had fallen on the floor. Above the poem, 'If Milly Comes for Christmas', was a poor illustration of a West Highland white terrier.

'Oh *that*!' I took the page from David's hand. 'It's a daft little thing I wrote myself. You won't be interested.'

'Read it to me. I like dogs . . .'

'I don't think—'

'. . . and it's about Christmas. Read it . . . please?' For the first time, my young grandson got into bed.

I ought to explain: I love English, so much so that I teach it at a sixth-form college. I am not a writer, however, and definitely not a poet. Oh, I can ramble endlessly about iambic pentameters and heroic couplets, dissonance and doggerel. In fact, thinking about it now, I probably know too much. When it comes to writing, I am so overcritical that I pan whatever I'm going to write before I've put pen to paper. The thought of my own grandson judging something I've written, even a trite little poem, almost terrifies me. But by now he had snuggled right down, pulled the duvet over his head and muffled another 'Please'.

I took a deep breath. 'As it's Christmas . . .'

If Milly comes for Christmas
I won't feel so alone
We'll sniff around the strawberry patch
Dig up that juicy bone
Other dogs, they know it's there
I growl and make them run
This bone is for a special dog
Who's lots and lots of fun

If Milly comes for Christmas
She'll teach me not to bark
At scary shadows in the yard
She doesn't mind the dark
I'll let her doze all afternoon
Upon my snuggly bed
The floor is cold but I don't mind
If I sleep there instead

If Milly comes for Christmas
I'll need no brand new toys
I'll go to bed on Christmas Eve
And never make a noise
When Santa comes a-calling
We'll wag our tails like mad
And tell him how the kids are good
Even if they're bad

She won't be here for Christmas
It happens every year
I wonder what she's doing
And why she can't be here
Milly is my mummy
We've never met, you see
But somewhere, far across the world
I hope she thinks of me

For a few moments there was no movement or noise from beneath the duvet. Then, still muffled: 'Is that it?'

'Yes. I told you it wasn't very good.'

'Does Milly ever come?'

'I don't know.'

'You wrote it. You should know.'

'I don't. That's the point of the poem.'

Another short silence.

'I want Milly to come this Christmas,' said David.

'Not this year, but maybe next.'

'Why did you write it?'

'Oh, well . . . you know how much I like terriers, especially Westies.' I tucked the poem into my pocket. David was still beneath the duvet. Maybe he had exhausted himself, I thought, anticipating the arrival of Santa and those reindeer in need of a comfort break. Either that or the poem had been so dull it had drained the adrenaline from his bloodstream. I took the opportunity to settle him down for the night. 'Well, it's gone eleven o'clock . . .'

'That poem,' blurted David. He was still beneath the duvet. 'It's about you and your real mummy, isn't it?' Out of the mouth of babes ... for a few moments I was entirely thrown.

'What ... what makes you say that?' My attempt to appear casual was defeated by the waver in my voice.

'Mummy told me you were adapted.'

'Adopted. Yes.'

'She said you had a first mummy who couldn't look after you.'

'That's right ... so she asked Great-Gran to do it.'

'Was your first mummy called Milly?'

'I doubt it.'

At this point David threw back the duvet and sat up. 'So you don't even know her *name*!'

'No.'

'Why couldn't she look after you?'

'I don't know.'

'What is she like?'

'I have no idea. I was only very small when she gave me to Great-Gran.'

'Did she call you Sophie?'

'I don't know but that's my name now.'

'Does she look like you?'

'I've no idea.'

'You mean ... you could have passed her in the street without knowing?'

I nodded.

'That's weird.' Another short silence. 'I think she must be very pretty.'

'Oh, well, it's nice of you to say that but I've already got your Christmas present.'

'Mark thought you were my mummy.'

'That's very flattering.'

'He said he would.'

'Would what?'

'You know ...'

'Well, I ... how old is your friend?'

'Eleven.'

'*Eleven!*'

'When I told him you were my nan he said you were gilf. What does that mean?'

'No idea,' I lied. (Goodness me, what are these kids watching!?) 'Now I really think it's time you tried to get some sleep.'

'Mark says I was adapted, too. *Was* I?'

'No, he's just winding you up. Older kids do that to younger kids.'

'But if I was only a baby when it all happened, like you were, I wouldn't know, would I?'

'Look.' I pointed to a small ridge in my nose. 'See this? Now, see that?' I touched him in the same spot on his nose. 'It's special to you, your mummy and me. It proves I'm your real nan and that mummy is your real mummy.' It seemed to settle him down. Maybe his friend's comments had worried him for some time. 'The sooner you go to sleep, the sooner Santa can arrive and the reindeer can relieve themselves.' I kissed him and turned off the light.

'If I were you I'd want to know,' he said as I went through the door.

'Know what?'

'Who they were . . . my real mummy and daddy.'

'Goodnight, David.' I closed the door. I was going to tell him my adoptive parents (my father is no longer with us) *had* been my 'real mummy and daddy' but he had taken in enough for one night, especially in a heightened state of excitement. I paused on the landing and thought again of Debbie Harry. She has never considered looking for her natural parents. 'I know who I am,' she said. 'To look for them would be an insult to my adoptive family.' I often wonder which two gene pools crashed together one dark night to create such a beautiful, talented 'accident'.

With David in bed, it was time to wheel out Henry the rocking horse from the garage. Dapple grey with large, doleful eyes, he's an antique but still in full working order. As a child I spent hours perched on his red leather saddle, rocking to and fro, sucking my thumb and stroking his mane, especially when I was upset. I hadn't

16

wanted to part with him, even to Helen, but felt duty bound as it was a family heirloom and David was now old enough to ride him. Next to the horse we left another poem, this one written by my great-grandmother.

Henry's poem
Let me take you for a ride
On a journey whence you came
Over hills and rivers wide
Keep tight hold upon my reins

If the way seems hard to you
Never let your doubts prevail

Make all speed and look for clues
Yonder through the rain and hail

Saddle up and ride again
Ask and I will hear your call
Doors will open at my name
Dare to trust me through it all
Look and you will find, I'm sure
Everything you're searching for

'He's been! Wake up. He's been! He drank the sherry. The carrots are half chewed.' It was 5.30 a.m. and David was already downstairs. 'Smell those bags!'

Matt has still not let on where he got the horse manure.

Chapter 3

Sticks and stones may break my bones . . . but words will never hurt me . . . Testing . . . now then . . . where was I? I can't mention Lucy without talking about her mother. The first time I saw Mrs Pitcher she was barking instructions at removal men. The Pitcher family were moving into our road. It was the summer of 1966. Fast-talking and fast-walking, she believed she was right, about everyone and everything, every time. The Pitchers lived next door but one to us in Leehart Gardens. Their 1950s semi was pretty much identical to ours, though Mrs Pitcher enjoyed pointing out the improvements they were going to make to theirs.

Talking of doing up houses . . . Emms has a big thing about that lanky bloke with the Bradley Wiggins sideburns . . . name escapes me . . . Kevin something . . . Google the Omniscient will reveal all . . . yes, here you go. I'm talking about Kevin McCloud. He presents *Grand Designs*, the TV show where earnest couples splash the cash building a dream home, from what's left of a crumbling castle or water tower or the like. The programme always goes something like this: it's just before Christmas, the money has run out and rain is seeping through tarpaulin sheets where the roof should have been three months ago. The subcontractors have downed tools and the wife has been knocked up (after a McCloud visit, couples become uber-fertile, it seems). Will they deliver the dream or get divorced? Such tension – enough to crack a few panes of top spec, eco-friendly insulating glass.

It's at this point I nudge Emms: 'Here comes the ad break.' During commercials for B&Q and Homebase, Emms tells me not to be so cynical but, sure enough . . . we rejoin the hapless pair, selling (finally) that bungalow they couldn't shift in Folkstone, moments before the bank forecloses on them. Now with all the money they need, the tarpaulin comes off and workers swarm all over the building like ants.

It's early summer. McCloud strolls up the drive, shakes the man's hand and ritualistically kisses both cheeks of the woman (it must be in the contract). He waltzes admiringly round the finished structure, sips a celebratory glass of Chardonnay and tsks when he finds out how far over budget they've gone. Finally, hands in pockets, he saunters towards the camera to do his epilogue that goes something like this: 'Before embarking on their dream these two people read the story so far of this intriguing building, because every house has a narrative: individual, insistent, idiosyncratic. They've listened to the bricks, to the mortar, listened and learned and lovingly plotted the next breathtaking chapters in an ongoing story of style, elegance and craftsmanship. Here is a tale that proves sheer, dogged determination and attention to detail pays off – and how . . .' Walks out of shot to rising theme music.

I mock but McCloud is right. Every house tells a story and every street, for that matter. Take Leehart Gardens in South Croydon, where I grew up. Three hundred yards from a railway station, you could smell the smoke and steam from engines hammering their way from London down to that small town on the south coast. The first two houses built in the close were grand Edwardian affairs: detached, six-bedroomed mini-mansions with absurd turrets and servants' quarters in the eaves. Designed individually by rival architects, they still face each other across the street, an architectural gunfight at the OK Corral. But the end of the Great War signalled a decline in landed opulence. Harder times for the rich meant those orchards were sold off and, between the wars, a series of large but inferior semis constructed, destroying woods that must have offered such delightful fruit in early autumn.

Our house, a small and depressingly sensible post-war semi, was built a little further along the road as it sprawled towards the station. Last in the close, and by all means least, came an unsightly block of early 1960s flats, thrown up while we still lived in the road – all picture windows, shallow balconies and flat roofs. To this day, the road is a real dog's dinner and I love it. Elegant, like a carefully designed new development, it isn't. Eclectic, disjointed and lived in, it certainly is.

Leehart Gardens reminds me of another dog's dinner, Selhurst Park. Crystal Palace's ground has four entirely different stands, built in four time periods, from Archibald Leitch's initial construction, opened in 1924 and looking much the same almost a hundred years later, to the Holmesdale Road two-tiered development, opened in 1995 and replacing the last open terrace. Compare this, if you dare, to Arsenal's ground. The Emirates Stadium, which cost a cool £390 million and opened in 2006, is a jaw-dropping work of art, but therein lies the problem. The essentially primitive game of football was not designed to be played in the hallowed aisles of a cathedral. The sleek lines of new stadia lull us into a stupor. Football belongs to something dishevelled, rambling, incoherent. The 'beautiful game' is about skilful movement and fine passes but it's also about mud, sliding tackles and bellowed profanities. Putting a football team into an identikit, all-seater stadium is like giving a young boy the most expensive keyboard for Christmas and saying: 'It cost a lot of money. Give us a nice tune.' Half an hour later he is having a whale of a time, playing in the cardboard box it came in.

Or, putting it another way: what match was most celebrated at Christmas 2014? One played a whole century ago, in a frozen turnip field, with turned-up helmets for goalposts and a tin can for a ball.

Which reminds me ... I recently joined a Facebook group called *Lost Football Grounds*, a pictorial lament for long-lamented terraces and decrepit stadia wedged between row upon row of tiny, terraced houses ... while I'm thinking about it I might as well look it up ... here you go ... thirteen thousand people have already joined the group with hundreds more applying. Members post fuzzy, black-and-white pictures of their favourite old grounds and recall, with great affection, being splattered by the white shit of an incontinent pigeon at Chesterfield's Saltergate stadium, or getting soaked to the skin by horizontal rain sweeping in from an angry sea at Blackpool's Bloomfield Road.

Funnily enough, I can't seem to find a similar Facebook group emotionally recounting tales of excellent corporate hospitality, comfortable seats and five-course meals at today's modern stadia. These new venues are homogenized, 'non-places' in the urban landscape

– safe, sanitized, soporific. Football has deserted the working classes who, as a tsunami of flat caps, poured out of factories at lunchtime on Saturday bound for their local ground. Now it's for the middle classes in mallified out-of-town sites where football stadia rub shoulders with fancy boutiques, posh restaurants and hotels.

So, having typecast myself as a grumpy old fan harping on about some glorious golden age, let me argue against myself. On Monday 11 July 1966, the Pitcher family arrived in Leehart Gardens. I'd just turned fourteen. Later that day, the opening match of the 1966 World Cup took place between England and Uruguay. Standing on the Wembley terrace cost 7s 6d (37.5p) – a lot of money back then. It wasn't a problem for Godfrey Henderson who, at the time, I considered a good friend. But then, neither of us had yet encountered Lucy Pitcher.

The Hendersons lived in one of those Edwardian minimansions. Godfrey's father was some kind of theatrical impresario in the West End ... I'm racking my brains to recall his first name ... Cecil, that's right. In those days a middle-aged man's first name was privileged information. You certainly never used it ... to do so would be considered impudent. Nowadays, a six-year-old thinks it's perfectly acceptable to call me William, Billy even. I draw the line at Shears.

Anyway, Mr Henderson was a rich, pipe-smoking, bearded leftie. Our other neighbours were less wealthy but politically blue, which created an intriguing tension when general elections came around. Godfrey was sixteen at the time and impressively cool ... apart from his name, which belonged to a bygone age. I only knew of one other Godfrey – legendary England wicket-keeper Godfrey Evans, who had already retired from international cricket by then. Godfrey hated his name, especially when *Dad's Army* hit the BBC and the oldest, dodderiest, leakiest character in the platoon shared his moniker. He insisted on being called Hendo, which was fine at school but didn't work at home. When I called round and asked for Hendo, Mr and Mrs Henderson would blank me.

The thing was, I loved their house. It was so much bigger and grander and unexpected than ours. Mr Henderson travelled the world, watching foreign theatre, music acts, circuses even, with strange-sounding names – anything that might do well in Britain. He brought back foreign food with him, spicy and exotic. It smelled strangely wonderful to a kid brought up on a post-war diet of sausages and fish fingers. I tasted my first curry, hot chicken madras, at the Hendersons' – a rite of passage in more ways than one. Best of all, though, Mr Henderson was a friend of the stars. All the way up two long flights of stairs hung framed, professionally taken photographs of him with famous celebrities – actors, musicians and comedians, mainly. I remember seeing pictures of Shirley Bassey, Morecambe and Wise and Michael Caine to name but a few. It was impressive stuff, especially when my own parents were bog-standard professionals (estate agent and state-registered nurse). On a couple of occasions I arrived at the house to see a smartly dressed young man on the point of leaving.

'You know who that is, don't you?' Mr Henderson said, cheerily waving off whoever it was.

'No.'

'Well, give me six months and you will.'

Godfrey was in trouble regularly for bunking off school early, to hang out with friends at the local technical college. He had a motorbike and played guitar in a garage band with aspirations. On this particular day, though, it wasn't music he was excited about. He stopped me outside the science block and suggested sneaking off to Wembley to see England play Uruguay. We didn't have tickets but he reckoned we might get lucky and grab a couple from a tout. I had never been to an England match. I dashed home early, telling my mother that games had been cancelled. I ransacked my post office savings book. I had just about enough.

We needn't have worried about getting into the ground. At least ten thousand tickets were left unsold. I've often wondered what happened to all those spares because, if you want an original ticket as a souvenir from that entirely forgettable first game of World Cup 1966, sellers are now asking for an astonishing £40 on eBay. According to auctioneers, the longer England's sad record at succeeding World Cup Finals goes on, the higher memorabilia prices will go for anything to do with that glorious tournament.

It makes you think . . . somewhere, someone may have a £400,000 bundle of unused tickets sitting in a cupboard, gathering dust. And value.

What I'm trying to say is: just because the England team was ranked second favourites to Brazil in 1966, the country didn't go into the tournament on a tide of optimistic patriotism. Our football wasn't deemed world-beating and the atmosphere in the ground was hardly electric. In fact, at the end of the game I remember the crowd booing, loudly. I wasn't sure whether it was because Uruguay simply defended for their lives, and gained a creditable 0–0 draw, or because England had failed to score in an international at Wembley for the first time since 1945, more than twenty years before. Being my first England match, I kept the report in the following day's *Daily Telegraph*. The reporter was none too impressed, either: 'The trouble, I am afraid, was that England could not build up moves quickly or accurately enough to outsmart a packed defence. The Uruguayans marked them tightly, tackled them hard and often late, pushed them, obstructed them and threw them out of stride. When one remembers that there are better defences than this lying in wait for Mr Ramsay's men in the later stages of the competition, one's hopes tend to sag.'

The report sounds antiquated, as if HM The Queen herself, who was there to open the tournament, expressed 'one's own frustrations' at the outcome. When I got home my parents gave me a roasting for going AWOL during a school day but I expected that. I knew it would be a long time before the World Cup Finals returned to the home of football.

Interestingly, two members of England's team that night didn't make the final eleven for the World Cup Final itself. One of them was Jimmy Greaves, already a legend before the tournament got under way and tipped to be our match winner, if we reached the final. Injured in the third group game, he was replaced by Geoff Hurst for the quarter-final against Argentina. Hurst kept his place for the last two games, even though Greaves was fit again. The rest is history. Seeing Hurst bag that hat-trick in the final must have made the nippy little Spurs striker think it was all over. By his own admission, it was.

'I danced around the pitch with everyone else,' he said later, 'but even in this moment of triumph and great happiness, deep down I felt my sadness. Throughout my years as a professional footballer I had dreamed of playing in a World Cup Final. I had missed out on the match of a lifetime and it hurt.'

The other player in the team that night who didn't make the team for the final was John Connelly. John *who*? Connelly was one of the World Cup's nearly men, an almost national legend. You might remember him dashing down the wing for Burnley, Manchester United, Blackburn and Bury . . . you might remember him playing twenty times for England, scoring seven goals . . . you might remember him for his highly successful fish and chip shop, Connelly's Plaice, in Brierfield near Burnley. Connelly played at the World Cup Finals. He almost became a household name like Bobby Charlton, Nobby Stiles and Gordon Banks; almost but not quite. John Connelly was the Troy McClure of 1966.

Astonishingly, the only players to receive winners' medals after the tournament were the eleven picked for the final. A long campaign by fans led, eventually, to the entire twenty-two-man squad being honoured by Prime Minister Gordon Brown in 2009 – among them, Greaves and Connelly. Recognition, at last, for Connelly, a player who didn't get the media coverage of Londoner Greaves, probably because he came from the unfashionable, egg-chasing town of St Helens and spent his entire club career in the north-west. Reward for his achievements came just in time. He died in 2012, just three years after receiving a 1966 winners' medal.

I take personal inspiration from John Connelly. I've been waiting in the wings for a long, long time. Like the amiable northerner, I'm not the most fashionable, I grant you but I think I've got something to offer. Mrs Pitcher never thought I would come to much and for years I've been pretty much overlooked . . . but this is my time. Come to think of it, the first time I actually saw her daughter was the day of England's next World Cup match against Mexico. Was it love at first sight? Well, I didn't actually see the whole of Lucy. That delicious moment was still a long way off. No, all I saw on the day we took on Mexico were those legs.

Chapter 4

'So, Mrs Daggert, you think my Shannon is an epileptic moron.'

'Of course not, Mrs Elliott.'

'Well, you put her in with the other morons.'

'No, no . . . you've got the wrong end of the stick. We're in the middle of an activity in my English Literature class. I've divided the students into several groups – Gammas, Deltas, etcetera, etcetera. Shannon is one of six Epsilon-Minus Semi-Morons. The idea is that—'

'So you *do* think she's a moron.'

'No, I—'

'And why is she a Minus? It isn't helping her self-confidence.'

'I'm not suggesting—'

'She wants to be an Alfie.'

'Of course she wants to be an Alpha. Everyone does. That's the whole point of the exercise, to reveal how we treat and envy one another, based on things like social status, possessions and physical appearance. Have you read the book, Mrs Elliott?'

'What book?'

'*Brave New World.*'

'Who's it by?'

'Aldous Huxley.'

'Never heard of him. Did it come out recently?'

'1932.'

'Can't you afford any new books?'

Sophie Daggert tries her level best to stay cool, calm and collected but the person at the other end of the phone is Mrs Elliott, Shannon's mother. 'Shannon's mother' is a phrase used frequently by staff at Woodfield Sixth Form College, with rolled eyes and 'not' and 'again' wrapped around the phrase like verbal bookends. Students do not often call their mothers in the middle of class, to moan about their teachers. But this is Shannon Elliott.

Sophie makes it clear to Mrs Elliott that there is no particular reason why her daughter is with the other Epsilon-Minus Semi-Morons. Whoever drew a black card in class 2B (Epsilons dress in black in Huxley's novel) has ended up in that group. Huxley's cynical vision of a genetically modified caste system begs a discussion of those predetermined differences between us. Like all human beings, she explains, Shannon and her fellow students endlessly compare themselves with one another for looks, money, intelligence, girl-friends, boyfriends, cars, mobile phones. Arbitrarily dividing them into groups of haves and have-nots gets right under their teen-age skin and introduces them to a major theme in the book. She has asked Shannon and the rest of the Epsilons to carry the Alpha group's bags, books and coats. At the same time they must open and close the doors of the classroom for them, bowing submissively. It's what happens in Huxley's novel.

'And this phone call proves the point of the exercise,' says Sophie. 'It's unfair.'

Mrs Elliott rings off abruptly, probably because she hasn't a clue what Sophie is talking about. Sophie puts the incident out of her mind, and asks the class to write down, anonymously, the physical feature they dislike most about themselves – and collects in the results.

'Right . . . six of you think you're too short,' she reports. 'Three, too tall. Two of you would like to do something drastic to your ears. Six more think your backsides let you down, while five others don't like the size of your breasts. Two of you think your hair is too curly, four think it's too straight and three more would like a new set of teeth. Counting up . . . we have thirty-one replies out of thirty-two. Perhaps someone thinks they're perfect.'

The rest of the class look at Gareth Hillier and groan. He says nothing and smiles: a smug smile revealing a set of shining Alpha teeth.

'Imagine!' says Sophie, brandishing a copy of Huxley's classic. 'Imagine not one, not ten but ninety-six identical Gareths, out of the same test tube without any physical flaws.' She opens the first page of the book and reads. 'A bokanovskified egg will bud, will proliferate, will divide, from eight to ninety-six buds, and every bud will grow into a perfectly formed embryo, and every embryo into a full-sized adult. Making ninety-six human beings grow where only one grew before. Progress.'

The idea of ninety-five more Gareth Hilliers thrills only Gareth Hillier and a couple of girls at the back of the class. Sophie explains more of Huxley's dystopia where natural reproduction has been abandoned and children are raised in hatcheries and conditioning centres. Marriage, natural birth, parenthood and pregnancy are considered too obscene to be mentioned in casual conversation.

'So you would never know your parents,' says Lisa Stonebridge. Sophie nods. 'Well, no change there, then. I was adopted.'

'Me too,' says Sophie. It is the first time she has ever told a class and can't think why she has. There is a moment's silence, as if everyone is looking at her differently.

'See, I've no idea where I got this.' Lisa holds a clump of curly, deep-red hair that fizzes in all directions. 'Every time a middle-aged ginge walks past me in the street I wonder if I got this from them.'

'I know what you mean,' says Sophie. 'I've spent all my life wondering who I look like.'

'When I'm eighteen I'm going to find out.'

Sophie nods her approval.

'Have you tried?' says Lisa.

'No.'

'Why not?'

'It wasn't encouraged when I was your age. Besides, the law has changed.'

'It's a bit scary because you never know what and who you will find.'

Chapter 5

Friday 8 January 2016

Teachers must respect students as if they are Alphas, while they can treat us like Epsilon-Minus Semi-Morons. That's the ironic way of it these days. Of course, if Shannon hadn't had a mobile phone on her, the chances are she would have forgotten all about a stupid incident in class today. I can't be bothered to detail it here. Suffice to say that the college principal, Jack Staniscliffe, asked me to apologize to Shannon's mother for 'any offence caused'. I am still seething. When I'm getting a class to engage with a new book, it's best not to start with the book itself. I look for a theme from the story, one that engages the class at a personal level, and work back to the book. It backfired on me today, that's for sure. It makes you wonder if it's all worth the effort.

As for telling the class I was adopted. It just came out. I know that, objectively, it's no big deal but I had never told any class before. Maybe the conversation with David had played on my mind. It would be an exaggeration to say I heard an audible gasp from the class but there was a definite reaction.

This diary was never supposed to be about the first few days of my life on planet Earth. It was going to be about setting down markers, to see if I'm finally moving on after Daggert. It doesn't seem to be working out like that, though. Wondering who gave you the colour of your hair (mine is an unspectacular dark brown) is one of the most obvious things you think about when you've been adopted. There are others, though. I must have been about eleven, maybe twelve, when I watched a medical programme on TV, *General Hospital*, I think. One of the doctors was treating a patient with Huntington's disease. They called it Huntington's chorea at the time. The doctor was explaining to a nurse how the nerve cells in the brain get progressively worse and the brain itself slowly deteriorates. Your personality changes, your speech gets slurred, your moods swing violently and – this is the thing I remember most – an early sign that you have the disease is fidgeting. Now that was something I did as a child, endlessly. I was told off time and again for it at school. One teacher even called me Fanny Fidget and it stuck.

Looking up the disease in the dictionary was probably the worst thing I could have done. I found out it wasn't a disease you catch. It is inherited through a faulty gene (though I didn't understand what genes were at the time). In that moment I realized I had no idea of my birth parents' medical records. Perhaps that's why I had been given up for adoption: they could no longer look after me. I lay in bed that night, trying desperately not to fidget with the decorative frills on the duvet, imagining my incontinent birth father on a bed somewhere, body jerking like Frankenstein's monster, shot through with 64,000 volts. By the morning, I was convinced it was just a question of time before I died a mashed-up vegetable, incapable of feeding and toileting myself.

I couldn't talk to Mum and Dad about it. How would they know what ailments beset my birth parents? In any case it would have been a sort of betrayal to ask. I had no reason to believe they loved me any more or less than my sister, Chloe. She is five years older than me and their flesh and blood. Of course, like all siblings, Chloe and I fell out. When I was about seven, with our parents out of the house, I had taken a pair of scissors to her favourite teddy bear and cut off all its hair, in the sure and certain knowledge that it would grow again. Chloe was furious. She grabbed me and pinned me to the floor.

'Time you knew the truth,' she said.

'What truth?'

'About where you *really* came from.'

'I already know,' I said. Mum and Dad had told me many times: they had personally chosen me from a room full of tiny babies.

'That's what they *say* happened but you weren't chosen at all.'

'Yes, I was,' I said, still pinned to the floor. 'They *had* to have you because you were stuck inside Mum but they *chose* me from dozens of others.' It was my only weapon.

Three inches from my face, Chloe shook her head and sneered. 'They collected eight Sugar Puffs tokens and exchanged them for you.'

'I don't believe you. You're, you're lying . . . you're *lying*.' The trouble was it all sounded shockingly plausible to my seven-year-old ears. Every few months, cereal manufacturers used to offer an enticing new set of things to collect. Who could resist sending off for a *Star Trek* phaser, Woody Woodpecker mug and bowl and (my personal favourite) a Winnie the Pooh honey pot company kit? Why wouldn't they offer a new baby? I wriggled free and ran upstairs, crying. Several hours later, when my sister had gone to her friend's house, I confronted Mum and Dad.

'Chloe says I came free with Sugar Puffs,' I announced. Dad was behind a broadsheet newspaper. He said nothing. 'She said you sent off eight tokens and got me in return.'

'She's wrong,' said Dad. His voice was flat and matter-of-fact. I still couldn't see his face. 'It was four.'

'What do you mean?'

'Four tokens for a girl, eight for a boy.'

Mum, who had overheard us in the kitchen, came into the lounge and told him not to be so cruel, he was only joking. She then repeated the classic 'chosen' story I had heard many times. Dad 'received word' from London that a number of new-born babies needed a home. Where they came from and why they appeared in London was never explained. Besides, what did it matter? It all sounded wonderfully mystical, only a notch or two down from the angel Gabriel telling Mary she was going to give birth to the saviour of the world – so lie back and think of Israel.

Mum and Dad didn't go up to London on a donkey but in Uncle Peter's light blue Hillman Minx, the one with half-moon sidelights that look like glass eyebrows. The way Mum told the story I presumed she and Dad were the first, perhaps only parents allowed into the holy of holies, probably part of Buckingham Palace, where dozens of babies were beamed down from the Starship Enterprise. While all the little innocents gurgled happily before them, one positively glowed. I was the brightest, prettiest and best behaved, so they chose me. I calmed down and, when my sister returned, stuck out my tongue at her on the stairs. Having said that, for years afterwards I checked the offers on the back of every cereal packet known to mankind . . . just in case.

Around this time it occurred to me that the natural order of things meant that the first-born baby in every household came from inside the mother and the second was chosen in London. It seemed plausible, in fact sensible. I went round the playground telling all my friends who were born second that this was how families worked. Logically, they must be adopted. I was also convinced that the only child ever born on Christmas Day was Jesus and that anyone who claimed to be born on 25 December was lying. I was forced to apologize to one very upset classmate, I think her name was Lynne, who had been born on Christmas Day, had an older brother and, as her parents explained forcibly to Mum and Dad, was definitely not adopted.

Monday 18 January 2016

Jack Staniscliffe sent an email asking the English Lit team to stay behind at 'cop' today. At least I thought he had. I didn't know what the acronym 'cop' stood for but thought twice about asking anyone for fear of appearing ignorant and out of touch. A search in Google offers a hundred and thirty-five different definitions of cop, from cost-only payment to contingency operations procedure. Taking another tack, I asked June, a colleague, if she was going to the meeting.

'What meeting?' she replied.

'The one with Jack at cop today.'

'Don't know anything about it. Besides, I have to pick up the kids at a quarter to five. Any meeting after hours is impossible on a Monday.'

I was surprised June hadn't been invited but deduced from her comment that the meeting was scheduled for some time after 4.30 p.m. I still hadn't worked out what cop stood for but, logically, the only definition that made any sense was close of play. Daggert referred to it when cricket was on TV. Goodness knows how it got translated into email jargon. I turned up at Jack's office, just after 4.30 p.m.

'Ah, Sophie, thanks for popping in,' he said, closing the door behind him.

'Aren't the others coming?' I said.

He shook his head. 'No need. It's about the new curriculum.'

'Oh, well, I would have thought head of school should be here.'

He waved away my protest and began to go through some of the set text options for the new Women in Literature section of the A level syllabus. Did I think we should do D. H. Lawrence's *Women in Love* or maybe Jeanette Winterson's *Oranges Are Not the Only Fruit*?

'Well, I—'

'Only, it's difficult to judge . . .'

'I don't think it's for me to—'

' . . . being a man in my fifties. I'm not really in touch with what motivates teenage girls. I've observed you in class. You connect with them.'

'I . . . well, thank you, though the class is split fifty-fifty in terms of gender.'

'I used to talk these things over with Ginny.'

Jack has been separated from his wife for the past eighteen months. There is little hope of reconciliation. Ginny was deputy head at a local primary school before completing her Masters at a summer school in Nottingham. Daggert had no time for summer schools. Under the guise of intellectual advancement, they are where the bored, middle aged and middle class go looking for a furtive fling, as far as he was concerned. Why I should mention Daggert's views here, I don't know. It's as if he is still in the room, reading every line, challenging every opinion. Anyway, he wasn't wrong in Ginny's case. She hit it off with a student from the Ivory Coast, several years her junior. They both signed up for a module called *Education: Developing an International Context*. Ginny, it seems, passed with distinction. She promptly dumped poor old Jack and is now said to be heading up a primary school in Abidjan.

I began to rabbit on about Winterson's novel. Jeanette, the main character, describes her birth and adoption (there it is again) with images from the biblical narrative of Christ. From an early age, she believes she will emerge as a Christ-like figure who will help save the world. As she ages, however, it becomes clear that her true quest is simply to find and accept herself. Her lesbian desires contradict the world-view she has accepted all of her life . . . but it became clear that a distracted Jack – he was playing with the cap of a fountain pen – wasn't listening. I stopped talking. He hardly noticed.

'How long has it been for you, now?' he said, after a few awkward moments of silence.

'I'm sorry, I don't know what—'

'Since you lost your husband.'

'Daggert? Almost two years.'

'You've coped very well.'

'Thank you, it's not been easy.'

'No . . . losing someone. It takes time, they say.' He studied his rather dull brogue shoes and brushed an invisible piece of fluff from his suit. As a rule, I'm happy enough to listen to others facing difficult times. In fact, it can be therapeutic. However, when you are alone with the principal, and the principal is a man, without a partner, it's a different dynamic.

'At first, I felt light-headed, unhinged, as though my brain had been sucked out,' I said. 'I expected grief to be about crying and sadness, not tiredness and a complete inability to focus.'

'Yes, I know what you mean.'

'And it isn't the big things so much as the little things. The last car Daggert and I bought together was falling apart but I couldn't bring myself to trade it in. I wasn't ready to let another part of him, of us, go.'

Jack nodded and fiddled with his pen again, putting the cap on and off, on and off. He's not an unattractive man – maybe just over six foot tall with sharp, intelligent eyes and brooding eyebrows. Before the split with Ginny he walked more confidently, at times bombastically down the corridors. His shoes had steel caps on the heels. It made his footsteps unmistakable. I noticed how worn down the heels are now. That's why we can't hear him coming any more.

'Ginny was, I mean is, very good on detail,' he said. 'She can remember the title of a film or the name of a restaurant from years back. I'm hopeless when it comes to practical information.'

I could have taken the conversation two ways: risked it and talked him through his personal situation or ploughed on with the meeting's official agenda. I was spared making the decision by a knock at the door and the arrival of an IT consultant, to talk through software upgrades.

'What? Now?' Jack glanced at his watch. 'I was expecting you at eleven o'clock.'

'The last call took longer than expected.'

'It's five o'clock.'

'Yeah . . . sorry about that.' He didn't seem at all sorry. Jack had badgered the company for a week. Now, at the wrong time as far as he was concerned, their man had turned up, awaiting instructions.

'I'll have to sort this out,' he said to me. 'I'm sorry.'

'It's not a problem,' I said.

'Look, before you go.' He picked up a brochure from his desk. 'I'd like you to attend this day conference. It's called *Sixth of the Best: Your College, Your Future*.' He passed me the brochure. 'It could be quite useful, what with all the political manoeuvrings over education.'

I was surprised to be asked. I glanced at the date of the conference. It was in half-term.

'Well, if you think it's worth it. How many of the staff are going?'

'Just the two of us.'

Chapter 6

Jack and Jillio went up a hillio . . . water, water for to find . . . Better play that back to make sure I rounded my vowels . . . hmmm . . . not a bad rendition of this daft little poem. Could be more rounded on the 'o' of Jillio. Mrs Pitcher would have an opinion about that. My first verbal encounter with our brand-new neighbour was in the local corner shop, a couple of days after she moved in. Close up, her narrow face tapered down to a prominent chin. Whether her thin, greying hair was in a severe bun I cannot remember but that's how she wore it most of the time – taut, bunched, imprisoned. She was shaking her head at the price of a loaf. My mother, ever mindful of the Bible she lived by, reminded us to 'love the stranger in your midst' (or words to that effect). I did my duty.

'I'm William,' I said. 'Good morning.'

'Good morning,' said Mrs Pitcher.

'I live next door but one. How do you do?' I held out my hand. Mrs Pitcher studied me over the top of her glasses. Her hand was pale and cold. 'I saw you moving in.'

'Did you now? What a long day. We were quite past it by the end.'

'Where were you living before?'

'A rather long way away.'

'Which town?'

'Nowhere you will have heard of.' She waved a hand and turned, as if that was to be the end of the conversation. I persevered.

'Have you been watching the World Cup?'

'Now that's about soccer, isn't it? Goodness me, no. We don't have a television set.' She paused, as if she wanted to say she had better things to do than watch television, especially 'soccer' on television, but thought better of it. 'I don't like sport. Nor does our Lucy.' She peered at me again, for a little longer this time. I got the impression I was to be very careful how I behaved with 'their Lucy'. I was about to ask about the rest of her family but she ended

35

the encounter. 'Give my regards to your parents. I shall compliment them on their son's fine manners when I meet them.'

I couldn't make out her accent. It sounded posh but strangled. The vowels in 'past' and 'rather' were like the crosses from our wingers, Connelly and Paine: far too long.

'She's originally from Liverpool, I'm told,' said Mum when I got home. 'She teaches elocution.'

Dad smirked at me. 'You could do with a lesson or two.'

Mum nodded. 'She'll have you talking like Kenneth Wolstenholme in no time. He's a northerner but you'd never know . . . voice like velvet.' Mum knew nothing about football except Kenneth Wolstenholme. As far as she was concerned, all men should aspire to be similarly dashing and smooth. She never tired of reminding us that, as a bomber pilot and squadron leader in the war, Wolstenholme had won a DFC and Bar. His style of commentary was that of a home counties medical consultant with an easy bedside manner. During those tense summer days of 1966 he called an anxious nation to his surgery and in rich, reassuring tones calmed us all with shots of verbal Valium. 'And there's Martin Peters, who, oh dear, can do a lot better than that . . . and will do through the course of the game . . . and there's Mexico's number six, Diaz, from a lovely-sounding place, Guadalajara . . . a colourful people, the Mexicans; always play with a lot of verve.' Years later, it sounds stilted and patronizing but then we are all children of our time.

'What's wrong with the way I speak?' I said.

'Nothing at all,' said Mum. 'Until you go to the other end of town.'

Most of my friends lived in Thornton Heath and it was all too easy to lapse into pseudo-cockney after a day spent in their ribald company. One thing was certain, however, I wasn't going to sit opposite Mrs Pitcher, reciting poems about dogs in green kennels, or brown cows on wet, Spanish plains. Later that day Alf Ramsey was interviewed on TV, in the build-up to England's second game against the Mexicans. He sounded his usual self: clipped and constipated, a cross between *Dad's Army*'s Captain Mainwaring and Parker, Lady Penelope's chauffeur in *Thunderbirds*.

'There's someone else who's had elocution lessons,' said Dad. I didn't believe him at the time but it was true. By the middle of the 1960s it had become positively unfashionable to speak with anything other than a regional accent but it was all too late for Dagenham's most celebrated son and knight-to-be.

England v. Mexico was scheduled to kick off at 7.30 p.m. I had to kill time before the game. Several days earlier I had promised to bash out a letter to Kevin, a lad of my own age whose family had owned the house now lived in by the Pitchers. I was quietly devastated when I heard Kev was moving, to East Anglia of all places. We had lived in and out of each other's houses and ruined two perfectly good lawns playing football and cricket for hours on end. We knew we would miss each other massively but, being lads of fourteen, weren't going to admit it. Pulling out my Imperial typewriter I wrote up my meeting with Mrs Pitcher, dramatizing it a bit, knowing Kev would be entertained by it all. I kept a carbon copy of the letter, which is why I remember the details so well.

While I was busy typing, it occurred to me that Mrs Pitcher had only mentioned a daughter. Maybe she had a son, too. I stood up and opened my bedroom window. It was a warm, balmy evening in high summer. A sweet smell drifted up from below my window. They say the honeysuckle releases perfume in the evening to attract moths. I breathed in deeply. A row of surviving apple trees from the old orchard provided a visual barrier between our garden and theirs. You could only see one small section of the Pitchers' lawn from my window. I glanced down, more in despondency than expectation. What I saw has stayed with me for the rest of my life: a pair of young and perfect female legs, feet together pointing skywards, big toes touching, absolutely still. Whoever it was could do faultless handstands. Her skirt wasn't long but what there was had fallen back over her midriff to reveal a pair of white knickers wrapped tightly round the curves of the sweetest backside. I could only see down to her waist, the fence obscuring the rest of her body. 'Blimey,' I muttered. It suddenly occurred to me that I looked like a peeping tom. Maybe somebody was watching me, watching her. I ducked away from the window and shook my head. 'Blimey.'

'Wolstenholme is on, love,' called Dad downstairs.

'Be right there,' said Mum.

'The match is on, Billy,' called Dad upstairs.

'Down in a minute.' As casually as possible, I glanced out of the window again. She had gone, whoever she was. I hadn't seen her face. I needed to see her face. Seven seconds. That's how long I had seen those legs for but they are still burned indelibly on to my retina. Seven seconds. That's all it took Bobby Charlton to gather the ball near the halfway line, accelerate like a startled gazelle, shift left then swerve to the right before thumping a right foot pile driver that was still rising as it flew past the despairing dive of the Mexican goalkeeper. In those seven seconds the ball had travelled seventy yards. In the second half, Roger Hunt got another goal, tapping in from close range after the Mexican goalkeeper spilled a shot from the hapless Greaves. A win against France would see us through to the quarter-finals. However, there were now more urgent matters to attend to. With a careful air of indifference I said to Mum: 'You know that card you've bought to give to our new neighbours? I'll drop it round to them if you like . . .'

I've just taken a phone call: an urgent one. Life has a nasty habit of getting in the way of a good reverie. It was from the head honcho at the Diocese of Southbury, Mark Pettigrew.

Pettigrew is diocesan secretary, effectively CEO of the diocese. He phones me when a 'potentially damaging situation', or PDS, arises. The newspapers never tire of a dodgy vicar, especially if he's arranging secret love trysts – a word beloved by the red tops but used virtually nowhere else – with a parishioner. The perfect dodgy vicar story will involve, say, a mother-of-three flower arranger. The perfect dodgy deed will take place late at night in the vestry, preferably with a twelve-inch sterling silver candlestick wielded creatively in the dodgy mix. Pettigrew is facing a cathedral-sized, double-whammy PDS, involving a dodgy priest *and* an eccentric organist at St Stephen's, Biddington. I know both priest and organist, though not well. The incumbent, Father Nicholas Ledgard, MA, BSc is one of the poorest preachers I have ever slept through. More at home in the senior common room than the parish office,

Ledgard is distant, distracted and quite incapable of making small talk, a serious failing in a close community like Biddington. He has, however, grabbed a few headlines recently with his fight to save the town's ancient pond.

The organist, Eric Carter, plays the instrument as if taming a snorting stallion, all nimble legs and flailing arms. Like most artists he is highly strung. A few Sundays ago, after numerous disagreements with members of the choir and Ledgard, he finally lost it. As the choir processed to their stalls for a confirmation service led by the bishop, no less, he thundered out 'Send in the Clowns'. Later that week, with the coffin of a well-known alcoholic being carried down the aisle, he played a thinly disguised version of 'Roll Out the Barrel'. I began to realize why he was acting bizarrely, even by his own standards, when Pettigrew told me the nature of the problem.

'Who else knows about this?' I said: the first question in these situations.

'A whistleblower from the church who has promised to keep quiet until things are sorted.'

'Is anyone likely to tip off the media?

'No, but it's only a question of time.'

'I'll go down first thing tomorrow.'

'You know the score.'

'Hand holding and mouth gagging.'

'Yes,' said Pettigrew. He paused. 'And if needs be, I'll do the KKs.'

'It's gone that far?'

'Indeed.'

So. Where was I? Oh yes, I was going to take that card round to the Pitchers. I know, I know . . . what did Pettigrew mean by the KKs? If necessary I'll explain later. Hopefully, it won't come to that.

I have no idea what the card said. It is too long ago. We all signed it and, next morning, a Sunday, I got up early, washed, splashed on some cheap aftershave, pulled a comb through my hair and waited impatiently until about midday. Of course, I hoped Mrs Pitcher wouldn't answer the door. I wanted to place the card in the hands that belonged to those legs. Out of pure habit, I rang the doorbell three times, in short, sharp bursts. That's how Kev had known it was me. Unfortunately it gave the impression of urgency, as if something was wrong. Mrs Pitcher came rushing to the door.

'Oh, it's you,' she said, opening the door halfway. 'Is anything wrong?'

'No, sorry,' I said. 'I was in the habit of ringing three times for Kevin, who used to live here. I'd like to give you this.' I held out the card, straining to see if anyone was behind her.

'Who is it?' called a young female voice from the landing.

'One of our new neighbours.' Mrs Pitcher smiled politely and took the card.

'From the house opposite?' I heard footsteps coming downstairs at speed.

'No, next door but one.'

'Oh.' The footsteps slowed up. The first rejection and we hadn't even met. She leaned half-heartedly over the bannisters, her wild, brown hair tumbling down in front of a lovely, open face. She scooped back her hair, gave me a warm if fleeting smile and waved. 'I'm Lucy.' Her voice was higher pitched than I expected: definitely northern. 'Nice to meet you.' She ran straight back upstairs. It wasn't *that* nice to meet me because she hadn't yet met me. I could only presume that the top half I had just seen was connected to the bottom half of the evening before. Dear God, I hoped so.

'We didn't know who to write to on the card,' I said. 'So we just put "To our new neighbours". Is Lucy your only daughter?'

'Ye-es.' Mrs Pitcher looked at me over the top of her glasses again. Another warning.

'I hear you're from Liverpool.'

'Well, after a fashion.' Another long vowel.

'Well, it's nice to have you as our new neighbours.'

I walked down the garden path, glancing back at the Pitchers' first-floor bedroom windows. I hoped Lucy might be looking down. No such luck. I had clearly made no impression whatsoever; unlike cool Hendo who probably had no idea she even existed. Until that moment, he had been a sort of mentor, someone to aspire to. Now he was someone to be envious of. A rival. Life would never be the same again.

I can't remember what I did immediately after that first visit to the Pitchers' house. I probably read reports of the England match and watched some other World Cup group games on TV. The summer holidays were upon us. All that time to kill. All that time to dream. Of course, I surreptitiously checked out their back garden, now and again. All right: every ten minutes, for several days. She didn't reappear.

It was the first time I had ever had those feelings, wishing I could find a way to talk to a girl, finding out all about her. In bed, when I turned out the light, I tried to recall her face. I wasn't certain it was her I could see. I only had a few glimpses to work from, but I knew she had to be mine. Some day. Somehow. I hoped I would bump into her at the corner shop, or on the top deck of a bus; anything short of ringing that bell again and asking to speak to her. That would be suicide. I had to figure out a natural way to make contact. I had to get into that house without blowing my cover. Of course, the other problem was Hendo. I needed to keep a keen eye on him as well. I tried to prepare myself for the inevitable – seeing him and Lucy together. It was bound to happen. He was cool. He played guitar in a band; I sang in a church choir. His father could introduce Lucy to Terence Stamp; my father could introduce her to stamp duty. I moped about, unable to concentrate on anything, even the build-up to England's vital game against France. Then . . . why not? The unthinkable just a few days before became a possibility, then a must. It would be a sacrifice worth making. I waited until England v. France was about to kick off, with Mum cooing all over Wolstenholme again.

'I've been thinking, you're right about my accent,' I said. 'I don't want to ruin my chances of getting a good job when I finish school, just because I sound like a cockney. What about having a word with Mrs Pitcher about some elocution lessons at her house?'

Chapter 7

Of course, had I not told 2B I was adopted, we might have discussed Graham Greene's *The Power and the Glory* this morning with a greater degree of objectivity. The portrayal of a flawed priest on the run in 1930s Mexico is classic Greene: dark and intense. Religion has been outlawed and suppressed ruthlessly by the authorities. The book's central character had led a decadent, indulgent life as a parish priest but is now pursued relentlessly by a young police lieutenant who despises the Church for addressing people's spiritual rather than material needs. He is sure · the new, revolutionary government can end poverty. The priest believes that the Church provides hope for the poor and oppressed. He is, however, haunted by his own sinful past. Hounded from town to town, he runs into Maria, a woman with whom he had a brief, illicit affair. He also encounters Brigida, their illegitimate daughter. Mocked because of her ignominious parentage, she is less than thrilled to meet her disgraced father.

'There's your answer, Lisa,' said Gareth Hillier, holding up the book. 'I bet the priest is a ginge.' One or two of his friends suppressed a giggle but the rest of the class groaned their disapproval.

'You're such a wanker,' said Lisa.

'Well, I mean, they're all at it,' said Gareth, defending himself.

'Who are all at what?' I said.

'These men of God – so called.'

'Doing?'

'Young girls, if they're not doing young boys.'

'That's a very cynical view.'

'Greene is cynical.'

'In what way?'

'About everything and everybody. None of his characters are likeable. There isn't one moment of humour or light relief in this book.' He tossed it on the desk in front of him. 'It's depressing.'

He has a point. Greene sucks all the oxygen out of his own story, presenting a parable of futility in a parched, abandoned corner of the world. Under an unrelenting sun, insects hurl themselves into lamps or are crushed underfoot. The priest battles with a stray dog over a bone with a few morsels of meat on it – a pathetic scene and one in which hunger and the will to live win out over human dignity. One character, neurotic, hysterical and perpetually afraid of dying, confines herself to bed, hardly ever coming out from under a mosquito net. It's a world to which 2B's suburban seventeen-year-olds cannot relate.

However, dig deeper and as characters go, the priest is symbolic of our confused times. Morally weak and changeable, he had taken advantage of people's veneration by indulging in drink and fathering a child. In a cruel twist of fate, he is now the last symbol of religion for miles around. Mortal danger doesn't entirely cure him of his vices, yet he is unable to leave the people behind, so thirsty are they for rituals he had once taken for granted. Despairing over his own weakness and inability to be truly humble, he, paradoxically, attains true humility. His final struggle is over the love he cannot deny for Brigida, his illegitimate child.

'This was the love he should have felt for every soul in the world: all the fear and the wish to save concentrated unjustly on the one child,' I read out to the class. 'He prayed, "God help them," but in the moment of prayer he switched back to his child beside the rubbish-dump, and he knew it was for her only that he prayed. Another failure.'

As the class ended, and the students filed out, Lisa asked if she could have a 'quiet word'.

'Take no notice of Gareth,' I said, closing the door behind us.

'Never have, never will,' said Lisa. 'He doesn't bother me. This does, though.' She held up a copy of *The Power and the Glory*. 'It's too close to home.'

'In what way?'

'The young girl . . .'

'Brigida.'

'She's angry and ashamed when she finally meets her father.'

'And you're worried you'll feel the same?'

Lisa nodded. 'A middle-aged man tapped me on the shoulder in town the other day. He was wearing a tatty shell suit and trainers. We had the same coloured hair and a similar shaped face. He wanted me to buy the *Big Issue*.'

'Oh, I see. Well, it's highly unlikely to be your father and anyway, there's nothing wrong with selling the *Big Issue*. He wasn't begging.'

'I know, I know . . . but it was embarrassing. Gareth is bound to see him. He'll make some kind of comment.'

'So he *does* bother you.'

Lisa shrugged. 'Maybe . . . but it's more than that.' She looked at the floor. 'These programmes on the telly, where they find your natural parents for you, it's usually about the mother being reunited with her child, hardly ever the father.'

I smiled. 'You end up having no idea who the father is.'

Lisa nodded. 'Finding my mother isn't going to be enough. I need to know who my father was, too. If I was the product of a drunken shag . . . you know . . . after closing time behind the pub, I've got to find out, even if it hurts. Not knowing is driving me nuts.'

'Well, you haven't long to wait before you can make some enquiries.'

'I know.' She paused. 'But it would help if someone else was on the same journey, a person I trust, sort of in parallel.'

I looked at her closely for a second. She gazed back at me, imploringly. 'You mean you want me to . . .'

'Yes.'

I shook my head. 'I'm not ready.'

'I think you are.'

'Lisa, I lost my husband recently.'

'I know, it must be very hard for you but I can just tell you feel the same way as me.'

'Well, I'll think about it.'

'Thanks. And thanks for being my fave teach.'

With that, Lisa grabbed her bag and ran out to join her friends.

Finally started to unpack Daggert's books, CDs, magazines and whatever else today: a significant moment. I sold our detached house three
months ago and downsized into a two-bedroomed cottage, built in
the 1890s. It's small but atmospheric with a modern kitchen diner
that's bigger than you might expect. There's a wood burner in the
lounge and it's crackling and blazing away as I write. Heated pine sap,
what a gorgeous smell! Until today, all Daggert's personal effects were
stacked in cardboard boxes in the spare bedroom, gathering dust. They
say that when you lose a 'significant other' you can choose to wallow
in the past or try to build a wall between you and those memories and
begin a new chapter in your life. I've attempted the latter, not always
successfully, I admit. Today I felt strong enough to dispense with a little
bit of the past but it has come back to hit me hard.

Daggert was a chartered surveyor. As well as stacks of professional
equipment – damp meters, manhole keys, laser measurers and the
like – he left behind clutter; loads of it, including dull professional
journals and text books from his student days. I'm told that, in my
situation, it's important to keep only the things that have real emotional value and discard the rest. I felt disloyal dumping the journals
into recycling bags but I have no use for them and they are beginning to give off that damp, musty smell.

He was also into amateur dramatics. Buried beneath dozens of
copies of the *Estates Gazette*, *Building Surveying Journal* and a pile of
England rugby programmes (I doubt Daggert missed more than three
or four internationals at Twickenham in twenty years), I came across
some of his scripts. I had no idea he had kept them all. As I thumbed
through the text, his absurd sense of humour poured from every page.
I dissolved. In fact, I absolutely howled – as quietly as possible; these
walls are thin. It did me good to let it out but the only way I can deal
with the memories is to write them out of my system . . .

The script took me straight back to the day we met. I was still
a student, in the last year of teacher training. In the holidays and to
supplement my grant (mercifully, still a grant in those days; I fear
my daughter will never fully pay off her student loan), I worked at
Aladdin's Cave, a fancy dress and costume hire shop near the centre

of Redhill. Though the pay was poor it was more fun than doing the usual student postal rounds at Christmas. I had to dress up as an elf, in a short, layered tutu skirt with red and green striped tights and green platform boots! The best part about working in Aladdin's Cave was that customers usually arrived in high spirits, ordering all sorts of costumes to wear over the festive period. This was the 1980s and we did a steady trade in Freddie Mercury, Crocodile Dundee, Tina Turner, Boy George, Wonder Woman and Madonna. And I should give an honourable mention to Zippy, George and Bungle.

One afternoon, a couple of weeks before Christmas, a young man in his mid-twenties wandered in, looking distracted and intense. His dark, curly hair appeared similarly confused.

'The parking meters are all taken,' he said. 'I've had to leave my car on a yellow line. Can you keep an eye on it?' I nodded. The council had recently introduced restricted parking on a number of roads near the town centre, stirring heated debate in the local press.

Aladdin's Cave had thousands of outfits to choose from, on two large floors. The young man didn't ask for any particular costume, just walked up and down the rows, stroking the stubble on his chin, scribbling notes on a piece of paper. I thought he might have been sent incognito from head office to take stock. I pointed him out to Mrs Gladwin, the manager of the shop. She just shrugged her shoulders. He went upstairs. More than twenty minutes elapsed before curiosity got the better of me. I saw him standing at the far end of the floor, near the Ghostbusters costumes. He had his back to me and was shaking his head.

'Anything wrong?' I said.

He wheeled round, startled. 'No, no . . .'

I nodded at the costumes in front of him. 'Well, if there is . . . you know who to call.'

'Ha . . . yeah.' He laughed, loudly. 'That's good. In fact, it's excellent.'

'Well, it's not *that* funny,' I said, though I was pleased I had been unusually quick on the draw.

He reached for his paper. 'I might be able to work it in.'

'Into what?'

'Your joke, into *Cinderella*. We're putting it on at the village hall.'

46

'Ah, so that's why you're here.'

'Sort of . . . I'm looking for another character, something more . . . *today*. I've got the stock characters: Cinders, the Ugly Sisters, Prince Charming and Buttons. I'm looking for another character to give it a contemporary twist.'

I walked towards him and folded my arms. 'What about the Fairy Godmother appearing in front of Cinderella, waving her wand sweetly, only for a Bill Murray-type Ghostbuster to burst in, shouting: "On the floor, everyone, I've got this covered. She's really a witch."'

He laughed, stroked his chin again and studied me intently. He had deep brown eyes that sparkled with more intensity than all the glitter in our glam rock section. He began talking about the outfits on offer. My Christmas elf outfit was becoming more embarrassing by the minute. We talked for a few more minutes and I measured up the Ghostbusters costume before disappearing downstairs, fearful the manager might have rumbled what was going on. I went into a pathetic daze, eyes on the stairs, hoping he'd come down and talk more. Finally, I did what I had been asked to do, and glanced out of the shop window. A parking meter attendant was prowling round his car. She had written out a notice and was about to stick it on the windscreen. I called upstairs to our new customer. He came flying down and argued with the attendant but to no avail. She walked on, leaving him standing by the car. He didn't move for about a minute, then put his notepad on the bonnet and started scribbling.

'Don't drive off, don't drive off,' I said under my breath. At least I thought I had.

'He'll be back.' Mrs Gladwin rolled her eyes and shook her head. Moments later, he returned.

'She'd written out her ticket before I saw her,' I said. 'I'm so sorry.' He didn't seem at all bothered. In fact, there was a huge grin on his face.

'She's given me another idea for the panto,' he said. 'A parking attendant is just right.'

'In *Cinderella*?'

He nodded. 'Everyone will relate to the fuss going on in the local paper. Do you have a costume I can use?'

'There isn't a huge demand for parking meter attendants,' said Mrs Gladwin, matter-of-factly.

'We've got a sexy policewoman,' I said. 'It's a bit on the revealing side.'

His face lit up. 'Could you customize it?'

'We'd have to rework the cap and find a shoulder bag.'

'And alterations will cost,' said Mrs Gladwin.

'I've got a budget,' he said.

I checked the list. 'There's only one in stock.' We went back upstairs and I found the uniform sandwiched between Mr T. and Del Boy. 'Whether it fits will depend on who's wearing it, of course.'

'She's about your height and build,' he said. 'It would be helpful if you tried it on.'

'No *way*,' I said. 'That's not in my job description.'

'Please?'

'Absolutely not.'

'Of course she will.' Mrs Gladwin was standing at the top of the stairs. 'All part of the service.' She was smiling broadly. I glared at her. A few minutes later I was standing self-consciously by the changing-room door.

'You look . . . amazing,' he said, eyes like saucers. 'You'll be perfect for the part.' It took a second or two for the penny to drop. I stopped and turned round. He was grinning. 'We're rehearsing tomorrow evening in the village hall, at seven o'clock.'

'Oh no . . . you're not getting me on to any stage,' I said. 'I even refused to be the back end of a donkey in a nativity play.'

'You'll steal the show.' With that he thanked Mrs Gladwin for her help, ripped the parking ticket off the windscreen and drove off.

I turned up at the village hall, of course. Well, you're only young once.

*

Writing this up has left me completely wrung out (yeah, yeah, I'm a big feeb, Daggert, no need to remind me). I'll relate what happened on the final night of *Cinderella* another day. Suffice to say, I had no idea about the bizarre world of amateur dramatics. Under the curly wigs and flagging moustaches, codpieces and laddered tights, hormones bubble and passions seethe.

Chapter 8

St Stephen's, Biddington, is an old church in an ancient town, so ancient that it's mentioned in the Domesday Book as Bodin's tun ('tun' meant farm or village). 'Despite being a favourite for London commuters, with attendant urban sprawl round the railway station,' says Wikipedia, 'the town retains an ancient, market town atmosphere.' The Hoops and Garters, a pub dating from the fifteenth century, is the oldest timber-framed building in a narrow high street. It serves up an impressive range of real ales. Behind the pub and in front of St Stephen's lies the holy trinity of green, cricket pitch and pond.

'More than a million ponds throughout the UK have been filled in during the past century,' bemoans St Stephen's incumbent Father Nicholas Ledgard, strolling round the pond's edge, hands behind back. 'Many dated back to Saxon times and were a key local venue for washing and drinking water.' Along with the wife of St Stephen's organist, Eric Carter, Ledgard has successfully led a much-publicized fight to save Biddington's ancient watering hole.

'Your mallards look in fine fettle,' says Billy.

'Ugh, non-stop shitting machines,' says Ledgard. 'They ruin the water. Trouble is, the kids love 'em.'

'Oh, well, you've some nice goldfish in there.'

'Dumped illegally and another source of faecal debris. Even worse, the road drains were hammering the pond with oil and salt. Preserving a natural pond is all about ensuring a careful ecological balance. It's now fed from a clean water source and the natives have returned – newts, frogs and all their little pals.' Ledgard has a long, thin neck with a protruding Adam's apple that bounces up and down, like a trapped frog making repeated bids for freedom. 'If you want to understand the science, ask Norma.' His pasty, academic face brightens at the sound of her name. 'Without her, the campaign would have failed. Quite a lady!'

Norma is Eric Carter's wife. Billy takes a deep breath. 'Which leads me to the reason for my visit.'

'Yes, I'm sure she would do the same for other parishes and other ponds.'

'That's not quite what I had in mind.'

'You've heard the rumours, then?'

'Yes.'

'I can confirm that Carter *is* barmy. How Norma put up with him for so long beats me.'

'Well, putting him to one side . . .'

'A sensible thing to do.'

'. . . I'm led to believe Norma Carter is now living with you in the vicarage.'

Ledgard nods. 'And not a day too soon, for her sake.'

'You must realize it poses problems.'

'How so?'

'Your wife . . .'

'I know, I know. Flissie must be mad to shack up with that buffoon.'

'That isn't what . . . I need to be sure I've got this right. You've willingly swapped partners and your wife is now living with the organist, Eric Carter.'

Ledgard smiles. 'And it's all very amicable, though I fail to see what Flissie sees in him.'

By now they are in Ledgard's untidy, book-lined study. He brings in two instant coffees, tapping the 'Keep Biddington Newtiful' slogan on his mug. 'Norma's idea. She's become a bit of an expert with the local media. When you call it a day, William, she'd be a first-class replacement.'

'They're taking a very dim view of it at diocesan house.'

'That's understandable. It will take people time to adjust.'

Billy stares at him. 'You must realize your actions bring the Church into disrepute.'

'It depends how you look at it.'

'And when word gets out, the media will go into a feeding frenzy. I'm not here to slap your wrists, I'm here to protect you.'

Ledgard shakes his head and smiles. 'I appreciate you're only doing your job, Shearwater. However, I think you'll find people are much more broad-minded these days. We all make mistakes. My marriage to Flissie had been all but over for years. Norma and I have nothing to hide. Let them send as many reporters as they like. We'll deal with them, one at a time, candidly and openly. Nothing wrong with exercising a little godly glasnost, eh?'

'It's not that simple,' I said.

'Oh, it is.' Ledgard folds his arms, defiantly. 'Norma and I are in love. We will ride out the storm and continue to serve the spiritual needs of the community. As Virgil wrote: *omnia vincit amor*. Love conqu—'

'Yes, I know what it means.' Billy reaches for his briefcase and pulls out a file. 'Does the name Julie Challenor ring a bell?'

Ledgard's eyes narrow. He puts his mug on the coffee table in front of him, studies the newt, sits back and crosses his legs. 'You've done your homework.'

Billy shrugs and points to the report in front of him.

'This is below the belt,' says Ledgard. 'It all happened more than twenty-five years ago. The case was never heard.'

Billy nods. 'It came before new procedures were put in place. Miss Challenor was persuaded not to pursue the matter.'

'That young girl came on strong to me during my first curacy. We are prime targets. You know that, William.'

'Of course, but I'm struggling to understand why you were ever alone with her in the vicarage.'

It is Ledgard's turn to shrug his shoulders. 'We all work on our own. You know that. We can't have a third party with us twenty-four hours a day.'

'The report says you saw her several times, always on your own. In fact, you insisted she came round when your wife was out.'

'That's an exaggeration.'

'She was fifteen.'

Ledgard purses his lips. 'She told me she was eighteen.'

Billy continues to read from the file. 'She claims that, on several occasions, you ran your hand up and down her exposed thigh.'

'She was upset. Her father was violent and vindictive.'

'As you did so you sang a nursery rhyme: "I love little pussy, her coat is so warm . . ."'

Ledgard blanches. 'It . . . it comforted her.'

51

'You then asked if you could unhook her brassiere and . . .'

'That only happened once, at her suggestion.'

Billy shakes his head. 'It occurred several times, so frequently, in fact, that when she came to the vicarage with a new bra that unhooked at the front, you expressed surprise. When you next met, alone in the parish office, you asked her if she was wearing her "front loader".'

Ledgard stands, suddenly. 'OK, that's enough. What do you want?'

Billy shakes his head. 'This isn't a film, Nicholas. I'm not here to blackmail you. I'm trying to find a solution.'

'You've dug the dirt.'

'No spade was required. There are other complaints listed, notably when you were a visiting lecturer at Archbishop Winchelsea College, some ten years ago.' Billy tosses the file on the coffee table and looks Ledgard straight in the eyes. The wind drops from his sails. He sits down, body shaking, head in hands.

'I've been a fool in the past.' Now he is holding back the tears. 'They were just silly infatuations. The feelings I have for Norma, I've never experienced anything like them before. What we have is so right. It comes from another place, somewhere divine.'

Billy hesitates. The report in his hand details how, more than two decades before, Ledgard told a young, vulnerable Julie Challenor how the love he felt for her transcended anything he felt for anyone before her, they were just silly infatuations. He decides not to twist the knife any further. 'So . . . what are you going to do?'

Ledgard stares at the floor. 'You think I should give up Norma.'

'I'm not suggesting anything. I'm discussing the situation with you.'

'But that's what you think I should do.'

'You must be the judge.'

'And if you were in my position?'

'Well, you can tough it out and wait for your relationship with Norma to be splashed all over the popular press. Ironically, your recent campaign to save the pond has lifted your public profile at just the wrong time. When the papers find out you're bonking your co-campaigner, who happens to be the wife of the church organist, they won't believe their luck. "Priest gives me the best vibrato I've ever known," says organist's wife. Put 'em up, knock 'em down. That's their way.'

Ledgard breathes in deeply. 'Or?'

'You can go straight round to the Carters, try to put things right with Flissie and, if you are both sensible, pack your bags. On Friday we'll send in a removals van to clear the vicarage and put you both in a safe house miles away, before anyone in Biddington knows what's going on. On Sunday, the bishop will lead the service you were supposed to take at St Stephen's.'

Ledgard looks stunned. 'What will he say at the service?'

'That you left suddenly for personal reasons. He'll urge everyone to pray for you and your family at a trying time for you all.'

'That won't stop the speculation.'

'We'll worry about that later. This way we close ranks and stay in control.'

Ledgard shakes his head. 'You're a bastard, Billy.'

'Like you said, I'm just doing my job.'

Ledgard stands, digs his hands deep into his pockets and sighs. 'I'll see Flissie this afternoon.'

'You're doing the right thing.'

'But two can play at this game, Shearwater.' He gives his visitor a long, pasty stare. 'If I ever get some dirt on you, be under no illusion. I'll get my own back.'

*

As soon as Billy gets into his car, he phones Pettigrew. 'Ledgard's talking it over with his wife. I think they'll take our offer and be gone by Friday.'

'Excellent, Billy. Thank you,' says Pettigrew. 'I've located an empty vicarage where they can stay for a month or two while we do the KKs.'

'Who do you have in mind?'

'A priest in a rural parish up north. He's built a model railway that runs out of a spare ground-floor room and along the vicarage garden. The track extends more than two hundred and fifty feet, around flowerbeds, into a shed and back to the house. I've seen the pictures. It's incredible. There are, however, reports that he's rather too fond of showing his Hornby 00 star class chassis bottoms, with pickups, to a succession of young choirboys.'

Chapter 9

I love little pussy . . . her coat is so warm . . . and if I don't hurt her . . . she'll do me no harm . . . The rhyme has been running through my head ever since I returned from St Stephen's, Biddington.

Father Nicholas Ledgard has convinced himself that his relationship with the organist's wife is the Real Thing. In his eyes was the faraway gaze of an infatuated teenager. Love makes a fool of us all but it's supposed to when you're fifteen. It's a different kind of foolishness when you're in your early fifties. It's a dangerous kind of foolishness when you're in your early fifties, the parish priest and pulling out all the extra-marital stops with the organist's wife. It reminded me of a recent survey on romance that came to one simple conclusion: being in love is how we feel about the person we are with at present, being infatuated is how we define previous relationships.

Ledgard sees himself as 'saving' Norma Carter: a standard psychological play. The talented, suppressed wife is liberated from an insensitive, overbearing husband by a caring, compassionate third party. I've heard all that before. But godly glasnost! That was a new one even to me. A wife-swapping, loved-up Ledgard is bad enough but now he is threatening to go Billy Joel and play the honesty card. Pettigrew was right. We have one holy mother of a PDS on our hands. We will now put this other priest, the one with a passion for model railways and choirboys, in some quiet corner of our diocese. Another distant diocese will get Ledgard. An ideal knock for knock. Or doing the KKs: a phrase borrowed from insurance companies that translates well into diocesan HR. It's a fair exchange of bad apples, moved on to new barrels before they go entirely rotten. Some fade into obscurity. Others have to be moved on again but at least a moving target is harder to hit.

As I told Ledgard, I was only doing my job. And Norbert 'Nobby' Stiles was only doing his job when he tackled Jacques Simon, fifteen minutes from the end of that third group match against France. I remember it vaguely but I've been winding down after a stressful day by watching highlights of the match on YouTube. By Stiles's own admission, it was a shocking tackle, very late and very dangerous. It left Simon, a genuinely talented player, writhing in pain. Inexplicably, the referee waved play on. Callaghan crossed the ball to Hunt, whose downward header was fumbled by the French goalkeeper for England's second goal. We were through to the quarter-finals, to a universal chorus of disapproval. The French press called Stiles a brute and a beast. So big was the international outcry that some members of the FA suggested Alf Ramsey should drop Stiles for the next game against Argentina.

When you consider the swarthy, manicured gods of the current game, built like brick shithouses but with the stealth and acceleration of a panther, Stiles looks like a gawky no-hoper. He is to football what Woody Allen is to celluloid: the quintessential anti-hero. On the surface, Nobby had nothing going for him. He was short, thin, had poor vision and his hair fell out prematurely. After his teeth were forcibly ripped from his jaw during a match early in his career, he wore dentures. And I mean . . . Norbert. The name alone leaves you scratching your head. How do you pronounce it? The French way? Who was going to call him Nor-bear? He grew up in Collyhurst, a proud, working-class area of north Manchester where pretentiousness is a mortal sin. Was it to be Norbert, as in sherbert? No wonder he became Nobby, though that must have created its own problems in the playground. Maybe for the very reason everything seemed against him, Stiles became a tenacious tackler loved by Alf Ramsey. Indeed Ramsey regarded Norbert as genuinely world class (yes, he called him by his full name, but what would you expect after those elocution lessons?) Ramsey defended him resolutely and refused outright to drop him for the next game. 'If Stiles doesn't play, the team doesn't play,' he said.

Let me reflect on it another way. There are unfashionable jobs that have to be done while other people take the glory. Perhaps Nobby's father, an undertaker, subconsciously prepared Stiles junior for a messy, underappreciated role for England. Similarly, someone had to put in a crunching tackle or two on Ledgard. It fell to me. He won't thank me for it. He may regard me as a bit of a bastard but I have his best interests at heart.

*

I fell asleep over my computer after dictating that last sentence. I dreamed I was alone at Ledgard's untidy desk. I could smell honeysuckle drifting up from below my bedroom window, even though I was on the ground floor: very strange. Lucy came in, wearing that red knitted mini-skirt and a front-loading bra, unhooked. She stood close to me, very close, and asked me what I was doing. 'Preparing the main thrust of my sermon,' I said. I turned the pages of *The Shape of the Liturgy* by Gregory Dix with one hand, and ran the other up and down her smooth, white thigh. *I love little pussy . . .* That infernal nursery rhyme was running round in my head in endless loop. Ledgard burst into the room. 'Gotcha,' he said. 'I knew you couldn't be that squeaky clean.' He reached for the phone with a victorious glint in his eye that frightened me wide awake again.

Chapter 10

Tuesday 16 February 2016

I've never been a political person. I have opinions, of course, but keep them to myself. Daggert got agitated enough for the two of us. Every time an election came round, I promised faithfully to sit up with him and watch the results come in. He would perch a TV at the end of the bed and cheer and curse. The sad truth is, I was always out for my own count before the first returning officer hereby declared. So when Jack Staniscliffe asked me to join him today at *Sixth of the Best: Your College, Your Future*, I wasn't up to speed on all the politics surrounding my profession. I'm well aware we're under financial constraints but structural change in education has been at the bottom of my mental agenda for the past two years.

I'm not naive. I was aware there could be more to it than a professional connection. On the other hand, I was flattered. There are more qualified members of staff he could have asked. If he was looking for a female colleague to accompany him, for whatever reason, there are several younger and more eligible than me. I also considered the hostile reaction from my colleagues. With all this in mind, I politely refused to join him at the conference but he insisted. It was none of anyone else's business, he said, and as it was to take place over half-term, it didn't interfere with any lessons. He wore me down. With mixed feelings, I eventually agreed to go. It would be churlish not to have done so.

Our destination was Chamberlain Manor, once a stately home, now a conference centre somewhere in undiscovered Surrey. I still haven't a clue where. I do know I spent more than two hours getting ready, mainly because I had never been to a conference of this kind before. Hair up? Hair down? Hair sideways? Maybe Sinéad O'Connor. But you have to be truly beautiful to shave it all off. Neutral colours? Neutral colours with colourful scarf? Power heels?

57

It reminded me of those romcom clichés where, before an important event, the heroine tries on outfit after outfit. Knowing we will die of boredom in real time, the producer mercifully jump cuts each change of clothes. All the time I could see Daggert behind the sports pages of *The Guardian*, grunting his disinterested approval at every change. How can you miss such a uselessly reassuring presence?

For once, the main roads out of Redhill were mercifully free of heavy traffic. By the time we hit the leafier roads of Surrey, we were over the early, awkward small talk. 'So, Jack.' I said. 'Why me?'

'Why you what?'

'At this conference.'

Jack smiled. 'Because, since I became principal eighteen months ago, you've shown absolutely no interest in me.'

I laughed nervously and shifted position on my heated leather seat. 'I'm sorry about that.'

He waved away my apology. 'Most of your colleagues are on the make. When they've done something they think is impressive, they make sure I know all about it. Take our new head of geography. I forget his name . . .'

'Peter Bryant.'

He nodded. 'Yes, Bryant. I'm fully expecting him to cc me in on one of his morning dumps.'

I burst out laughing, something I hadn't done for a very long time. 'That's just the kind of comment my husband would have made.'

'Think I would have got on with him?'

'Daggert? Definitely.'

'Lucky man. All I ever get from you is a polite nod or wave. At first I thought you must be intensely shy but the speed with which you scurry away when you hear me coming makes me think you must find me repulsive.'

I put my hand to my mouth. 'No, I—'

Jack gestured. He hadn't finished. 'But the more you avoided me, the more intrigued I became. The students like you and the work they deliver is of consistent quality. You have a winning way. There must be a secret.'

'I take no notice of school inspectors.'

Jack smiled. 'Well, none of us do. It has to be more than that.' I told him how, when I began teaching, I asked a class what they most looked for in a teacher.

'I thought it would be excellent subject knowledge, attention to detail, efficiency – the kind of things beloved of Ofsted,' I said. 'It was none of the above. Most of all, they wanted to be shown kindness and respect. If I show respect to my students, they respond. It's a two-way street.'

'Interesting,' he said, 'but I'm old school. Assume complete control of the bastards. When I was deputy head of a primary school I adopted the HPB method for assemblies: a hymn, a prayer and a bollocking.'

I shook my head. 'Typically male.'

Jack nodded. 'Well . . . in one way I was right. There *is* more to you than meets the eye, though what meets the eye is worth it in its own right. Or does that comment prove I await reconstruction?'

I smiled. 'Oh, I don't think women will ever reject a little flattery.'

'It isn't flattery.'

'Well, I accept your compliment but you hardly know me.'

'Hence this trip.'

'There isn't much to discover.'

'That I can't believe. Of course, the best way to find out about someone is to rifle through their bookcase and record collection.'

'Ah . . . if a soul had windows.'

'Favourite film is an alternative.' He gave me an enquiring look.

'What – ever? Easy. *Local Hero*.'

'The one with the telephone box?'

I nodded. In the film, MacIntyre, a 1980s hot-shot executive from Texas, is sent over to the fictitious Scottish coastal village of Ferness to buy out the locals and build an oil refinery. He discovers a quaint, close-knit community of eccentric locals in woolly jumpers who gradually seduce him with their easy-going lifestyle. He must close the deal that will spell the end of a village he grows to love. The deal falls through and a sombre, bewitched MacIntyre reluctantly returns to his empty, soulless Houston apartment, pockets stuffed with stones and shells that smell of the North Sea. The film's final shot is of the phone box in Ferness, the village's only link with the outside world.

It rings unanswered with Mark Knopfler's Celtic anthem ripping out the viewer's heart.

'Forsyth's script, Puttnam's production, Knopfler's music . . . it's shatteringly beautiful, the saddest, deepest comedy ever made,' I said. 'Daggert and I watched it whenever it came on TV. We always ended up in pieces. Damn! That's the second time I've mentioned him in a minute. I promised myself I wouldn't bore you.'

Jack shook his head. 'You're not.'

'You *will* stop me if . . .'

'I'll do no such thing.'

I explained how Daggert had wanted to go to Pennan, where part of the film was made.

'If I remember correctly, the American . . .' said Jack.

'MacIntyre.'

'Yes, MacIntyre shovels coins into the payphone, calling his boss back home.'

I nodded. 'The phone box has become a shrine. In fact, it's a listed building. Just before Daggert was diagnosed, we arranged a holiday in Scotland, taking in Pennan. We never made it. Before he died he asked me to go, for the two of us.'

My visit to the tiny village is something I will never forget. I stayed overnight in Dundee before driving up the east coast, beyond Aberdeen. On the way I played the film's soundtrack on the car's audio system, pointing out the scenery to Daggert. He never answered. In fairness, an urn strapped into the passenger seat would struggle to do so. I drove to my hotel in Banff and took a taxi to nearby Pennan. I didn't fancy the drive back in the dark, along unfamiliar coastal roads. It was mid-afternoon when the taxi turned down a narrow, steep road and emerged on to Pennan's single street, a row of white fishermen's houses, gable ends pointed to the sea. It was eerily quiet. Behind one dwelling someone's washing billowed in the wind, a reminder that, while most of the properties are now holiday homes, a few people still live and work in the village.

I ambled along the main street to the harbour, breathing in the salty air. Brightly coloured leisure craft and a couple of fishing boats bobbed on the tide. I looked back at the village, set below a steep cliff that rises like a frozen tsunami of dour Scottish rock. This one-street village is a natural theatrical stage. If someone strung a high rope from two poles, one at each end of the street, a stage curtain could be strung along its length. I replayed scenes from the film in my head: the spectacular northern lights, the arrival of the Russian fishing boat, the village dance, the hermit Ben's idyllic beach. No one on a motorbike came racing by, a comic device in the film, but I imagined it nonetheless.

I passed the telephone box several times before finally going in. Daggert had made a card for me to attach to the wall. On the front was a scenic view of Pennan. Inside it said, 'Ah, bugger it. I meant to say cheerio,' the final line of dialogue in the film. He had signed the card, 'Jonathan Daggert, and there are two g's in Daggert'. I stood in the telephone box for a while. It was another closure, another irretrievable part of a husband I had to leave behind. I welled up as I shut the payphone door and walked to the shore, only a few yards away, and scattered his ashes to the rising tide. The tears flowed but they were cleansing and resolving. I had just put the cap back on the urn when I heard the dull thudding ring of the payphone's bell. MacIntyre! It had to be MacIntyre. No, Daggert! *It was Daggert!* It must be a sign. I was in a crazy dream. I would wake up at any moment. I didn't want to wake up. I ran to the phone, brushing back the tears. The call must be for me. It couldn't be. It had to be. I reached the phone box as a woman, probably in her sixties, smartly dressed with a large flower in her lapel, stepped out of it. She smiled and pointed to Daggert's card. 'Someone has a great sense of humour.'

'My ... my husband wrote it.' I tried hard not to appear hysterical.

'You must introduce me.'

'I'm afraid he's dead.'

'Oh, I *am* sorry.'

'Did ... did you answer the phone?'

'Answer it?

'Just then.'

'It wasn't ringing.'

'But ... I heard it ...'

She smiled again. 'Lots of people do. The place is enchanted.' She looked at the urn. 'Ah.'

'Now I feel stupid.'

'Don't.'

'I could have sworn . . .'

'How about a coffee, or something stronger?' She guided me into the Pennan Inn. A large picture of Burt Lancaster, best-known star of the film, adorns one wall, the film's official poster another. The woman ordered two large Gaelic coffees.

'Thank you,' I said. 'I feel such a fool. Your mind plays tricks.'

The woman smiled again. 'Tell me all about . . . Daggert, is it?' It's a cliché worn as smooth as the pebbles on Pennan's shore but it was as if we had known each other for years. She listened as I rambled on about Daggert, amateur dramatics, teaching, Ofsted, my house, my adoptive parents, my daughter and grandson. She said I should make a point of finding my natural parents. Absolutely. Definitely. Groups of people came and went around us. The inn slowly emptied. The woman pointed to the toilets and excused herself. It gave me a chance to ask the barman if he knew who she was.

He shook his head. 'She came in earlier and said she was waiting for someone. I presumed it was you.'

'Have you any idea where she's from?'

'She said she lives on Skye, though it sounds as if she comes from somewhere south of the border.' I glanced at my watch. I was shocked to see it was past 11 p.m. I asked the barman if he could recommend a local taxi service. He nodded towards a cab parked up by the shore. I went outside. No wonder Bill Forsyth made such a play of the night sky in the film. Thousands of stars shone like diamonds spilled on to a jeweller's cloth. The taxi driver tucked away his newspaper when he saw me coming.

'I just need to thank someone,' I said and went back to the inn. There was no sign of the woman. Anywhere. The barman hadn't seen her leave. It was baffling. I couldn't even remember her name. Perhaps she had never given it to me. I left my contact details at the bar and climbed in the back of the taxi, my mind in a foggy whirl. To this day I have no idea who she was . . .

We pulled up in the car park of Chamberlain Manor as I reached the end of my story. Jack had listened attentively (I hope I hadn't bored him) but he was now preoccupied with the day ahead. He became Staniscliffe, the college principal, striding purposefully towards the conference centre. I struggled to keep up with him and chided myself for not choosing flatter heels. I also regretted telling him so much about myself. Some of the mystery and magic of a tale so intimate dissipates with its telling.

I soon discovered I had made too many presumptions about the conference. I imagined we would slip into a packed auditorium and bag a couple of seats near the back. The moment we walked through the centre's arched, antique doors into an oak-panelled reception area, I realized I had completely misread the situation. For the first time I looked through the conference programme. Jack was giving the keynote address! What the hell was I doing here? I made quietly for the door. Too late. Jack introduced me to an 'old colleague' called Colin something. I smiled politely and shook his clammy hand. I didn't want him to think I was involved in some way with Jack but I'm sure I sounded far too defensive. I blurted out that I was there because I was researching a Masters. The only subject that came to mind in that moment was the one Jack's wife had studied at summer school, with traumatic consequences. Jack looked at me, curiously.

Colin, whose name was Fletcher, said he was covering further education in Scandinavia in his seminar.

'Oh, that's interesting,' I lied.

'You're welcome to join us,' he said, 'though I doubt Jack will let you out of his sight.'

Jack said we had to leave directly after his address. I wasn't aware we were under time constraints but, suppressing my thankfulness, I nodded and walked swiftly into the conference theatre.

It was the first time I had seen Woodfield's new promotional video. Our own gorgeous Gareth Hillier is the star, and I have to say, the college has never looked so slick: a sharply edited, high-intensity film can give a wonderfully distorted impression. I wouldn't have a clue how to put together a film like that. Daggert called me a technosaur. I even baulked when Jack's predecessor insisted all our lessons were to be presented on overhead projectors. You read that correctly: overhead projectors! Chalk and talk had worked perfectly well for me. OHPs, unwieldy and cumbersome, were out of my comfort zone. I had just reached an uneasy truce with felt-tip pens and acetate when

Jack, newly installed as head, sent out a further decree. No longer would we clatter and rattle OHPs along the corridors from class to class. Now we all had to present lessons using these shiny new data projectors bolted to the ceiling.

The sad truth is that I've never had the patience to master our brave new media. I like words. I still cram too many on to one PowerPoint slide. I can't help myself. I have no idea how to fly in whizzy graphics, either. My presentations are unimaginative. Against all the odds, however, most of my students pass their exams, many with distinction.

'Crazy, isn't it?' said Jack, as if reading my mind. 'We've spent thousands on a state-of-the-art film to win new students, to try and beat another local college spending the same sort of money to win the same students. Why doesn't this government go the whole hog and demand that lighthouses compete against one another? Because of budget constraints, two in every three sixth-form colleges have been forced to drop courses. For some inexplicable reason, our colleges pay VAT whereas local authority-maintained schools are exempt. We could have ten more teachers with the money. Instead we are letting experienced staff go . . .' He prowled and growled round the lectern, the Jack Staniscliffe I remember when he first arrived at Woodfield, before the summer school incident.

It had turned windy by the time we left the conference: large gusts that would make even Sinéad fumble for a comb. By the time we reached the car I resembled a scarecrow but fought the temptation to flip open the mirror on the sun visor. Oblivious, Jack secured his seat belt, fired up the engine and apologized about Fletcher. I said I was the one who should say sorry. I wasn't really doing a Masters. Jack asked me if I knew what happened to his wife at summer school.

'Vaguely,' I replied but I knew everything, of course. What better way to brighten a dull day in the staff room than chinwag about the principal's wife running off to Abidjan? I know things about Jack I'm not sure he knows, and plenty of other things that probably aren't even true. It was time to divert the conversation away from all things Ivory Coast. 'I did start a Masters,' I said, 'looking at the way novels are adapted for films.'

I've thought a lot about this. A novel takes, on average, more than twelve hours to read so we'll often spend several days on it. A good one indulges us in leisurely foreplay, building up remorselessly to a satiating climax. A film, by contrast, is a sensual car crash. We are at the mercy of speeding celluloid that cannot turn back, dwell or diverge. And we cannot know what the characters are thinking without resorting to those phoney voiceovers used only in comedies. Dialogue is an external expression of thought, that's true, but do the words we hear reflect what the character is really thinking? And once spoken, they are no longer thought. Films often compensate by overstressing facial expressions. I rambled on about this for far too long, discussing novel after novel, film after film. I do that when I'm nervous: anything but painful silence. Jack chipped in, now and again, out of politeness I imagine.

By now we were about a mile from my house. He asked me how I would describe what would happen in the next couple of minutes, if I were writing the screenplay. There was mischief in his eye, the kind a camera would dwell on before cutting to me for my reaction. That's the great advantage of film. It cannot convey thought but it can reflect the points of view of different characters, all in the same scene. Novelists trying to do the same will usually fail. When I read a novel I am intimately fused to the point of view of one person in that chapter. I see the world through their eyes and their eyes only. I played along by asking him what genre of movie we were in.

'I was thinking of an intelligent, romantic comedy,' he said.

I really hadn't seen that coming. 'What does your character think of the female lead?'

'Hmmm.' Jack slowed the car. 'Well, let's say he had hoped he might find the odd gold nugget but hit a lode-bearing seam.'

'Now he really is flattering her and she isn't one to be fooled.'

'Funny . . . I can't see that in the script,' said Jack. He pulled up outside my house but kept the engine running. 'My character knows he's damaged goods but he values people with integrity and the lost art of conversation.' I was now living the tension-filled moment of a thousand romcoms. The engine was still running! If the female lead asks the male lead into her house, she could be deemed presumptive or too easy. On the other hand, if she politely thanks him for his company and gets swiftly out of the car, is that rude and ungrateful? What was I thinking? This wasn't a date in the first place. There again, Jack was my boss. I couldn't win.

'My character has a bereavement from which she is still recovering,' I said. 'She would ask your character in for a coffee but she isn't ready to cross that line.'

Jack was silent for a few moments. 'Another bit of improvisation there.' He smiled ruefully. 'My official script has your character throwing caution to the wind.'

'Taking the yolo line.'

'Yolo?'

'You only live once. The students use it all the time.'

'Ah, so that's what it means.'

'Don't think me ungrateful, Jack. I've enjoyed today. I'm just not ready.'

'Of course. I understand.'

'Also . . . you're the principal.'

'Is that just a convenient excuse for the fact that you don't see it working at all?'

'Maybe. I'm not sure.'

'Well, I'm glad I asked and that I didn't chicken out.'

We exchanged a few more pleasantries. I got out of the car and he drove off. It could have been me but he seemed to stay a little too long in first and changed into second with a hint of anger. But maybe that was me, writing the screenplay.

Chapter 11

There was a crooked man . . . he walked a crooked mile . . . he found a crooked sixpence . . . upon a crooked stile . . . OK. I'm up and running again after returning from North Downs Radio, where I was a special guest on the late-night phone-in, *Pillow Talk*. I can confirm that Alan Partridge's nocturnal ramblings are not just a clever caricature. Every night at 10 p.m. something peculiar happens across the country. Owls hoot. Coffin lids creak open. The living dead rise and call their local radio stations. The subject they discussed on tonight's show: would you eat the snails in your garden? Olive Reed-Westbrook, the guest on *Pillow Talk* before me, breezily explained how she collects a few dozen 'gooey gastropods' (her phrase) in a bucket and covers them with a pair of old tights. For the following week she feeds them lettuce, onion and stale bread, 'to grit out their guts', before plunging the whole lot into boiling water. Ten minutes later, they're ready to serve.

'And the taste?' asked presenter Harold Bristow, grimacing.

'Subtle and earthy. Snails are best served with butter, olive oil, garlic and parsley,' said Olive, who told us how she 'hails from Irons-bottom', the sort of place one doesn't just come from, it seems.

'I'm told they're a bit on the chewy side.'

'They can be. I dice them up if I have guests for supper.'

'Guests! Do they know what they're eating?'

'Of course . . . most are pleasantly surprised. They're rich in protein, snails.'

It was the turn of the undead to grab those telephones, for and against Ms Reed-Westbrook's predilection for *helix aspersa*. 'Not for me, they taste like burned rubber bands' . . . 'Love 'em, yummee' . . . 'I cannot think of anything worse than cleaning and eating such a disgusting creature' . . . 'Loved *The Magic Roundabout*, loved Brian, think before you eat.' And so it went on for the best part of fifteen minutes, either side of the local weather and community noticeboard.

'Talking of slow-moving creatures.' Harold turned to me at last. 'My special guest has been a long time edging his way to the top but, judging by recent reports, he's coming out of his shell.' That's rich: being punned with faint praise by someone stuck at the foot of the media ladder. 'And he's a man with a mission, to bring back the heart and soul to the troubled world of our national game. I'm delighted to welcome to *Pillow Talk* author and chaplain, Canon William Shearwater.'

The joys of modern technology mean I was able to download the interview on to my computer.

Bristow: Now then, William, your books are calling on the authorities to put football back on the straight and narrow. All power to you! I used to look forward to the World Cup but Blatter and gang have corrupted the tournament. Mind you, it hasn't been the same since that game against Argentina in 1986. Maradona's 'hand of God' and all that.

Me: Well, it depends which continent you're on. Some would argue that, twenty years earlier, we cheated South America – and specifically Argentina – out of the World Cup.

We won it fair and square in 1966.

It was fixed.

You seriously believe that?

Most South Americans do. They're convinced the whole tournament was rigged, as part of a conspiracy to prevent a South American team from winning. Brazil had lifted the Jules Rimet Trophy at the previous two tournaments and were hot favourites. But lenient refereeing meant Bulgaria and Portugal were given free rein to kick Pelé and gang out of the 1966 finals.

That's highly contentious. As a team, Brazil were poor.

Maybe, but the same people will point out that an English referee sent off two Uruguayans in the quarter-final against Germany:

Uruguay lost four–nil. And it was a German, Rudolf Kreitlein, who sent off Argentina's captain Rattin in the infamous quarter-final which England won one–nil.

Just coincidences . . .

Perhaps but other things were going on behind the scenes.

Like?

Uruguay were supposed to play all their group matches at Wembley but, believe it or not, the stadium's owners refused to cancel a scheduled greyhound race! The match between Uruguay and France was moved to the dilapidated White City Stadium, built for the 1908 Olympic Games! It was a fix.

Hang on. Whose side are you on?

I'm not interested in taking sides. I want to get above all the petty nationalism and recover football's soul.

But what about all the bribes?

At the risk of repeating myself . . .

It depends which continent you're on!

Exactly. In Africa, Asia and Latin America, Sepp Blatter is Jesus, Mother Teresa and Martin Luther King rolled into one. He's been the champion of poor countries that rely on FIFA's funds to develop their sporting facilities.

In return for votes.

Hmmm . . . those in glass houses! In the run-up to our bid to host the 2018 finals, an England team travelled to Trinidad and Tobago to play the national team. The sole purpose of this was to buy up its executive vote, in the shape of the notorious Jack Warner. Another friendly in Thailand was cancelled after Thailand failed to vote for England. No vote? No game: a transaction as corrupt as they come.

So what are you exactly campaigning for?

The restoration of the people's game to the people. Football has lost touch with its origins. We need to turn the game upside down. It must be governed by its grassroots. Internationalism must replace patronage.

All right, if you had your way, what's the first thing you would do?

Instigate root and branch reform of football at every level, not just FIFA. Those appointed to lead our game should be of proven integrity and honesty. I want nothing less than total transparency. I am also calling on the England team to tour the developing world in pre-season – not to flog shirts or hoover up FIFA votes but because continents like Africa have given the world game so much and been rewarded with next to nothing in return . . .

I've just got home at well gone midnight and replayed the interview. I think it came over OK. I'll put a link to it on my website tomorrow. The house is quiet. Emms is asleep. Come to think of it, she was probably out for the count before I hit the airwaves. She is a lark. Me? More of an owl. I have to wind down slowly, which is why I keep this verbal journal late at night. Whatever the time, Emms never tunes in when I'm on TV or radio. 'I don't want to inhibit you,' she says. The truth is, she gets bored hearing me trot out the same old stuff, and who can blame her? When you've been together as long as we have, it's rare to discover new things about each other, though it wasn't always the case.

We first met at my father's local estate agency, Shearwater and Finch. Dad hoped I would take over the business, so after A levels and with little idea of what I wanted to do for a career I gave it a go as a junior property negotiator. At the time, estate agency was going through radical evolution. Hundreds of small, independent firms were being gobbled up by super-charged national chains: in much the same way independent corner shops have been forced out of existence by Tesco, Sainsbury's and the rest. There were plenty of crooks around at the time, the kind who could teach even FIFA a thing or two. To compete meant being sharp and resourceful. I was neither. To be a good salesman it helps if you emotionally engage with whatever you're selling. I tried but lack any real passion for bricks and mortar.

When I began working for my father, the firm's receptionist, I forget her name, was boisterous and loud with a dried-out smoker's face and a rasping cackle. She decked herself out in a succession of trouser suits (purple and burnt orange were *de rigueur* in the early 1970s), and insisted on telling every visitor how her two-year-old daughter was ridiculously advanced for her age. To everyone's relief she landed a job at a rival agency. The following Monday, at exactly 9 a.m., our new receptionist crept in through the front door – a school-leaver starting her first job.

'Hello, I'm Emma Dawson. I . . . I think you're expecting me.' It was barely a whisper. Her coat was buttoned up so tightly at the neck I thought she might choke. For some reason I also noticed the large brass buckles on her stylish patent leather shoes; or maybe I noticed the legs before the buckles. A mass of straight brown hair fell across her face, protecting her from the world beyond. In those first few days I tried but failed to get more than a sentence or two out of her before that hair descended again, like curtains at the end of a theatrical play. She was the opposite of boisterous and loud, however, and that was all that really mattered.

Everything changed following the cock-up at Collison Court, as we now call it. Several weeks after Emms joined the firm we had one of those impossible days: people off sick, cars breaking down, clients and customers screaming for attention. With no one else available, my father took her with him to measure up a couple of properties that had to be put on to the market that same day. Her next job was to rush back to the office, type up the particulars and post them out to dozens of prospective purchasers.

Only big companies, much bigger than ours, could afford one of those shiny new machines they were calling photocopiers. We were still using an archaic Gestetner duplicator. That meant taking a black-and-white Polaroid photo of the front of the property, typing up the details on a paper stencil, inking up the duplicator and running off a few dozen copies in the print room. In her haste to make the last post, Emms put the photo of a house in Kensington Gardens on the particulars of a flat in Collison Court. And vice versa. Next morning, people were arriving at our offices requesting viewings – of the wrong property. Mortified by her mistake, Emms revised the particulars and scurried upstairs to the print room to run off more copies. I held the fort below, promising enquirers that corrected details would be available shortly. The details didn't appear. Apologizing, I went upstairs to the print room to find Emms bending over the duplicator. She was trying to pull out a piece of paper stuck in the rollers. Tears were splashing all over the machine, her face smudged with ink.

'What's happened?' I said.

'Stupid bloody machine.' She kicked it. And again. 'I'll . . . I'll never get the hang of it. I keep messing up.' The room was no bigger than a large cupboard. I was forced to stand very close to Emms and the strange fusion of Estée Lauder Eau de Parfum and warm duplicator ink was surprisingly arousing.

'Let me have a look.' I touched her for the first time, an instinctive squeeze of her hand. Now my hand was covered in ink as well.

'Oh no, sorry,' she said.

I waved away the apology. 'Leave this to me.' It sounds heroic but I knew how temperamental the printer could be. 'Take a couple of minutes and, if you think you're OK, keep them happy downstairs until I've printed these out.'

'OK, thanks.' She hesitated, as if wanting to return the friendly gesture, looked at her hand, shook her head and disappeared. It took ten minutes to free up the paper jam and run off the particulars. What I saw when I arrived downstairs has lived with me ever since. Emms was engaged in intense conversation with three couples, suggesting ways both properties could be improved.

'You could take out a wall here.' She had even drawn a sketch. 'Glass sliding doors would give you much more light in the living area. Your other option . . .' When she saw me she stopped. I gestured to her to carry on. There and then, one of the couples made an offer on the flat, for the full asking price.

'I'm sorry,' she said, when the office was empty. 'I was just trying to keep them here, like you said. It was the only thing I could think of.'

I've often wondered about that day; how life might have taken a very different course if it hadn't all gone wrong. If the correct Polaroid photo had been on the correct particulars, we might never have discovered Emms's hidden qualities. I may never have ended up marrying her. She may never have taken over Shearwater and Finch.

There again, if it hadn't all gone wrong for Jimmy Greaves, Alf Ramsey might not have played Geoff Hurst against Argentina in 1966. After England's final group game against France, Hurst reckoned he had little or no chance of playing in the World Cup but that evening he found Jimmy Greaves staring at an ugly great hole in his shin. One man's misfortune became another's opportunity. 'I knew at once that I would play against Argentina in the quarter-final,' said Hurst. 'I didn't know whether to laugh or cry.' As the sun beat down on Wembley the following Saturday afternoon, and with just fifteen minutes of the match left, Ray Wilson pushed the ball down the wing to Martin Peters. The West Ham midfielder sent it on a wide arc to a point just short of the near post. With the elegant Rattin now off the pitch, Hurst met the ball unmarked and headed it neatly past the Argentinian goalkeeper. One goal was enough to put England through to the semi-finals of the World Cup for the first time.

In the build-up to the tournament, the mercurial Greaves had been deemed the man most likely to win the cup for England with a flash of individual brilliance and inspiration. He was also the kind of maverick Alf Ramsey didn't easily relate to. Greaves's impact on the game had little to do with coaching, planning and preparation; nothing, in fact, to do with the manager. Come to think of it, he was like Lucy: all mesmerizing flair and individuality, but someone who, finally, didn't fit the system.

Greaves's injury solved a problem for Ramsey. He abandoned his traditional wide players and turned England into those famous wingless wonders. Greaves, like Lucy, was a luxury he couldn't afford. It was a hard-working eleven that took on Argentina that day with a midfield that lacked style and flamboyance but would prove difficult to beat. To his mind, Ramsay had found the formula for success.

I can't help thinking the same of Emms. She came along at just the right time, offering the right formula. She is uncomplicated and single-minded. On the surface, she lacks flair but put her in the right context and she is the consummate team player. We work well together because she has her world and I have mine. The passionate spark between us may ignite only occasionally these days but you can't have everything. After all, Geoff Hurst never hit quite as high a note again after the World Cup in 1966. He didn't need to. And neither do we.

Chapter 12

Looking back, it would have been easier if my mother had told me all I need to know about my adoption at a significant point in my life: my eighteenth birthday maybe or when I gave birth to Helen. Instinctively, we both knew the day would come somewhere down the line, though we never admitted it to each other. Today was the day, however . . .

I took her for lunch at the award-winning Tinnivelli Tea Rooms, which doubles up as a fair-trade gift shop, selling fancy wooden hearts, sweet-smelling candles and soaps. My own heart in mouth, I came clean.

'An adopted student of mine wants to trace her birth parents,' I said. 'She's nervous about it and would like us to share our journeys.' I glanced at Mum for a response.

'Oh, I see.' She tried to disguise the hurt but her smile was thin and forced. 'I have to tell you there may be . . . complica-tions.' Her eyes never met mine. She even failed to put her coffee cup down securely in the middle of the saucer: unprecedented for a lady meticulous in manners, especially at the Tinnivelli Tea Rooms.

'Complications?' I said.

Mum took a deep breath. 'These TV programmes, where they reconnect adopted children with their birth parents . . . they only show you happy reunions. It wouldn't be good for ratings if they showed the other side.'

It took me a few moments to absorb her comment. 'You think I'm going to uncover some dreadful secrets.'

'People only give up their babies if they can't manage. And if they can't manage, there's usually a problem, that's all.' She stared at the pattern of roses on her misplaced cup. 'To us you were perfect from the moment we saw you. That's all that mattered.'

I squeezed her shaking hand. It had turned cold and clammy. 'Look, even if I discover the Queen of Persia gave birth to me, you will always be my mum.'

She couldn't look me in the face. 'I shouldn't be so selfish but sharing you will be . . . difficult.'

'You will still have me. I just need to know.'

'For the student's sake.'

I nodded. 'To be honest, for mine, too.'

'Yes . . . yes, of course.'

I was aware that we had passed through a door into a place where our relationship would never be quite the same again. We had spoken of the unspeakable: my life before I was handed to her. As a child I romanticized about my unknown history. Perhaps I was the product of a tryst between a handsome prince and his beautiful lover. I imagined their giving me an eyebrow-raising name like Cassandra or Calypso, two characters in a fairy story I read over and over again. When I was ten or eleven Blondie was top of the charts and I fell in love with Debbie Harry. I wanted her voice, looks and name. The advent of adolescent angst soon dispelled the fantasy. I steeled myself for disappointment: I was more likely to be a Sharon, Kimberly or Charmaine – once fashionable names consigned to the scrapheap of popular taste.

'The thing is, I don't have a copy of your adoption order,' said Mum. 'When we moved, I foolishly put a box of important documents and mementos next to a box of rubbish. When we got to our present home I couldn't understand why we brought a box of rubbish with us. I was devastated.'

Of course, she may have been lying but what was the point of pushing her? The whole conversation was already difficult enough.

'That must have been awful, I'm so sorry,' I said when I really wanted to scream. I changed the subject, made small talk and then drove her home. Reaching my own home, I read up my next move on the web. It seems I have to apply for my original birth certificate that may provide my mother's name and address at the time of the adoption. It may also give me my father's name. The whole project comes with a big string attached, though. I was adopted before November 1975, and that means I must have counselling before I can access my records. I'm told this is to soften the blow if there is sensitive information about the adoption. It also 'helps adopted people understand some of the possible effects of their enquiries'. I've booked in for a session with our local social services department.

At least I'm finally on the trail.

Monday 29 February 2016

That angry gear change, when Jack dropped me off after the conference, has bothered me ever since. It was totally out of character. You usually associate such petulance with a boy racer but Jack had driven like a gentleman until that moment. Of course, I may have imagined the whole thing. Maybe his foot slipped off the clutch or something. I would have settled for that but his mood has changed over the past few days. He is going out of his way to avoid me.

Wanting to put my mind at rest, I arrived at work a lot earlier than normal this morning. Jack is always up with the lark so I reckoned I might engineer a chance meeting with him in the car park. It's stalking, I know, but an early morning conversation, with hardly anyone else around, seemed the best way to sort things out. No more than three minutes after parking up, I heard the shrill ring of a bell. Lisa jumped off her bike and knocked on the window of my car.

'Hello, miss,' she said. 'What are you doing here so early?'

I wound down my window. 'Getting my thoughts together, Lisa. Another long day ahead.'

'Well, what do you think about this?' Her head was virtually in my car. On it was a purple knitted hat with drooping earflaps. It would make a great tea cosy.

'Promise you won't laugh.' She had one hand poised on the hat's oversized pompom.

'Lisa . . . you *haven't!*'

'You've got to promise.'

'That lovely hair, you've cut it off.'

'Yes and no.'

'I don't understand.'

'You've got to promise.'

'Promise.'

'Ta da.' On one side of her head, luscious red hair tumbled down to her neck. The other side was completely bald.

I must have looked horrified. 'What*ever* possessed you . . . ?'

'It's called Brave the Shave. I'm trying to raise a thousand pounds for Cancer Research. I sold half my hair yesterday. They handed over fifty quid to start me off.'

'What about the other half?'

'They can have that when I get to nine-fifty. Until then, doing this raises my profile. Everybody here will know what I'm doing and why. I've already raised seventy-three pounds by putting a selfie on Facebook and Twitter. Loads of people have liked it and donated. I don't even know some of them but my friends and family have shared it.'

'You're very brave, Lisa. What did your mum say?'

'She thinks I'm mad. Sometimes she's a bit overprotective, if you know what I mean. Especially since my dad left.'

For the next five minutes, Lisa told me about her difficult situation at home. As she did so, Jack pulled up, offered us both a brief nod of the head and strode towards his office. I couldn't interrupt Lisa. It was all a bit frustrating but my 'chat' will just have to wait until another day.

Friday 4 March 2016

In ascending order of significance and chronology, the buildings I've least wanted to enter in my life:

- Big school
- Tunnel of Love with Kevin Grant
- Tunnel of Love with Andrew Simmonds
- Orthodontist's
- Bat cave at Chester Zoo
- 47 Yew Tree Gardens, Hooley

- Twickenham
- Coin-operated public toilet with dodgy lock, Tooting
- Mayday Hospital, Croydon
- Greenfern House

I've been reminded many times of my first day at 'big school'. It was an occasion to put on a bottle-green uniform, a couple of sizes too big, and puff out your chest. Instead, overcome with nerves, I locked myself in the toilet. I took my first ride through the Tunnel of Love with Kevin Grant when I was thirteen. I wanted to be with Andrew Simmonds. A week later, I took the same ride with Andrew Simmonds but wanted to be with Kevin Grant. Seven days is a long time in politics and teenage passion. As for 47 Yew Tree Gardens: a year after the Tunnel of Love I had to go to a party there. I knew Kevin would be swanning around with his stunning new girlfriend. The orthodontist and a public toilet with dodgy door: I hardly need justify trepidation of any kind. Then there's Chester Zoo: hundreds of rabies-infested bats hanging upside down in the dark, echo-locating. You've got be joking. Twickenham? Daggert's first home. Mayday Hospital? Daggert's last stop.

All of which brings me to today and the way I walked around Greenfern House, home of our local authority's adoption team, as if circling the walls of Jericho.

'It's taken me what little courage I have to come in,' I ventured to Carmel Withers, who has been assigned my case. 'I prowled outside for half an hour.'

'The last person to do that was propositioned,' Mrs Withers replied, without humour. There's a saying by Maya Angelou, one I have taken as a watchword in teaching. 'People will forget what you said. They will also forget what you did. But they will never forget how you made them feel.' Mrs Withers made me feel like a child banished to the naughty step. Did I realize that my life and those of others around may be changed for ever if my search was successful? Did I appreciate the hurt it could cause my adoptive family? Was I using the search as an excuse for not facing up to family responsibilities? Was I looking for the father figure I had lacked since my adoptive father had died? Was I aware how intrusive my search might be, not only for my natural parents but for members of the families they might now have?

I left Greenfern House in tears. If this was how it was going to be, I figured there was little point in going through with it all. I got home, kicked off my shoes, poured a generous glass of sloe gin, slumped on to the sofa and turned on the TV. After a few pointless minutes of channel hopping, I switched on the computer. The top post on my Facebook page was from Lisa. *Nearly there. Not sure whether people are giving out of sympathy or admiration. #Whocares? Last count was £823. #stilldraughtyuptop*

Accompanying the post was another picture of her head. On the shaved part it read '£177 to go'. They say youth is wasted on the young. Not in Lisa's case. The girl is inspirational: so positive and determined. I need to harness a bit of her exuberance. I am now chiding myself for being so sensitive this afternoon. I am telling myself that Mrs Withers was only doing her job: protecting person or persons unknown, in a complicated situation. She could have been a little more understanding, more human, but I've got to get over that if I am to carry this through.

Chapter 13

Round and round the rugged rock the ragged rascal ran . . . Notice my superior articulation . . . giving the letter 'r' the respect it deserves: something England's current manager struggles to do. *Wound and wound the wugged wock* . . . It's an aural car crash, a Hodgson house of horrors. When he was first appointed, the headline writers had a field day: 'In Woy we twust' and 'Bwing on the Euwos'. If he really wants to win the World Cup, Roy would do well to follow Sir Alf and one William Shearwater: invest in elocution lessons.

At the very hour a Eusebio-inspired Portugal contested a World Cup semi-final with England, I was sitting opposite Mrs Pitcher, receiving my first lesson in dynamic diction. The cool, crisp scent of a spruce and fir air freshener almost overpowered the front room of her impeccably clean house. Constable's *Haywain*, ubiquitous in the 1960s, gazed down from the wall. A grandfather clock plodded out the long minutes. No matter. I was inside Lucy's home at last.

If truth be told, I could speak perfectly well. It just depended what company I kept. Each morning I dropped off the letter H at the school gates and picked it up again later: a form of childcare for misbehaving consonants. Ensconced in the Pitchers' front room, I therefore had to invent a pronunciation malfunction. A lot of my contemporaries chose to say 'free' when talking about the number three. I suddenly had the same problem.

'Ah, so you're struggling with the unvoiced "th" with no vibration of the vocal cords,' said Mrs Pitcher.

I nodded. 'The trouble is I was born in Fort Neef,' I said, in my best south London dialect. 'Just down the road from Fort William.'

'I can't hear a Scottish accent.'

'No, what I mean is . . .' The joke wasn't worth explaining.

'To ensure the correct sound, friction must occur between the tip of your tongue and your top front teeth. Not teef. Look.'

Her lips were thin and mean. 'You need to stick your tongue out between your teeth, not too far, leaving just enough space to let the air out.' I felt stupid but obeyed. 'That's it . . . slowly. Try to avoid an explosion of air.' I obeyed again, pretending to find it difficult. After a few more deliberately botched attempts, Mrs Pitcher handed me a piece of paper.

'This should help,' she said. 'I'll ask the questions. You give me the answers. Is it Thursday today?'

'No, it's Tuesday the twenty-sixth of July,' I read.

'Will Thursday be the third of the month?'

'I don't think it will be the third of the month but the fourth.'

'So tomorrow will be the twenty-eighth?'

'No, the twenty-seventh. The end of the month means we are thankfully nearer pay day.'

'Good, let's do that again . . .'

Unbeknown to me, an enthralled, throbbing throng of 93,000 were in the throes of thanking Bobby Charlton, who, at full throttle, had scored two thrilling goals. Meanwhile, Nobby Stiles had thoroughly thwarted the threat of the Black Panther, Eusebio. Portugal had been thumped. We were through to the final.

After half an hour, and with no sign of Lucy, the vocal exercises had become pointless and tiresome. I needed to wriggle clear of Mrs Pitcher and try my luck another day. I explained that my mother was working nights at the hospital and had asked me to take our dog for a walk, before it got dark. That was when I heard the first squeak and bump. Mrs Pitcher immediately looked up at the ceiling and rolled her eyes. Another bump. Another squeak. Bump. Squeak. Bump. Squeak. Now it gathered pace. Being very sheltered, I thought it must be someone jumping up and down on a bed.

'She's at it again,' groaned Mrs Pitcher, 'imagining a far country, where all is bliss and blessing. Most evenings she has a go. She should have grown out of it by now.'

I had no idea what Mrs Pitcher was talking about and was too polite to ask. Her daughter was at home: that was all that mattered. 'I think I'll have a couple more attempts at those sentences,' I said. I was so excited I forgot to fake an 'f' on think.

'There, it's coming naturally now. Well done.' Mrs Pitcher turned back to the page in front of her. 'Is it Thursday today?'

'No, it's Tuesday the twenty-sixth of July,' I replied. Bump. Squeak. Bump. Squeak. Bump. Squeak. Bump. Squeak. Bump. It gathered even more pace and then stopped, abruptly. Now an agitated Mrs Pitcher wanted to end our session but I was determined to stay.

'Will Thursday be the third of the month?' she read.

'I don't think it will be the third of the month but the fourth.'

'So tomorrow will be the twenty-eighth?'

'No, the twenty-seventh.'

I heard light footsteps on the stairs and suddenly Lucy Pitcher was there, peering into the front room. She was wearing a peach-coloured woollen dress with puffed shoulders and flared sleeves. It had been crocheted with row upon row of tantalizing see-through triangles, rectangles and circles. It was also short. Wonderfully short. Maybe three inches below see level, as we used to say at school.

'Hi,' she smiled.

'The proper greeting to any visitor is hello,' said Mrs Pitcher, before I could reply. 'You've been watching too many American films.'

It was Lucy's turn to roll her eyes. 'Hello . . . William, isn't it?'

I nodded. 'But most people call me Billy. Or Shears. It's short for Shearwater.'

'Isn't that a seabird?'

I nodded. 'Some migrate more than eight thousand miles to breed.' What was I thinking? After lying awake in bed, rehearsing dozens of impressive opening gambits, I ended up sounding like Valerie Singleton on *Blue Peter*.

'It's an unusual surname.'

'There aren't many of us around.'

'Not surprised, if you have to travel eight thousand miles for a date.' Her eyes sparkled, mischievously.

Mrs Pitcher gestured to the back door. 'Never mind migrating seabirds. Those guinea pigs of yours need feeding, girl.' The word 'girl' came out rhyming with 'sell', the first hint of a Scouse accent she had worked so hard to lose.

I attempted to defuse the tension. 'My sister has a guinea pig.'

'Really? What type?' Lucy leaned against the door.

'Abyssinian.'

'With hair in those swirly rosettes?'

I nodded. 'His name is Banjo.'

Mrs Pitcher gathered up her books and papers. 'In Peruvian restaurants guinea pigs are a delicacy, served up complete. Head, legs, the lot.'

I must have looked shocked.

'Take no notice,' said Lucy. 'Mother doesn't like animals of any kind. Only a few human beings are acceptable, for that matter.' She hesitated, scrutinizing me closely. 'I've got two female smooth hairs at the bottom of the garden. Do you want to see them?'

'You bet.' I got up too quickly, almost tripping over the leg of my chair. I chided myself for a bad first impression: Valerie Singleton and overeagerness, an appalling combination.

Mrs Pitcher seemed surprised at Lucy's invitation. 'I hope the shed is in a decent state,' she said. 'Lucy wanted those little rats. Keeping the shed clean is her responsibility.'

The Pitchers' garden was the same length as ours but we had a greenhouse at the end instead of a shed. Lucy had come downstairs barefoot but put on a pair of flip-flops and grabbed a transistor radio.

'What's the scene like?' she said as we walked down the garden path. Scene? I must have looked blank. She gestured with her hand to the neighbourhood. 'What happens round here?'

'Oh, well ...' I could hardly tell her about the forthcoming church choir outing that included high tea and a gentle stroll round the gardens at Sissinghurst Castle. I remembered reading of incidents involving mods and rockers on the south coast. 'Brighton can be a good day out.'

'Day out?' she giggled. 'I wasn't thinking of a Darby and Joan coach trip, just somewhere to have a bit of a blast.' What exactly constituted a blast? I dared not admit my ignorance. Had I been standing at the exact point of detonation, I still wouldn't have known. The guinea pigs squeaked with anticipation: a very different pitch from the one emanating earlier from upstairs.

'They know your footsteps,' I said.

Lucy nodded and opened the shed door. 'Sorry about the pong.'

'Can't smell anything,' I lied.

She smiled. 'It's the only place I can turn on.'

I looked at the radio in her hand. 'Aren't you allowed to listen indoors?'

She giggled and tuned the transistor to Wonderful Radio London, a pirate pop station. The first song on was 'I Want You' by Bob Dylan. Whenever I hear it, I'm back in that shed.

'I love Dylan,' she said. I mumbled some kind of affirmative, though I knew little of Bob Dylan at the time and when the song finished asked if there was any chance of switching to the Home Service. She turned away and failed to suppress another giggle. 'What's so funny?' Everything about me seemed to amuse her.

'Nothing . . . it's just . . . you're so . . . so *square*!'

That stung. It still does. It's impossible to overestimate the power of that noun, delivered from one teenager to another five decades ago. My shapeless half-sleeve shirt and dull grey slacks (for that's what our mothers called them) told the painful truth: I was now on the official register of square offenders. I hadn't yet found the courage to drag myself, sartorially, into the swinging sixties. Polo neck sweaters, chunky corduroy jackets and Chelsea boots, the ones with elastic side panels, were daringly fashionable. Unlike me, Godfrey Henderson had all of the above. I envied his money, style and sideburns, for which he regularly received the ultimate badge of honour: after-school detentions.

'I just want to know the World Cup score,' I said.

'Isn't that over yet?' she said. 'It's such a drag.'

'We're playing Portugal.'

'Is "we" England?'

'Do I look Portuguese?'

Lucy folded her arms and studied me. 'You seem very agitated.' She put her hand round the back of the guinea pig cage and thought twice. 'Can I trust you?'

'I'm not sure what you mean,' I said. She looked at me again, then pulled out a large box. Still smarting from being called four-sided, I feared more humiliation.

'Look . . . I . . . I don't smoke.' It sounded so weak.

'Nor do I,' she replied, 'At least, not tobacco.' She pulled some Rizla cigarette paper out of the box, the type my grandfather used to roll his own, and laid it on top of the cage. 'One of the prefects at school got me into this. These leaves are from the top of a flowering female plant. They can really send you.' She made a filter tip out of a piece of card and laid it at the end of the joint, then distributed cannabis evenly along the length of the paper. 'Too much and it won't close properly.' She tucked and rolled up the back half of the joint (though I had no idea it was called that at the time), licked the sticky strip of paper and sealed the lot, lightly twisting it to keep the contents from falling out. 'Here.' She held out the finished article. 'See what you think.'

Twenty minutes later I was spreadeagled on the floor of the shed, glassy-eyed and giggling about seabirds trying to pronounce the unvoiced 'th' in a mid-air mating ritual. Or something. Two disinterested guinea pigs lay on top of my stomach, remorselessly chomping their way through dandelion leaves.

'This is crazy,' I said.

'It makes me less crazy,' said Lucy. 'They reckon I'm hard to handle and the problem's all up here.' She pointed to her head. 'This stuff fills in the holes.'

'When can I transfer to your school?' I said. 'It sounds . . . a bit of a blast.'

Lucy was sitting on a stool. 'Being sent away to boarding school at seven is miserable.'

'Why did you go?'

'Dad travels a lot on construction projects and mother couldn't cope with me on her own. It's very strict. We're in uniform six days a week.'

'What, even Saturdays?'

'Until lunchtime.'

'I can't imagine you in school uniform,' I lied. St Trinian's was my mental point of reference and an arousing one.

'Anyway, Mother got what she wanted. I no longer have much of a northern accent.'

'Funny, that.'

'My accent?'

'No. The way you call your mother, Mother, and your father, Dad.'

Lucy looked at me intently. 'I'd never realized that . . . wow.' She was quiet for several seconds.

'Do they know anything about this?' I held up the remains of my joint.

She shook her head and looked at the door. 'No one gets past that. But just in case, the guinea pigs' droppings overpower the smoke.'

A few minutes later, I heard a car pull up and a garage door open. 'That'll be my . . . father,' said Lucy. 'You're right. It sounds strange.' It occurred to me that, if Mr Pitcher was anything like his wife, he wouldn't take kindly to finding me holed up in a garden shed with his daughter. Head spinning, I stood up and put Lucy's guinea pigs, still chomping remorselessly, back in their cage.

'Maybe you should bring Banjo round,' said Lucy, breathing over my shoulder. It was a small shed and I could feel one of her breasts nudge softly into my back. 'Who knows what might happen were the three of them to become close friends . . . I doubt Banjo could control himself.' It is probably an unreliable memory, a product of wishful thinking, exaggerated with the passing decades. All I know for sure is that my legs, already unreliable from the inhalation of tetrahydrocannabinol, almost gave way.

'Thank you, God,' I mouthed silently. I was no longer in full possession of my senses or limbs but I congratulated myself for fluent articulation of the unvoiced 'th'.

'Lucy!' I've often wondered what would have happened next if at that very moment Mr Pitcher hadn't called out to his daughter. It was more a loud hiss, yards from the shed. Lucy swore quietly and hurriedly tidied away what was left of the cannabis. 'He never comes down here,' she muttered. 'Something must be wrong.' She stepped out of the shed. I crouched on the stool, awaiting my fate.

'I need your help, love,' said Mr Pitcher. 'It's your mum.'

'What's happened?' said Lucy.

'Don't worry, it's not like that. I've got a new framed picture for her birthday. I need somewhere to hide it. She never goes in the shed . . .'

'Not now.' I could hear the tension rise in Lucy's voice. 'There's no room.' There was room enough but smoke still hung in the shed like an early morning mist in autumn.

Mr Pitcher seemed unconvinced. 'Let me see if we can move something.'

I could think of only one way to resolve the problem. 'Hello, Mr Pitcher,' I said, stepping out of the shed. 'I'm Billy, from down the road. Lucy was showing me her guinea pigs.'

'Yes . . . yes,' said Lucy. 'Billy's sister has one. An Abyssinian, with those twirly rosettes.'

'Oh.' Mr Pitcher was taken aback to see me. 'Well, I . . .'

'Why don't you bring the picture down to our house and we'll keep it there for a few days, until Mrs Pitcher's birthday?'

'Well . . . that's very kind of you. Billy, did you say?' He held out his hand. 'I'm Bernard but everyone calls me Bernie.' He had a quiet northern accent. I couldn't work out where it was from. Everything about him seemed the opposite of Mrs Pitcher: unassuming and genial. Lucy went into the house to engage her mother while Mr Pitcher (it would never be Bernie for me) lifted the framed print from the boot of his car.

'Have you any idea if we beat Portugal, Mr Pitcher?' I said, as we walked to my house.

'I think so,' he said. 'I heard something on the car radio.'

I punched the air. 'Do you know the score?'

'No idea. Not interested in football, me. Now Rugby League, that's a man's game.'

My parents offered Mr Pitcher a cup of coffee. They got on well. So well it occurred to me that, if I wasn't careful, I may not see Lucy again that evening.

'I didn't thank your daughter for her guided tour of the shed,' I said, as Mr Pitcher got up to go.

'Well, you'd better come back with me,' he said. We walked to the front door of his house. 'I've been thinking . . . one good turn and all that . . .'

'What kept you?' Mrs Pitcher met us in the hall.

'Our new neighbours. And I'd like to repay their kindness.' He explained that most of his colleagues were not football fans and those that were had been unimpressed with England's performances in the World Cup. 'One of our clients gave us some complimentary tickets for the final but none of us wants to go. Could you use any, Billy?'

'Use any?' It came out in a strangulated gasp. If the cannabis had reduced my knees to jelly . . .

Lucy joined us in the hall and pulled a face. 'That's a shame. I thought they might be tickets to something interesting.'

'Godfrey, who lives over the road, he's a big England fan,' I gushed. 'He'll definitely want to go, too.' I wasn't thinking, of course. I should never have mentioned Hendo. I was too excited to think strategically. After all these years I am still kicking myself. Some regrets last a lifetime.

'Do you mean that boy with the unkempt hair and those strange-looking whiskers?' said Mrs Pitcher, haughtily. I nodded.

'On the other hand,' said Lucy. 'A day out at Wembley could be a lot of fun . . .'

Chapter 14

Saturday 12 March 2016

I turfed out more boxes today and found the review of Daggert's *Cinderella* in the local paper. Reading the review and the script took me back to nights of rubber daggers and cardboard shields, nylon tights and plastic warts. Egos, too, bigger than the giant in *Jack and the Beanstalk*, uglier than Cinderella's sisters.

Talking of those sisters . . . I made my first appearance in Scene Nine of *Cinderella*, at the Palace Ballroom. A transformed Cinders has already arrived in her coach, unrecognized by Griselda and Lolita, played by two men, of course. Daggert had rewritten two scenes at the last minute, adding me as Rita, the parking meter attendant. It wasn't a large part but then I had never acted before. The ball is in full swing when all eyes turn stage left . . .

ROYAL
ANNOUNCER   My lords, ladies and gentlemen, please welcome your host for the evening, His Royal Highness Prince Charming, MSc, MBE, KFC, B&Q.

Fanfare sounds as the Prince, in tetchy mood, walks in giving a royal wave without enthusiasm.

GRISELDA   [*curtsying*] Sire.

LOLITA   [*curtsying*] My lord, my liege.

PRINCE   [*bored*] Yes, yes, yes . . . where's the grub?

GRISELDA   Well, I can be quite tasty.

LOLITA   Pah! [*sticks out a false bosom*] His Royal Highness wants a bit of crackling [*looks Griselda up and down*] not a pudding.

GRISELDA   I've turned a few heads in my time.

LOLITA   And stomachs.

With his back to audience, Prince moves away from Griselda and Lolita and tucks into the food. Rita appears in wings.

ROYAL
ANNOUNCER   Your Royal Highness, my lords, ladies and gentlemen, may I introduce er . . . [*puzzled, looks at sheet*] . . . I don't seem to have any . . . who are you exactly?

RITA   Never mind my name.

Dressed in a traffic warden outfit, Rita pushes announcer to one side and enters, notebook in hand, to off-stage boos and wolf whistles. Griselda, Lolita and Cinderella look put out as she walks past them.

RITA   Right then, who owns the jewel-encrusted, gold-plated carriage registration no. D857XBN?

Prince Charming, still eating with back to audience, puts up his hand. Rita walks slowly across front of stage, milking boos and wolf whistles from audience, and taps Prince on the shoulder. Prince turns.

PRINCE   [*instantly attracted*] Oh, I *say*! How lovely.

Griselda, Lolita and Cinderella look even more put out.

RITA   Are you aware of the helpful new traffic regulations in the town centre? [*off-stage boos*]

PRINCE   Of course. With the revenue from the parking meters I will be able to pay another servant to clean out the ashtrays in my carriage [*to audience*] after a sneaky backhander to our local councillors. [*more boos*]

RITA   Are you aware your carriage is parked on a double yellow line?

PRINCE   Oh no, it isn't.

RITA   [*with audience*] Oh yes, it is.

91

PRINCE	Oh no, it isn't.
RITA	[*with audience*] Oh yes, it is.
PRINCE	Well, I can park wherever I want. I'm a Prince … and this is a Saturday.
RITA	I don't care if it's a Sunday.
PRINCE	That's my fun day.
RITA	Rules are rules, even if it's just another [*invites audience to join in*] manic Monday.

Rita sticks a parking ticket on Prince Charming and exits stage right, to the Bangles' 'Manic Monday' and a chorus of boos and wolf whistles.

Several members of the cast advised Daggert that most of the audience wouldn't know that Prince wrote 'Manic Monday' but that didn't stop him slipping it in. It was his production.

I appeared once more, at the story's denouement. Prince Charming and his willing valet Dandini are looking for the owner of the glass slipper left behind by Cinderella. He has searched high and low, to no avail.

The scene opens at Baron Hardup's house, home to Griselda, Lolita and Cinderella, who is cleaning the fireplace in the corner. Curtain opens with a song playing, 'Agadoo' by Black Lace. Griselda and Lolita are each holding a shoe and singing.

GRISELDA
AND LOLITA   Grab-a-shoe shoe shoe
Push a foot inside and see
Grab-a-shoe shoe shoe
Soon the Prince will marry me.

Song finishes. Griselda studies her shoe.

GRISELDA	My future as a princess is waiting.
LOLITA	Your future is waiting on a princess!
GRISELDA	Prince Charming will be banging on my door soon enough.

LOLITA   But eventually you'll have to let him out.

GRISELDA   [*goes to the window to look for the Prince*] Hello, there's a soldier outside.

LOLITA   [*joins her at the window*] That's no soldier. It's that parking meter attendant and she's coming up our path.

Two loud knocks on door. Griselda and Lolita open it. Rita is holding a giant pumpkin with a parking ticket on it.

RITA   Does anyone here own this?

CINDERELLA   Yes. I do.

RITA   It's parked illegally.

LOLITA   A pumpkin? Parked illegally?

RITA   It was seen leaving the ball at speed, as if by magic.

GRISELDA   The only magic vegetables round here are the mushrooms.

LOLITA   And you must be on them, love.

There are two more loud knocks at the door. Lolita opens the door to Dandini.

DANDINI   All rise for His Royal Highness Prince Charming MSc, MBE . . .

LOLITA   [*rolls eyes, joining in with Dandini*] KFC . . .

GRISELDA   [*rolls eyes, joining in with Dandini*] B&Q.

DANDINI   His Majesty requires all members of the household to sit down and put out their right legs.

LOLITA AND
GRISELDA   At last!

Rita exits stage right. Griselda, Lolita and Cinderella all sit down on the sofa. A tired, crotchety Prince Charming enters stage left and addresses audience.

PRINCE   Another town, another street
                Another pair of sweaty feet
                Corns and bunions, flaky skin
                Six-inch toenails growing in

                Warts, verrucas, blisters too
                Veins all varicose and blue
                Athlete's foot, arthritic toes
                Where this girl is, heaven knows

                Should I ever lose the crown
                And find myself with plebs cast down
                I'll carve a living out, you'll see
                And make a bob or two, or three

                Learned lawyer, male nurse
                Driver of a slow, black hearse
                Of every job I'll make a fist
                But *never* a chiropodist.

Dandini tries the slipper on Lolita.

GRISELDA   No chance. Her feet are so big even clowns stop and
                stare!

The slipper won't fit. Dandini tries it on Griselda. Her foot is also too big.

GRISELDA   [*trying to squeeze foot into slipper*] If I could . . . just . . .
                take off . . . the VAT.

Dandini tries the slipper on Cinderella. Her foot fits perfectly.

PRINCE   My heart is full, my joy complete
                An end to stalking women's feet
                I've found a girl who gets top marks
                Her slippers always come from Clarks
                So here am I, on bended knee
                Cinderella, marry me!

You know the rest. The Prince bags his bride. The sisters beg
forgiveness. The cast belt out a final number. The mayor bids all

farewell. The audience braves the cold air. The cast bevvy the night away. That's the theory. It didn't turn out quite like that on the last performance of Jonathan Daggert's legendary *Cinderella* . . .

I soon learned that, given the right part, every coarse actor will be the stand-out performer. Or that's what they believe. Conversely, hell hath no fury like a leading lady scorned. Cinderella was played by Janice Gresham, a former student of ballet, poised for a big break in the West End. She had the kind of Bambi brown eyes that made her a shoo-in for Virgin Mary in the school nativity; and those ballet disciplines gave her an enviable, if slightly robotic deportment. While awaiting the inevitable call from her theatrical agent, Janice had a temporary job meeting and greeting shoppers in a local supermarket. Poised for the big break is an accurate description because even in the foyer at Tesco her heels seemed permanently joined. Her feet pointed out at strange angles, too, as if the Dance of the Sugar Plum Fairy was about to begin behind her in cooked meats.

She sizzled enough herself to win the close attention of Colin (Griselda) and Mike (Lolita). After rehearsals, they vied for her attention at The Grapes, our local across the street. Her eyes were only for the producer, though (she was learning fast) and Daggert spoiled everything by adding a new character, to be played by a novice. Yes, it was just a cameo role. No, she wouldn't have a major part to play. Yes, she would be in two scenes, that's all. No, she wouldn't steal the show. In spite of these assurances, Janice was less than thrilled at my inclusion. Daggert and I weren't yet an item and when I arrived at rehearsals, Colin and Mike now had someone else on whom to practise chat-up lines.

On the final night of the panto, a blinged-up mayor and mayoress took their seats in the front row alongside other local notables and a reporter from the *Echo*. Behind them sat row upon row of scrubbed-up, badged-up, toggled-up Brownies and Cubs. Half the town, it seemed, had turned up as well, with standing room only at the back.

I got an inkling something was irking Janice before she went on for her first scene. It may have been because Colin and Mike promised to get me drunk on Earl Grey tea after the show (I had told them I was teetotal, which was untrue). Daggert was giving me more attention than her as well. In fact, she wouldn't look me in the eye. And I wasn't the only one. I've seen county court bailiffs get a warmer greeting than Cinderella's Fairy Godmother that night. When the same lady waved her magic wand and said, 'You shall go the ball,' Cinders gave the 'yeah, whatever' look I see every day on the faces of my students.

It didn't help when, without warning, Daggert played Shirley Bassey's 'Big Spender' as I walked on stage for the first time, something he kept back for the final performance. The whistles, boos and cheers reached a new height. Being panto, my job was to play to the crowd. At least, that was my defence. I stopped centre stage, invited more audience response, and then threw my traffic warden's hat at the mayor. That probably pushed Janice to the edge but it wasn't until the last scene that she hurtled over at full tilt.

The idea of my arriving at Baron Hardup's house with a parking ticket on a pumpkin was pure Daggert. And I think Janice would have kept her cool if the scene had played out as scripted. Colin and Mike, however, planned some high jinks for the final night. As I headed for my exit stage right Lolita and Griselda picked me up, dumped me on the sofa and sat either side, linking arms with me to prevent my moving. Cinderella was left alone on the armchair.

You could almost hear something snap in Janice's highly strung brain. She grabbed the pumpkin and with both hands threw it with venom into Lolita's solar plexus. The humble pumpkin, cultivar of the squash plant and remarkably rich in antioxidants such as lutein, xanthin and carotenes, generally weighs in at something between four and six kilogrammes, close on a stone in old money. Thrown down from height it feels considerably heavier. Griselda got up to restrain Cinders but those ballet lessons kicked in, literally. If Griselda had been a true sister, the pain would not have been so intense. He (she) lay doubled up on the stage floor. Lolita, still holding his (her) stomach, tried to calm Cinders, who slapped him across the face.

Until this point, the Brownies and Cubs had hardly joined in on key moments, even the 'he's behind you' and 'oh yes, he is'/'oh no, he isn't' interludes. Now, however, they clapped and roared their approval. Those Ugly Sisters were getting their comeuppance at last. Persuaded by the children, most adults in the audience presumed the scene had been rehearsed and delivered to perfection. They joined in the applause. I beat a hasty exit. Much to everyone's relief backstage, Prince Charming lived up to his name and smoothed the audience with a brilliant piece of improvisation.

'Hands up who likes Donatello?' he asked. Cub and Brownie hands shot to the sky. 'What about Leonardo?' More ascending hands. He explained how the fighting skills of all four Teenage Mutant Ninja Turtles, hugely popular at the time, had been granted to Cinderella by her Fairy Godmother.

'Heroes in a half shell,' he sang.

'Turtle power!' sang back the kids.

'Let's do that again . . . Heroes in a half shell . . .'

Lolita and Griselda recovered their poise. The panto ended without further unforeseen incidents. When Daggert came on to take a bow at the curtain call, I half expected Cinderella to stretch out a leg and push him over. She didn't. He was the producer. She was learning.

A few days later the following report appeared in the *Echo*.

CINDERELLA: PANTOMIME MEETS PUNK

Time was when political activists joyfully subverted the medium of pantomime to ridicule oppressive powers. Consider the end of the eighteenth century: Britain is at war with France, and violent confrontations between government and citizens are the order of the day. Into the predictable world of pantomime bursts a character with white face and red cheeks, pie-crust frill and baggy trousers, cavernous mouth and elastic face. As war raged, Joseph Grimaldi's hilarious antics embodied the freedom of British culture in contrast to our humourless enemies, the French. Grimaldi became one of the great satirists of his age, offering ludicrous commentaries on fashion, technology, transport and political authority.

If Jonathan Daggert hasn't studied Grimaldi, call me the clown. He overlooks no political target, local or national, in his excellent and highly original production of *Cinderella*. Take those infernal double yellow lines in the town centre, for example. He mocks our jumped-up local bureaucrats by casting a saucy traffic warden, with watchful eye on both

Prince Charming's jewel-laden carriage and our mayor. And the prince himself, usually wimpy and two-dimensional, gets a cultural makeover. Tormented and tetchy like Prince Charles, Charming, played by architect Tim Masters, finally redeems himself, overcoming a stultifying diffidence with wit and wisdom. Daggert's clear message to today's Buck House cast: shape up or ship out.

But it is his reconstruction of the principal character that proves the most surprising and satisfying. Not for Daggert the poor-little-me, virginal victim. Instead we encounter an altogether darker, damaged adolescent. Cinderella, played by ballet graduate Janice Gresham, pouts and simmers with frustration, rage even. Gresham, a star in the making, provides an unexpected and delicious dénouement. Her pugnacious attack on the Ugly Sisters, beautifully choreographed, was a tour de force. If you want to see what happens when *Swan Lake* meets the Sex Pistols get a ticket for the next Jonathan Daggert production. *Puss in Boots* is likely to be on the agenda, I hear. I dread to think what size Doc Martens Puss will be wearing.

Janice got a minor role in the West End and moved in with one of the lighting engineers. That's the last I heard of her. *Puss in Boots* never happened: Daggert was too busy revising for his finals. The company staged *Aladdin* instead, written and produced by Tim Masters, who had played Prince Charming. He wanted me to play Princess Badroulbadour but, as well as not being able to spell it, I didn't fancy playing the part without Daggert around.

Thinking that through led me to buy the *Daily Mail* today. The paper has my number, of course: female, middle class, middle of the road, middle aged. They call it fascism in oven gloves and it's not hard to work out why. A new cause of cancer is splashed across the *Mail*'s pages with monotonous regularity: this month it will probably be peshwari naan bread and rising house prices, next month answering machines and being too tall at fourteen. We are warned that one puff of cannabis will turn us into paranoid schizophrenics, losing all respect for Her Majesty The Queen, people carriers and Waitrose.

But I bought this issue because an article caught my eye: 'Are You Looking for a Father Figure?' I wouldn't have given it a passing thought before my first counselling session with Carmel Withers. I was never close to my adoptive father and he died when I was in my early teens. Did he leave, or even create some kind of void? I have no idea. What I do know is that Daggert burst into my life, all drive and self-assurance, setting whatever agenda needed setting (in his opinion). And I ran with it. Maybe that's why I responded to Jack: another dominant personality.

And where am I in all this? When will I make decisions on my own? It was easy enough on stage, as Rita. When I chucked my hat at the mayor it was just a bit of fun. The *Echo* reviewer deemed it a political act. Had I thought it would be construed as political, I wouldn't have done it. I'm not that brave. Then I think of Lisa, with enough courage in class to admit she was adopted, call gorgeous Gareth Hillier a wanker and shave off half her hair to raise money for a good cause.

It's a sobering thought to be a middle-aged teacher and find your mentor is a student in your class.

Chapter 15

Here we go round the mulberry bush . . . the mulberry bush . . . the mulberry bush . . . Nicholas Ledgard will be as good as his word, if an unexpected call from an old friend today has anything to do with it.

'William, it's Kristina.'

'Kristina? Crazy Kristina?'

'One and the same. It's been forty years.'

'Dat is . . . ongelooflijk.' It's one of the few Dutch words I know. With added guttural, it is much more satisfying than our own 'unbelievable'.

She laughed. 'So . . . you still remember the words I taught you?'

'Zeker. Where are you phoning from?'

'Utrecht.'

'Ah, back home!'

'And still into theology.'

'In what capacity?'

'Professor.'

I gave a low whistle. 'That's . . .'

'Ongelooflijk! I was never very good at anything else.'

We chatted for several minutes. There were so many people we had known all those years ago. In a short but eventful chapter of my life, Kristina Erkens was sandwiched somewhere between Lucy and Emms. We met at university, on her first day. I had returned before the start of my second year, to help with Freshers' Week. Like most of our Dutch cousins, Kristina spoke excellent English, drank strong lager, mocked the British apology for coffee and kept a pouch of tobacco in the breast pocket of her tight cheesecloth shirts. She would leave morning song, gasping, and roll her own outside the chapel.

For a reason I can no longer fathom, we clicked. Too quickly. The first week of term was a whirlwind. By the end of week four the storm had blown itself out but not before we sat alongside each other for the official year photo. To my eternal embarrassment, her head is lolling on my shoulder.

'I'm calling because . . . do you know someone called Nicholas Ledgard?' she said.

'Ye-es.'

'He phoned me just now.'

'What? In Utrecht?'

'Yes.'

'Why? Do you know him?'

'No. He said he was writing an article on theological responses to climate change. I've had a couple of papers published on the subject.'

'But I don't see why . . .'

' . . . it has anything to do with you?'

'Yes.'

'He said he had seen the photo. *Our* photo.'

I groaned. 'Goodness me, what were we thinking?'

She laughed. 'We look sweet.'

'Yes, well . . . my family will never let me live it down.'

'You had a lucky escape – that's what my husband says. Anyway, this Ledgard, he seemed a bit too interested in . . . you and me.'

'What do you mean?'

'He asked more questions about our relationship than the disappearing polar caps. He seemed a bit . . . griezelig.'

'Yes, creepy sums it up.' Ledgard is digging up the dirt. He wants revenge. I was pondering what to do next, if anything, when I received another call, this time from a freelance reporter. He was at Wembley Stadium for my speech and wondered if I had any personal memories of the 1966 World Cup. Would being at the final qualify, I said? When I gave him my account of Saturday 30 July 1966, he couldn't believe his luck . . .

*

Being fair to Lucy, she didn't come on strong to Hendo. Perhaps Hendo and I were so pumped up for the final, we wouldn't have noticed. It was hard to concentrate on anything, or anyone, other than the match ahead, though Hendo did go on about his motorbike. I was secretly chuffed when Lucy pulled a face and said she would never ride on the back of anything with only two wheels.

We changed trains at East Croydon. The platforms were heaving with England fans sounding klaxons and clanging handbells. We wore top hats with rosettes all over them. I don't remember seeing anyone in replica England kit but there were plenty of shirts and ties, even on the terraces. I also waved a Union Jack. After all, to most English minds we were playing for the pride of the British Isles. Our Celtic cousins would support us, just as we would support them in a similar situation. At the far end of the platform Lucy, unimpressed by testosterone-driven jingoism, spotted a small, grey-haired man holding a German flag. He looked dapper in suit and tie.

'How awful, being alone on a day like this,' she said. 'I'm going to have a chat.' Hendo and I looked at each other and shook our heads. The time for talking to the enemy was after the game, when we would politely rub his nose in it. With no respect for received culture, Lucy sat next to the foreigner.

'Guten Morgen, ich bin Lucy,' she said.

'Ich bin Rudiger,' he said. 'Erfreut, Sie zu treffen.'

They exchanged a few more words in German but it soon became clear he knew far more English than she knew German.

'We're going to the game.' Lucy pointed at the map he had been studying. 'Travel with us.' Hendo looked at me. I looked at Hendo.

Rudiger smiled warmly and shook his head. 'I am watching the match at my hotel.' He shrugged. 'I have no ticket.'

Lucy reached for the inside pocket of her windcheater. I looked at Hendo. Hendo looked at me. Lucy looked at both of us. 'Dad brought home four.' Of all the . . . I mean . . . when you think of . . . and she gives it to a *German*! Rudiger sat speechless for several seconds. I thought he was going to cry. Needless to say, being English, Hendo and I smiled through clenched teeth and shook hands with our new travelling companion. Thanks to Lucy, we also had to make polite conversation with . . . a *German*!

'You know our town?' I said, when Rudiger had recovered his poise. The large-scale street map in his hands covered the Croydon area.

He laughed. 'I know it better than you. Before the war I flew to your airport hundreds of times. I am a pilot.' Hendo looked at me. I looked at Hendo. We were suddenly impressed.

'When the war started, your blackout made no difference. I could fly blindfold to Croydon Airport.'

'You were in the Luftwaffe?' Hendo gawped.

'Yes.'

'Fighters or bombers?'

'Bombers.'

'Which one?

'The Dornier Do 17.'

'The Flying Pencil!' said Hendo. 'I made the Airfix model.'

Rudiger sighed. A faraway look came into his eyes. 'Before the war I dropped off the mail.' He put his hand up high. 'And then . . .' Accompanied by his own descending whistle, he slapped his hand on his knee several times. 'Boom, boom, boom.' All insensitively graphic but we were teenagers in the presence of a genuine Second World War bomber. Respect.

'I imagine you're visiting old friends,' said Lucy.

Rudiger shook his head. 'Just paying a final visit to some places that mean a lot to me.'

'Like the old aerodrome,' said Hendo.

'Not so much.' The map was marked at several points. At first, we thought they were pubs or churches.

'I think this was one of mine.' Rudiger pointed to an 'x' in Galpins Road, Thornton Heath. 'Boom,' he said. 'And probably these two in Wharfedale Gardens. Boom. Boom.' He squeezed Hendo's arm. 'But let's forget all this, we are friends again, until this afternoon.' I looked at Hendo and discreetly pointed to Rudiger's right arm. You could see the wings of an eagle tattoo where the cuff of his shirt met his wrist.

I changed the subject and soon wished I hadn't. 'Whereabouts in Germany do you live?'

Rudiger sighed again. 'Dresden,' he said. In one February day in 1945 at least 25,000 people were killed when Allied bombers dropped more than 3,900 tons of high-explosive bombs and incendiary devices on the city. 'My wife died that night. I lost every-thing . . . everything.'

'I'm sorry,' I mumbled.

'They were sad days but we cannot dwell on the past.' He held up his ticket. 'I cannot thank you enough. I spoke to my wife this morning and she told me to expect a miracle. You are that miracle.'

'I'm glad you've married again,' said Lucy, brightly.

'I haven't.'

I looked at Hendo, Hendo . . . well, you know the rest. Had we been on our own, the two of us would have melted into the crowd. Lucy, however, had warmed to her new friend and all the tickets were in her pocket. By now we were sitting together on a crowded underground train bound for Wembley Park.

'Do you have any pictures of your wife?' said Lucy.

Rudiger reached into the right-hand pocket of his jacket. 'Es tut mir Leid . . . I mean, sorry . . . wrong one,' he said, pulling out some sandwiches in a plastic wrapper.

'And an apple to finish. Very healthy,' said Lucy, spotting a round bulge in the same pocket. 'Unless it's a cricket ball.'

'They don't play cricket in Germany,' I said.

Rudiger smiled and patted his pocket. 'For supper, possibly my last.' He found a crumpled photo of his wife. 'So beautiful.' We all nodded. She was blonde with a heart-shaped face and engaging smile. Lucy studied the photo intently.

'She looks lovely,' she said.

'You're very kind, thank you.' Rudiger's eyes began to water.

'They've let Beckenbauer play.' I deftly changed the subject. The tall German midfielder, just twenty years of age, had received a sec-ond booking against Russia in the semi-final. Nowadays he would receive an automatic ban from the final but back then FIFA had a formula allowing them to bend the rules. Each caution had to be confirmed at one of their meetings. If the booking was not con-firmed it didn't mean the referee had made a mistake, it simply meant no further action was necessary. Way before the corruption scandals, FIFA officials were already skilled at turning a blind eye.

'Who?' said Rudiger.

'Beckenbauer.'

'Will he win you the match?'

I was puzzled. 'He's one of your players.'

'Ah . . . oh well . . . we have to stop Greaves.'

'He's not playing.'

Rudiger's eyes narrowed. 'Whoever plays, Germany must win. Make no mistake. It is death or glory.'

We reached the stadium early and got drenched in a sudden downpour. I'll never forget Lucy, soaked through, standing there at the turnstile, about to watch her first-ever game of football, the World Cup Final. She took a photo of us all on her Brownie 127 and when the stadium opened, Hendo and I rushed to the front of the standing enclosure. After getting drinks, Lucy and Rudiger joined us there. The atmosphere, already electric, went into overdrive as the two teams came out. When the band struck up West Germany's national anthem, Hendo saw Rudiger instinctively raise his right arm in a Nazi salute and turn it into a harmless wave to nobody. At least, that's what he said after the game. To my mind it was a product of Hendo's fertile imagination but it's true to say our German friend celebrated Helmut Haller's opening goal of the final with unbridled enthusiasm; and Haller was, like Rudiger's wife, of pure Aryan stock.

Geoff Hurst headed an equalizer minutes later. Hendo and I punched the air and hugged each other. Both of us wanted to hug Lucy but didn't want to embarrass ourselves. Of course, if she hadn't looked so damn gorgeous we would have thought nothing of it. She took no notice of the celebrations. Even without a little help from a joint or two, she seemed preoccupied. Rudiger simply shook his head and muttered something to himself in his mother tongue.

I remember very little about the second half, except that we were on top for most of it. Finally, the pressure paid off. Germany's Horst Hottges, attempting to clear eight yards from his own goal line, swiped at the ball and slipped. The ball looped in the air. Following up, Martin Peters swept it home. Hendo and I jumped up and down in joy. Hunched and helpless, Rudiger stared out over the perimeter fence.

'I've been thinking about the photo of Rudiger's wife,' Lucy said to me as the game restarted.

'What about it?'

'It's puzzling me.' I didn't take much notice. Minutes later, people all over the stadium were whistling to remind the referee it was almost full-time. West Germany won a free kick yards from the English penalty area. The most heartbreaking moment of my young life was about to happen. In a packed penalty area, the ball broke kindly to Wolfgang Weber who stabbed home from three yards to equalize. Hendo and I hung our heads in misery. Rudiger smiled and looked up to the heavens. We were heading for thirty minutes of extra time.

'That photo,' said Lucy, taking me to one side. In the intense emotion of the moment it was hard to believe she could be concerned about the photo of a deceased German girl. 'I've seen her face before.'

'Impossible,' I said.

'I'm sure of it. I just can't think where.'

In spite of West Germany's late equalizer, we were well on top in extra time. Ball had a shot tipped over. Charlton hit a post. After ten minutes, we witnessed the defining moment of the 1966 World Cup Final. Ball to Hurst. Hurst swivels, shoots. The ball beats Tilkowski in the German goal, rattles the bar and drops down behind him. Which side of the line? From where I was standing it looked a good goal. Not for Rudiger. Not for a man who knew all about things dropping at speed from a great height. Swiss referee Gottfried Dienst consulted with the man who was to become the most famous linesman in history, Tofiq Bahramov. Bahramov was adamant: the ball had crossed the line. Rudiger spat out some more unintelligible German and stabbed a finger at where Bahramov was mentioned in the programme.

'The man is a Soviet,' he said. 'This is about the war. This is his revenge.' Unknown to us at the time, Bahramov, said to be Russian but actually from Azerbaijan, really had fought against the German army during the war. An apocryphal story relates how, on his deathbed, he admitted a pro-English prejudice. When asked why he allowed the goal to stand at Wembley he is said to have replied, 'Stalingrad.'

All Hendo and I cared about was that we were winning. Five left . . . four . . . three . . . every one of those last minutes felt like an hour. West Germany pushed forward relentlessly, looking for another equalizer.

'Got it!' said Lucy, suddenly.

'Got what?' mumbled Hendo, eyes fixed on the pitch.

'The woman.'

'Which woman?' Haller aimed a long, hopeful cross into the box. Banks collected. More whistles.

'Rudiger's wife. The one in the photo.'

'What about her?' Hunt tracked back to tackle Held.

'That wasn't his wife.'

'Who was it, then?' Oooh. Close. Seeler just failed to connect with a header yards from our goal.

'It was Eva Braun.'

'Eva Braun? Hitler's bird, you mean. They committed suicide together,' said Hendo. It was as if someone had poked him awake. 'Bloody hell, this bloke's a nutter.' Rudiger's eyes were closed. He was muttering some kind of mantra. 'Hey, Mr Luftwaffe, can I have a bite of your apple?' said Hendo. A very strange request with fewer than two minutes left. Rudiger didn't reply. He kept his eyes closed and hand firmly in his jacket pocket. Hendo turned to Lucy. 'That isn't an apple, it's a fucking hand grenade. Remember what he said?'

'Death or glory,' said Lucy.

'Quick . . .' If I still regret mentioning Hendo as a likely recipient of those spare tickets, it is nothing to the remorse I feel for not seizing that moment. 'On my back, Lucy. Now!' A giggling Lucy threw her arms round Hendo's neck and climbed on board. In a couple of seconds they were over the low wall that separated us from the greyhound track. I followed them. We dodged a couple of policemen and ran full pelt towards the pitch. We just kept running until we were on the grass. The referee blew the whistle at last and Hendo tripped and collapsed in a heap with Lucy sprawled all over him. They were both laughing hysterically. All three of us were given a severe ticking off by the police. They didn't believe our story, of course, but no matter. On the train home, Hendo and Lucy only had eyes for each other. They say two's company and three . . . in an instant I had become part of the crowd.

Chapter 16

We started on the First World War poets in class today: Owen, Sassoon, Blunden, Rosenberg. It's riveting stuff, albeit shocking and depressing, with death and destruction shot through every page. I needed ice-breakers for what I knew would be a heavy lesson so I had asked the class to find some amusing epitaphs. They came up with auctioneer Jeremiah Goodwin's headstone, 'Going, going, gone', and 'In memory of Jane, beloved wife of Thomas Carter, marble cutter. Similar monuments: 250 dollars'. My personal favourites, though, were US talk-show host Merv Griffin's 'I will not be right back after this message' and Clement Freud's 'Born 24.4.24 Best Before 15.4.09'.

I explained how, before 1914, families largely accepted death and bereavement as the will of God. After the war, Victorian culture was largely abandoned. The old 'beautiful death' and elaborate funeral processions disappeared, replaced by a new type of culture, less ornate and more sombre. Grief, once openly expressed, was avoided. Ritual was reduced to a minimum. The spiritualist movement gained mass appeal, too, suggesting the war dead could live on in disembodied form.

All of which was lost on Kelly Summerton who raised a bored arm and asked what part of what I was going on about would be needed for the exam. I doubt it made any impact on gorgeous Gareth, either, who may have good reason to look down at his crotch and smile but was far more likely to be sending and receiving texts. For once I let it go. I had other things on my mind, specifically another meeting after school at Greenfern House. Carmel Withers had some information about my adoption. I found myself counting away the hours. At the end of class I mentioned the meeting to Lisa.

'I'll come with you, miss,' she said.

I frowned. 'Well, I'm not sure if . . .'

'Please.'

'I've no idea what to expect.'

'That's the point. It's a learning curve for me.'

After a lot of consideration, I agreed.

'I wonder where your mum is living,' said Lisa. We were in a waiting room outside Carmel Withers' office.

'It could be anywhere.'

'What if she wants to meet you?'

'After all these years, it may be too much.'

'I'm all excited, miss, so I can't imagine how you feel.'

'Terrified.'

Lisa put her arm round my shoulder. Educational protocol means I dare not touch a student without a third party in the room: crazy but true. These days you never know who is going to accuse you of improper conduct. But we were out of college and, frankly, I no longer cared. I needed support and Lisa was an unlikely provider.

Carmel Withers took a sideways glance at my young companion as we entered the room. Her hair was enough to frighten anyone. 'Your . . . daughter?'

'A good friend,' I said. Lisa beamed.

'Well, Lisa, I trust you will appreciate the sensitive nature of the situation.' Mrs Withers pulled out a file from a dull grey cabinet drawer that screeched on its runners.

I explained Lisa's own background. 'She understands perfectly and that's why she's here.' It seemed to allay Mrs Withers' fears. I strained to look at the papers in her hand.

'I wouldn't want you to leave with neckache,' she said, flatly.

'Am I being that obvious?'

Mrs Withers managed a thin smile. 'I would hand the whole file over to you but it's a bit more complicated than that. Look, there's no easy way to say this. I'm very sorry to have to tell you your birth mother is no longer with us.'

I knew it was possible, even likely. The news still hit me in the pit of my stomach. I went into numbed shock.

'Oh, miss, I am sorry.' Lisa put her arm round my shoulder again. 'Are you all right?' I nodded but I wasn't. After all these years: and then . . . nothing: the end of the road before it had begun. I tried to be brave but ironically Lisa's sympathy made it impossible. The floodgates opened. I shuddered into a fit of uncontrollable sobbing.

'You will understand now why we encourage people to be very careful before embarking on their search,' said Mrs Withers.

I nodded but it was a few minutes before I could pull myself together. 'When did she die?'

'In 1969.'

'That's . . . ages ago! What else do you know?'

'I can only give you limited information. Before November 1975, promises of lifelong confidentiality were given to birth parents and families. Your mother's family have requested no contact.' If my mother's death was a body blow the notion of her family making the effort to disown me was even harder to take. 'However, I can give you a summary of information about your adoption.' She passed me a typed sheet, while keeping the file firmly closed in front of her.

Gender: female

Date of birth: 3 March 1968

Weight of baby: 6 lb 12 oz

Place of birth: Mission of Grace, Bognor

Mother is 16 years old

Occupation: Not known

Nationality: British

Religion: C of E

Father: Name withheld. Knows about the baby.

'Oh God,' I said. 'She went through all that when she was still a child.'

'It wasn't uncommon,' said Mrs Withers. 'It still isn't. But we don't send girls away now. Many unmarried mums went to the Mission of Grace to give birth. As places go, it was a good one.'

I shook my head, trying to take in what I was reading, imagining myself at sixteen, far away from my mother and father, giving birth for the first time, in the company of strangers who would take my baby away for ever.

'What about my father?' I said.

'We're not sure if he is still alive.'

'His name isn't here.'

'No.'

'But you don't have his death certificate.'

'No.'

'So, if he is alive I could contact him.'

'It all depends.' Mrs Withers explained that, as far as she knew, my father hadn't added his name to the Adoption Contact Register. Until he does, there's nothing I can do. He has the right to remain unknown to me. This was almost too much to bear. Knowing I would never speak to my mother was painful enough but my father's reticence put the seal on it. I felt disembodied with grief.

'All these years,' I murmured. 'All these years and he hasn't tried to find me.'

'It's not quite as simple as that,' said Mrs Withers. 'A long-lost daughter arriving on the doorstep could have a profound impact on his family and friends. It may be an incident he has put behind him and that is why he has to be protected by law.'

'I'm an incident,' I mumbled. 'An accident. A car crash.'

'Oh, miss, don't say that,' said Lisa. 'You're our best teacher. Everyone says so. We love you. Even Gareth.' It was a sweet thing to say but I was too distressed to feel anything. I kept thinking of my adoptive mother's words: the TV programmes only show you happy reunions. There may be, what was her word? Complications.

'I can, however, give you two letters,' said Mrs Withers. 'The first letter was written to the adoption agency by your mother. The other is a reply. They are all I have. Would you like to read them?'

Would I like to read them? My mother's letter was handwritten, in a style astonishingly similar to mine. The characters are fat and very loopy. I still have no idea of her name or where she lived but something of her personality is locked in that letter. I am gazing at it as I write.

2 March 1969

Dear Mrs Osborne

A year ago tomorrow my baby girl was born. Giving her up for adoption was the hardest thing I have ever done. Part of me died inside. I will never get over it. Most of all I hope she is happy with her new mummy and daddy. Not an hour goes past without my wondering how she is and where she is. There are so many things I long to tell her but I am leaving that to Henry. I told him everything and I know he will pass it on, when the time is right.

Yours sincerely
(name withheld)

4 March 1969

Dear (name withheld)

Thank you for your letter. You can rest assured that your little girl is in very good hands. She is progressing rapidly and is the apple of her parents' eye. I am told that on her first birthday she kept pointing to her pretty cards and saying little made-up words of her own to them. I understand that she is quite taken with Henry who keeps a watchful eye over her at all times.

Yours sincerely
Edith Osborne (Mrs)

'Henry!' I gasped.

'Who's Henry?' said Lisa.

'My rocking horse. I was told he belonged to my great-grandmother. I had no idea where he really came from. I passed him on to my daughter, Helen, at Christmas.'

Mrs Withers studied my file, careful to ensure I could see no part of it. 'I don't see any reference to a rocking horse here. I imagine it was a personal request by your mother, probably

112

allowed on the strict understanding that nothing could point back to her or her family.'

I left Mrs Withers confused and conflicted: a cocktail of grief, elation and frustration. I drove Lisa home, thanked her for supporting me through it all and then phoned Helen, hardly drawing breath for ten minutes. 'And you'll never guess what else I found out. Henry belonged to my mother! She must have written Henry's poem, too. Isn't that amazing?'

Helen went quiet. 'I didn't realize.'

'None of us did, love.'

'No, the thing is . . . I don't know how to say this but . . . I've sold him. He was too big for our house.'

Someone might as well have punched me in the face. The one crumb of comfort I had gleaned from the whole experience, the one physical item handed down to me by my own dead mother, had been disposed of.

'Who did you sell him to?' It came out as a strangled whisper.

'An antiques dealer offered me six hundred pounds. I couldn't refuse. David wasn't fussed either way and we need the money. I'm so sorry. If I'd known . . .'

I wanted to scream. I mean, really let rip. 'Do you have details of the dealer?'

'Somewhere, yes, but it was weeks ago.'

'I don't care.'

'He's probably sold it on.'

'Then I'll find whoever owns it and buy it back.'

'Mum, it's just an old rocking horse.'

'I'll pretend I didn't hear that.' I really can sound like the teacher I am when I want to.

Writing it all out has enabled me to cool down a bit. I am being a bit harsh on Helen. After all, I did give Henry to her. He was no longer mine. But, other than my mother's sad and painful letter and her poem, he is all I have of her. I may have got the whole thing out of proportion. I may be overreacting. But I know one thing and one thing only. I have to find Henry. I have to find him – and bring him home.

Chapter 17

Half a pound of tuppenny rice . . . half a pound of treacle . . . that's the way the money goes . . . pop goes the Ledgard . . . I didn't expect to see the weasel tonight. He popped up at an *Our Goal: The Soul* presentation at Portcullis House, a public meeting room in the House of Commons.

I was in full flow at the lectern, addressing another room of somebodies in suits, when a familiar Adam's apple crept in at the back. It threw me for a few seconds. I was charting the way football owes its very foundation to local churches: twelve clubs that have played in the first division over the past twenty-five years or so (I use 'first division' in a generic sense) owe their origin to God-botherers: Aston Villa, Southampton, Bolton Wanderers, Everton, Tottenham Hotspur, Barnsley and Fulham, to name seven. Ironically, those early pioneers were so successful they got the red card for their troubles. What started as a community resource became a commercial juggernaut.

But not everything is lost. Punk football is on the rise. Community-owned clubs are springing up from the grassroots. FC United of Manchester is owned and democratically run by its supporters and has risen dramatically through the leagues. Best of all, it sticks to its principles: opposing, for example, the changing of kick-off times from traditional slots. When the club reached the first round proper of the FA Cup, its management refused to move the match to a Monday, to accommodate TV coverage. Their argument? Monday is a working day for the average fan. Monday night football is a TV invention and does not benefit supporters. The club was forced to comply by the FA, but not before making a point that resonated with tens of thousands of fans from hundreds of clubs.

I concluded my address by calling on everyone present, representing parliamentary constituencies, community groups and sports associations, to join together and bring change to an industry rife with greed, corruption and exploitation: but to do that we must be beyond reproach and transparent in our dealings. Afterwards, I did some radio interviews, keeping a discreet eye on Ledgard. He busy-bodied around the floor, engaging in conversation with various notables. As the crowd thinned out we found ourselves together, next to the table with my books on sale.

'This is an unexpected pleasure.' I shook his hand, politely.

'I was in town and passing,' he said.

'I didn't know you were interested in our national game.'

'Well, in spite of your "investigation"' – he used air quotes – 'there are things you still don't know about me. I enjoy the odd game or two of soccer.'

Yes, Ledgard used the 's' word. Seasoned fans will know why I privately recoiled. We invented the word here in Britain and until the 1960s used it freely as an alternative to 'football'. But our American cousins woke up to the game at last and used the 's' word to distinguish association football from their own sport bearing the same moniker. Consequently, we rejected it. For an Englishman to use it, without being aware of its loaded background, says everything.

As for the sentence itself: a true fan cannot simply enjoy 'the odd game or two'. Supporters of less successful clubs, and that's most of us, will admit that the odd game or two sticks out in the memory as enjoyable. A 6–0 thrashing of a bitter local rival, after a decade or five of humiliating defeats, lives long in the memory; but to genuinely enjoy that victory it is necessary to endure every depressing defeat along the way. A true fan implicitly understands the nature of Calvinism. He does not choose to follow. He was chosen to follow, predestined for a lifetime of long, dark tunnels at the end of a chink of light; of black clouds at the end of a silver lining. Yet he perseveres, on rain-swept Tuesday nights in Barnsley, with the stubborn, irresistible faith of a prophet who has no doubt. Ledgard knows none of this devotion. He was not at the House of Commons for the love of the game. He was on the snoop.

'Kristina tells me you phoned her,' I said.

'Yes, she was very helpful.' He was expecting my comment and played it calmly out of defence.

'Something to do with melting polar caps.'

'Indeed.'

'What magazine are you writing for?'

'Yes, well, it all depends . . . there are a number of options.' He mumbled titles I had never heard of. I doubt they even exist.

'She said you took a keen interest in our brief relationship.'

'Oh, I wouldn't say that.'

'Your questions surprised her.' I gave him a warning stare.

'Something to hide, Shearwater?'

I gave him another look. 'How's the new parish?'

'Depressing.'

Ledgard is a dog with a bone. Disturbingly, he reminds me of myself in those long, summer weeks of 1966. The euphoria of England's triumph ebbed away and the rest of the summer stretched ahead. I wasn't going to give up on Lucy that quickly. The time was best spent improving my diction still further . . .

*

'You'd be surprised,' said Mrs Pitcher, 'how many people down here in the south make a cut-price offer sound like a female pig.'

I looked at her blankly.

'Say the word sale,' she said.

'Sale.'

'As I feared. Your "l" was more like a "w". Sale sounded like sow.' She was right and this time I wasn't faking it.

'Let's work on some "i" sounds with "l" endings,' she said. 'Repeat these words after me. Style.'

'Style.'

'Try to keep the corners of your mouth back. If they come forward you'll get a "w" rather than "l" sound. Say mile.'

'Mile.'

'Better. Tile.'

'Tile.'

'Good. Now try a complete sentence. She'll walk a mile down the aisle in style.'

'She'll walk a mile down the aisle in style.'

'A bit lazy on the last "l" but otherwise acceptable.'

I would have walked a million miles, down any old aisle, if someone was all smiles at the end of it.

'Has Lucy got her photos back from the chemist?' I had a sinking feeling she must be over the road, at the Hendersons.

'I'm not sure. She's at the Plaza,' said Mrs Pitcher. Even worse. She must be with Hendo. He hadn't wasted any time.

'Oh really? What's on?' I said.

'*The Family Way*. She likes Hywel Bennett.'

As well as Bennett, the film starred Hayley Mills. While the lads at school drooled over Raquel Welch, Hayley rang all my adolescent bells: a cute, gentle blonde with ocean-blue eyes and lips full and sensuous in cinematic close-up, no 3D glasses required.

'She gets the northern accent all wrong,' chided Mrs Pitcher. I hadn't noticed. I *had* noticed Miss Mills taking off a good deal of her kit for the first time. 'Lucy is tired of the film now. When you've seen any picture a dozen times, it becomes boring.'

'She must be a big fan.'

Mrs Pitcher shrugged. 'She needs the money.'

'You mean . . . she *works* there?'

'Started last week, as an usherette.'

I made some excuse to finish the lesson early, flew home and checked out screening times at the Plaza, a tiny one-screen studio sandwiched between a car showroom and a five-storey office block. If I got on my bike and caned it I could make the final showing, walk Lucy home and come back the next day for my wheels. I was out of breath when I reached the Plaza. I locked up my bike behind the cinema. I tucked in my shirt. I smoothed down my sweaty hair. I walked calmly into the foyer.

'You've only missed the adverts,' said the woman at the box office. I felt a tap on my shoulder.

'This way, sir!' Lucy shone a torch in my eyes and giggled.

'What are you doing here?' I made sure I was surprised to see her.

'Do you like it?' She pointed to her grey uniform.

'You look like an air hostess.'

She laughed and tore my ticket in two, gave half back to me and put the other on the end of a dangerous-looking skewer. 'Are you waiting for anyone nice?' She gave me a coy look.

'No.' I suddenly felt exposed. 'I was . . . bored, now the football's over.'

'If you'd told me you were coming, I'd have got you in for free.'
She looked at me with those mischievous eyes and led me into the
gloom. The place was almost full. 'Here.' She pointed to an empty
seat with her torch.

'Hendo!'

'Billy!'

We tried to look pleased to see each other. In a way, we were. It
was just that . . . I hardly need explain. Lucy went back to the foyer.

'I thought you'd seen this film already,' said Hendo.

'I have. Like you!'

'Give us a shout . . .'

'. . . if you want your back scrubbed,' we said together. It's a line I
will always remember from *The Family Way*. Hayley, playing a young
bride, is about to take a bath when a male friend bursts into the
room. She is only partially covered: a good enough reason to see the
film again, several times.

We both queued up to buy a choc ice from Lucy at the interval:
it was the least we could do. As the credits rolled, Hendo disappeared
without a word. He wouldn't do that unless . . . he must have gone
for his motorbike. He was going to give Lucy a lift home. Then I
remembered her saying she would never ride on anything with two
wheels. I helped her clear up the rubbish between the seats. Within
minutes we had finished and turned off the lights.

'There's a proper Charlie outside, papping his horn,' called the pro-
jectionist from the foyer. Someone had parked a bubble car, banana
yellow with a white flash, right up by the cinema door, more on the
pavement than the road. The entire front of the tiny vehicle was a
door that opened on a hinge. Out stepped Hendo, like a grinning
jack-in-the-box, holding up three fingers and pointing at the wheels.

'Your friend . . . he's . . . utterly mad.' Lucy was entranced.

'Sixty-two quid. Exchange and Mart,' said Hendo. 'What do you
think?' The engine spluttered noisily.

'It sounds like a motorbike,' said Lucy.

'It *is* a motorbike, a pregnant one. Thirty miles per hour in thirty
seconds. Given a following breeze, she can reach forty-seven!' Hendo
gestured to us both. 'Come on. Get in.' It was nice of him to offer
but there was room for only one more on the single bench seat. And

it had to be Lucy. I rode home on my bike but never saw the bubble car arrive. Half an hour later I went out on my bike again and saw it parked a couple of hundred yards from our street. The windows were steamed up and I heard a female giggle or two as I rode past. I was envious but resigned. Hendo had three wheels. I wasn't old enough to drive. He had sideburns. You could wipe mine off with a flannel. He played drums in a band. I would never be allowed to play drums in my house. On the other hand . . . next day I went down to Pipers, the local music store, and using all my savings bought my first guitar for five guineas. And a copy of Bert Weedon's *Play in a Day*.

*

If an event is significant it's amazing what detail you can recall, however far back it may be. It wasn't a flashbulb memory: the kind where you hear shocking news on a global scale, the deaths of John Kennedy or Princess Diana, for example. It was a defining moment on a personal level, though. They say you are in the most formative time of your life between the ages of fifteen and twenty-three. Things and people you encounter are likely to shape you for the rest of your life.

Talking of which, Emms has just walked in from a reunion in Oxford. Back in the 1970s, she was one of only four female students on a fifty-strong estate management course at the polytechnic. Understandably, the girls stayed close and three of them still meet up occasionally. This time they decided to stay overnight in the city of dreaming spires, without partners, like the starry-eyed students they once were. I've never understood what they find so riveting about the brickwork of Keble College. And when their conversation turns to moisture meters, tenant law, measuring rods and theodolites . . . Maybe I'm just threatened. It's role reversal. I should be the one donning hard hat and waterproofs, striding my way over waterlogged construction sites.

'Ledgard turned up tonight,' I said.

'Ledgard?' Emms hung up her coat in the hall.

'You know . . .'

'Doesn't ring a bell.'

'Biddington.'

'The one who saved the pond?'

I nodded. 'With a little help from a female friend.'

'Good for him.'

'It was more complicated than that, if you remember.'

'I don't.'

I reminded her about Ledgard's infidelity.

'He might have been happier with the organist's wife,' she said. 'Fiona's a new woman since she left Tom.'

I explained how the two situations were completely different: Ledgard had a chequered history, whereas Fiona and Tom, who met one night at the polytechnic folk club, had simply grown apart, slowly and remorselessly.

'Ledgard contacted Kristina,' I said.

'What, your Kristina?'

'She's not my Kristina.'

'She still likes you.'

'Don't be silly.'

'You were well suited.'

'I hardly think so.'

Emms smiled. 'Anyway, Fiona's invited us to her nineteen-sixties fancy dress party next week. I said it would be right up your street and accepted.'

I must have looked horrified. 'You know I hate parties and, anyway, they're your friends.'

'Only because you don't want them to be your friends, too.'

'But . . . a party?'

'You know, flower power, peace and love, all to a session of sixties karaoke songs. It will be . . . a gas.'

What better way to blight the memory of a wonderful, turbulent decade than by joining a bunch of middle-aged obsoletes, kitted out in tie-dyed T-shirts that didn't flatter the first time round. We'll turn on not to sweet-smelling hashish but a heated discussion about the cost of nursing care for elderly parents. We'll tune in not to subversive, under-the-pillow pirate radio but a damned karaoke player. And the only thing that drops out will be a set or two of ill-fitting dentures.

I can't wait.

Chapter 18

I didn't see Jack this morning so much as ambush him. I must have disgraced myself with such a display of raw emotion, and so early in the morning. When he agreed to find cover for my lessons this afternoon, I thanked him, probably a little too profusely.

We were back on *The Power and the Glory* in class. I explained how Graham Greene skilfully sustains tension as he describes the last days of the whisky priest. Hunted like a fox by the reforming lieutenant, we forgive his moral failings because he is only too aware of them himself. He is no longer a paragon of religious virtue but human and fallible, like the rest of us. He has the opportunity to escape but agrees to hear someone's confession, knowing it is a trap. This final, selfless act leads to his Christ-like capture and execution.

I am not sure I was convincing. There was too much tension in my own head. It's hard to sound enthusiastic when you are willing the minutes away. My final morning class finished at 12.45 p.m. I would have to put my foot down to reach the auction in time. To make matters worse, Henry was scheduled as an early lot. And I had to contend with Adam Farrell.

'I've finished the assignment, miss,' he said, at the end of the lesson.

'At last. Where is it?'

'On my computer.'

'I need a hard copy.'

'I'll email it to you.'

I shook my head. 'I must have it on paper.'

'That means I've got to go all the way over to the library to print it out and bring it back here.'

Oh, the hardship! 'That's right.'

'But I could email it.'

121

'And then *I've* got to print it out.'

Of course, being in a rush, it would have been easier to accept the essay electronically, but I dare not establish a precedent. All the students would follow suit. Watching Adam saunter over to the library and back, clowning around with a couple of friends en route, was almost more than I could bear.

I seem to be at perpetual war with new technology: whether it's a parent calling a student on her mobile during class, Gareth gazing down at his crotch as he texts or Adam trying to send me an essay by email. Maybe that's why I am drawn to the mythical town of Ferness in *Local Hero*, where everything is slower, easier. The only way to access the outside world is to shovel ten-pence pieces into the coin slot of a red telephone box. As MacIntyre discovers, being one of the world's information poor has therapeutic benefits. Of course, I am only at war with technology when it suits me. I entered the postcode of the auction rooms into my satnav and let Darth Vader guide me towards the M23 and Brighton. Daggert and *Star Wars* . . . that's another story.

'Depart,' breathed Vader, from deep inside his helmet. 'Your destiny lies with me.'

It is a long time since I believed I had any sort of destiny; that I will arrive anywhere, ever again. In a galaxy far, far away, I'm a piece of space junk drifting round a collapsed planet. I turned out of the school car park. Today, if I was lucky, I might at least recover something of personal value. I reached the motorway in good time but hadn't factored in a traffic jam behind a three-car pile-up. 'Come on . . . please . . . come on . . .'

'There is a route to the Dark Side that is ten minutes quicker. Take the next exit,' said Vader. I hesitated. I had taken his advice on previous occasions: the alternative roads had proved slower. Should I risk it? I couldn't make up my mind.

'I find your lack of faith disturbing,' chided Vader.

'Feel the fucking force.' I surprised myself at the outburst. I rarely swear. It drew a sympathetic smile from a young man in a stationary car alongside me. I took the alternative route and, sure enough, hit more traffic – all of us sent there, no doubt, by Vader, John Cleese and Ozzy Osbourne. In a fit of pique I veered off down a side road hoping to find a short cut, narrowly missing a post office van. Now I found myself halfway up a cul-de-sac in a quiet residential neighbourhood. Curled up on a garden wall, a tabby cat looked at me, yawned and went back to sleep. I thumped the steering wheel in frustration.

'Make a U-turn,' breathed Vader, without sympathy. 'Then, take a right turn. Sense your way.'

I was spared more bizarre instructions by a phone call from Helen. She was full of remorse about selling Henry. Consoling a hysterical daughter was one thing but I was still several miles from Brighton and fighting my own emotions. I would have to find somewhere to park and then register for a bidding card. I had never bid for anything at an auction. How much would Henry cost? If he was genuinely rare, I feared the sky might be the limit and I'm struggling to make ends meet as it is. I looked at some signposts. Now I was completely lost. Once more I was forced to throw myself on the mercy of a once-heroic Jedi knight.

'Proceed as indicated,' he said. 'Don't make me destroy you.'

This time I got lucky on some minor roads. I switched off Vader as he began telling me that 'the circle was now complete' or some such nonsense.

The auction had already begun, the room three-quarters full. I asked a sales clerk outside the room if I could see Henry. He told me it was probably behind the stage and would be wheeled out when it was 'offered to the floor'.

I went into the room and sat down at the back, next to a woman about my age who looked familiar but I couldn't place her. A professional dealer by the looks of it, she was friendly enough.

'Eyes on anything nice?' I asked.

'A Victorian looking glass and kaleidoscope. You?'

'A rocking horse.'

'Are you a dealer?'

'No, it's a personal thing.'

'Well, good luck. There are some hard-nosed people here today.'

The truth is, I was way out of my depth and a jumble of nerves, not made any easier by the speed and urgency shown by the auctioneer, who must be ex-military.

'Lot forty is a grey Silvercross child's pram with reins,' he barked, with a back straight enough to have seen serious action in Iraq and Afghanistan. A minute later his gavel came down like a gunshot in Basra. 'Sold for two hundred and sixty-five pounds.' Henry was next. I tried hard not to fidget with the catalogue. Under stress, old habits return. Someone had replaced my heart with a bass drum and was thumping the canvas with a sledgehammer. The moment I saw Henry I knew I would have to fight the temptation to stand up and tell everyone that this had all been a terrible mistake. The antique wooden toy wheeled out before you all has been mine for decades and that, if none of you mind, I am just going to take him home where he belongs.

'The next lot, forty-one, is a Collinson vintage dapple grey rocking horse, early twentieth century, with . . .' A colleague gestured to the auctioneer from the wings. 'Sorry, I'm told this lot has been withdrawn. Moving on to lot forty-two . . .' I have no idea what lot forty-two was. I was in shock. I accosted the clerk outside the auction room, who told me Henry had been collected about an hour before. I phoned the dealer. 'Sorry, Danny Bingham is not available to speak to you right now but if you'd like to leave a message . . .'

I tried several times, and got the same message, before the woman sitting next to me bought me a cup of coffee.

'What about the kaleidoscope and looking glass?' I said.

'Never mind those. Henry means a lot to you. If he's supposed to come back to you, he will.'

There was nothing more I could do except thank her and drive home, Darth Vader on mute. I got clogged up in the school run and rush hour before finally arriving at my house. Danny Bingham was still unobtainable. He had only given his mobile number to Helen. Without a fixed line I had no idea where he lived. That was probably deliberate. And, of course, he had done the deal for cash and not given her a receipt.

I had a shower and threw some tasteless (maybe it was me) pasta into the microwave and rustled up an uneventful side salad. I poured myself a glass of wine. And another. I had to calm down. It was just a wooden horse. Helen needed the money. She had done nothing wrong. It would have been nice, though, if she had advised me of her plans. I would have lent her some money, to tide her over. Perhaps she was too proud to ask. We've all been there. There again, Matt never liked Henry. Yes, Matt may have wanted to get rid. Being fair, their house is probably too small for a rocking horse. Maybe I should have waited until they moved. On the other hand, keeping hold of an heirloom is selfish, especially as David liked riding Henry. Round and round and round went my thoughts. If only . . . how come . . . where is . . . why did . . . ?

I drifted in and out of sleep during *The Apprentice*. I remember Alan Sugar telling one of the contestants: 'If you nod your head any longer I'll put you on the back seat of my bloody car.' A couple of minutes later I dreamed he was giving the contestants their latest task: getting the highest amount for a Collinson vintage dapple grey rocking horse. I told Sugar the horse wasn't his to sell. He fired me.

The doorbell shocked me awake. It had to be Helen. To be honest I wasn't sure if I could cope with her. I had had enough for one day. But it wasn't Helen.

It was Henry.

Chapter 19

Bobby Shafto's gone to sea . . . Silver buckles at his knee . . . He'll come back and marry me . . . Bonny Bobby Shafto . . . Emms didn't like my outfit, mainly because it wasn't an outfit: dull black trousers, white shirt, uneventful shoes.

'But this is authentic,' I said. 'It's what I wore in the sixties.'

'And yesterday.'

'Exactly. I wasn't fashionable then. I'm not now.'

By contrast, Emms slapped up for the party with ghostly pale foundation cream, mascara and eye shadow. She sported a flared, A-line dress, pink and black in big alternating squares, with a tantalizing top-to-bottom zip at the back. Last on were chandelier earrings, false eyelashes that bristled like a toilet brush, a pair of white, flat-heeled go-go boots and a 1960s perfume recently reborn – Oh! de London – splashed with profligacy.

I was tempted to pull out an old paisley shirt from the loft. It doesn't fit properly now and besides, it would have been a betrayal. The fashions meant little to me at the time. I was captivated more by the underlying spirit of the decade: music, art and politics colliding together in a glorious creative flux. Some argue that swinging London was a hyped-up reaction to the ration book blues of the 1950s; that a fortunate set of political and economic conditions gave our generation the longest gap year in history. Perhaps we really were the first to live out Peter Pan's imperative never to grow up. At the time, all we knew was that we had the keys to a playground of endless possibility. Never mind the marijuana, transformation filled the air. It wasn't just about fads and fashions, more a social and political apocalypse. We really did think the world would change, that we were on the verge of a 'new way of doing things', the dawning of the Age of Aquarius and all that. Of course, I didn't understand any of this at the time. I had nothing else to compare it with. I went along for the ride.

'So, tonight . . .' Emms pulled her dress straight in the long mirror. 'Are you going to be your usual self or good company?'

'Well, that depends on the drink.'

'But we agreed. You're driving back.'

'Who said anything about me?'

'I don't get you.'

'Your friend Lizzie.'

'What about her?'

'Out of her skull last time. And when she started on the karaoke . . .'

We were among the first to arrive at the party. I figured the earlier we got there, the sooner we could withdraw gracefully. In fact, Fiona had turned her large, Edwardian semi into something very groovy. Beanbags littered the main lounge. Two lava lamps bubbled away pointlessly. Framed posters on the walls featured Bob Dylan (the *Blonde on Blonde* cover), Jimi Hendrix, Jefferson Airplane and the Hollies. In one corner of the smaller second lounge, 'Dedicated To The One I Love' by the Mamas and Papas played on a vintage Dansette record player.

'My Dansette had a smell,' I said.

'They all do when they warm up,' said Fiona. 'Like baked fish.'

A leather-clad Diana Rigg smiled enigmatically across the room at the bare-cheeked Athena Tennis Girl. A Gibson semi-acoustic guitar had been placed carefully on a stand. Centrepiece was an electric wall clock with sunburst metal rays.

'Borrowed it from my folks,' said Fiona. 'They've had it on their wall since I can remember. What do you think?'

'Love it,' I said. 'And this takes me back.' The door from the lounge to the kitchen diner had been removed for the night and replaced by a bead curtain. 'I haven't heard that death rattle in years.'

The air was thick with scented candles and smouldering joss sticks.

'Handmade in India by Dalits,' said Fiona. 'Sourcing products from disadvantaged communities is terribly important. It picks up the spirit of the decade, don't you think? With our love we could save the world.' Fiona is gushingly right on.

'That aroma!' I breathed in deeply.

'Cedarwood Absolute. It's cedar of the highest quality, with a touch of sweetness. Works wonders on nervous tension.'

'You don't strike me as . . .'

'Oh, I'm neurotic. Three years ago I bought a book called *How to Worry Less About Money* but I've been too anxious to read it. Now I'm worried if I wasted my money.' I asked her how long she had been channelling Woody Allen and we were in the middle of an interesting conversation – as to whether Allen had made neurosis fashionable – when a middle-aged man wearing an orange crushed velvet suit and ten-gallon hat strode into the room.

'I must take exception to one of your posters, Fiona,' he said.

'Oh, which one?' said our host.

'The Tennis Girl.'

'It *is* a bit on the rude side.'

'That doesn't bother me.'

'So?'

'Wrong decade.'

'Really? I was sure . . .'

'Here.' The man thrust his iPhone at Fiona. 'Definitely nineteen-seventies, though there is a dispute as to which year. The poster was publicly torn to pieces in the Middle East as an example of western sexual decadence.' He looked up and waved, as if we must all be intrigued who was now among us. 'I'm Roy.'

I discovered Roy was a chief librarian, which probably accounts for his attention to detail.

'And you?'

'A writer and a chaplain in the Church of England.'

'Supposedly committed to the poor, yet the second largest land-owner in the country.' The old myth lingers.

'I think you'll find the Forestry Commission owns the most land,' I replied smoothly. 'Followed by the Crown Estates and the National Trust, then the Ministry of Defence . . .' Faced with unsupporting facts, Roy lost interest.

'A chaplain, eh? The one at my school touched me up before choir practices.'

Overhearing our conversation, and its potential for conflict, Fiona banged a spoon on the table. 'My apologies to everyone over the anachronistic poster but I've tried to be entirely authentic with the food.' She unveiled a table of liver sausage, frankfurters, prawn cocktails, ox tongue, stuffed celery with cherry tomatoes and peaches encased in gelatine. One half of a grapefruit, wrapped in silver foil, was punctured with cubes of cheese and pineapple on cocktail sticks. And what 1960s bash would be complete without a cheese fondue? We tucked in, reminiscing about the dull diets of our parents and the globalization of food since the war. Twenty minutes later I was enjoying some football banter with Fiona's new partner, Francis, when Roy, imbibing a powerful home-brewed beer, imparted more insight to the assembled company.

'You know what they say about the nineteen-sixties . . .' I wondered how long it would be before someone trotted out the cliché. I rolled my eyes and mouthed along with him. 'If you remember them, you weren't really there.'

'Bollocks,' I said. Emms kicked me but I paid no heed. 'You're a chief librarian, Roy. You must have read the definitive social history of the decade, Dominic Sandbrook's *White Heat*.'

Roy looked startled. 'It . . . rings a bell.'

'Sandbrook argues that hardcore hippies were few and far between. The love-ins. The drugs. The happenings. Mostly, they're a myth. Just one in twenty of all young adults in Britain had tried an illegal substance by the end of the decade. Most of us looked more like, well, librarians than hippies. Your saying about the nineteen-sixties is entirely redundant.'

'Well, you church people . . . got your kicks in other ways, I suppose.'

'What are you insinuating?' It was getting personal.

'Oh, I think you know what I mean.'

'No, spell it out.'

'My own experience was not unusual.'

'Have you reported it?'

'No.'

'Why not?'

'It was a long time ago.'

'If you think you've got a case, lodge an official complaint.'

Enter Fiona again with her spoon, under the instruction of Emms, as I discovered later, and in the nick of time. I don't usually rise to the bait but the man is uninformed and insufferable.

'Time to celebrate the decade in song,' said Fiona. 'Over to you, Roy, for the karaoke.'

I groaned. If 'I Will Survive' is on the playlist, they should pass a law preventing inebriated, middle-aged divorcees from being within a mile of a karaoke machine. In Japan, where this contraption was invented, they've learned their lesson. Singers in bars are offered a sound-proofed booth with monitor and microphones. They can croon as loudly as they like: to themselves. I have no problem with people giving it all they've got but that's why bathrooms and cars were invented. Digitized backing tracks are the bastard child of music technology. Karaoke is doing for musicianship what satnavs are doing for map reading: making an entire generation illiterate. Give me Hendo's garage band any day – out-of-tune guitars, screeching feedback and drums hammered to oblivion. I dumped myself in a corner of the room. Emms's fears had been realized. I was now my usual self.

'In Japan, everyone has to sing at least one song on karaoke night,' said Roy. 'Who's first?' I slumped further into my purple beanbag. Singing would be entirely against my principles. If, however, I refused to take part I would be deemed a party pooper. Fiona's Francis got things off to a reasonable start with a version of Creedence Clearwater Revival's 'Bad Moon Rising'. The evening rushed south after that. Emms's friend Lizzie offered us Petula Clark's 'Downtown'. If I was alone and life was making me lonely I now knew the place to avoid. Some songs are so difficult to sing that no self-respecting citizen should even hum them – 'Bridge Over Troubled Water', 'You've Lost That Lovin' Feeling', and the ironically titled 'Silence is Golden' to name but three. Like lambs, Roy led all of them to cacophonic slaughter.

Then came the duets. Two couples I had never met were well off key on 'Somethin' Stupid' and 'River Deep Mountain High'. Murdering classics should be a capital offence. I looked around. No one else seemed to care.

'Right, I've heard most of you. Now it's my go,' said Roy. 'I have no partner so I need someone to join me. Someone who hasn't yet sung.' He pointed at Emms. She looked at me. I shrugged. Roy had lined up Sonny and Cher and 'I Got You Babe'. He put his arm round Emms's waist. He might have let it slip further down. I couldn't be sure in the steamy gloom. My toes curled with embarrassment. The odious man was all over her.

I couldn't blame him for trying it on, mind. She was the smartest woman there, by some distance. Maybe he was doing it to spite me, or is that my ego talking? I was surprised how much Emms played along. It wasn't like her. Only one thing for it: if you can't join them, beat them . . . I slipped into the next room and tuned up the Gibby. It was in good nick. Francis is a guitar freak. When the karaoke stopped I reappeared, finger-picking some six-string ragtime.

'I realize that live music isn't as good as the real thing.' I nodded at the karaoke player. 'But I'm going to sing a song anyway and I'd like you all to sing along.'

The Engelbert Humperdincks and Cilla Blacks of this world were part of the 1960s, of course, and I've nothing against their stuff. But the writer of the song I was about to deliver defines the special atmosphere of the decade: the fusion of popular music, politics and social statement. I say song. It is one-tenth song and nine-tenths rapping ragtime.

The lyric doesn't promise much by the way of political unrest but then 'Alice's Restaurant' started out as a throwaway number, to open a new eating house in Great Barrington, Massachusetts. All that changed after its author, Arlo Guthrie, son of dustbowl balladeer Woody, was arrested for littering on Thanksgiving Day 1965. While playing the rag to live audiences, Arlo, then just eighteen years old, began recounting the tale of his bizarre encounters with the police, courts and Vietnam draft board. 'Alice's Restaurant', eighteen minutes and twenty seconds long, is now a classic anti-war anthem, played all over US radio every Thanksgiving Day: the true spirit of the 1960s, very much alive and kicking half a century later.

I didn't do the whole rap, though I know every word. That would have been pushing it. Some people sang along to the chorus. Others looked blank. No matter. I had contributed to the party, as well as preserving my personal integrity. Ten minutes later Emms suggested we set off home, earlier than I expected.

'Well, that was embarrassing.' She slammed her seat belt into the slot.

'What do you mean?'

'Roy is Fiona's friend.'

'I don't understand.'

'You embarrassed him. He was trying his best.'

'All I said was . . .'

'Never mind what you said. Your body language was appalling.'

'I hate karaoke.'

'And didn't you let us all know . . . again. I'm almost embarrassed to tell you that Roy has invited you to a book club at his library, to talk about your books. Heaven knows why.'

*

It's gone 3 a.m. now. Emms is asleep. I've come downstairs and had a couple of brandies. I have to admit, her criticism stung and that's why I've talked it all out to my confessor. These reflections are becoming pure therapy.

Two good things have happened, though. The *Church Times* interviewed me several weeks ago. I forgot all about it until opening the current issue. They've given me the whole of the back page and included my experiences at the 1966 World Cup Final. I was careful not to include real names. That would tempt fate. In all these years I've never mentioned Lucy to Emms and, in her current mood, I'm not about to start. The interview also covers the night I played in a band at the Big Top, Bishopsgate, an event now regarded as seminal in the history of 'experimental and progressive art' in the UK. It didn't strike me as being much to write home about at the time but it's reached mythical status over the years.

Bishop Maureen read the article, too, and emailed me. In her mid-fifties, articulate and culturally engaged herself, Maureen is the first woman to be appointed to high office in our diocese. Many years ago she was lead singer in a punk band called The Sound of Mucus. Needless to say, on the day of her recent appointment, the media dug out her old publicity photos. Decked out in standard grey clerical attire, it's hard to believe Maureen ever sported a safety pin through her nose and rocked up with a scarlet mohican, ballet tutu and black Doc Martens.

She isn't a football fan, so I am surprised she has asked me to take her to a match. Intriguingly, she doesn't want to sit in the directors' box, though I could arrange that with the owners of Crystal Palace. She wants to be with the 'ordinary punters'. I explained that the people who bought the club in 2010 are ordinary punters with money, but I know what she means. I have suggested attending an away match where we'll sit with the hardcore, raucous Holmesdale Fanatics. The atmosphere will be energetic, ill-disciplined and hostile. People will leap about mindlessly. She will be overcome by nostalgia.

Chapter 20

Helen had nothing to do with the courier delivering Henry to my door. The only other person who knew I was going to the auction was Jack.

I bought a top-quality bottle of French red wine from a local all-night supermarket and pulled up outside his house, an older style Georgian-styled property with an in-and-out gravel drive. There were lights on in the lounge and hallway so I reckoned he must still be up, even though it was past 11 p.m. I knew all manner of things might happen after he opened the door but I no longer cared. For the first time since Daggert, I felt genuinely excited: the fall-out would have to take care of itself. I grabbed the bottle and crunched up the drive, heart pounding yet again. Reaching the porch, I took a deep breath and rang the bell.

Through stained glass in the front door I saw the outline of a woman walking towards me. Hurriedly, I hid the bottle under a nearby bush. The door opened a few centimetres. 'Who is it?' said Jack's wife, Ginny.

'I'm Mrs Daggert,' I said. 'I teach at your husband's college.'

'Oh.' Ginny glanced at her watch.

'I'm sorry it's so late.'

'Jack!' she called, then opened the door wider and looked me up and down, the way women do. 'It's one of your staff, a Mrs . . .'

'Daggert. Sophie Daggert.'

'Sophie Daggert.'

'I'm calling about Henry. I wanted to thank Mr Staniscliffe.'

'Henry?'

'Yes, Henry,' said Jack, marching into the hall, 'a student with a particularly difficult background. I asked Mrs Daggert to let me

134

know what happened after the college closed. I forgot to give her our phone number. Do come in.'

I stepped into the hall. 'I can't stay,' I said. I'm not blessed with the ability to think quickly but a student came to mind who had been involved in a fracas with a friend in the college refectory. 'I've had a long phone conversation with Henry's parents about the incident at lunchtime,' I said. 'His father may come in next week but wouldn't say when. I thought you ought to know.'

'Forewarned is forearmed and all that. I appreciate your letting me know.'

Ginny Staniscliffe was still giving me the not-so-discreet once-over as Jack and I discussed Henry's poor attendance record, behaviour in class and troublesome family background. We were so convincing I began to think he really exists. Ginny seemed persuaded and left us alone to finish our conversation.

'Thank you,' I mouthed and pointed to my purse.

Jack shook his head, then said loudly: 'Let's hope Henry behaves himself from now on. I'll see you on Monday and thanks again for putting my mind at rest.'

I pointed to the bottle of wine underneath the bush. He nodded and waved me off. So Ginny has returned from Abidjan. That will be hot news next week. I was puzzled, relieved and deflated: a strange cocktail. I still have no idea how much Jack paid for Henry. Whatever it was, I intend to pay him back. But the bigger question is – why did he buy him in the first place? Ginny's unexpected return makes things even more confusing.

Saturday 26 March 2016

I sent an email to Lisa to tell her Henry was back, though I didn't say how! Within minutes she came round to see him. It isn't usual for students to call in on teachers at home but Lisa is fast becoming the exception that breaks every rule. As for her and Henry: it was love at first ride.

'I've always wanted one of these, miss,' she said, rocking to and fro. 'I don't know how your daughter could have let him go.'

'Well, he's back and that's all that matters.' I brewed some coffee and came back to find Lisa studying Henry's black hooves.

'I've been thinking,' she said. 'About the letter and poem.' I had been thinking about them myself. In fact, I could probably recite both by heart, I've read them that many times. 'The letter says, "I told him everything and I know he will pass it on, when the time is right." What do you think she meant?'

The words had played on my mind, too, but getting Henry back had preoccupied my thoughts. 'Well, he's never revealed anything to me in all the years I've known him.'

'But you weren't expecting him to.'

'True.'

'Now you are listening.'

I couldn't disagree. 'You think my mother might have carved some kind of message into Henry?'

Lisa shrugged. 'I can't see anything. Besides, that might be too obvious. Maybe she used invisible ink.'

I asked Lisa if she was a fan of the Secret Seven. She said she never liked their music.

'That's S Club Seven,' I said but she wasn't really listening. We were on Google, looking up everything posted there about invisible ink. Some forms of secret writing (so we discovered) are revealed through heat. We applied a hot water bottle to various parts of Henry: to no avail. Then Lisa remembered how her parents mark expensive items with ink that can only be read under ultraviolet light. We went shopping in town and I bought a banknote checker, used to detect forged currency. Once again, Henry refused to talk.

'My mother was very young and it was a long time ago,' I said, despondently. 'Maybe we're expecting too much.'

Lisa shook her head. 'The poem tells you to look for clues. When you think about it, she would have had to be very careful not to get caught. It's up to us to solve the puzzle.'

'You'd make a good Columbo,' I said.

Lisa asked me how discovering America had anything to do with my adoption. She knows nothing about junior sleuths and dishevelled detectives but has something in common with them all: she never gives up. We sat on the floor and fell silent. Every now and then I gave Henry a kick, to send him rocking. No matter how much oil I put on his moving parts, he squeaks.

'He has very kind eyes, don't you think?' said Lisa, at last.

I nodded. 'When I was little I stroked his mane and told him my troubles. He always listened. After a ride, I would rest my head on the back of his neck, put my hands round his tummy and sometimes fall asleep. Once I fell off and—'

Lisa snapped her fingers. 'His insides! We did that horse in history. They led it into the city with people hidden inside.'

'The wooden horse of Troy.'

'That's the one. Maybe there's a message *inside* Henry.'

We took off his red leather saddle and stirrups and searched high and low for any sign he had been opened up and carefully put back together. We tapped every area, hoping to find a hollow section but drew another disappointing blank. Lisa asked to stay the night. She was certain that together we could solve the puzzle. I couldn't see any real reason why not. We spent several minutes on the floor. With one foot I nudged Henry in the darkness. 'Don't squeak, speak,' I said.

We watched an episode of *Columbo*, recorded several weeks ago. A recent article suggested Peter Falk's interpretation of the tatty tec is a constant re-enactment of David and Goliath. The murderer is invariably rich, powerful and assumes intellectual superiority. By contrast, Columbo turns up in a battered, backfiring Peugeot and crumpled coat. He appears preoccupied, naive and in awe of the illustrious suspect, but it's all a guise. Remorselessly, he outwits the bigshot murderer.

Man against the odds: a theme beloved of Hollywood. In ancient myths and legends he was the prototype of our modern heroes and heroines. Adventurous and resourceful, they fight for good against evil. Our books and movies constantly recycle these characters in modern settings. By now it was 2 a.m. and all had gone quiet. I was thinking how Ben Knox, the old beachcomber who lives in a driftwood shack in *Local Hero*, is one such example, when Lisa, who had drifted off to sleep on the sofa, suddenly woke up and grabbed the poem.

'Yes . . . yes . . . I thought as much, miss. It's staring us in the face. Read the poem again, carefully.' I scrutinized the piece of paper. It looked no different. I held the paper to the light. Nothing.

'Look at the start of each line,' said Lisa.

Henry's poem
Let me take you for a ride
On a journey whence you came
Over hills and rivers wide
Keep tight hold upon my reins

If the way seems hard to you
Never let your doubts prevail

Make all speed and look for clues
Yonder through the rain and hail

Saddle up and ride again
Ask and I will hear your call
Doors will open at my name
Dare to trust me through it all
Look and you will find, I'm sure
Everything you're searching for

'Let . . . on . . . over . . .' I shook my head.

'Not the whole word, just the first letter.'

My jaw dropped.

'It *is* the same saddle you've had all these years, isn't it?' said Lisa.

I nodded. We leaped from the sofa, falling over each other like two drunks. There are two parts to Henry's leather saddle. The top is a soft padded cushion. This is stitched into the larger lower section, studded at intervals, which lies flat over Henry's back. I grabbed a Stanley knife and ripped into the stitches. My hands were shaking so much I cut myself. Lisa took a turn. Sure enough, between the padding and the bottom section of the saddle we pulled out something I had sat on, unknowingly, for more than

138

forty years: an envelope with a heart drawn on the front. My hands trembled too much to open it.

'Shall I?' said Lisa. 'I'll be very careful.' She pulled out several black-and-white photos, faded with age, of a young girl holding her baby close. 'Oh, miss . . . this must be your mum. She was beautiful . . . those eyes . . . they're your eyes . . . oh, miss.' It's hard to express the emotion to people who have always known their parents, but in that second I was complete. I looked like someone else.

'Any idea where these were taken?' said Lisa. One of the photos was set against a bridge by a fountain, another by a train at a station. I shook my head. Neither place was recognizable but that may have been because of the tears that squeezed out of my eyes. In every shot my mother was holding me tightly, as if she would never let me go.

'I wonder who this little bunch were,' said Lisa. Tucked inside a football programme of the 1966 World Cup Final she found an out-of-focus photo of two teenage boys wearing top hats and England rosettes. Next to them stood an older man with a German flag. There was a painting, too, of a sad child walking across a field of flowers, trailing a piece of string with bunting, a small silver necklace and an advert for some kind of pop festival at the Big Top, Bishopsgate, in London. Circuses were held on the same site in the nineteenth century and it had become a leading music venue in the 1960s (so we later discovered on the internet). The line-up mostly featured groups I've never heard of. One of them, Second to None, are still going strong, I think. The MC was trapeze artist, later to become film director, Garry Kite, a bit of a hero of mine. I searched for a letter from my mother, or even a short note, without success.

'She's gone to all this trouble without saying who she is,' said Lisa. 'I can't believe it.'

I explained how the laws back then were very strict. My mother would face prosecution if her name had been discovered on any of the mementos.

'I would have taken the risk,' said Lisa. I explained that she had been born into a very different world.

'They didn't give a shit for the real mums back then,' said Lisa. 'Sorry, miss, for swearing . . .'

Lisa's frustration mirrors my own but at least I now know something about my mother. I am mesmerized by the photographs. As I write this I am picking them up and putting them down, one by one, again and again, trying to imagine where my mother was at the time and what was going through her mind. It may be decades later but the way she is holding me, heals me. Lisa is right. Her eyes, the shape of her face, her hair: I'm looking at a teenage me. I want to know who she was and what happened to her. Why did she die so young? Who were the two boys at the turnstile? Are any of these people related to me? Lisa found her phone and took a copy of the best photo of my mother and me. Eventually, I pulled out the camp bed in the spare room for Lisa and we both grabbed a few hours' sleep. Before she left in the morning, Lisa hugged me at the door.

'Don't give up, miss,' she said. 'Remember what Henry says in his poem. Those last two lines. He isn't going to dump you halfway.'

After she left I read it again and tried to believe.

Look and you will find, I'm sure
Everything you're searching for

Chapter 21

When I was a young boy my father said to me . . . listen here, my son, you're CPFC . . . here we are, you'll know us by our noise . . . pride of south London, the famous Palace boys . . .

'Are *all* the chants gender specific?' Bishop Maureen was shouting in my ear, trying to be heard above the hubbub at West Ham's Upton Park.

'Hadn't really thought about it,' I said.

'As for the one about south London being wonderful because it's full of . . . I've jotted it down . . . tits, fanny and Palace. It's all very dick-waving alpha male.'

Maureen's language is more colourful than the average bishop. I smiled, ruefully. 'Have a heart. Where else can they be so politically incorrect?'

'There, you've bought it, too. This notion that men should reclaim spaces where they can be proper men, like the good old days.' She was smiling but I was being told off. 'Football is a misogynist's outpost, like Australia. We might as well be listening to an album by a male voice choir, featuring oppression's greatest hits.'

I played along. '*Now That's What I Call Sexism.*'

She frowned reprovingly. 'Even your official song excludes females.'

'What's so wrong with "Glad All Over"?'

She glanced at her copious notes. '"Other girls may try to take me away . . ." More macho posturing.'

I laughed. 'Methinks the lady doth protest too much. Or is that comment gendered?'

'Shakespeare put "methinks" at the end of the phrase, not the start. Most people get that wrong.' There are those who find Bishop Maureen difficult, if not impossible. She's informed, pedantic and high risk but she pushes me and I can't help rising to the challenge.

'At least,' she said, 'they haven't sung "Get your tits out for the lads".'

'They changed the words at Palace,' I said. 'When one of our former players came on as a substitute they sang "Get Moritz out for the lads".' At least that got her laughing. Bubble machines pumping at full pelt, the home fans bellowed out their own anthem, "I'm forever blowing bubbles", as the teams warmed up.

'Fuck off,' bellowed a man behind us.

'Wankers,' shouted another, with helpful, explanatory hand actions. Maureen didn't seem to notice. I smiled and shook my head. She looked at me, enquiringly.

'I was thinking about the good old days,' I said. 'The vicar at my church wouldn't go to matches because of the bad language but let beat groups, as he called them, play in the church hall. Now I'm with a bishop who doesn't bat an eyelid at profanity but gets peeved at a pop song.'

Maureen smiled. 'I used to shout far worse obscenities on stage. It would be hypocritical to tut-tut now.'

We were looking around us and talking about the way football fans were increasingly middle class and middle aged when a tall, gangly man in his late fifties pushed his way along our row and stopped next to Maureen.

'Excuse me for asking but your face is familiar,' he said. 'Didn't you used to be in The Snots?'

'Rumbled!' Maureen grinned and shook his hand. 'Nice to meet you . . .?'

'Grant. Grant Wellings. I've got all your LPs in my loft. If I'd known, I'd have brought them for you to sign. Next best thing . . .' He handed her a matchday programme.

'On this page?' Maureen pulled out a pen.

'Anywhere will do . . . loved "Bambi, Your Mother's Dead (Get Over It)", by the way. What happened to you all?'

'You know how it is . . . husbands, babies, Damascus road encounters.'

'Shame . . . I didn't know you were Palace.'

'I'm not.'

'Oh . . . well, thanks anyway.' He glanced at her signature. 'Is this your new band?'

'No, it's who I am.'

'What . . . Bishop Maureen? Fuck! I mean, sorry, I didn't realize.'

'No problem.'

The man sloped off, blessed and bewildered.

'The *Snots*?' I said.

'That's what our close fans called us, a sort of shorthand.' The match kicked off. 'So . . . when is everybody going to sit down?'

'Half-time.'

'I thought you weren't allowed to stand.'

'You're not but if you sit down you won't see the game.'

Either through boredom, excitement or aching legs, Maureen went for a comfort break after half an hour. By that time the score was 1–1. She didn't return before half-time. She didn't even return during half-time. I went looking for her, presuming she had been waylaid by more former fans or called up by the diocese to deal with a new crisis. I had settled in for the second half when my phone vibrated: a text from the good lady. Maybe 'good bishop' would be less gendered, or just 'bishop', so as not to imply value judgement.

Met 2 girls in ladies, both upset. Seeing them home. Sorry! Hope u win. M.

Being consistent, she should have said 'two young females in the toilets', but there again, that would be ageist. Whatever Maureen wanted to talk to me about would have to wait. It was Palace's last ever match at Upton Park, before West Ham's move to the Olympic Stadium. The score was 2–2 at full-time. Quite a few people hung around at the ground afterwards, reminiscing about past victories and defeats. On the train back I received another text.

Girls delivered safely. M.

Intrigued by my encounter with their former lead singer, I googled The Sound of Mucus again: an interesting if brief history that comprised three albums, one Top 30 hit, followed by 'internal artistic differences' and an acrimonious split – the story of hundreds of bands.

I never quite got punk rock. They say its chief architects were Malcolm McLaren, the Ramones and the New York Dolls. I don't

143

buy that. The true creator has never received credit, perhaps because he always wore a posh suit and tie with a pointed handkerchief in his breast pocket. Pre-punk guitar legends like Eric Clapton, Pete Townshend, Brian May and Keith Richards name him as mentor. In spite of that, I contend the man who gave us punk rock was none other than Herbert Maurice William 'Bert' Weedon, OBE.

To this day, no self-respecting guitarist dare play 'Bobby Shafto' in a folk club. It's the first song in Weedon's *Play in a Day* tutorial and the entire audience knows it to be so. All guitarists remember how their fingertips hurt like hell as, for the first time, they coerced those stubborn digits into the C chord position. 'Bobby Shafto's gone to sea . . .' and then the G chord . . . 'Silver buckles at his knee . . .' and back again to C . . . come on, you can do it . . . there you go . . . 'He'll come back and marry me . . .' Of course, there's another factor at play. Those lyrics. In spite of all the practice I put in on that late summer's day, I couldn't rush out of my bedroom and show family and friends, least of all Lucy and Hendo, how I had mastered a song about a sailor (a sailor!) crossing the ocean with shiny things dangling halfway up his legs.

Clearly, those original punk rockers took Weedon at his word, though. At the end of the first day they knew a couple of chords. Why bother with day two and 'There is a Tavern in the Town' with its three chords and pinkie-stretching seventh? Sod that. All they needed now was a drummer, a manager and the ability to grab a microphone and belch loudly at will. Popular music forms have always been used as vehicles for dissent but where folk, for example, stirs and inspires, punk snarled, spat and stomped.

I was looking at jpegs of a young Maureen, splattered in saliva while crowd surfing at the Screen on the Green – a renowned punk venue in London – when the doorbell rang.

'Bishop!' said Emms. 'What a nice surprise.'

'I hope I haven't disturbed you.'

'Not at all.'

'I had to leave the match early.'

'Billy was saying.'

'I wanted to apologize.'

144

I clicked off Google Images and came to the door. 'No need. Come in.' It was the first time Maureen had been to our house. Being freelance, a sort of 'loose canon,' I'm not one of the diocesan inner circle.

'I really wasn't intending to slope off like that,' she said. It transpires that one of the two fifteen-year-old girls, Gemma, had locked herself in a cubicle, crying. Lizzie, her best friend, talked to her through the door, telling her she had got everything out of proportion.

Gemma had agreed to go to the game with boyfriend Carl, nineteen, as long as Lizzie went, too. Neither of the girls liked football so they would be company for each other. To make conversation on the way to the game, Lizzie, who had never met Carl before, asked him what he was studying at college. He told her he was a trainee chef. Lizzie said the only thing she could make that anyone actually eats is a Chelsea bun. Carl said he refused to make Chelsea buns because he hates Chelsea. That made Lizzie laugh and the conversation turned to the kind of food Carl prepared that week and who for. As far as Gemma was concerned, Lizzie was too interested in Carl's week and Carl was too interested in telling her about it.

Things really kicked off just before the game began. Fuelled by warm, gassy beer, Carl told Lizzie he could imagine her cooking really slowly and simmering on a low flame. She replied by saying 'you get the best cream when you stiffen it up' or words to that effect. Gemma, who was also half-cut (her words), stormed off to the ladies.

'I managed to talk her round and the three of us went for a drink, outside the ground,' said Maureen. 'Neither Gemma nor Lizzie were in a fit state to be left on their own so I accompanied them home. By the time we got there, they were the best of friends again. It reminded me of my own experience several years ago . . .'

Maureen's long path to a bishopric, she explained, began one night after an ill-tempered Sound of Mucus gig in Great Yarmouth. Following a monster row to end all rows with the lead guitarist, live on stage, she refused to return home in the band's microbus and went drinking alone in a nearby bar. Next day she woke up on the settee of someone's front room that, she said, 'smelled like her grandmother's – of coal and lily of the valley'. A woman in a passing car, by the name of Hazel, had found her lying in the gutter and taken her home. A middle-aged spinster, Hazel knew nothing about punk rock. Maureen knew nothing about Old Testament prophets and social justice, the subject of an essay her host was writing at the time, towards a degree in theology.

'When Hazel saw my hair it reminded her of the prophet Ezekiel,' said Maureen. 'She told me how, to make a point to the corrupt elite of the day, Ezekiel set one third of his hair on fire, scattered another third around the city and threw the rest to the wind. He saved a few hairs to sew into his clothing. It was right up my street.'

Hazel introduced Maureen to the rest of the prophets and their passion for dissent and bizarre protest.

'Hosea, Jeremiah and Joel were all proto-punks,' said Maureen. 'Before meeting Hazel I saw the Church as the means by which the establishment controlled the masses. She showed me that, in its purest form, it is the perfect vehicle through which to fight for social justice. I quit the band and got ordained.'

I remarked how the incident at West Ham must have rung bells.

'More than that.' Maureen was striding around now, pulling hard on a cigarette as she spoke. It was curious to see a woman in a purple blouse and dog collar, inhaling in our lounge. 'I think you're on to something, Billy. Your campaign to see football and the community come together again, let's make it happen.'

I must have looked shocked, as well as delighted.

'I can see it working on two levels,' she went on, 'the structural and the personal. We join forces with the fans feeling exploited and disinherited by fat cat businesses controlling the game. We campaign with those fans for change. The game mustn't slip irretrievably from the grasp of young and less privileged people. On the personal level, we form a support network for fans like Gemma and Lizzie. Most clubs already have official chaplains who are seen in the directors' box. They lead special services and support charitable events at the ground. All well and good but after our visit to West Ham today, I realized what's missing. Each club needs a chaplain for the fans, one who is never seen in a suit and tie but sits with the noisy bunch and travels on the supporters' coaches to away games.' Now she was really warming to her idea. 'Maybe they could have "FANS' CHAPLAIN" across the back of a replica shirt. When a Gemma-and-Lizzie-type incident happens, they are there to help, an integral part of the community, serving it, supporting it when required. Not pontificating, like . . . like a bishop.'

When she gets going Maureen is a true force of nature.

'I could see you heading up something like that,' I said.

Maureen looked horrified. 'I can't imagine anyone worse. The media would hark back to my punk days and dig up more people I insulted. No . . . it has to be someone who is articulate, with no historical baggage and who understands the game at every level. They have to be credible with the fans, too. I've done my research. There's only one person who fits the bill perfectly and I'm looking at him right now.'

Chapter 22

Today it was my turn to see someone arrive, unexpectedly, on the doorstep: on a Tuesday morning, at 7 a.m. Being in the shower I didn't hear the doorbell. It was only as I came out of the shower that I heard someone knocking, knocking, knocking on the front door. I edged back the bedroom curtain, opened the window slightly and saw a familiar car parked outside.

'Jack!'

'Sophie, I'm sorry to call so early. Could I . . . ?' He gestured to the front door.

'Give me a minute.' Just as well he couldn't hear my language as I threw myself round the bathroom, kitchen and living room. After a couple of deep, calming breaths in the hall, I opened the front door.

'I need to explain a few things,' said Jack. 'The college car park is hardly suitable . . .'

'Of course, come in.'

'Ah, so this is Henry!'

'What do you think?'

'He's magnificent.'

I told him how Lisa had helped me locate the photos and mementos. He pored over them. 'After all these years. I knew buying him was the right thing to do.'

'You must tell me how much he cost,' I said. 'I want to pay you back.'

Jack shook his head. 'There is no question of that.' His father, it transpires, walked out of the family home when Jack was six. 'That day we put up some beanpoles in the garden, all very exciting at the time. He let me plant the seedlings and said: "You'll grow up quickly, too. Be sure to look after your mother." He walked down the path and out of our lives, without any warning, never to be seen again.'

'That's awful. You must have been devastated.'

'I have no idea how my mother coped. My father was a travelling salesman and she was convinced he had another family somewhere. When I was old enough, I began searching for him. I called his old customers and friends. I visited his favourite haunts. No one could throw any light on his whereabouts. He didn't drink. He wasn't violent. My mother adored him. So did I. He may have had a nervous breakdown but I still have no idea if he is dead or alive. That's why, when you told me about Henry, it struck a nerve. I knew you had to have him back.' He stood to go. 'And now I've explained all that . . .'

I was holding the photographs in my hand and had to stop myself from fidgeting, anxiously. 'Before you go . . . I need to say something. When I called round the other night, I wasn't expecting to see Ginny.'

'You and me both.'

'Is she back for good?'

'Who knows?' He got up and walked to the front door. 'Next time, maybe I will be the one to leave.' He gazed at me steadily, held my hand to his lips and kissed the back of it.

'I need to know,' I said. 'If Ginny hadn't been—'

'Yes. Now, before things become too complicated for us all, I had better go and pretend to run a sixth-form college.'

I smiled. 'Well, think of me first thing as I lead a discussion on Philip Larkin's poetry with 2C.'

'The one about unhelpful parents, I should imagine. I'll be disappointed if I don't receive a complaint from a mother about foul language in class.'

I hugged Jack briefly, sympathetically. And then he was gone, though I noticed the gear change was gentler, more resolved.

*

'Larkin's insistence that his poems make no wider cultural comment is itself an intellectual statement. What do you think?'

It was now 9.10 a.m. and too early for 2C to be up with the Larkins (unforgivable, I know). I tried another tack. 'Some argue that he writes for the common man, but doesn't enjoy his company? Do you think that's true?' Too abstract. One more go. 'Or maybe, like some feminist critics, you see violence in Larkin's depiction of women.'

Rhiannon Batey put up her hand. 'Miss, I've shared that picture of your mum.'

'Me, too,' said Megan Ryan.

'And me.' Several students nodded. The room stirred from slumber.

'Picture? What picture?' I said.

'The one of your mum holding you when you were tiny,' said Daniel Hamilton. 'Lisa in 2B posted it on Facebook.'

'Yeah, she asked us to share it,' said Megan. 'Your real mum looked just like you.' More nods.

'We hope you find out her name,' said Rhiannon.

My head was spinning. 'Whoah! What's all this about? What's going on?'

Daniel pulled out his iPhone. 'Here, I'll show you . . .'

*

'You should have asked me first, Lisa!' We were sitting in my car in the college car park at lunchtime. It was the only place we wouldn't be interrupted. On the way there, three students from the School of Engineering stopped me in the corridor and wished me well in my search. I've never spoken to them before. I don't even know their names.

'I wanted to surprise you, miss,' said Lisa.

'You succeeded.'

'I didn't mention you by name.'

'You didn't need to. All your friends have.'

'I thought you'd be pleased.'

'Facebook and Twitter. I don't do all that stuff.'

'But miss, when I put pictures up for my cancer appeal I got a great response.'

'That's totally different.'

'The page I created for you is doing even better. It could go viral.'

'I'm not with you.'

'People share pages with friends. Then those friends share with their friends and the whole thing takes off. There are dozens of comments already. That's a sure sign. One person said . . . let me find it . . . here . . . *Someone, somewhere knows who this lady was. You deserve to know the truth, Sophie. Good luck, we're right behind you.*'

'Who wrote that?'

'Stuart Croft.'

'Who's he?'

'I've no idea.'

'That's the problem. I feel . . . exposed.'

'I did when I cut off my hair. Loads of people laughed at me. You've got to be prepared to lose before you gain.'

'But Lisa, there are legal implications. I shouldn't be in possession of that photograph.'

'I know. That's what I told . . .' she hesitated.

'Told? Told who?'

'Oh, one of the people who added a comment on the page.'

'What did you say?'

'That the authorities used to treat young mums like shit.'

I shook my head. 'You must take down the page right now. I don't want the police knocking on my door.'

'But miss, think about it. All that's happened is that you've found an old picture or two in a rocking horse and you want to find out more about them.'

I shook my head. 'I wish it was that simple.'

To be fair, Lisa had done a lovely job, superimposing my mother's face on a vintage wanted poster, the kind you associate with the Wild West. Below her face ran the headline: 'Do you recognize this woman?' I watched as, reluctantly, she reopened the page on her iPhone. 'Look, it's been shared thirty-four times since we walked to the car!' I stared at her. 'All right, miss. Sorry.'

Crestfallen. Dejected. Neither word does justice to Lisa's changed mood as, a yard behind me, she silently trudged back into the college, hands deep in her coat pockets.

It was almost impossible to get any kind of concentration out of my remaining three classes. Every student, it seemed, was keen to help me discover my mother's name – and come round for a ride on Henry.

*

151

When the phone rang just before 9 p.m., I froze. An overheating sense of guilt led me to think it must be the police. Then I hoped it was Jack. I had no reason to believe it would be him, of course. I was genuinely excited at the thought and that surprised and unnerved me. It turned out to be Helen.

'What's all this about?' she said.

'What is *what* all about?'

'That photo on Facebook.'

'You mean . . . it's still on the web?'

'Still? I've only just seen it.'

'I must have another word with Lisa.'

'Who's Lisa?'

'A student.'

'The photo is incredible. It says you found it in Henry's saddle. I can't believe I'm looking at my real grandmother. Why didn't you tell me?'

'I . . . I didn't want to upset you.'

The truth is, in all the drama, I completely forgot to call her. I explained what had happened and wanted to know how the news had reached her, especially as I had seen Lisa take down the page.

'You've got a lot to learn about the internet, Mum,' said Helen. 'Once the story is out there, it's out there. Your friend Lisa may have taken it down but if someone else had already copied and pasted it on to their own site, there's no saying how far it will travel. Henry has well and truly bolted.'

Chapter 23

A frog he would a-wooing go . . . Heigh ho! says Rowley . . . A frog he would a-wooing go . . . Whether his mother would let him or no . . . Soon after buying the bubble car, Hendo quit school and got a job with the local greengrocer. I'll never forget the day he chugged up in that dark green Bedford panel van for the first time. It was early 1950s style, with a split windscreen and wide, horizontal metal bars for a radiator grill. In flowery writing on the side it boasted 'Munton Moffett High Class Fruiterers'.

'Perfect, eh?' he grinned.

'It's . . . I don't understand,' I said.

'You soon will.' He opened up the back doors. 'Hop in.' Though empty, the van stank of cauliflower and cabbage. I still heave at the smell of cabbage, especially when it's simmering in a pan.

'So this is your future.' I clambered in the back, breathing through my mouth. 'Delivering fruit and veg.'

'You're joking.'

'So . . . ?'

'Bubble cars weren't designed to take drums. At a push I can transport all PFF's gear in this old lady.'

'Who or what are PFF?'

'It's the new name of the group. It was much longer and very French before. We decided yesterday to shorten it, to three initials. I can fit the gear and Lucy into the van. Last but not least . . .' He nodded at me and grinned. 'We need a roadie.' It was the first time I had ever heard the term. 'Someone to help us load in the gear and set it up at the gig.' By 'gig' he didn't mean a light two-wheeled carriage pulled by a horse. 'We'll be paid so you'll get your share.'

'But . . . I don't know anything about sound systems.'

'You'll pick it up.'

'I've got homework.' I sounded like a regular goody two shoes.

'Most of our engagements are at weekends.' Hendo picked up a rogue cabbage that had rolled under the driver's seat then slammed shut the van's back doors.

'What have your parents got to say about it all?' I said.

'Dad ran off to the circus at fourteen.' Hendo booted the cabbage halfway down Leehart Gardens. 'That's where he met Mum. They can hardly object.'

I pointed across the road. 'Will the Pitchers let Lucy go?'

He shrugged his shoulders. 'It's worth a try.'

It was time to know the truth, however painful. 'Are you two . . . you know . . . ?'

'You, me and Lucy – we're just friends.' He smiled. I was being used as cover. 'We've got a gig tomorrow night in Sydenham. Up for it?' What else would I do that was more interesting? Besides, if Lucy was going . . .

The following evening we loaded up the Bedford to its ceiling with drums, guitars, microphones and Vox AC-30 amplifiers. I could only just get in, right at the back. Hendo drove and Lucy, naturally, sat in front on a warm, comfortable passenger seat.

There was another way of looking at it all. Sandwiched between two AC-30s, I was playing a minor part in an ongoing historical revolution. Some academics argue that social change is principally politically driven. I would contend that technologies, in this case amplified sound, also play their part in transforming history. Think about it. Without amplified sound Hitler couldn't have whipped millions into a nationalistic frenzy at open-air rallies, Churchill couldn't have brought a resolving calm on the radio, and Dave Davies couldn't have given nightmares to a million shocked parents. *Dave Davies?* For it was Mr Davies, guitarist in The Kinks, who sliced the speaker cone of a little green Elpico amp with a razor blade and linked it to an AC-30 amplifier, similar to those each side of me in the van. The distorted sound he got on his guitar, utilized on 'You Really Got Me', was considered by some a depraved abomination: to others, a defining moment in the history of the instrument.

The point is that we consume amplified sound constantly through radio, TV, cinema, telephone and the internet but, like me, sitting that day on a damp patch of squashed melon, rarely give it much thought. At the other end of the van Lucy had only happy thoughts. Hendo chatted away to her. I spent most of my time making sure his bass drum didn't topple on me.

The pub was depressingly shabby but the smell of smoke and beer was a welcome change from essence of vegetable. In one corner of the pub's function room, an old boy supped his pint while he read the sports pages of a newspaper, probably eking out the long hours before returning to his flat. Further along sat another man, black and in his early twenties. As I went past, clutching a couple of microphone stands, he touched my arm.

'What sort of stuff do you play?' His voice was deep and rich.

'We're keeping the blues alive,' said lead guitarist Andy, plugging his instrument into the amp. 'You'll love it.'

'That's very decent of you,' said the man. 'Without your help we might forget our enslaved past.'

'We just dig the music,' said Andy.

'Yeah, you kids have a tough life, getting up for school every day. That kind of suffering can only be expressed in twelve bars.'

I had walked into a cultural and political minefield but was too young to understand. I looked at Andy who said nothing more and carried on sorting out his guitar. Remembering my manners, I introduced myself to the stranger. 'Pleased to meet you, I'm William. William Shearwater. And you're . . . ?'

'Curd,' he said. 'Blind Lemon Curd.' I couldn't see a white stick. Andy gestured to me to join him by the amp.

'He's taking the piss,' he said.

'I don't get it.'

'Later. Here . . .' He threw me some gaffer tape and I set about securing leads to the floor. When I looked round, Mr Curd had disappeared. Twenty minutes later I went out to the van and found him talking to Lucy.

'Billy, this is, how do you pronounce it . . . Mumamba?' she said. The man nodded.

'We've met,' I said. 'I thought your name was—'

'Your friend . . .' Mumamba cut across my comment, pointing to the joint in Lucy's hand. 'She needs to give this up. Marijuana users display

155

impaired neural connectivity in specific brain regions involved in a range of executive functions like memory, learning and impulse control.' That wasn't exactly what he said. I found that last sentence on the internet just now. Let's say they were words to that effect: it all happened a long time ago.

'Mumamba is a medical student at University College London,' said Lucy. 'He's from Lusaka.'

I looked blank. 'I'm not sure where Loose—'

'Lusaka,' said Mumamba. 'Capital of Zambia.'

I was going to say I had no idea where Zambia was but Lucy put an arm round Mumamba's shoulder and said: 'He also plays electric guitar.'

Mumamba knew what I was thinking. 'Unbelievable, isn't it?' he said. 'Some of us have had electricity for almost two years now.'

'That's good.' Once again, I was too naive to understand invective. I still feel embarrassed thinking about it.

'I think our new friend should play tonight with the group,' said Lucy. I wasn't sure how Andy, leader of PFF, would take it but Lucy had Hendo wrapped round her little finger. Hendo persuaded Andy. So, an hour or so later, Mumamba glanced through the band's song list and plugged in for the band's second set. To this day I don't know what he did to extract such an astonishing sound out of Andy's spare beat-up Fender. True, he twiddled a few knobs on the AC-30 but I've fiddled with the same knobs ever since and get a sound resembling a mushy pea convention. Maybe it was something to do with the controls on the guitar's pickups. Even the way he tuned up was different class and when he pulled out the bottleneck and hit those blue notes (diminished thirds, fifths and sevenths, to be technical), conversations tailed off all over the function-room floor.

Unexpected events like Mumamba's one and only gig with PFF have the power to inspire or demoralize. Before he plugged in that Fender, I had decided my days as a guitarist were best buried at sea with 'Bobby Shafto'. But I went home and tore into 'There is a Tavern in the Town' with renewed gusto. At the other extreme, Andy gave up on the blues, claiming it was dying as a popular music form. Besides, he said, there was a new sound coming over from the USA. PFF must change or die. The catalyst behind all this was a young lady called Lucy Pitcher. I was beginning to understand how she collected people. Well, males anyway: first me, then Hendo, then Rudiger, then Mumamba. I mention all of this only because Bishop Maureen has similar powers of persuasion . . .

*

It was Maureen who landed the big media fish at this morning's *Our Goal: The Soul* bash in Birmingham. Maureen is an ecclesiastical whirlwind. Everything she does is like a punk rock single – short, fast and loud. While she cajoled journalists into attending the event, I set up the photo opportunity outside Aston Villa's ground. My thinking was straightforward: football needs to rediscover the simple vision of its founding fathers. One such patriarch was William McGregor.

A Scot by birth, McGregor moved to Birmingham in 1870, setting up a drapery business. He helped manage a football club run by members of the Villa Cross Wesleyan Chapel. With the club now called Aston Villa, and firmly established as one of the leading clubs in the country, McGregor wrote to several others, suggesting they form a 'football league', playing each other home and away in the course of a season: two points for a win, one point for a draw. The rest is sporting history. McGregor's huge contribution to the game was recognized in 2009 when a bronze statue in his memory was erected outside Villa Park: in his hand, that momentous letter. It seemed the perfect place to inform the media of our plans. Aston Villa are rightly proud of the great man's legacy and when the club's officials heard what we were planning they offered us the directors' lounge in which to hold a media reception. Maureen politely turned them down.

'It sends out all the wrong signals,' she said. 'This is all about the fans. We need to be seen outside, in the street, not in the corridors of power.' Not bad, eh? That's punk football for you. It's hard to believe she has only been to one match in her life.

I stood underneath the statue of McGregor and, with a gaggle of journalists, camera crews and photographers around, explained that he was, truly, the Jimmy Hill of his time: a visionary, bursting with new ideas and limitless energy for the game. It was McGregor who insisted that clubs in the newly christened Football League shared gate receipts. For decades, wealthier clubs were unable to dominate the competition – until, that is, some people had the bright idea of fixing something that wasn't broken and formed the Premier League.

The success of McGregor's brainchild directly inspired the creation of similar competitions in a host of other countries. As chair of the Football League and Football Association, McGregor became one of the first football celebrities, writing a weekly column for the *Birmingham Gazette*. He even endorsed a special type of football boot called the 'McGregor lace-to-toe'.

'He was also a member of a church in Aston, for forty years,' I concluded. 'Reminding us that power for good lies in the hands of the local community, of whatever faith or persuasion. Ordinary people can still bring down the mighty if they pull together. Twenty thousand Liverpool fans proved that when they walked out of Anfield at the seventy-seventh minute of a match against Sunderland, protesting that the highest price ticket in their new main stand had been set at an astonishing seventy-seven pounds. In the face of such orchestrated, visible dissent the club backed down. If we join together, we can bring about change. We will bring about change.'

That was the cue for Maureen to wheel out her new chaplains: not the real thing – yet – but two theological students, male and female, in replica shirts with 'FANS' CHAPLAIN' across the back.

'They will always wear away kits, and that's deliberate,' she said. 'Our chaplains will identify with hardcore fans who follow their clubs round the country.' Hardcore! She's even picked up the language. Her tale of meeting the girls at Upton Park followed before she, too, pointed to the statue behind her. 'McGregor's own minister, the Reverend W. G. Percival, described him as a "genial, kindly, honest sportsman" and "a man of absolutely unblemished personal character". I am delighted there is somebody today who can step into the great man's shoes, a man beyond reproach, who will head up this new initiative. Canon William Shearwater . . .'

More interviews followed. More photographs. BBC Midlands Today and Sky Sports did us proud. I was on TalkSport and BBC Radio Five Live earlier this evening and while I've been jabbering away into this microphone, the online newspapers have loaded up reports, too. 'The Blessed United' is the headline in the *Mirror*: a clever allusion to the superb football novel by David Peace. 'Well, I'm damned . . .' begins the report. I like 'Cheers for Shears' in the *Mail* and the *Sun*'s 'Never Mind the Cassocks, it's Bishop Maureen'. All very tongue in cheek but you expect that from the subs, even if the heading often bears no real relation to the story beneath.

Out of the blue I also had a call today from a researcher at the BBC who is putting together a documentary for BBC4 on influential cultural events of the 1960s. He had read my interview in the *Church Times*, specifically how I had been in a band at the 'happening' at the Big Top, Bishopsgate, now regarded as an iconic event in the UK's cultural history. Would I like to be interviewed as part of a retrospective?

I've spent many a long year mastering the media. It's like holding the devil's tail. You have to be sure you've thought through all the implications of what you are doing. You need to be aware of all the angles the journalist is likely to take before you give him the information he is looking for. It's all about thinking like him. Being one step ahead. I've created a reservoir of goodwill over the years. They like me. They trust me. I mean, look at this coverage! Though I say it myself, all the hard work is paying off at last.

Chapter 24

My first thought was that it had to be Jack again. No one else would knock at my door so early in the morning and so insistently. I didn't even bother looking out of the window. I ran downstairs and opened the door expectantly, only to discover a man, probably in his late twenties, standing in the porch. He was dressed casually with a canvas satchel slung over his shoulder and sported a fashionable black, bushy beard.

'Mrs Daggert?' he said.

'Ye-es.'

'Tim Harvey.' He put out his hand. 'Slipstream.'

'Slipstream?'

'The press agency.' I had never heard of it. 'We want to help you trace your mother.'

'How did . . . ?' I panicked and slammed the door in his face.

I imagine he was used to that because he leaned down and spoke through the letter box. 'Lisa told me. I believe she's one of your students.'

'Oh God, oh God,' I said to myself. 'Lisa, what have you done?'

'We only want to help.' All I could see were two rows of teeth and that bristly beard. 'In the same way we helped Lisa with her fund-raising. She's a great kid.'

'She shouldn't have put that up on Facebook.'

'But . . . you want to find out about your mother, surely?'

'Not if people start knocking on my door at all hours.'

'I only want to help, honestly.'

'This could get me into all sorts of trouble.'

'I don't understand. You've every right to know the name of your mother.'

'The authorities don't think so.'

'How do you mean?' I heard him dump his bag on the porch floor and take something out: probably a notebook. 'It would be so much easier if you told me what you do and don't want me to say. I'm on your side, believe me.'

'I'd rather you went away.'

'But if I don't cover the story another reporter will, without making sure of the facts. There's already enough on Facebook to run something. I want to make sure you're happy with what goes out.'

'No newspaper will be interested.'

'You must be joking. You've been literally sitting on a secret photograph of the mother you never knew for more than forty years – and she was trying to tell you all along through a poem. It's a slam dunk.' A slam dunk! I would have no idea what that meant if I hadn't overheard conversations between students. Every generation coins new phrases. It's only natural. But faced by a class of sixteen year olds, it's easy to say one thing and find it means something else to them. I asked a girl if she had 'done the D' yet, meaning work for her distinction. The entire class collapsed in laughter. I was informed that in their parlance 'doing the D' involved manipulation of the male sexual organ.

'Let me in and you stay in control of the story.' Tim Harvey wasn't giving up. 'If you let the other reporters cover it without talking to you, they'll make things up, believe me.'

He was right, of course. I remembered what Helen had said on the phone. Thanks to Lisa, Henry had already bolted. Five minutes later, after he promised he would check everything with me before putting anything out, I opened the door.

'Any idea which paper will run the story?' We were still in the hall.

'The *Daily Mail* are gagging for it.'

'You've already told them?'

He nodded. 'It's perfect for them.'

'If he was in a grave, my husband would be spinning.'

'Yeah, I understand, but forget the politics. The main thing is that we use the paper's readers to find out more information for you about your mother.'

'The main thing is that I'm not sent down!'

'Mrs Daggert, we'll only be asking the *Mail*'s readers if anyone knows anything about a photo you've found in an heirloom. That's all. I'll write it in such a way that we avoid legal issues.'

I sighed and reluctantly took him through to the lounge.

'So this is Henry!' he said. 'Awesome.' For more than half an hour he scribbled away in his notebook. I made him read back his notes. There was another knock at the door.

'That'll be Holly,' he said. 'Our photographer.'

'You're not—'

'If you don't mind.'

'I do mind.'

'The thing is, if we don't take any pictures our competitors will hang around outside your house for hours and take some of you putting out a bin, or getting into a car.'

'That's ridiculous. I'd look shady, like a criminal.'

'Exactly.'

These people know how to wear you down but, I have to say, Holly was a sweetie. She even suggested what I might wear for the 'shoot', as they call it. We went through all the photos and chose the best ones together. When the two of them left, I slumped to the floor, in a state of nervous exhaustion.

'Daggert . . . Daggert . . . Daggert . . .' I kept saying, over and over. 'Where are you, just when I need you? Why did you have to go like that?'

*

I'm still wrung out and it's late afternoon: so much for charting the process of recovery through bereavement. I feel back beyond square one. Helen has badgered me endlessly to go over to her house. Rather than mope for the rest of the evening I've decided to drive over and stay the night. It will be the first time since Christmas.

Helen and Matt hadn't expected to see anything other than the photo they had spotted on Facebook. The picture taken at the World Cup Final intrigued them even more.

'You don't suppose . . .' Helen gave me a sideways look.

I shrugged my shoulders. 'Maybe.'

'All these years I've been cheering for England and I'm a quarter Fritz.'

I shook my head. 'He looks too weird and old. No, it must be one of the two boys. At least, I hope so.' The photo is black and white, out of focus and was taken from too far away to make out much detail, especially as they are wearing crazy hats. We looked in vain for family resemblances.

'Maybe the taller boy has it,' said Helen.

'Let me . . .' I shook my head. 'Can't see it myself.'

'If any of these people are still alive, this photo is dynamite.'

I reminded her how our birth relations are protected by law.

'I know,' she said, 'but what if the media were to get hold of it?'

I shook my head. 'I've learned my lesson. I didn't even mention this one to the reporter.'

While Helen and I were talking, Matt had been on Wikipedia, looking up the groups mentioned on the leaflet advertising the 'happening' at the Big Top, Bishopsgate. Only one is listed.

'Second to None formed in nineteen-sixty-six,' he read. 'Their first album, *Psychic Delia*, released in the so-called Summer of Love in nineteen-sixty-seven, reached the Top Forty of the UK album chart. *Psychic Delia* is best described as early progressive rock, a popular genre in the late sixties. Their best-selling single, 'Hoops and Garters', peaked at number sixty-four in the UK charts in nineteen-sixty-eight. They became a favourite on the underground concert circuit. Fronted by Neil Price, they have recorded a total of twelve albums and are still touring.'

'And we know about Garry Kite.'

'He became a leading film producer. He's still going, if not quite so strong.'

*

Before I left I put young David to bed. When I finished reading him a story he said: 'I'm sorry Milly's dead.'

'Milly?'

'You know . . . your real mummy.'

'Oh yes, of course . . . my poem. Well, we don't know her real name.'

'She'll be Milly to me until we find out her real name.'

'That's nice.'

'What happened to your daddy?'

'We don't know.'

'Are you going to find out?'

'Maybe.'

'Are you hoping he's thinking of you?'

'Why do you say that?'

'In your poem you said you hoped Milly was. I would be wondering if he was thinking of me.'

'Yes,' I said. 'Yes, I do wonder.'

Chapter 25

'This'll interest you.' William Shearwater folds back the *Telegraph*'s Money section. 'An eight-thousand-square-foot eco mansion, built in Grasmere under the watchful gaze of Kevin McCloud and Channel Four's *Grand Designs*, is to be transformed into eight studios and apartments.'

Emma Shearwater is at the other end of the breakfast table, coffee cup in hand. 'Really?' she says. Not a tell-me-more 'really', but a distant, humouring 'really'. There is something much more interesting on an early page of her *Daily Mail*.

Billy presses on regardless. 'Nestled on a hillside overlooking the lake, the seven-bedroom family home and luxury self-catering guest house has been on the market at two and a half million for three years but hasn't sold.' The story involves his wife's hero. It is only a question of time. 'Situated just above the busy town, the house was designed by its owner, architect Robert Carney. The geodesic roof, if that's how you pronounce it, was marvelled at by *Grand Designs* presenter Kevin McCloud.' Billy emphasizes the last five words, to no avail. 'McCloud described it as "awe-inspiring" but Carney said: "It's an obscene waste of space for a small family. I built it juiced up on ego."'

'That's amazing.' Emms shakes her head.

'I knew you'd be interested.'

'All that time.'

'And effort.'

'I hope it works out OK.'

'He may not get his money back.'

Emma glances at her husband, over the top of the *Mail*. 'Get back what money for what?'

'You've not been listening.'

'To what?'

'Exactly.'

'This poor woman.' Emma taps the page in front of her. 'She was adopted as a baby but had been sitting on a photo of the birth mother she never knew, for decades! Astonishing.'

'Sitting?'

'Her mother had hidden it in the saddle of a rocking horse.'

Billy is admiring the wooden floor of Robert Carney's folly, reclaimed from a redundant junior school in Appley Bridge, Lancashire. The mention of a rocking horse, however, piques his interest.

'What type is it?' he says.

'A wooden one.'

He looks at his wife with scorn.

'Well, I don't know what type exactly. Anyway, that's not the point.'

'Is there a picture?'

'Here.' Emma holds up the newspaper. The *Mail* has devoted a page and a half to the story. There is a huge picture of the horse and its owner. She, in turn, is holding the photograph of a young girl and her baby.

'That's . . . that's, my God, that's . . . a Collinson,' murmurs Billy.

'Are you all right?' says Emma. 'You look like you've seen a ghost.'

'The horse . . . it's . . . our family owned a rocking horse like that.'

'You've never mentioned it before. Maybe it's the same one.'

'It can't be.'

'What about the young girl in the picture?'

Billy studies the photo carefully. 'No.' There is a quaver in his voice. He coughs. 'It's the horse.' He gathers himself. 'My parents sold one for a few shillings. It must be worth hundreds of pounds now.'

'Into the thousands,' says Emms. 'Here.' She hands Billy the *Mail*. He reads the article carefully.

'You're right. It's quite a story.'

Emms nods. 'It's like that programme on TV, where they reunite parents and children.'

'*Long Lost Family*,' says Billy.

'That's the one. You'd think her birth relatives would come forward, wouldn't you? The poor thing lost her husband recently as well. She's a very attractive woman. Looks a lot like her mother from the photo. Someone will recognize her, surely.'

*

That afternoon, Billy cries off a couple of meetings and drives to Redhill. He turns into Walkers Lane: a leafy cul-de-sac with Woodfield Sixth Form College at the end of it. He watches students pile out at the end of classes, hesitates, then turns the car round to leave. Before he can engage first gear, someone taps on his window.

'Billy!' It is Jason Roxburgh, from ITV's regional news.

Billy winds down the car window. 'Oh . . . hello, Jason.'

'What are you doing here?'

'I . . . well, I was going to ask you the same thing.'

'I've been sent to cover this teacher story. The one in the *Mail*.'

'Thought as much.'

'So, what about you?'

'I've been sent to, er . . . keep an eye on you. It's one of our colleges.'

'Oh, great,' says Jason. 'Maybe you can help. The principal won't let us in.'

'I'm not surprised. It's a personal issue.' Billy raises the window and engages first gear. Jason taps hard on the window again.

'But I'm under pressure from my editor.' He is talking through the glass. 'She says it would make a cracking "And finally" for tonight's show.'

Billy opens the window again and shrugs. 'I can't go against the principal's decision.' Seeing the conversation, two more people come up to the car.

'This is Canon Shearwater,' says Jason Roxburgh. 'He does communications for the Church of England. He knows the college . . .'

'Well, I don't know it well,' says Billy. 'It's not on my patch.'

'Madeleine from the *Mirror*,' a woman says, thrusting a hand through the car window into Billy's. 'Can you have a word with Mrs Daggert for us?'

Another woman leans in through the window. 'We promise not to be intrusive. Sorry . . . hi, I'm Hannah Rimmington, from the *Telegraph*. Weren't you in our paper the other day?'

'Yes, but this is a different story.'

167

'Something to do with football?'

Billy nods. 'But it hasn't got anything to do with this situation.' For another minute or so Billy tries but fails to extricate himself from Madeleine and Hannah, two very determined young ladies. Behind them he notices three more reporters and two photographers, listening to the conversation. His car is now surrounded.

'Billy, I've got the principal on the line,' says Jason, 'a Jack Staniscliffe.' He thrusts his mobile into Billy's face.

'Look,' says Billy. 'I'm not here to—'

'Please?'

Reluctantly, Billy takes the phone. 'Mr Staniscliffe, is it?'

'Ah, Canon Shearwater. We've not met but I'm so grateful you've dropped by to help us.'

'I . . . I don't want to intrude.'

'You're not intruding. Please come to my office. Mrs Daggert and I would be enormously grateful for your advice.'

'I'm not here in an official capacity, Mr Staniscliffe.'

'Forget the formalities. Call me Jack. It's all hands on deck right now. You're a godsend.'

Billy's foot slips off the clutch and the car stalls as he drives to a reserved parking space. Jack Staniscliffe comes out of his office to greet him.

'Do call me Billy.' He shakes Staniscliffe's hand.

'Well, Billy, I can't say how relieved I am to see you. Sophie is teaching but she'll be free in a few minutes. Can I get you a drink?'

'A coffee would be gratefully received,' says Billy, 'but I wouldn't want to disturb Mrs Daggert.'

Jack waves away his misgivings. 'She will be grateful for your help. The college telephone has rung all day long. We've even had a radio station in Wisconsin call us for an interview, would you believe?'

Several minutes later there is a timid knock on the principal's door.

'Sophie, come in, and meet Canon Shearwater,' says Jack. 'He's here to help us cope with the media.'

'That's good of you, Mr, I mean, Canon . . .' says Sophie.

'Please, call me Billy.' He shakes her hand.

'We've never had to handle a situation quite like this before,' says Jack. 'Perhaps you could guide us.'

'Well . . .' Billy takes a deep breath. 'The reporters at the gates, they're only doing their jobs. Treat them with dignity and you've a greater chance of seeing that dignity returned.' He drafts an official statement, to be delivered by Jack, and suggests Sophie slips quietly away, over the college playing fields, while the reporters are taken a cup of tea at the gates.

'I am so grateful, Billy,' says Sophie hugging him, briefly.

Billy and Jack give out cups of tea to the reporters, and Jack reads the bland, holding statement.

'While Mrs Daggert is "overwhelmed" by the interest shown in the tracing of her birth family,' he says, 'she now needs to concentrate on her teaching and would ask people to respect her privacy, and that of all the families involved, concerning such a personal matter.'

The reporters, having been sent down to interview Sophie, explain to Billy and Jack that anything less than that will kill the story.

'I understand,' says Billy. 'If you're under pressure from your editors I'll talk to them myself.' He does so, in a couple of cases. And then reluctantly, one by one, the reporters pack up and leave.

'I imagine we'll see them again,' says Jack.

Billy nods. 'But now you've time to work out how to respond.'

'And you'll help us . . .'

'Well, no, you'll need to talk to Carol Feeney.' Billy gives Jack her phone number. 'This is her patch, not mine.'

'We'd much rather work with someone we know we can trust,' says Jack. 'Sophie is a fine teacher and we wouldn't want this to escalate any further.'

But Billy has already waved and walked to his car.

Chapter 26

Twinkle, twinkle, little star . . . how I wonder how I got into this mess . . . My voice sounded more like a squeak when I saw an article in the *Daily Mail* this morning. It was the first time I had seen a picture of Lucy in more than forty years. And the first time I had seen my daughter, ever. So Lucy is dead. And she's been dead for years and years. After I got over the initial shock, I felt a strange elation. At least she hadn't blanked me for all that time.

I made an excuse to Emms and headed to my study, quietly grabbing a bottle of whisky on the way. I poured myself a long one. I told myself to stay calm, think clearly. So Lucy gave birth to a daughter called Sophie. I was surprised to discover she teaches in Redhill, a matter of a few miles away. One of her students, with a strange hairstyle, is helping her search for her father.

I told myself to stay calm and think clearly. Someone, somewhere is bound to identify Lucy. Sophie will find out her mother's name but, thank God, nothing in the story points back to me. Hendo knows what happened, but I haven't seen him for decades. My own parents died years ago. Even if they are still alive, Lucy's parents are unlikely to disclose my identity, not after the trouble Mrs Pitcher took to ensure no one knew her granddaughter even existed. The whole point of the adoption was to protect both families' good name. That's how they saw and did things in those days.

I have considered owning up but it would be the end of my career: a man of the cloth, living a lie for decades, campaigning for football to clean up its act? Hardly. When Lucy told me she was expecting a child, it was the turning point in my short life. I was just a regular kid trying to cope with a traumatic event, but no one will care about that now. I'm there to be shot down in flames.

I told myself to stay cool . . . to stop . . . stop and think . . . but I couldn't just sit at this desk. I had to get out. I cancelled a couple of meetings and drove to Redhill. Sophie teaches at Woodfield, a

Church of England sixth-form college. I thought I might catch a glimpse of her, from a distance. Until I did, she wouldn't seem real. Whatever the case, I thought the drive would give me a chance to calm down and consider what to do next.

Until this afternoon I had no reason to visit Woodfield. It's outside the Diocese of Southbury, which means it's not on my patch. At one point, I almost turned round and came back – to pack my bags and disappear across the Channel until the heat dies down. What heat, I kept saying to myself? No one knows you are Sophie's father. No one will find out, either. You are protected by law. Mrs Pitcher saw to that all those years ago. Calm down. Then the panic crept back and I decided to give myself up, throw myself on my daughter's mercy, tell her I was just a child when it all happened and beg her forgiveness. But I thought about Emms and the rest of the family and the distress it would cause; and that inevitable phone call from a chortling Nicholas Ledgard.

Stomach churning, I turned slowly into Walkers Lane: a leafy cul-de-sac with Woodfield at the end of it. The chances of catching sight of Sophie were minimal but I reckoned I might be lucky. However, after a few moments I came to my senses. This was tantamount to stalking. I told myself to get a grip and go home. I reached the college gates and began turning the car round but before I could engage first gear and drive away, someone tapped on my window: Jason Roxburgh, from ITV's regional news. My heart sank. I've worked with Jason on a number of stories. He's a decent bloke but not someone I wanted to see today of all days. He talked me into chatting to the principal of the college. Surrounded by him and half a dozen other journalists, I really had no option but to do my job.

My whole body trembled as I drove a few yards to the college car park. In a few moments I would meet my daughter in the most bizarre circumstances. I had imagined meeting him or her thousands of times but never like this. The truth is, I can't bear to watch *Long Lost Family*. It's too close for comfort. The format is predictable but no less emotional for that. A lost daughter, say, is tracked down and both she and the grieving mother are overcome by the news.

They exchange letters and photographs. They agree to meet. A suitable venue is arranged – a park, say, where the mother took her daughter for one last walk before giving her up for adoption. The mother wants to explain that she never wanted to let her daughter go. It was forced upon her. Can she ever, ever be forgiven? There are healing tears of reconciliation and a new, happy rest of their lives together . . .

Jack Staniscliffe was alone in his office. I was trying hard to concentrate on what he was telling me but every time I heard approaching footsteps, I felt sick with apprehension.

More footsteps, a woman's heels, echoed along the corridor, a knock at the door and there she was: pink and flustered, her hair pulled back unfussily to reveal a diamond-thin face. It was Lucy's face, reborn: her ridiculously even features older, wiser and even more compelling for it. Her eyes met mine, confidently, warmly. I shook her hand. The formalities were bizarre. Not for me the moment of release, where relatives cry a swollen river of tears, hug one another as if their very lives depend on it, then walk around serenic lakes, arm in reconciled arm.

They both looked at me expectantly. The adrenaline surged, subduing emotions that kicked and raged. The first thing to do, I explained, was to come together as a team and make decisions corporately. Every person in the team, from receptionist to principal, must stick to the agreed course of action, no matter what external pressures are exerted, at whatever time of day or night. Public statements should be agreed by all and, if necessary, copies printed and given to reporters. Further media enquiries must be routed through one nominated person, acting as spokesperson for all.

We agreed a statement, to be delivered by Jack. We also agreed that Sophie should slip quietly out of a back door, across the playing fields. As she turned to put on her coat I noticed the sweeping curve of her neck, white and ski-slope smooth. I was standing behind Lucy in the guinea pig shed all over again. I chided myself. Whatever was I thinking?

'I am so grateful, Billy,' she said and hugged me, affectionately. 'Really grateful.'

'I'm just not doing my job,' I said. 'This isn't my patch, you see.' She laughed. Thank God, because the comment was as weak as my legs. I caught a delicious scent as she leaned towards me. I'm pretty sure it was Chanel. The fresh orange, jasmine and rose were subtle and inviting.

We took the reporters cups of tea, and Jack read them the bland, holding statement. I killed their story but it was all I could do. I gave Jack Carol Feeney's phone number. Woodfield is on her patch.

'With due respect to Carol, we'd much rather work with someone we know we can trust,' said Jack. If only he knew.

I left in a state of nervous turmoil. I am still in it, though documenting what has happened today gets things in some sort of proportion. Fortunately, Emms was out when I got home and has been out all evening. I'm not sure where. I am grateful for such a small mercy.

*

I had just finished that last sentence when the phone rang. I glanced at my watch. It was gone eleven. 'I hope you don't mind my calling, only I didn't have a chance to thank you properly this afternoon.' It was Sophie Daggert. We talked for the best part of an hour. It might as well have been ten minutes. And we were far from through when Emms pulled up and put the car away in the garage.

'If you have time for a coffee, I would value your advice on a very complicated situation,' concluded Sophie. 'You have been so helpful . . .'

Oh. Dear. God.

Chapter 27

Canon Shearwater's unexpected appearance outside the college gates reminded me of that classic urban legend, the one where the driver of a car picks up a hitchhiker by the side of the road. They begin to chat and the hitchhiker warns the driver to get ready for a momentous event in the near future. With the car still travelling at speed, the hitchhiker disappears from the passenger seat. While I've never heard of a vanishing media consultant, Jack called Canon Shearwater a godsend. Appearing as he did from nowhere I wouldn't disagree, so I couldn't let this crazy day end without thanking him again. He was at the end of a traceable landline so at least he is human. An angel would have only a mobile number.

The first phone call of the day had been very different. My mother rang before I went to work. She was upset. Very upset. As usual, she could only see her point of view. Her first words were: 'You could have warned me.' Not even a 'Hello, love, how are you?'

'About what?' I said.

'This article in the *Mail*.'

'I wasn't sure it would appear at all,' I said, 'let alone which day.' Perhaps I was remiss not to call her, but in spite of what Tim Harvey had said I was certain the *Mail* wouldn't run the story. How wrong can you be!

'Well, the first I heard about it was from Hilda just now . . .' Hilda is my mother's friend at the YWCA lunch club for senior citizens. They meet there every Monday and Thursday for a meal and a moan. It would be uncharitable to call Hilda a sour bitch but I just have. Hilda's own sons and daughter rarely, if ever, visit or call. It's obvious why. Mum is under her spell and always returns home upset on Monday and Thursday afternoons.

'I wish you had told me where Henry really came from,' I said.

174

Her reply was typically brusque. 'What good would that have done? Besides, I've always disliked rocking horses. They take up too much room.'

'Then why did you keep him?'

'Whoever the girl was who gave birth to you' – she has never used the term 'your mother' – 'insisted on it. Now we know why. Besides, your father liked Henry for some reason. It's all very upsetting.'

'I hoped you would be pleased for me, finding the photo.'

'Well, I'm just glad . . .' She paused. 'Glad that . . . hopefully, your mind can be put at rest.' I'm certain she was going to say she was glad that 'the girl who gave birth to you' is no longer alive – but thought better of it. 'She does look terribly young,' she went on. 'I wonder if the boy who had his way with her is still alive.' Had his way! So I was a two-minute job in the bike sheds or the bus shelter, as far as she was concerned, and I've been saved from the appalling consequences of such a union. The silly thing is that I regard her as my 'mother'. She has never needed to stress the point. Sometimes her insecurity drives me mad.

The story in the *Daily Mail* is 95 per cent accurate. Some of the descriptions are exaggerated but I can live with that. I am surprised at the amount of coverage they gave Lisa (not that I'm not grateful to her). Slipstream already had a photo of her from her fund-raising drive. It featured prominently, especially in the online version. What she says is embarrassing: 'Mrs Daggert is the best teacher ever. She's the only person I know who really understands what it feels like to be adopted . . .' She mentions staying overnight at my house. I'm sorry she told them that. It would have helped if I had known Canon Shearwater before all this began. I'm sure he would have helped me manage things better.

After I put the phone down to Mum, Jack called. He said I could have the day off, to let the heat die down. But I wanted to work. I wasn't ill and besides, I didn't want to be alone in the house. When I arrived at the college, I was overwhelmed by well-wishers in the car park. Everyone had either read the story or been told about it. In fact, because most of the information in the *Mail* had already been all over Facebook, the discovery of the photo was now old news to most of my students. All they wanted to know was whether anyone had come forward with new information. There's nothing reliable, yet.

We were back on the war poets in class, in particular Siegfried Sassoon. In Sassoon's 'Base Details', the commanders have the power of life and death over common soldiers, staying out of the line of fire themselves by remaining at 'the Base'. Sassoon's officers are caricatured as red-faced, fat and lacking in self-awareness as they claim 'we've lost heavily in this last scrap', the understatement of 'scrap' indicating they have no understanding of what battle on the front line is really like. What better way to introduce Sassoon than through clips from *Blackadder Goes Forth*? If there has been a better satire concerning the futility of war, I have yet to see it.

I showed a clip from the final episode. Blackadder is about to join his troops as they go over the top, to their almost certain death. Colonel Melchett, portrayed as a blustering buffoon by Stephen Fry, asks Private Baldrick if he is 'looking forward to the big push'.

'No,' says Baldrick. 'I'm absolutely terrified.'

'Don't worry, my boy,' says Melchett. 'If you should falter, remember that Captain Darling and I are behind you.'

'About thirty-five miles behind,' adds Blackadder, sardonically.

We were discussing the similarities between Sassoon's poetry and *Blackadder Goes Forth* when I received a message from Jack. I had to see him immediately in his office.

'The *Telegraph*, the *Mirror*, the *Times*, BBC News and BBC Radio Surrey want to interview you.' He read the list from a page in front of him. 'Some of them are outside the college gates. They've told me they will wait all day, if necessary. I've told them not to come on to the premises or I'll call the police. Hopefully they'll give up and go home.'

'I'm so sorry. If I had thought . . .'

He shrugged his shoulders. 'These things happen. What's most important is protecting the good name of the college. Try and focus on your lessons for the day.'

Doing that was almost impossible but I did my best. I was surprised not to see Lisa in class. I hoped there weren't people camped outside her house, too. Every now and then I left my class for a few seconds, to check the college gates. Several reporters were standing there, chatting to one another, taking calls on their mobile phones. Two or three had cameras round their necks. Surely there were more interesting stories to cover.

It was well into the afternoon when Canon Shearwater arrived, from nowhere. He is in his late fifties or early sixties, I would say, has piercing blue eyes and, most surprisingly, seemed dressed a little too casually for a day's work about town. He seemed agitated. Perhaps preoccupied is the right word. He said, 'This isn't really my patch,' and 'I don't want to intrude,' several times, as if he hadn't expected to find himself there at all. Once Jack explained the situation, however, he took control. In fact, I witnessed a master class in crisis management. Of course, we can all make things work on our own turf. Give me my classroom and a subject I love and you can shut the door and leave me to it. It's a different matter walking into a place you have never been before, as Billy did (well now, I've used his Christian name for the first time, though it feels too familiar), and organize people you don't know – especially in a volatile situation. It was very impressive.

Before they smuggled me out of the back door (I felt like a criminal!) Jack asked Billy for his business card.

'Sorry, I don't think . . .' He felt around in his pockets. 'No, I've none with me.' For someone so organized, it was a surprise.

'I'd like to call you, if I may, for further advice,' said Jack.

He shook his head. 'You need to speak to Carol Feeney. This is her neck of the woods.' He was quite insistent. 'From my own experience, I would expect things to blow over in a few days. That might be best for everyone.' Before I left I hugged him, on impulse. Maybe it was a bit unprofessional but I wanted him to know I appreciated his help. He returned the embrace warmly. He has the most piercing eyes.

I returned home to find a dozen voicemails and more than twenty emails waiting for me. The voicemails were from friends and family, congratulating me on the article and wishing me well. Most of the emails, sent on by the *Daily Mail*, are from people who 'definitely' recognized my mother. 'It's Brenda Catchpole from Hatch End,' says one. 'I always thought she had a secret or two. She died in 2012.'

Ms Catchpole's recent demise renders that suggestion impossible. A couple of people have sent photos featuring young girls similar to my mother: maybe, maybe not. One man, in his late sixties from Fraserburgh in Scotland, poured out his heart, saying he has waited more than fifty years to see his lost love again, Fiona McClelland. 'So that's why she left me,' he said. 'You must be my daughter. I can see the similarities between us. When can we meet?' One email is from an ex-pat in Charlotte, North Carolina, but I think he's just homesick.

I understand now why Carmel Withers said it is important to share this journey with someone I know and trust, someone older than Lisa. But no one comes to mind. Every twenty minutes or so the sound of a croaking frog on my computer tells me more emails have arrived: each one offering another name. Without two or three emails identifying the same person, independently of one another, there's no point in pursuing any of them at this stage, is there? I'm not sure. And my mother's words haunt me: 'These TV programmes . . . they only show you happy reunions.'

Out of curiosity, I entered 'Canon William Shearwater' into Google. There are stories about him all over the web. I had no idea about this *Our Goal: The Soul* campaign but then I never read the sports pages. According to Wikipedia he's a media consultant and author who's been married for almost forty years. As for Carol Feeney, I'm sure she's perfectly good at her job, but from her photos on Google she looks too young and inexperienced for this kind of situation: only a gut feeling, but I'm usually right about these things.

I found Billy's phone number easily enough and summoned up the courage to call him. It was already late. It's much later now. We talked for almost an hour. He particularly wanted to know how hard I had tried to locate my birth parents through the official routes and if I had had any joy at all. He seemed quite knowledgeable about the law as it pertains to children once deemed 'illegitimate'. He asked me about the circumstances of my adoption, whether I had been happy as a child and, in particular, about the relationship with my adoptive parents. He wanted to know about my job, my favourite authors, films and even the music I listen to. I'm a bit retro in that regard.

'Am I rabbiting on?' I said.

'No, no ... I'm intrigued.'

'Only, it's very late. I don't want to keep you up.'

'You're not.'

'Do I sound a bit ... desperate?'

'How do you mean?'

'Well, you know – a widow in her forties, on her own, trying to put her life back together ...'

'You don't sound at all needy.'

Even if he wasn't being sincere it was a nice thing to say. Towards the end of the conversation I asked him if I could seek his advice again. He suggested this Carol Feeney person would be best. He was quite insistent. I said I would value a chance to meet up again, maybe just for a coffee, before talking to Carol. He was reluctant to do so as Woodfield 'isn't on his patch'. He must have said that half a dozen times today. I am disappointed because I think we would get on.

As I was talking to Billy (maybe I should go back to calling him Canon Shearwater) my mobile was on silent and buzzing. Several calls had come in. They were all from the same number: Lisa's. She had left a voicemail.

'I'm really sorry, miss ... so sorry. I'm sure you're asleep so I won't ring again. I'm so, so sorry ...'

Chapter 28

Pussy cat, pussy cat, where have you been? . . . I've been up to London to look at the Queen . . . Bishop Maureen arranged a meeting at the Eutychus Trust this morning. If *Our Goal: The Soul* is to make any headway we need funds and the trust is well known for awarding grants to projects it deems 'creative and community centred'. For a few short hours I was grateful to have no time to dwell on events of the past few days.

Maureen suggested meeting outside Mansion House underground station at 3 p.m.

'That's some distance from the trust's offices,' I said.

'Best part of two miles.'

'There's another station much nearer.'

'I always walk the last mile or more, to any destination in town. It's good for the mind and body and we can talk as we walk. We're after their money so be prepared for a grilling!' She also suggested, firmly, that as she would 'purple up' I should don some serious clergy clobber. It intrigues me how ordained women quite happily sport unflattering dog collars and clerical shirts. Indeed, before women were ordained, clergymen tended to dress more informally. Perhaps because they fought so long for the right to be revs, women wear godly gear with more pride. I have to say, though, Maureen scrubbed up well this morning, in figure-hugging suit, purple blouse and gold cross necklace. I looked dull by comparison: beauty and the priest.

The Eutychus Trust would have taken no notice of me had I applied for funds on my own but an impassioned letter from a newly appointed female bishop with a colourful past cannot be so easily ignored. We are asking for £200,000 over the next three years. Winning the award would mean we can take on a staff member or two and appoint the first fans' chaplains. I will also be free to spend most of my time on the campaign. I would no longer need to play Red Adair and deal with Nicholas Ledgard-style blow-outs.

Maureen walks as fast as she talks and I struggled to keep up with her. I wasn't going to admit I have a nagging problem with my left hip and that I may eventually need a replacement.

'This Adam Johnson case,' said Maureen.

'The Sunderland footballer?'

She nodded. 'We need to make that central to our presentation.'

'I'm not with you.'

'He groomed a girl of fifteen. She was standing outside the ground after games.'

Needless to say, I knew about the case. It's been all over the papers for weeks. Johnson, sent down for six years for sexual activity with a child under sixteen and child grooming, began texting the girl while his partner was pregnant with their child. He met up with her twice, knowing her age.

'Imagine how that poor girl must have felt, before telling her parents what happened,' said Maureen. 'And then there's the traumatic court case to endure, at such a tender age. One of our chaplains could have supported her, and the family, behind the scenes.'

I hadn't really envisioned *Our Goal: The Soul* being directly involved with fans in this way but, as Maureen pointed out, it fitted the trust's remit. There are plenty of supporters' groups protesting vociferously at rising ticket prices and the poor management of their clubs. Virtually nobody is caring for the punters, the casualties of the system.

'We all make mistakes,' she said, walking half a yard ahead. 'But Johnson dug himself in deeper by not coming out with the truth from the start. He lied to his girlfriend. He lied to the club. The deceit did for him.'

I cleared my throat, to ensure she didn't pick up any hint of a voice that threatened once more to tremble. 'Yes,' I said, a tad too firmly. 'Yes . . . I'm sure you're right.'

We turned a corner. Well, Maureen turned a corner and I caught up with her.

'I recognize this road.' I was happy to change the subject. 'That new block of flats . . .'

'The Tangerine Tree used to be there.'

'Yes, the Tangerine Tree.' I stood at the entrance to the flats. 'It's where I entered my first vulva.' A strange comment, admittedly. I received a reproving look from my companion: the Americans call it the 'hairy eyeball'.

'You like Swedish cars, then,' she said.

'No, you heard me right. I did say vulva.'

I had to explain myself, of course. PFF were invited to an experimental event at the Tangerine Tree, around November or December 1966. My memory is a bit hazy but I'm sure Hendo's father got tickets through his theatrical contacts. It was a 'happening', in the true 1960s meaning of the term, and possibly one of the first in London. Happenings are difficult to describe because each one was self-consciously unique. Put another way, there are as many definitions of a happening as there were happenings. Michael Kirby, in his book *Happenings: An Illustrated Anthology*, suggests they were a 'purposefully composed form of theatre in which diverse alogical elements, including nonmatrixed performing, are organized in a compartmented structure'. Confused? Gary Botting, a Canadian theatre critic and playwright, sheds more darkness on it all: 'Happenings abandon the matrix of story and plot for the equally complex matrix of incident and event.' Oddly enough, a children's TV series offers the most accessible description. Happenings would have been a long way from Gerry and Sylvia Anderson's minds when they dreamed up their puppet show, *Stingray*. Each week, however, its opening gambit is as near as it gets to a perfect definition: 'Anything can happen in the next half-hour ...'

In his essay 'Happenings in the New York Scene', Allan Kaprow wrote: 'Visitors are now and then not sure what has taken place, when it has ended, even when things have gone "wrong". For when something goes wrong, something far more right, more revelatory, has many times emerged.'

Which brings me back to my first vulva. The Tangerine Tree was filled with Nag Champa incense, dry ice and strange (for the time) Indian sitar and tabla music: droning, dreamy, hypnotic. Projected on to a large screen were the words 'Wall of Illusion'. Strewn across the floor were hundreds of old car tyres. We could rearrange them, roll them along the floor, build rubber castles out of them and, if we lacked imagination, sit on them. I recall a beat poet coming on to the stage in a straw boater and reciting some self-indulgent stanzas from halfway up a ladder. More sitar and tabla followed. More dry ice. More poetry, this time from a woman who bounced on a small trampoline as she recited her work. I never found out why. There was no why. We had to discover our own meaning.

Hendo and Andy decided to search for deeper consciousness at a local pub. They missed the stage curtain being drawn back to expose the tour de force: a large inflatable silver vulva, some twenty feet high (though it may have grown in size over the years). I have no idea whether it was anatomically accurate. At the time, I wouldn't have known. One by one, five maybe six actors came down the vagina (a wet, inflated inner tube) and squirmed their way, head first, on to the stage, wiping a greasy white substance off their faces. I imagine this was a symbolic reference to vernix. They struck up improvised dance sessions with the audience then invited us to crawl back up towards the womb.

Lucy, who may well have been high, grabbed me by the hand. We squeezed into the vulva, laughing stupidly, and in almost total darkness crawled up the long, narrow vagina. I bumped into someone in front of me who was unsure whether to go along the left or right fallopian tube. I fell back on Lucy, giggling. I felt the soft curves of her body below me and her hot breath on my ear. I pulled her closer to me. She pulled my shirt loose in the darkness and ran a hand up my back. 'Budge up,' said a lad behind us. We had to move. The most delicious forty-five seconds of my short life were over. Kaprow was right. When something goes wrong at a happening, 'something far more right, more revelatory, has many times emerged'.

I offered Bishop Maureen a judiciously edited version of these events.

'What a difference a decade makes,' she said.

'Not quite your scene . . .'

'The whole hippy thing was so pretentious. It was ripe for ridicule.'

'We were just having fun. You punks were the only ones to get all flustered and serious about it. Thank God Ian Dury came along to pop your own pretentious bubble.' I had clearly hit a nerve but just as the conversation was getting interesting we arrived at the Eutychus Trust.

The presentation went well. I always feel diffident about asking for hard cash, albeit for a worthy cause. Maureen has no such misgivings. The grilling never materialized and all the buying signs were there. However, we won't know whether we've landed the big prize for a couple of weeks. Afterwards Maureen treated me to a meal at a cosy Italian restaurant in the West End.

'Bottle of red?' she said.

'Bottle of white,' I replied. 'It all depends upon . . .'

Maureen laughed. 'I know where this is going.'

'But you punks hate singer-songwriters.'

'Now you're caricaturing me. I still put my feet up to Carole King.'

For the next half-hour we swapped notes on everything from Donald Trump to the Middle East, Calvin's *Institutes* to Joe Strummer.

'I hear you play a bit yourself,' she said.

'Not seriously. My long and illustrious career began and ended at a happening in Bishopsgate. I was an overnight failure.'

'The happening at the Big Top, Bishopsgate is the stuff of legend.' She looked genuinely impressed. 'What happened? Who else was on the bill?'

It was time to be vague again. 'It's a long and dull story. I'll bore you with it another day.' My former life was beginning to intrigue Maureen, a little too much.

When I got home, Emms wasn't around. Come to think of it, I've dictated all this and I'm still not sure where she is. She hasn't phoned. Ah. My mobile was on mute. I set it like that when I met up with Maureen. I'd best turn it on. I'm still reeling from five voicemails, all from Emms.

'Don't forget you're speaking at Roy's book club at the library tonight . . .'

'You've not forgotten about tonight, I hope . . .'

'Billy, where the hell are you . . . ?'

'I've had to apologize to everyone here . . .'

'Billy, you really are such a fucking selfish idiot . . .'

Chapter 29

Tuesday wasn't the worst day of my life. That was the day I lost Daggert. It wasn't the most shocking, either. That was when we discovered his condition was terminal. Tuesday, though, was so crushing, so humiliating it has taken me two days to find the courage to sit here and write it up. I would rather pretend it never happened. But this journal has been therapeutic. Once events are recorded here, I consign them to history. I can begin to move on.

I woke at 5 a.m. In fact, I'm not sure if I slept much after three. That's not unusual. The amount of administrative paperwork involved in teaching these days, on top of the marking, report writing and whatever else, means you are permanently under deadlines that have little to do with teaching. I sometimes think the worst invention ever was the personal computer. In the old days a bank of secretarial staff would be in place to help with administration. Now, because the technology is available to us all on desktops, we do the work secretaries used to do – as well as the job we had before. And because we have the same technology at home (usually bought out of our own pockets) we are expected to continue working there as well, at all hours. I can never leave my job behind.

Monday night was even worse than normal. I kept thinking of Lisa's voicemail. I tried to call her back but she had switched off her phone. Lying alone in the darkness, molehills become mountains. When my phone rang at about 7 a.m. on Tuesday morning, I thought it would be her at last. It wasn't. It was Jack, calling from home. I was relieved to talk to another human being. A stupor befuddles your brain when you are on your own for long spells.

'It's . . . about Lisa Stonebridge.' When he hesitated, I instinctively feared the worst. This was going to be a difficult conversation. 'I've had her mother on the phone.'

My heart sank. 'Oh dear, what's wrong?'

'She is concerned about, how can I say this . . . your relationship with her daughter.'

'My what?'

'All this publicity in the papers.'

'It's got nothing to do with Lisa.'

'She sees it differently.'

'You're not suggesting—'

'I'm not suggesting anything. I have to deal with any complaint in a professional manner.'

'Yes . . . yes, of course.'

'Can you come to my office when you arrive?' I had never heard him sound so cold and formal.

'Jack, what's this about?'

'As I said, it's best if you come straight to my office.'

He rang off abruptly, leaving me in a state of panic, my stomach in knots. I tried phoning Lisa again. Her phone was still switched off. I dressed and rushed to work without coffee, let alone breakfast. I arrived before Jack and waited outside his office, as if sent there for detention. I must have looked as bad as I felt because one of the Latvian cleaners, who knows little English, looked at me sympathetically and gestured towards the coffee dispenser. I waved away his offer, politely. Finally, Jack marched down the corridor and beckoned me into his office.

'You'd best close the door behind you.' He pointed to a chair.

'I don't understand . . .'

'The article in the *Daily Mail* has put Mrs Stonebridge on edge. She thinks you are undermining the, er . . . *wonderful* relationship she has with her daughter.'

I was stunned. 'What do you mean "undermining"?'

'I believe Lisa wants to find her natural parents when she turns eighteen.' I nodded. 'As far as Mrs Stonebridge is concerned, Lisa made that decision under your influence.'

'But it's not like that. She's the one who asked if she could—'

Jack put up his hand. 'I believe you. However, the way in which you've taken Lisa under your wing has left you wide open to criticism.'

'She specifically asked to be involved in my search. At times she implored me.'

Jack began juggling with his pen. 'Sophie, Mrs Stonebridge is a divorcee with only one child. She fears Lisa could strike up a wonderful relationship with her natural parents.'

'And dump her in the process? That's highly unlikely . . .'

'Not to her mind. The story in the *Mail* brought her insecurities bubbling to the surface.'

'But Lisa engineered all that publicity.'

Jack shook his head. 'I'm afraid that's irrelevant. You are her teacher. From a professional point of view, you should have kept your distance.'

'Oh God.' I put my hand to my mouth. 'She stayed over.'

'Yes, that was a big mistake.'

'She slept on the couch but there wasn't any—'

'There doesn't need to be. Mrs Stonebridge thinks you're grooming her daughter.'

'*Grooming* her? That's ridiculous.' I began to shiver, maybe through shock and anger. Maybe fear.

'I agree, it is ridiculous,' said Jack, 'but all these cases in the papers are making everybody twitchy. I have to be seen to act responsibly and professionally, in the interests of all parties. There is an official complaints procedure and we have to go through it. Hopefully Mrs Stonebridge will have calmed down overnight but I am expecting a formal letter from her some time today.'

It was suddenly all too much. I put my head in my hands and burst into tears. Given a chance I would have willed myself out of existence, there and then.

'Have you talked to Lisa?' I said, but it came out more like a hoarse whisper.

'Briefly, yes, and she fought doggedly to prevent her mother making a complaint. It only exacerbated Mrs Stonebridge's fears.'

'That I have some kind of hold over her daughter . . .'

Jack nodded. 'I think we all need a cooling-off period. I'm suggesting you spend the rest of the week at home.'

I must have looked horrified. 'But . . . that implies I'm being suspended.'

Jack eased back in his chair. 'Sophie, take a few deep breaths. One way and another, it's been a stressful few days.'

I had no choice but to get in my car and leave. But I didn't go home. I drove round in a daze, not knowing where I was most of the time. Just going. Anywhere would do. Anywhere at all. The act of travelling, however mindlessly, made me a moving target. I might have choked to death, stuck behind a hissing, grumbling Eddie Stobart lorry on the South Circular Road, but at least no one could get me there. A couple of hours later I found myself at one of the bridges over the Thames. I know it well. When we started going out, Daggert hired a rowing boat nearby. We splashed about a bit, enjoying the first electrifying days of a relationship that just felt ridiculously right. At a small, intimate restaurant, facing on to the river, we had a meal and talked for hours. The restaurant has changed a lot but it's still there.

I sat at a table in the open air. The sun was warm. In its own aloof way it was attempting to comfort me. I saw a young couple, much the same age as Daggert and me at the beginning of our relationship, trying and failing to row in the same direction. They fell around laughing. The boat rocked idiotically from side to side. I felt myself well up. An older woman approached me, notepad in hand. I didn't look at her directly, hoping she wouldn't see my emotional state. I failed.

'Hey now, what's with the tears?' she said.

'Oh . . . I'm just being soft.' Presuming her to be a waitress, I asked for a cappuccino.

'Waiting for a friend?' she said.

I shook my head. 'Just remembering him.'

'He was pretty special, I imagine.'

I nodded and pointed to the couple in the boat. 'That was the two of us, years ago. I asked him to help me up from the floor of the boat but he insisted on putting the oar in the right place first. I said . . .'

'Never mind the rollocks.'

I looked at her in amazement. 'How did you know?'

'Just call it an annoying gift.' As she walked away she said over her shoulder: 'He's laughing, too, by the way.'

Two minutes later another waitress came to my table.

'Can I take your order?' she said.

I looked blank. 'I've already given it to someone.'

'That's strange. I'm the only waitress serving.' I presumed the person I had spoken to was the manager and busy on another matter. In any case, I was too emotional to give the incident much thought. I drove back slowly. When I reached home I turned off every possible means of communication and, I'm not proud to say, drank myself into alcoholic oblivion, something I haven't done since I was a teenager.

I woke yesterday with a splitting headache to find some flowers from Jack. I don't know how to feel about him. Is he really in my corner? Does he have to be so objective about it all? I am confused and hurt. Eventually I turned on my computer. Among all the junk, a couple of emails caught my eye, forwarded from the *Daily Mail*. Two women from Liverpool claim to have been at school with my mother. They contacted the paper independently of each other, as well. One of them sent a primary school photo of her class. There's no doubt the eight-year-old girl highlighted in the photo is strikingly similar to my mother. Meanwhile, Melissa Blackwell, now living in Cumbria, claims to have been at Glenworth boarding school with her. She remembered Henry; more specifically his permanent squeak. That clinched it. According to both emails my mother was a Lucy Pitcher who lived in Liverpool until she was fourteen or fifteen.

I didn't know what to do next. This was everything I had been waiting for but I needed a steady hand on the tiller. I began punching in Canon Shearwater's numbers on my phone. Then I thought better of it. I knew what he would say: 'It's not my patch.' But I'm not ready to trust all these rollercoaster emotions to another stranger, to this Carol Feeney, whoever she is. Melissa Blackwell included a phone number in her email and I left a message with her to call me back when she gets a moment.

*

Melissa returned my call earlier this evening.

'Your photo,' she said. 'It's definitely Joose.'

'Joose?'

'That's what we called her at Glenworth. It started as Juicy Lucy and got shortened. You know how it is with kids.' She sounded well educated and articulate. I found myself raising my game in the diction department.

'I want to know all about her.'

'She fascinated me, did Joose.'

'How do you mean?'

'Like all boarders, she got homesick. But it went deeper with Joose. She was shy and withdrawn. Being an only child didn't help. Most of us had a brother or a sister at the school. When she got miserable, Joose had no one close to confide in. She disappeared into herself for long periods.'

Melissa told me that 'Joose' (I really don't think I can get used to calling my mother that!) could pass most exams without really trying, which was 'bloody annoying to be honest'. In fact, she was so good she skipped a whole year and was put in for her O levels a year early. She loved art but not the way it was taught at Glenworth. She went 'off-piste' (Melissa's phrase) and drew huge, surreal flowers that burst out of cracked pavements and towered over scenes of urban decay. I described the picture left behind in the saddle, of the sad child walking across a field of flowers, holding a piece of string. 'It sounds like one of hers. She always weaved her name in the flowers,' said Melissa. 'Look closely.'

I found the picture. 'No, I can't see the word Lucy anywhere.'

'She signed them Joose.'

I looked again. Sure enough, there it was, hidden between some jasmine and African daisies (I like my flowers, too!) Now there could be no doubt. I squeezed every last drop of information out of Melissa. On one occasion, she had stayed at Lucy's house outside Liverpool, where she had taken a few rides on Henry. 'Mr Pitcher was friendly enough but her mother was frosty. I'm not sure anyone was quite good enough to be her daughter's friend.'

To the surprise of everyone at Glenworth, Lucy never returned to take her O levels.

'We were never told why,' said Melissa, 'though there were plenty of rumours.'

'That she was pregnant?'

'Yes, but there were other issues going on.'

'Like?'

'She smoked weed in the woods behind the school, at a time when most of us had no idea what it was. There was talk she had got into something heavier. The whole drug scene was beginning to take off. You have to understand, Joose was bright and got bored very easily. She liked experimenting. She would try anything once.'

I sent Melissa a scan of the three fans at Wembley. She studied them carefully. 'Sorry, I don't recognize any of them,' she said, at last. 'You have to remember we were at an all-girls school. Any connection with local boys had to be clandestine. Rumours circulated, of course. We wanted to believe them but they were either without foundation or wildly exaggerated. I don't remember any stories about Joose in that way, though she always held her cards close to her chest.' She paused. 'She was no football fan, so I'm surprised to see a photo of her at Wembley. What month was the World Cup held in?'

I'm no fan myself and had to look it up. 'July.'

'So this would have been taken around the time her parents moved south. She would have been due back at Glenworth that September for our O level year but she never arrived. I missed her terribly. We had always been next to each other in the dormitory. She kept a supply of marshmallows under her bed. Any time of day or night she would give me one. I was devastated when she didn't come back to Glenworth . . .'

*

I put down the phone after more than an hour and a half and took stock of the strangest week of my life. I now knew the name of my natural mother, where she grew up, where she went to school, what she excelled at and her predilection for art, flowers, marshmallows and marijuana. Discovering all this had led to my being put on a form of gardening leave from my job. I thought it couldn't get more fraught than this. I was wrong.

The phone rang an hour ago. It was Melissa, extremely excited.

'A reporter from the *Daily Mail* phoned me just now. He was thrilled they helped you discover the identity of your mother. They are very keen to help you find your father as well so I sent him a copy of the three fans at Wembley. They are running it in the next two or three days. Isn't that exciting?'

Chapter 30

Billy pulls up outside a nineteenth-century mid-terrace cottage. Though small, it has an imposing front door of gnarled oak and French-style window shutters. He walks up the garden path past carefully tended flower urns. He tugs on the bell pull, a long slim iron rod. It generates a tinkling sound. The heavy door is ill-fitting and difficult to open.

'Canon Shearwater, welcome,' says Sophie. 'I can't thank you enough for coming.' She shakes the hand of her guest, warmly.

'Remember, it's Billy.' He kisses her on the cheek, briefly, politely.

'I didn't want to presume.'

Billy stands in the hall and studies a set of framed cartoon caricatures on the wall.

'Oh, those,' says Sophie. 'My father's work, years ago.'

'They're very good.'

'Thank you.'

'Wedgie Benn looks so young. And that one at the top, with the eyebrows . . . his name escapes me.'

'A trade unionist.'

'Woodcock! George Woodcock.'

Sophie nods.

'So your father veered to the left.'

Sophie shrugs. 'I'm not sure whether he drew them out of respect or derision. We never really clicked.'

'And this sketch.'

'That's of Bryn Aur, an old farmhouse above the Gwynfynydd gold mines in North Wales. It's jointly owned in trust by my late husband's family.'

'It looks idyllic.'

'It is. I go there to escape whenever I can. I've just brewed some coffee. Can I tempt you?'

'Of course.' Billy hangs up his jacket and stoops through a low doorway into a lounge dominated by a wooden rocking horse. 'Now then, I recognize this creature . . . from the paper.'

Sophie walks to the kitchen. 'And what a lot of trouble he has caused.'

'Yes . . . my word, yes. He dances a merry waltz, does this one.'

'The more enthusiastic the rider, the more he squeaks.'

'Really?' Billy smiles and rocks the horse gently with his hand. He glances at an array of pictures, books, CDs and a colourful quilt spread over a sofa. His eyes rest on the grate. 'Ah, alongside the coffee I thought I could smell the remains of a real fire.'

'Making it can be laborious after a full day at work.' Sophie is talking loudly from the kitchen. 'But I can't imagine this place without the aroma of wood and coal in the air.'

'I've lived in old vicarages where they've taken out some magnificent fireplaces in the name of modernization. Acts of desecration.'

'Absolutely. Moving from parish to parish and house to house must be quite challenging.'

'It has its drawbacks and benefits. You have to take the rough' – he runs a finger along the horse's mane – 'with the smooth.'

'Your wife must be very understanding.' Sophie brings a tray of coffee and biscuits through to the lounge. 'Especially when you receive calls from hysterical women demanding your advice.'

Billy smiles and is invited to sit on the sofa. 'Yes, I'm sorry to hear about . . . Mrs Stonebridge?'

Sophie nods. 'She's written a formal complaint.'

'That's a pity.'

'Jack is meeting with the board of governors today, to discuss my actions and whether the college has suffered reputational damage.' Sophie air quotes the last two words.

'And the story hitting the media again is not going to help.'

'Exactly. Is there anything we can do to prevent the *Mail* from publishing the photo of the football fans?'

'I need to see what they say in their email.'

'Yes, of course. I should have thought of that. If you don't mind, the computer is in the spare bedroom, up some creaky stairs.' Billy follows Sophie, who pauses on a tiny landing. 'It's smaller than my old house but much more atmospheric.' Billy glances into Sophie's bedroom. It is furnished with a shabby chic chest of drawers with antique mirror, matching wardrobe and double bed under sloping eaves. Some nightwear and a pair of knickers are lying on the bed. Sophie closes the door smartly and directs Billy to the smaller spare room with a sofa bed and desk. There are textbooks and papers on the sofa. A couple of receipts and a blood donor card are next to them. She turns on her computer.

'I'm afraid it will take a while to boot up,' she says. 'If Daggert was still around he would have ditched it by now. Sorry, by Daggert I mean my late husband, Jonathan. Everyone called him that, even before I met him. He was always first in line for the next version of whatever software was coming out. I never understood it all. I still don't – my students say I'm in danger of becoming a technosaur, if I don't stay up to . . . right, it's loaded . . . oh, you can't see that!' Sophie laughs in embarrassment. She clicks away a page that has loaded automatically. 'It's a daft diary I've kept since Daggert died. It was supposed to chart my journey through bereavement but it reads more like a disaster movie.'

'That's a brave thing to do.'

'Have you ever kept a diary?'

'Me? No.'

'But you've written books.'

'That's a different matter. When it comes to the history of football, I'm your man. On important matters, I've got nothing to say. At least, that's what Emma, my wife, says.'

Sophie clicks on an email from the *Daily Mail*: 'We are keen to update our readers with this new photograph. The story has already captured their attention and a new development will sustain interest. We expect to publish within the next seven days.'

'Hmmm, they do seem keen. I need to see the photo, if I may.' Billy sits on the sofa bed and studies the photo carefully. He shifts uneasily, glances at Sophie then again at the picture in front of him. 'It isn't of the best quality. In fact, it's almost impossible to make out any detail on the faces under those England hats, wouldn't you agree?' He does not wait for Sophie's confirmation and puts the photo face down on the arm of the sofa. 'Are there any others?'

'No, just mementos.'

'I'd be interested to see them.'

Sophie shows Billy everything she has found in the saddle. He shows no obvious interest in any of it.

'There's nothing more – at all?'

Sophie shakes her head.

'OK, let's look at the situation.' Billy drains his cup. 'Have you confirmed to the *Mail* that Lucy Pitcher was your mother?'

'No, her old school friend Melissa told the paper for me.'

'Then you need to go back to the paper and deny it.'

'But my mother *was* Lucy Pitcher.'

'Tell them Melissa means well but has the identity of your mother confused with someone else.'

'But she hasn't.'

'That's irrelevant. You must be entirely selfish and think only of saving your career.'

Sophie frowns. 'What about the other email, from the woman who knew her at primary school?'

'Another disappointing case of mistaken identity. You have received information from three more reliable sources since, offering alternative suggestions. You are pursuing these and will let them know the outcome in due course.'

'But that's completely false.'

'Do you think newspapers care about truth?'

'No, but I do.'

'You asked for my professional advice, Sophie, not a sermon. My approach will buy us time. We need to get you through this business with Mrs Stonebridge and out the other side.'

Sophie folds her arms and sighs. 'You talk a lot of sense, Billy. I've been so naive. I've brought all this on myself.'

Billy touches her arm. 'Hey, don't beat yourself up. You are a victim of circumstances beyond your control, of events before you were born.'

'I don't think I have the confidence to talk to a newspaper,' says Sophie. She asks Billy to do it for her. He explains that the *Mail* knows him too well. The reporter will presume Sophie has hired a media professional to manipulate the facts.

'Which is the truth,' says Sophie.

Billy smiles. 'You're a good student.'

'I can't believe that I'm learning how to lie from a clergyman.'

'You're also learning how to protect yourself from the likes of Mrs Stonebridge, who distort the truth. Sometimes it really is necessary to fight fire with fire.'

Sophie sighs again and phones the *Daily Mail*. She has a crib sheet in front of her, written by Billy. Reluctantly, the news editor agrees to hold back from publishing more until further notice, on the strict understanding that no other newspaper has received a copy of the photo. The *Mail* would like to retain the exclusive.

'Phew!' Sophie puts down the phone. She has stood throughout the call. 'I'm shaking like a leaf.'

Spontaneously, Billy stands and hugs her. 'That was great.' He feels her trembling.

Sophie's own act of spontaneity is to kiss Billy on the cheek. 'Thank you,' she says. He lets her go, reluctantly. 'I'll make some more coffee.' They head downstairs. 'Of course, if they don't publish the photo, I will be no nearer tracing my father.'

'You may discover he's German,' says Billy.

'Well, I did the O level.'

'Be careful what you wish for, *meine Liebste*.'

'What is so hurtful is that he has never tried to trace me.'

'Maybe he doesn't know how.'

'Maybe he just doesn't care.'

'I doubt that. They were different times. He could have been very young. His family may have had the final say.'

'But surely, after all this time . . .'

'The longer it goes on, the harder it may be to own up.'

'That's what the adoption people said. My mother thinks all was not quite right about my conception. With Lucy dying so young, maybe she was right. What do you think?'

'Oh, I don't think my views are relevant.'

'Don't tell me. It's not your patch.'

Billy smiles wryly. 'You're learning fast.'

Sophie grinds some coffee beans to medium fine. 'I used to hope I was the product of an illicit relationship between a handsome prince and a beautiful princess.'

'Princess or not, you inherited her looks.'

Sophie pauses, studies her guest and deposits the ground coffee in a filter. 'You said that with real feeling.'

'It was said with real feeling.'

'But I'm talking to a consummate liar.'

'How kind of you to say.'

'Seriously, it's a gift.'

'I wouldn't put it quite like that.'

'I would and I'm grateful.'

Billy hovers in the doorway to the kitchen. 'You have discovered that your mother loved you and regretted giving you up for adoption. Perhaps that's all you need to know.'

Sophie takes fresh milk from the fridge. 'I have an inkling where this is going.'

'You have?'

'You're afraid I'm going to find out I'm the product of a quick, lunchtime shag in the woods behind Glenworth boarding school, in exchange for a large packet of marshmallows.'

Billy laughs. 'I . . . well, I think that's being a little harsh on Lucy. She was worth more than that . . . from what I've heard about her.'

Still holding the milk carton, Sophie studies her guest again. 'I think you are quite taken by my mother.'

Billy clears his throat. 'If she was anything like her daughter I couldn't fail to be enchanted.'

'Now your pants are on fire.'

'I mean it.'

'Well, it's sweet of you to say. I'm sure Mrs Shearwater has surrendered to many a similar charm offensive.'

'Oh, Emms knows me far too well. By comparison, the news editor of the *Daily Mail* is a soft touch.'

Sophie pours the coffee. 'How did you meet her?'

'Emms? You cannot be genuinely interested.'

'Don't be silly. I'm a woman. We do the whole person, not just jobs, politics or, dare I say, football.'

'Boxing might be more apt. Right now, Emms and I are toe to toe in round five.'

'Oh dear. Why?'

198

Billy hesitates. 'For some inexplicable reason, I find myself want-ing to tell you.'

'Is that a bad thing?'

'I hardly know you.'

'That's a good thing. We have no history.'

Billy shakes his head ruefully. He hesitates again. 'You, Mrs Daggert, are dangerously intuitive.'

'Another lie. You mean nosy.'

'And fast on the draw.'

'Stay ahead or you're dead. It's the only way when you teach teenagers. You were about to tell me how you met your wife and why you're now at loggerheads.'

'I really wasn't.'

But Billy does tell Sophie how a young Emma Dawson arrived at his father's offices, coat buttoned up tightly and brass buckles glowing on patent leather shoes.

'Was she your first love?' says Sophie.

'Oh now, that all depends on what you mean by love.'

'I wasn't looking for Prince Charles's fudged definition.'

Billy laughs. 'What if I said we made a good team?'

'Or Sarah Ferguson's.'

'I'm not doing too well, am I?'

'You're evading the question.'

'Which prevents me from lying.'

It is Sophie's turn to smile ruefully. She teases out of Billy a full description of the 1960s party, the karaoke sessions, and in particular Roy, the chief librarian. He also tells her how he forgot the book club event, a faux pas not helped by his dining out with Bishop Maureen.

'No woman likes to take second place to anyone, bishop or not,' says Sophie.

'It wasn't deliberate,' protests Billy. 'I had a lot on my mind. And the relationship is purely professional.'

'That, as you said earlier, is irrelevant,' says Sophie. 'This bishop, she used to be a singer, didn't she?' Billy nods. 'They say it was a brave, pro-gressive move to appoint a lesbian ... I mean, it's generally assumed that she's gay.'

'By whom, exactly?'

'It was in the papers.'

Billy raises an eyebrow but says nothing.

'OK.' Sophie holds up her hand. 'When did the papers ever care about the truth?'

'My visit has not been in vain.' Billy moves forward in his chair and glances at his watch.

'I've one more question, before you go,' says Sophie. 'Lucy's mother and father. Do you think it's worth trying to find them?'

'I presume they asked for no contact, all those years ago,' says Billy. Sophie nods. 'Even if you did track them down I doubt they would be too thrilled to see you. That's if they are still alive, of course. I would let things be.'

Sophie stares at the floor, head bowed. She says nothing. 'So that's it . . . the end of the road.' She stifles tears. 'Damn, I promised myself I wouldn't be pathetic.' Billy reaches out and squeezes her arm. Sophie doesn't look up. A minute or two later Billy stands.

'It's been a difficult week, and these have been hard things to deal with,' he says. 'I don't want to make matters any worse. I'll give you a ring in a few days to find out how you are.' Sophie says nothing in return. She doesn't look up. Billy heads to the hallway, silently puts on his jacket and opens the front door.

'I meant to ask, how did you become a canon?' Sophie is still looking at the floor.

Billy pauses. 'I'm not sure what you mean.'

'Whatever made you go into the Church?'

With his back to Sophie, Billy looks up at the caricatures in the hall and the Welsh farmhouse, as if contemplating them.

'Guilt,' he says at last and without looking back at Sophie, closes the front door behind him.

*

Ten minutes later, Billy calls in at Bargain Booze and buys a small bottle of Courvoisier cognac. He takes a swig, slips the bottle into his jacket pocket and heads home. It is mid-afternoon. He takes a detour and parks up near his old school. Nothing's changed. He drives into town. So many shops have closed down. It's like a ruin.

He heads for the local multiplex cinema. Most of the films showing this week are of little or no interest. *Batman v Superman* looks like two rival pop stars trying to boost their flagging careers by recording a duet. *Spotlight* is more interesting: a team of reporters delving into allegations of abuse in the Catholic Church. Nicholas Ledgard, he recalls, had the cheek to review it in a recent edition of the *Church of England Newspaper*.

He decides to give both a miss, pulls again on the cognac and makes for the Blue Anchor, a haplessly titled watering hole a couple of miles from his home. He has a meal there, another drink and watches an evening's European football on the big screen. It is dull and undemanding. He drives home slowly, but not too slowly, aware that the alcohol in his bloodstream is probably twice the legal limit. The town is now full of young people out for the evening. He arrives home without mishap. Emms is watching *Holby City*. He doesn't want to get too close or she will smell his breath.

'I'm going to sleep in the spare room,' he says. 'It's been a long day.'

'The woman you visited earlier just phoned,' says Emms. 'The one with the rocking horse.'

'Sophie Daggert?'

'That's her.'

'What did she want?'

'Such a nice person.'

'Yes.'

'And what a story. She was on for ages.'

'But why did she call?'

'She's invited us both to a meal at her house tomorrow evening and I've accepted. I'd love to meet her.'

*

It has been half an hour since Sophie put down the phone to Emma Shearwater. Her front doorbell rings. She is upstairs in her dressing gown and glances at her watch. It is past ten. The bell rings again, followed by a knock on the door. Someone is determined to get a response. She looks down from her bedroom window. It is a woman she doesn't recognize. The bell rings again.

'All right, all right. Keep your hair on.' She walks downstairs into her hall and opens the front door a few inches.

'Where is she?' says the woman.

'I'm sorry, I'm not sure who you—'

'You know who I am. Where's my daughter?'

Sophie opens the door wider and looks closely at the woman. 'I really don't know—'

'That's a lie. I met you at the parents' evening.'

'But I see dozens of people.'

'I'm Lisa's mother.'

'Oh yes, Mrs Stonebridge. I should have guessed.'

'Where is she?'

'Lisa, you mean.'

'Of course.'

'I've no idea.'

'She's gone AWOL.'

'Oh dear. I'm sorry. Have you any idea where?'

Uninvited, Mrs Stonebridge pushes open the door, steps into the hall and looks over Sophie's shoulder. 'She must be here.'

'I can assure you she isn't.'

Mrs Stonebridge tries to push past Sophie, who blocks her way into the lounge.

'You have no right to barge in here,' says Sophie.

'You have no right to turn Lisa against me.'

'I've done nothing of the kind.'

'We'll let the court decide.'

'And we'll let the court decide about the way you are trespassing on my property.'

'If she's here they'll throw the fucking book at you.'

Sophie folds her arms. 'I don't take kindly to bullies, Mrs Stonebridge. I suggest you leave before I call the police.'

'Oh, I think the police will be round soon enough. You've messed with the wrong person.' Mrs Stonebridge marches out of the house, slamming the front door behind her.

Trembling with shock, Sophie pours herself a drink but before she is halfway through it the telephone rings. She lets it go to voicemail. 'Miss, are you there?'

Sophie grabs the phone. 'Lisa, where are you?'

'I can't say.'

'What's going on?'

'I'm not coming back.'

'Your mother has just left.'

'She thinks I'm there, doesn't she?'

'Lisa, you have to go home.'

'Not while you're not allowed to teach. If I had known how my mother would react . . . I'm so sorry, miss.' Lisa bursts into tears.

'Running away won't help anything. It only makes things worse.'

'You don't understand. She smothers me. I can't have a life of my own. Dad left because of her. What's happened to you is the last straw.'

'Lisa, you must tell me where you are.'

'I can't.'

'Are you safe?'

'Yes.'

'Are you with relatives?'

'I can't say. You would have to tell my mother.'

'Lisa, give your mother a call and tell you are OK at least.'

But the phone goes dead.

Chapter 31

Sophie sits pensively in Jack Staniscliffe's office. Jack fiddles uneasily with the top of his pen. 'This has become a little more complicated than I'd hoped,' he says. 'It transpires that Lisa is still only fifteen.'

'But she's in my A level class,' says Sophie.

'She was bright enough to jump a year at her old school.'

'I didn't . . . I mean . . . why weren't we told?'

'We were. It's easy to overlook in the admission process. We need to tighten up. Have you any idea where she is?'

'She wouldn't say.'

'We need to get her home.'

'She'll only return if I come back to school.'

'Ah. Therein lies the problem.' Jack stands, walks to the window and folds his arms. 'The board of governors suggested I deal with this matter by simply writing you a formal letter of warning and leaving it at that. They are very much on your side.'

'But you've since discovered Lisa's age.'

Jack nods. 'Which means I have no option but to suspend you pending an investigation.'

'But that's . . . crazy.'

'Of course it is, but in this day and age I have to be seen to act quickly and decisively. I'm really sorry.'

Sophie hangs her head. 'Mrs Stonebridge has nailed me.'

'We can keep the whole thing between ourselves for a few days,' says Jack. 'If you could persuade Lisa to return we may be able to talk Mrs Stonebridge round and resolve the situation with a minimum of disruption. If not, I will have no alternative but to make the suspension public knowledge.'

'And that means bad publicity.'

'Most likely, yes.'

'And Lisa won't return—'

'Unless you're reinstated. It's catch twenty-two. See if you can get her on the phone.'

Sophie calls Lisa's mobile but it goes to voicemail. 'I'm not sure I can handle much more of this.' She brushes away the tears. 'I might as well give up.' She asks Jack for the pen on his desk. 'I'm going to write my letter of resignation.'

Jack puts the pen into the inside pocket of his jacket. 'We can sort this out without going to those lengths, Sophie. I want you to stay . . . very much.'

*

It is the evening of the same day. Emma Shearwater is in Sophie's galley-styled kitchen, draining vegetables in a colander.

'I can't imagine what you are going through,' she says.

'I'm trying hard not to be the victim.' Sophie lifts a spinach and ricotta lasagne from the oven. It bubbles with escaping heat.

'That's very laudable but we all need support at times.'

'Well, your husband has been a bit of a hero.'

Emma glances at Billy, who is poking a real fire back to life in the lounge. 'He has his moments. How is your mother taking it all?'

'Not very well. Seeing the story splashed all over the newspapers hasn't helped. In many ways I sympathize with Mrs Stonebridge. Adoptive relationships can be intense. Lisa is very strong-willed.'

'That's as maybe,' says Billy from the lounge. 'The woman had no right to barge in here, whether her daughter is fifteen or fifty.'

Sophie sighs. 'I could have done with a man in the house to back me up, I'll admit.'

'Losing your husband must have been so hard,' says Emma.

Sophie nods. 'I mean, look at this place. It's so tidy. Daggert cluttered it up. Now everything is still in its place when I come home in the afternoon, just as I left it in the morning. I never thought I would find order so depressing.'

Emma smiles. 'You can live with Canon Shearwater if you want. His study is a disgrace.'

'But I know where everything is.' Billy is holding a broadsheet newspaper across the fireplace, to draw air up the chimney. 'Research shows orderly environments encourage you to play it safe. The messier your desk, the more creative you are. Cluttered minds lead to pathways and solutions.'

'A lame excuse,' says Emma, from the side of her mouth.

'Well,' begins Sophie, 'far be it from me to come between husband and—'

'Seriously, the time he spends on that computer of his.'

'Writing takes time,' says Billy.

Emma does not respond. Instead, oven gloves on, she carries two dishes of vegetables past Billy to the extending table in the lounge then returns to the kitchen.

'I'm sure Daggert found me impossible to live with,' says Sophie tactfully. 'The truth is, we all need each other, for different reasons.'

'Oh, don't take any notice of me,' says Emma. 'I'm still all hissy from the other night.'

'The book club.'

'He told you, then.'

Sophie nods. 'Maybe the fact that he mentioned it proves it was on his conscience.' She takes the main dish to the table and invites her guests to sit down. 'I believe you still run the estate agency, Emma.'

'In more of an advisory role these days,' says Emma. 'Estate agency has changed radically since the firm was formed in the fifties. I can't keep up with the technology, to be honest.'

'She's still the best negotiator I know,' says Billy, helping himself generously to sautéed carrots and cauliflower. 'The kids coming into the business may be wizards on their computers but they have no idea how to sell a house. This lasagne looks fabulous, by the way.'

'Thank you,' says Sophie. 'Daggert was the real cook around here. I've never had the patience to do it properly. Emma, how come you . . . ?'

'I know, I know – ended up running the family firm when it should have been his Canonship?' Emma points her knife at Billy.

'Everyone asks that,' he says.

'The truth is I'm just into property,' says Emma. 'I mean, take this lovely house. I can think of five people who would buy it tomorrow. I've already rehearsed selling it to them. That's sad.'

'Well, I've no intention of putting it on the market,' says Sophie, 'but I might have to if I lose my job.'

'It won't come to that.'

'I wish I was as certain as you. I thought I had hit the depths when Daggert died. This has ripped another hole in the bottom of a boat only just above the surface.'

'We should be looking after you, rather than the other way round.' Emma squeezes Sophie's arm.

'No, really, I'm delighted to have the company.'

'It's at times like these you need family around.'

'Well, my daughter Helen does her best but she lives some distance away and, besides, she has her own family to think about.'

'Do you have friends nearby?'

'A few but, how can I say this . . . they were mainly Daggert's. Does that sound strange?'

Emma looks ruefully at her husband. 'Billy has no time for my friends.'

'That's not true,' says Billy. There is a brief pause. 'I like Fiona.'

'Yes, you've got a soft spot for Fiona, I'll grant you. And who else?'

'Well . . .'

'Do you like football, Emma?' says Sophie, smartly.

'I was afraid you would ask her that,' says Billy. 'The answer is definitely no.'

'How did you both meet?' Sophie changes the subject yet again, even though Billy has already told her the tale. Now it is Emma's turn to reminisce.

'First love at first sight, then,' says Sophie.

'For me,' says Emma. There is another short silence punctured only by a log cracking in the fire. 'Billy has always said there was no one before me but I've never believed him.'

'And she's hung on to that for all these years,' says Billy.

Sophie takes a deep breath. 'Well, I've been the perfect host by asking all the wrong questions. I was going to offer you both some more lasagne but I'm afraid it might stir up unresolved conflict.'

'I would love some more,' says Emma, 'but this time I'm changing the subject and we're going to talk about you. Are you any nearer finding out whether your father is still alive?'

'No, I've—'

'I've suggested Sophie puts the search on hold for now,' interjects Billy. 'The last thing she needs is more coverage in the media. We need to resolve the situation with Mrs Stonebridge first.'

Emma nods. 'In which case, tell us more about your career. What made you study English literature? Shakespeare never did anything for me, I have to admit . . .'

*

'Well, Sophie is perfectly delightful,' says Emma, getting into bed. 'I'm so glad she invited us. There is something very familiar about her. I feel I have known her all my life.'

Billy kicks off his shoes. 'I'm worried about her emotional state. She doesn't deserve to lose her job over this.'

'You must do everything you can to help her, Billy,' says Emma. 'She seems so alone and vulnerable. Several times I thought she was going to cry. Promise me you will look after her.'

'I promise,' says Billy. 'I promise.'

Chapter 32

The phone rings in Billy's study. 'Canon Shearwater speaking.'

'Good morning, Billy, it's Jack.'

'Ah, Jack. I thought it might be you.'

'Whatever you've done, it's worked. Mrs Stonebridge has decided not to press charges.'

'I thought she might.'

'I can't thank you enough. Again.'

'It only took a phone call.'

'But you're not going to tell me who was on the other end of it.'

'No.'

'Fair enough. I'd like to tell Sophie the good news but no one seems able to trace her.'

Billy tells Jack that he and Emma were at Sophie's house for supper the night before last.

'Well, nobody has spoken to her since,' says Jack. 'Her mobile goes to voicemail. We're getting a little anxious.'

'You've tried her daughter?'

'Helen hasn't heard from her, either. It's not like Sophie to disappear like this, but I'm loath to make too much fuss. She's had a lot on her mind.'

'I presume Lisa is still missing.'

'I'm afraid so.'

'You don't suppose . . .'

'I find it hard to believe they would meet up, but you never know. If you have any idea where Sophie is, would you contact me?'

'Of course.' Billy puts down the phone. 'I have one idea,' he says to himself. 'It's a long shot and miles away. That's if I can find it at all . . .'

*

Five hours later Billy pulls into a car park in Dolgellau, North Wales. He checks his mobile phone. There is one text from Bishop Maureen. *Grant approved! Let's go ahead with the press conference.*

He fist-pumps at the news, wanders into the town square and buys a couple of local history books and an Ordnance Survey map. He finds a coffee shop, orders an espresso and spreads out the map on the table in front of him. Bryn Aur is marked at the end of a narrow road high in the mountains. One of the books provides a potted history of the Gwynfynydd gold mines.

> Two angry rivers, the Mawddach and Cain, torrent and tumble through its steep-banked valleys, but nothing else at Gwynfynydd rivals their endeavours. Boulders rest easy on the riverbed, worn smooth by the water's eternal clamour and dash. Grey, gnarled trees, protruding at drunken angles from overhanging rock, have all but forgotten how to grow. Sheep yawn and stroll between tufts of coarse grass, gazing impassively at passing strangers. Even birds of prey, drifting dreamily on warm westerlies, seem disinterested in swooping for the kill.
>
> All of which makes it hard to believe that this serenic jewel of nature, lying on an ancient geological fault, once experienced a frantic, Californian-style rush for riches. For it was here that feverish prospectors loaded up satchels bulging with newly mined gold and exchanged them for glasses of cheap wine in the streets of nearby Dolgellau.

Billy shakes his head. It is an area of the country he knows nothing about. He finishes his coffee and heads further north. Turning off an A road into the mountains, he follows a single-track road that crosses a fast-flowing river and meanders for miles through forests and farmland before becoming dangerously potholed. After crossing four cattle grids, it peters out yards from an old farmhouse on the steep slope of a mountain. He glances again at the map. This must be it. The nearest house is two miles back. The sun is still high but everything seems eerily quiet and deserted. There is one car next to the house. It is Sophie's. So he was right. He hesitates. She may be with a male friend. Worse still, he may discover Lisa. And there's another possibility he doesn't even want to consider.

He gets out of the car. Several sheep, chewing the cud relentlessly, are as unimpressed as the guidebook suggests. Somewhere in the valley he hears a river rushing to the sea. He prowls round the house of roughly hewn stone: grey, dour and unflinching. Smoke curls from the chimney. He takes a deep breath and walks towards the front door. Before he can lift the knocker the door opens.

'Billy! What . . . how did you . . . ?'

'I had a hunch.'

'But why? Something awful must have happened.'

Billy shakes his head. 'Everyone's worried about you, that's all.'

'And you've come all this way.'

'It's the least I could do.'

'When I heard a car I prayed it would be you. Does that sound pathetic?' She hugs Billy and begins to sob into his chest.

'Hey, it's going to be all right,' he says.

'Don't let me go.'

'I won't.'

Sophie attempts to gather herself. 'This isn't like me. I didn't know I was so upset. I'm sorry.'

'So am I.' He feels her warm tears on his shirt. He kisses her lightly on the forehead. He pulls her closer. She does not resist.

'I don't want to be a problem,' she says.

'You're not a problem, you're a delight.' He kisses her again and holds her tightly.

Sophie looks up into Billy's eyes. 'You're shivering. Are you not well?'

'It . . . it was a long drive.'

'I'm so sorry.' She eases away from her visitor. 'I've put you and everybody through it. I've been thinking only of myself. Come in, please.'

Billy stoops through a low doorway. The flagged stone floors are ancient and uneven. 'What an astonishing place.'

Sophie nods and smiles. She points Billy into the sitting room where a fire spits and snarls, sap hissing and sizzling from damp pine logs. He checks out a bookshelf full of thrillers, games and puzzles.

'Time-killers for a rain-swept holiday,' smiles Sophie. 'You're in North Wales.'

Billy spots a complete set of *Reader's Digests* from the 1960s and 1970s. He picks one out and stops at adverts for a dark green Morris Minor and a pink zippy dress. He smiles ruefully, places it back on the shelf and stops by a glass display cabinet sunk into a pine coffee table.

'Oh, that . . .' Sophie folds her arms. 'A ten-year-old Daggert was bored one summer. They're moths.'

Billy studies the caption below each exhibit. The ink has faded and is barely legible. 'A *Mormo maura* – or Old Lady,' he reads.

'Yes, a bit of a beast, that one. Daggert said that mounting them was the problem. You can't swat moths without squashing them. He sprayed fly killer round the room but it took ages to work. They were still fluttering when he glued them to the board. The Old Lady struggled so hard, one of her wings came off.'

'And you still married him.'

'You know how it goes . . . where you love you cannot break away.'

'Is that a song?'

'A poem.'

'You seem at one with your subject.'

'English literature?' Sophie shrugs. 'I was until I started to teach it. But you've not come all this way to talk about my failing career.'

'Well, I have – but it's not failing.'

Sophie points to the painting of a waterfall on the wall. 'I'm rushing downstream, without a paddle.'

Billy studies the painting. 'That's an impressive piece of work.'

'Daggert's brother did it. You are looking at the Pistyll Cain, near an opening to the old gold mines below us.'

'What, right below?'

Sophie nods.

Billy gives a low whistle. 'I had no idea any of this existed.'

'Not on your patch, you mean?' she smiles. 'We can walk there, if you like.'

'To the waterfall? Really?'

'Of course. You've come all this way so you may as well see the sights.'

As they amble through a pine forest, Sophie explains the history of Bryn Aur, how the dream of riches proved its economic ruin. The property depended on a fast-flowing stream to propel a watermill.

212

One morning, further up the mountain, some underground fire-works blasted a huge hole in the bed of the stream. No water, no income. Bryn Aur fell into disrepair until, decades later, the Daggert family bought it, restoring it year by year as a holiday hideout.

They pass the last visible remains of a large Victorian pipe that snakes downhill towards the river. More than eighteen inches wide, it has rusted to a deep orange-brown. Jules Verne-styled bolts, two inches in diameter, hold the twelve-foot sections of pipe together.

'I've only been here an hour and it feels like two weeks,' says Billy. 'This place, it's . . . it's another world.' He is standing on a bridge behind Sophie. In front of them the Cain rushes headlong over the falls and cascades into the ferment below, throwing a thin, misty spray across the valley.

'You need to tell me the bad news,' says Sophie.

'How do you mean?'

'You've not come all this way to gaze at a geological fault.'

Billy smiles. 'I have some news but it's not bad. Mrs Stonebridge has dropped her case against you.'

Sophie gasps. 'Seriously?' She hugs Billy. 'But . . . I don't understand. How? Why?' She looks hard at him. 'You've nobbled her, haven't you?'

Billy grins. 'After a fashion. Suffice to say a brief call to a friendly police officer gave me all the information I shouldn't be party to. She won't be going to court.'

'I knew it. You really are an angel. In a moment you will disappear, like the others.'

'The others?'

'I've met three recently, all women. One in Scotland, one in Brighton and another by the Thames. They all helped me, then vanished. Grief does funny things to you, they say. Am I losing my marbles?'

Billy shakes his head. 'My mother had dementia for the last four years of her life. It reached the point where she regularly asked me if I was her father. "No, I'm Kenneth Wolstenholme," I would reply. That cheered her up. Ten minutes later she would ask me the same question, and again ten minutes after that. In her last few weeks, her brain was so beaten up it couldn't send the command to her mouth to eat or drink. She would have died of thirst but for a saline drip. In the end, diamorphine took her away peacefully, thank God. The night she died I was in bed at home. She appeared in my room, looking in rude health. She smiled, said, "Goodbye, William," and disappeared.'

'She knew your name!'

Billy nods. 'That's what I cling to. Death heals.'

They fall silent for a while. 'I'm waiting,' says Sophie, finally.

'Waiting for what?'

'There's something else,' she says, 'another reason why you've come all this way. It's something much deeper. From the moment you arrived at Bryn Aur you've been preoccupied. In fact, from the moment I first met you.'

Billy smiles, weakly. 'Intuition is a dangerous gift. Emms has it in spades as well.'

'I hope she isn't intuitive enough to know what I am going to say next.' Sophie rests her arms on the parapet of the bridge and studies the river that rushes beneath her feet. 'I'm falling in love with you.'

'Oh.' Billy shifts awkwardly. 'I didn't see that coming.'

'Neither did I.'

'This is . . . difficult.'

'I'm not expecting anything in return.'

'That's not what I meant.'

'Admitting it relieves the tension, somehow.'

'It's not that I don't . . . it's just . . . impossible.'

'Of course it is. I came to Bryn Aur to give myself a good talking to.'

'And then comes a knock at the door.'

Sophie smiles, shakes her head and starts walking back up the mountain. 'I've told you because I want you to know why I must back off for a while.'

'Don't.' Billy puts a hand on Sophie's arm. 'Please.' He pulls her to him and holds her close again. Very close.

Sophie draws back. 'You are supposed to look embarrassed and say you are very flattered and all that but . . .'

'. . . you are in a vulnerable state of mind.'

Sophie nods. 'Exactly.'

'Then I would be lying.'

'You're good at that.'

214

'As you have reminded me several times.'

'You must at least do the decent thing and tell me I am confused and irrational.'

'I can't. Your feelings are misplaced, however, as are mine for you.'

'Your feelings? I'm not sure I understand.'

'You don't need to understand, just trust me. It's hopeless.'

Sophie stands still and looks at Billy. 'Poor Emma. You're going to tell me you've never had the courage to come out.'

Billy shakes his head, ruefully. 'That would be so wonderfully simple. No, you are the one thinking clearly and rationally, Sophie, though I cannot imagine why you might fall in love with me. I am the one who is hopelessly confused. Worse still, I long to tell you why, but I cannot, dare not fall in love with you, too.'

The path is steep and uneven. They walk on, mostly in silence, sometimes clambering over boulders, until the river sounds muffled through the trees. They reach Bryn Aur. Billy walks into the house and picks up his mobile phone from the kitchen table. 'There's a voicemail from Jack,' he says and puts the message on loudspeaker.

'Billy, some good news. Lisa has come home and will be in school tomorrow, I'm told. Hopefully we'll soon hear from Sophie and we can tell her the situation. Incidentally, I was surprised to see her picture of the nineteen-sixty-six football fans in today's *Express*. I thought they had agreed to suspend publication. Anyway, when you get this message give me a call.'

'Lisa is back, thank God,' says Sophie but Billy isn't listening.

'The photo,' he says. 'How did the *Express* get hold of a copy?'

'I've no idea,' says Sophie. 'I thought only the *Mail* had it. My mother's school friend must have given it to the *Express* as well.'

Billy calls up the story online. Sure enough, there is the photo, under the headline 'Who are you? Who are you?'

'Recognize any of these fans from the 1966 World Cup Final? Let us know,' runs the caption.

'You don't look very well,' says Sophie. 'I'll get you a drink.'

'Thank you.' Billy sinks into an armchair. While Sophie is in the kitchen he checks for text messages. There is only one. It is from Nicholas Ledgard.

Were you ever that young, Shearwater? Can't wait to chat.

Chapter 33

Tucked away in a London back street behind the Strand, Edward the Confessor is, according to the *Good Pub Guide*, 'busy and unpretentious, offering cask ales and a global beer selection. A menu of simple home-cooked food is served all day. There is no background music or sports TV.'

Billy and Nicholas Ledgard meet in the foyer. They do not shake hands. Underneath Ledgard's arm is a copy of the *Daily Express*.

'I can't imagine why you suggested this venue,' smiles Billy.

'No blaring jukebox. We can have a meaningful conversation,' replies Ledgard.

'And then, of course, there's the name.'

'Indeed. We are at the only pub celebrating the last King of the House of Wessex – though you have even more in common with a monarch before him: Cnut the Great.' Ledgard stares at Billy.

'I imagine that was meant to intimidate me,' says Billy, smoothly. 'If the crown fits . . .'

They walk into the pub, which is bustling with lunchtime customers.

'I have to congratulate you.' Billy points to the *Daily Express*. 'No one else has recognized me.'

'Nor did I at first, but during that interview in the *Church Times* you made one fatal mistake.'

'I said I was at the World Cup Final in 1966.'

'Precisely. I put two and two together. You are on the point of becoming a seriously big noise, too. All very bad luck, I'd say.' Ledgard tries but fails to conceal his delight. He points to the beer handles in front of him. 'What's yours?' He orders and pays for two pints of Bombardier. They find seats at the far end of the pub. Ledgard raises his glass. 'Here's to our carefully kept secrets.'

Billy does not lift his glass in return. 'It will be good to have your help tracking down the other two people in the photo,' he says. 'One of them may be Mrs Daggert's father.'

Ledgard splutters into his beer. 'Now you're taking me for a fool.'

'He can only be identified if he makes himself available.'

Ledgard shakes his head. 'Still using the law as a shield, eh, Shearwater? You can run but you can't hide.'

'It seems you want to exact some kind of revenge.'

'I'm thinking only of Mrs Daggert.'

'Of course you are.'

'After losing her husband like that, she deserves to know the truth.'

'Even if it sends shockwaves through innocent families?'

Ledgard points to the picture in the *Daily Express*. 'You and Mrs Daggert's mother . . .' He waits for Billy to offer a name. He does not do so. 'You must have been very young.'

'As opposed to a grown man who lures a child to his study to play with her Cnut.'

Ledgard laughs. 'Very good . . . *very* good. It's a shame the way things have gone. Given better circumstances I think we could have been good companions.'

Billy wraps two hands round his glass and stares into his beer, like a fortune-teller studying a crystal ball. 'You do realize that if you blow the whistle on me, I will have to blow a foghorn on you.'

'I have nothing left to lose,' shrugs Ledgard. 'My wife buggered off back to the organist five weeks ago. I was relieved, to be honest. And I loathe this church you've dumped me in – full of people who see themselves as "culturally relevant". They want me to abandon vestments, down-dress if you will, so I am more accessible to the common man. Next they'll be asking me to take up the guitar.'

'Bad news for a top-notch tat queen like you.'

'Tell me about it. We're all being squeezed out of mother church. Goodbye smells and bells, hello rock the flock. It's a fucking disgrace. Why, I know people who have to travel more than fifty miles to find a solemn high mass these days. Worse still, my PCC has gone all health and safety and wants to bring in one of these ghastly new e-censers.'

'The ones modelled on e-cigarettes?'

Ledgard nods. 'When did a bit of hefty censing ever harm any-one? Awe. Solemnity. Wonder. Asthma. It's all going up in e-smoke.'

Billy smiles. 'Over-ritualized worship doesn't cut the mustard for me. It's like a one-night stand: delightful while it lasts but you wouldn't want to hang around after the cigarette.'

Ledgard laughs too loudly. 'I have definitely misread you, Shearwater. You've got more about you than I thought. What a shame I've got to blow that whistle.'

Billy looks hard and long across the table. 'The media never tire of clergy and sexual abuse. I will have to disclose your sordid liaisons with young Julie.'

'Which will implicate a number of people, including three bishops who knew about my predilections and did nothing. More work you don't need, Shearwater, defending the indefensible.'

'You really want to take it that far?'

'As I said, I have nothing to lose.'

'Except your liberty. You'll be sent down.'

'All guns blazing.'

'That's a high price to pay.'

Ledgard takes a wallet halfway out of his breast pocket. 'And I'm willing to pay it.' He offers the wallet to Billy and puts it back in his pocket. 'On the other hand, if you really cared about your own flesh and blood, you'd tell her the truth. But there again, you've got to the top by being Mr Teflon. If anyone finds out what happened all those years ago . . .'

'You're not bothered about Sophie. You just want revenge.'

'I want justice.'

'Even if you end up in jail?'

'Yes.'

'You're insane.'

'I'm angry.'

'Yes . . . yes, I can see that.' Billy picks up a beer mat and taps it several times on the table in front of him. 'I could have a word with the powers that be about moving you to a tat-friendly parish where they still love a genuine smoking handbag.'

Ledgard smiles, ruefully. 'Nice try but I'm not biting.'

'After five years you'll receive a more than generous early retirement package.'

Ledgard shakes his head. 'You can't kick me into touch that easily.'

'I'm suggesting ways we can both get out of a difficult situation.'

'With you smelling of roses? No dice.'

Billy puts on his raincoat. 'Despite what you say, you have much more to lose than me, Ledgard. I will come crashing down, then fade into obscurity while you,' he points at his adversary, 'become someone's bitch in Wormwood Scrubs.' He stands and taps his head. 'I'd think very long and hard about what I've said.' He walks swiftly to the door of the pub, then into the rushing streets of London.

*

'In fact, Billy's just come in, looking the worse for wear.' Emma Shearwater is on the phone to Sophie. 'You can speak to him yourself, if you like.'

'I'd rather you talked to him first,' says Sophie.

Emma cups her hand over the phone's mouthpiece. 'I phoned Sophie to tell her she can have my ticket for the cup final.'

'I'm not sure that's a good idea,' mouths Billy.

'Nonsense,' mouths back Emma. 'You know I hate football. The ticket is always wasted on me.'

'But it's been twenty-six years since Palace last made a major final.'

'So what? Anyway, I've already made other plans.' Emma takes her hand away from the phone's mouthpiece. 'He says he would love to take you. He's here now.'

'Do you really want me at the match?' says Sophie, before Billy can speak.

'Of course. We are privileged to have tickets each year through the FA. Emma only goes for the hospitality.'

'I should be treating you, not the other way round. And I don't know the first thing about football.'

'Nor do Manchester United.'

Sophie laughs. 'I presume that's who Palace are playing.'

'And we'll get our revenge for losing the nineteen-ninety final.'

219

'Emma's right. You do sound a bit . . .'

'Tired and emotional? It's been a stressful day. Are you back at work?'

'Put it this way – there's a pile of essays staring at me from my living room table.'

'That's good news. And Lisa?'

'All present and correct. I'd still love to know what you found on Mrs Stonebridge.'

'That you will never know, no matter how Brahms and Eucharist I may be . . .'

Chapter 34

Young David came to stay last night while Helen and Matt went to a business bash in London. He told me he feels just as much at home in my house as his own.

'In fact,' he said on the phone, 'I think it's even better because you have a real fire.'

As soon as he arrived he cleared away the old ashes and laid the scrunched-up paper, wood and coal, in the way I had shown him last time. Striking the match is a big moment, an important ritual. What is it with males and fire? You'll never see men in the kitchen, chatting while they cook, but put them round an open fire and it's a sizzle scrum. They'll talk music, football, politics, anything – while fighting to turn the hamburgers and give the coal a prod. Very strange, almost primeval. I am flattered by David's affection for my humble abode. He said he also likes staying over because I don't mind reading him the same story again and again: in particular, *A Bear Called Paddington*.

'Read that bit where they find him at the station,' he said.

I began to read it for the umpteenth time, when out of the blue he said, 'Do you think you'll ever find your real daddy?'

I looked at him in surprise. 'Where's that come from?

'Paddington was adopted, wasn't he?' He had got the word right for the first time.

'Yes, by Mr Brown.'

'He never found out who his daddy was.'

'No, but he had a good life with the Browns.'

'Do you think you'll ever get married again?'

'Dear me. So many questions! Someone's got to like me enough first.'

'Mark likes you.'

'Ye-es. You told me that a while back but I think I'm a little bit too old.'

'What about that man who Mummy says you talk about a lot? She showed me a picture of him in the paper. He looks old enough for you.'

'That's Canon Shearwater.'

'Is Canon his first name?'

I laughed. 'No, it's what he is.'

'Does he shoot people?'

'No, it's spelled differently. It means—'

'Mummy says you really like him.'

'Oh, does she now!'

'She says you sound excited when you talk about him on the phone, like you used to when Grandagg was still alive.'

That threw me. I had to hold back the tears. I'm doing the same, thinking about it now. Sometimes you need the simple honesty of a child to confirm what you know to be true but have never admitted to yourself. I look forward to being with Billy. He is witty, authoritative and yet strangely vulnerable. What I hadn't realized is that other people have noticed my feelings for him, too.

'Canon Shearwater is a very nice man but he's married to a lovely lady called Emma,' I said.

'Can we bake some little cakes tomorrow?' The agenda had suddenly changed. Clearly, my love life was no longer of any importance.

'Yes, of course.' What I didn't tell David was that I am going to the FA Cup Final with Canon Shearwater. I have no idea what to expect. I know nothing about football. I'm sure I will be a hopeless companion and that Billy will wish he had taken Emms after all.

Chapter 35

'Look at our fans. It's fantastic. They've have had a tough few years.' Manchester United's Wayne Rooney is being interviewed on the Wembley pitch after his team win the FA Cup Final. But behind him the TV audience cannot hear United fans, only those of Crystal Palace, singing themselves hoarse – for the losers.

Watching the interview on a plasma screen, Billy's voice cracks with emotion and the exertions of passionate support. 'Tough few years? Try a hundred and eleven. Try waiting more than a century to win your first major trophy *ever*.' He is in Wembley's Bobby Moore Room, scene of his Christmas Eve address. This time he is with Sophie, surrounded by suits and summer dresses consuming what is left of the corporate hospitality.

'Bad luck, Shears.' A man slaps him on the back. 'There's always next century.'

Billy turns, his reactions slowed by the effects of inebriation. He stares blankly at the man. 'I'm not sure . . .'

'Armitage from Bailey, Harvey and Madge.'

The light of recognition dawns slowly. 'Oh yes . . . solicitors . . . in Sussex somewhere.'

'I sorted out your mother's will.'

'Yes, you're . . .' He looks at the man's Manchester United tie. 'I thought you were a Tesco bag.'

'I am.'

'But you're supporting United.'

'Brighton is my other club.'

'Other club? That's pathetic. No man can serve two masters. Here . . .' Billy fumbles around in his wallet and pulls out a £5 note. He throws it on the floor. 'This is what you and your two clubs are worth. Buy yourself some fucking glory.'

Armitage looks shocked. 'I was only trying to . . . I didn't mean . . .'

Sophie grimaces, tugs discreetly on Billy's sleeve and bends down to pick up the note. 'It's been an emotional day,' she says and pulls Billy away. 'We'd better get you home.'

'I'm fine,' he says.

'The drink has got the better of you.'

'At last, thank God.'

'You'll not make it to the underground.' They descend in the lift and walk slowly towards the taxi rank.

'Will Emms be at home?' says Sophie.

'She's never at home,' says Billy. 'She's staying with friends . . . somewhere or other.'

'Then you'd better come back to my house.'

Billy does not object. He slumps in the back of the taxi. Sophie gives instructions to the driver.

'They think it's all over,' murmurs Billy. His head lurches forward in an alcoholic haze. 'It really, really, really is now.' He sways with the motion of the taxi.

'I'm sad you lost,' says Sophie.

'Lost what?'

'The match.'

'Oh that . . . who cares?'

The taxi driver slows down at traffic lights, looks in his rear-view mirror then pulls back the glass window separating him from his passengers. He points to a sign in the back of the cab. 'If he chunders, it's fifty quid.'

'Tell him to fuck off,' slurs Billy.

'Sorry,' says Sophie to the driver. 'Take no notice. His team lost.'

The driver slams shut the dividing glass and revs the engine. It is a warning.

'I'm sorry . . . so sorry,' murmurs Billy.

'You've done nothing wrong.'

'I've done everything wrong.'

'You'll be fine tomorrow.'

'You don't deserve this.'

'I'm repaying a kindness.'

'I've not been kind, I've been cruel.'

224

To the motion of the taxi, Billy begins to doze again. He is about to topple on to the floor of the cab, when Sophie pulls him towards her. He lies across her lap, his head just below her breasts. He pulls her to him and nestles into her body, into her breasts. She strokes his hair.

'I love you, Billy,' she says, softly. He pulls her closer.

*

Billy is fast asleep when they reach their destination. Sophie pays the driver.

'He's not your husband, is he?' he says.

'How do you know?'

'You like each other too much.' It is said with a wink.

'I dare not leave him alone at his home.'

'Here, I'll help you get him inside.'

Together they guide Billy up the narrow stairs and into Sophie's bedroom where he collapses, fully clothed, on her bed.

'Give me a minute,' says the driver. He beckons her to leave the room. Two minutes later Billy is naked and asleep in Sophie's bed.

The driver comes downstairs. 'He's stark bollock up there. That's how we'd leave the drunks on school trips. He'll not do it again.'

'I am very grateful.' Sophie offers him another tip. He refuses to take it.

'You look like a decent lady,' he says. 'Good luck.'

*

At six o'clock the following morning, Billy stirs. He reaches for the bedside clock but it isn't on the cabinet. He feels around. There isn't even a cabinet. He notices an unusual and sensual aroma. It could be pomegranate, maybe plum. Head pounding, he opens his eyes. He props himself up on his elbows and looks round. The curtains are closed. He doesn't recognize the room; at least, not at first. Wait. Oh God. He pulls back the duvet. He is naked. He only sleeps naked after ... oh, dear God. He lies back in bed and puts his hands on his head. Think, for God's sake, think. He remembers the taxi. He remembers snuggling up to Sophie and feeling the sweet curve of her breast on the side of his face and her aroused nipple. He recalls her stroking his hair. Did he hear her say, 'I love you, Billy'? Wishful thinking, perhaps. After that, nothing.

He hears the clatter of a pan in the kitchen, a radio playing, then footsteps on the stairs and a gentle knock at the door.

'It's your room,' he says. Sophie enters, wearing a gold satin and lace dressing gown. Her hair is loose and free. She is holding a tray with two boiled eggs, tea and buttered toast, cut neatly into soldiers.

'How's your head?' she says.

'I've got two and they've declared war on each other.'

Sophie smiles, hands Billy the tray and sits on the side of the bed. 'Did you sleep OK?'

'I can't remember. In fact, I can't remember very much at all.' He pauses, choosing his words carefully. 'Did you sleep on the sofa bed?'

'Well, now . . .' There is a faint grin on Sophie's face. She pours the tea. 'Do you take sugar?'

'No, but I'm partial to paracetamol.'

Sophie holds up the three middle fingers of her left hand and takes a small box from the pocket of her dressing gown.

'Akela to the rescue.' Billy takes a swig of tea and swallows the tablets. 'I won't gain any badges with my behaviour, which has been quite reprehensible.'

'Quite reprehensible,' mimics Sophie. 'You are adorably old-fashioned, Canon Shearwater. I'm sure that, sober, you wouldn't make love to anyone but Mrs Shearwater.'

Billy's right arm spasms. He is in the middle of dipping a toast soldier into one of his eggs. Yoke and white spill down the shell.

'Maybe your old friend guilt is making an unwelcome return,' says Sophie.

'Something that has never left cannot come back.' Billy tosses his teaspoon on the tray, sighs deeply and looks straight at his host. 'Sophie, I need to know if anything . . . happened between us last night.'

'If I flung myself on a drunken priest of advancing years and demanded his body?'

'Well, I . . . no, no . . . you wouldn't have done that.'

226

'How do you know? You've never been trapped in a bedroom with me before.'

'I confess, I have thought far too many times of being in a bedroom with you. My behaviour concerns me, not yours.'

'Goodness, you're really worried.' Sophie leans across the bed and touches Billy's face, tenderly. 'Why am I such a problem?'

'It's not you. It's just that . . . I don't . . . do this sort of thing.'

'Affairs, you mean?'

'You could put it like that.'

'When did I suggest one?'

'You didn't, but—'

'Is it Emms?'

'This has nothing to do with her.'

'Do you still love her?'

'Of course.'

Sophie shakes her head. 'You said that much too quickly and far too defensively. The negative tension between you is palpable. Where was she last night?'

Billy shrugs. 'I'm not sure. Each of us has areas we keep separate from the other.'

'That's sad.'

'It works.'

'For you.' Sophie digs her hands into the pockets of her dressing gown. 'You are petrified of intimate physical contact and yet . . . you are drawn to me like a moth to a flame. It doesn't add up.'

Billy laughs nervously. 'How did I end up naked?'

Sophie explains.

'Thank God.' Billy cannot disguise his relief.

'You see?' Sophie wraps the dressing gown tightly round her. 'Your reaction tells me all I need to know.'

Billy grabs her arm. 'Believe me, Sophie, it's the exact opposite. Last night it was the demon drink, this morning it is carnal desire that is ripping me apart. What I wouldn't give to hold you, to explore you, to taste you, to, to—'

'Shipwreck in your thighs?'

'That's a perfect description. Where . . . ?'

'*Under Milk Wood*. Dylan Thomas was another drunkard.' Sophie sighs. 'Well, if the ship won't come to shore, the shore must do the decent thing.' She walks round to the other side of the bed and climbs in next to her guest. Somewhere in the distance, church bells start to ring. Transfixed, Billy holds a piece of toast above a boiled egg. Sophie runs a hand on to his leg. 'I thought so,' she says. 'Another soldier ready for action.'

'Sophie . . . Sophie, you can't do that. You musn't do that.' Billy grabs her hand. 'You can't because . . . I'm . . . I'm your father.'

*

Half an hour later, Sophie is lying on the living-room floor, her face pale and drawn. She is on her back, hands behind her head, recovering from a second bout of intense vomiting. Billy is slumped untidily in an armchair. He has told Sophie how her mother came into his life one summer's day and, months later, left for ever. Five decades of deceit had begun.

'I knew you could lie, but my, this one takes the crunch cream,' says Sophie. 'What kind of monster leads his own daughter to almost . . . I mean, what the hell have you been trying to do?'

'Hold on to my career, my wife, a few dreams – and you.'

'And the greatest of these? Let me guess.' Sophie is staring at the faintest of cracks in the ceiling plaster. 'And now you could lose the lot.'

Billy shifts uneasily in his chair. 'One of the sweetest moments of my life was when you click-clacked your way down the corridor at Woodfield.'

'It was Lucy you saw, not me,' says Sophie. 'You fell in love with her again, using your daughter as a vehicle. That's not affection, that's perversion.'

Billy shakes his head. 'I hadn't seen you grow up. I had no knowledge of you as a family member. I knew nothing about you. You walked into my life as a complete stranger. Fighting my attraction for you has been the hardest thing I have ever done.'

The room falls silent. Sophie begins pushing Henry with her foot. He squeaks rhythmically. 'I'm going to wake up in a minute and find Daggert sitting there. Please God.'

Billy reaches out and stops Henry with his hand. 'I'm sorry. It's difficult to explain . . . it brings back memories.'

He tells her of his first encounter with Lucy, the elocution lessons with Mrs Pitcher, Hendo, the World Cup Final and the happening at the Tangerine Tree. But at that point there is a knock at the front door. The excited voice of a child comes through an open window. 'Nan, I've done my own baking.' A small hand appears, clutching a fairy cake.

'Oh my God,' says Sophie. She glances at her watch. 'My family are here for Sunday lunch. I'd completely forgotten.'

Billy heads for the door. 'I would understand if you never wanted to see me again, Sophie, but there is much more I need to tell you, if you will let me – for your sake and mine.'

He politely acknowledges a bemused family in the tiny hall and leaves.

Chapter 36

From: William.Shearwater@btconnect.com
Sent: 22 May 2016
To: Sophie.Daggert@yahoo.co.uk
Subject: What you need to know

Dear Sophie

I know that nothing I write can make up for my appalling deceit but I must explain how and why you came into this world. At least you will know the truth – at last. If you then choose to have nothing more to do with me, I will understand.

I told you about the 'happening' at the Tangerine Tree and the incident with Lucy in the Fallopian tube. For weeks afterwards, I couldn't get it out of my mind. She was Hendo's girl but we were both roadies for PFF. That meant we spent hours side by side at a sound desk in down-at-heel clubs all over London. It's amazing what innuendo can be delivered when two people are twiddling knobs and pushing faders up and down.

For Hendo's father, Cecil Henderson, what took place at the Tangerine Tree was nothing short of an epiphany. We couldn't shut him up on the way home. 'This is it,' he said. 'The future is rock 'n' roll, theatre, poetry, jugglers, clowns – all coming together in a glorious state of creative flux.' The show at Bishopsgate was his idea. He called up Garry Kite, a trapeze artist before he became a film director. 'I'll put the acts together,' he told him, 'if you do one or two of your old circus tricks and MC the whole thing.' Once Kite was on board he booked the Big Top, Bishopsgate, formerly a circus venue and the only one big enough to take the show.

PFF were to open the show, but for several weeks beforehand the relationship between Hendo and Lucy had slowly deteriorated. They hardly spoke to each other on the way to the gig and had an almighty row in the Big Top car park. Both stormed off. A search party was sent out, led by Garry Kite. 'If we can't find Godfrey you'll have to take his place, Billy,' said Mr Henderson. I gaped at him. 'I haven't . . . I can't . . .' The truth is, I had often stood in for Hendo during the sound check but this was completely different. 'You know all the songs,' said Mr H. 'But what if I sing out of tune?' I said. 'The other lads will help you,' he said. I spent the next two hours rehearsing, hoping Hendo would turn up. He didn't.

If not fully in bloom, Flower Power was beginning to bud at this time. Word got round that Henderson's big night at the Big Top was the place to turn on. At 4 p.m., to Indian sitar and tabla, in poured the 'in' crowd: lads sporting paisley shirts, hip-hugging bell-bottom jeans with flower patches; girls wearing peasant blouses, tie-dyed T-shirts and skimpy halter tops. Many had those jangly ankle bracelets and handmade necklaces with bells as pendants. Once again there wasn't a chair in sight. Instead, the floor was covered with a thick layer of sawdust and scattered car tyres. Small circles of people sat cross-legged and rolled joints. Sitars droning, the rest of the lads in PFF turned on backstage for the first time. After my experience in the guinea pig shed, I politely refused.

We were due to perform at just before six. Mr K was to fly through the air on a trapeze, somersault into a safety net, grab a microphone and introduce PFF. Mad, I know. At just before six there was still no sign of him, or Hendo and Lucy. Mr Henderson had to MC. 'Playing for the first time with the band, I'd like you to give a special welcome to the one and only William Shearwater.' So, no pressure then. In fact, though I say it myself, I did OK. The other members of the band, however, were unaware of the debilitating effects of marijuana. They tuned in OK but forgot to tune up and giggled their way through the set. The sound balance was shocking, not that the crowd seemed to notice much. And if they noticed, they didn't care. Nothing was going to stop them having a splendid time.

I remember very little else about the evening except the poet on the trampoline lost her bearings and by mistake flew out into the crowd. She was caught by a bunch of lads sitting on tyres at the front. Was crowd surfing invented that day? Several websites and bulletin boards suggest it was. Mr K returned midway through the evening, without Hendo and Lucy. Neither of them showed up at all. Mr K did his thing, although much of it was lost on an audience that became less discerning with every passing hour.

Was the event a success? There were rumours that several A&R men were there to check it out. Some big stars sent out spies, too. A year later the Rolling Stones put together their ill-fated Rock and Roll Circus. A coincidence? A researcher from the BBC doesn't think so. He wants to bring together all the surviving artists from that night in Bishopsgate and recreate the event at a venue in Blackburn, of all places. It will be filmed as part of a major series on the 1960s, going out on BBC4 next year, celebrating the fiftieth anniversary of the Summer of Love. Second to None are still going strong but I'm not sure I can help him locate anyone else. PFF never performed again. Following the split with Lucy, Hendo lost interest and the other members formed new bands with different friends. Somehow, though, the legend of Bishopsgate lives on.

I have told you this because I am trying to understand why Lucy would choose to leave a flier of that event, of all things, in Henry's saddle. She wasn't even there.

Anyway, it has now turned midnight. Emms has returned and gone straight to bed. I still haven't explained how you came into being but I will do so tomorrow.

Billy

From:	Sophie.Daggert@yahoo.co.uk
Sent:	23 May 2016
To:	William.Shearwater@btconnect.com
Subject:	Re: What you need to know

Dear Billy

When I first met the woman at the adoption agency, Mrs Withers, she advised me I was about to embark on an emotional journey. She wasn't wrong. Ironically, the one person who gave me the kind of support I needed (other than Lisa in her own way) was the very person I was searching for. If you must know, I am still fucking angry and if I had any sense this would be a thank you and goodbye email. Are you really sure Emms has no idea about all this?

In a ham-fisted way, I'm trying to say that I've reached the end of my search. I've found my father and also found him to be the most engaging liar on earth. Maybe that's as far as it goes. Maybe we should keep 'who you are' as something between the two us, for the sake of all our loved ones. As for how I came into being: you haven't yet reached the point of my conception but I've already encountered bubble cars and bouncing bards, fake genitalia and flame throwers – and enough marijuana to keep the International Space Station in orbit until the twenty-second century.

It really doesn't bode well for the Big Moment. Right now, I'd settle for that simple lunchtime shag in the woods.

Sophie

From:	William.Shearwater@btconnect.com
Sent:	23 May 2016
To:	Sophie.Daggert@yahoo.co.uk
Subject:	Re: What you need to know

Dear Sophie

I can't blame you for feeling so angry. I would feel exactly the same way in your situation. But I hope you will let me finish what I set out to do. I need to tell you, for my own sake, though finding words to describe how your daughter was conceived is a strange occupation. If I were to recount a similar move-by-move account to my other daughter, Beth, she would run a mile. 'Too much infor-mation,' she would say, hands over ears. Describing close encoun-ters of an intimate kind is embarrassing and unnecessary within a family context. However, you do not have that context. You need answers to simple questions not usually requiring answers. Who? When? Where? Why? How? So here goes . . .

To say Mrs Pitcher was relieved when Hendo and Lucy stopped seeing each other is an understatement. She moved south to keep

Lucy away from the 'long-haired layabouts' of Liverpool, only to find her daughter hanging around with a long-haired layabout (with sideburns) in Croydon. Worse still, he drove a fruit and veg van: hardly the kind of young man in which her daughter should take any interest.

A few days after the Bishopsgate happening, she discovered Lucy's stash in the guinea pig shed. Apoplectic hardly does justice to her state of mind. There were several loud exchanges on the doorsteps of Leehart Gardens. For the first time I heard her true Scouse accent in all its shrill glory. I mean, if she had heard *me* shorten the first vowel in 'bastard' like that . . . The Hendersons, especially Mr H who 'should know better', were a bunch of reprobates who had led her innocent daughter astray. In fact, Lucy had introduced the evil weed to Hendo but Mrs Pitcher wasn't having any of that. Worse still, her irreversibly corrupted daughter now refused to go back to boarding school, opting to continue as an usherette at the Plaza. The Hendersons were entirely to blame.

I watched the drama unfold from my bedroom window. In a quiet moment I asked Hendo why he had gone AWOL at Bishopsgate. After all, he wasn't one to get stage fright. He never really explained himself and I put it down to a lovers' tiff. As for Lucy: when she wasn't working at the cinema she seemed to be permanently in her bedroom. I waited until Mr and Mrs Pitcher were out and called round a couple of times but she never answered the door. Then, out of the blue one afternoon, she phoned and asked if I wanted a free ticket to see *The Graduate* at the Plaza. I had already seen the film at another cinema, though I wasn't going to admit it. As a (just) fifteen-year-old I couldn't understand why Dustin Hoffman's Benjamin fancied Anne Bancroft's Mrs Robinson. Bancroft was thirty-six – well past it. Doe-eyed Katherine Ross, who played her daughter, was a babe. When I saw the film again in my forties, Katherine Ross seemed dull and gauche. As for the delectable Anne Bancroft . . .

I hung around in the foyer at the end of the film and offered to walk Lucy home.

'What did you think of the film?' she said. Before I could answer she said: 'Don't you love the last scene, where they hop on the yellow bus to get away from everybody?' We walked on for no more than a hundred yards and a green 403 double-decker pulled up at a stop next to us. 'Quick.' Giggling, Lucy grabbed me and in seconds flat we on the top deck. The back seat was free. She pulled me into it.

'Where are we going?' I said.

'Who cares?'

I looked at my watch. 'It's gone ten o'clock.'

'Don't be nesh.' I had no idea what the old northern word meant at the time. Something of the north remained embedded in Miss Pitcher. The conductor came upstairs, whistling: they always did in those days.

'Where to?' he said.

'The end of the line,' said Lucy.

'Chelsham Garage, then.'

Lucy giggled. 'Where's that?'

'Miles from here,' I said.

'Good. The further, the better.' There was no arguing with her. I had just enough for the fare. We were the last passengers on the bus when it arrived at Chelsham.

'Come on,' said Lucy. 'Let's keep walking.'

'But . . . it's just woods and fields,' I said. 'There's nothing down there. And look at the time.'

She took some persuading but finally relented. We began the long walk home. The following two hours will remain in my mind for several eternities. For the first time since our encounter in the guinea pig shed, I had Lucy to myself. And for the first and only time, she opened up to me. It's hard to remember what she said after so many years but the cool pretence disappeared. I began to understand why she wanted to escape. The real Lucy Pitcher was anxious and uncertain. As well as the break-up with Hendo, strained relations between the Hendersons and the Pitchers had taken their toll.

There's another side to this, which I didn't realize at the time. I've been through numerous personality tests over the years and every time I'm told the same thing. I'm a rescuer. I need to be needed. For some reason Lucy had become vulnerable. I wanted to save her: from the situation, from herself. I acted in a similar way with Emms when she first arrived at Shearwater and Finch. I even felt some compassion for Ledgard, in spite of his antics. And the old habit kicked in again when I met you.

Lucy and I had changed the world as we came in sight of Lee-hart Gardens.

'Billy, do you love me?' she said, out of the blue.

'Of course,' I said. 'It was love at first thigh.'

She laughed and raised an interrogative eyebrow. I recounted my first glimpse of her in the garden.

'But it's got to go deeper than that, hasn't it?' she said.

'Do you think I would allow you to bundle me on to a bus at ten o'clock at night, heading for a deserted bus garage, just to walk back home for miles, if it was skin deep?' I said. 'This has been the best night of my life.'

She pulled me to her. I would never have had the courage to do the same to her. We kissed for the first time. It was my first kiss ever. 'Listen, I'm not at work tomorrow,' she said, coming up for air. 'What are you doing after school?'

'Nothing.'

'My parents will be out. I'll leave the back door open.'

'What if . . .'

'No ifs . . . just come.'

To write this has taken me far longer than I expected, so I'm going to hit the sack and try and finish the story tomorrow.

Billy

From:	Sophie.Daggert@yahoo.co.uk
Sent:	24 May 2016
To:	William.Shearwater@btconnect.com
Subject:	Re: What you need to know

Dear Billy

Aaargh! How could you leave it there? Any well-crafted story is like good sex: it requires careful, well-judged foreplay, but this . . . this is slow torture.

I played the ending of *The Graduate* to a class, recently. We compared the action and music in the build-up to the church wedding with the very end scene, where Hoffman and Ross ride away in the bus. The breathless acoustic guitar of Simon and Garfunkel's 'Mrs Robinson', as Hoffman races to wreck the wedding, compares starkly with 'Sound of Silence', when Hoffman and Ross hardly look at each other in the last minute of the movie. The final, enigmatic message is, as one student said so eloquently: 'Oh shit, now what?'

My conception sounds a little more valued than I expected: certainly more interesting than that of my own daughter. 'The luteinizing hormone has been detected,' I said to Daggert, holding up a test stick. 'Which means?' He was watching rugby on TV. 'I'm ovulating,' I said. 'Hmmm,' he grunted. 'See you at half-time.'

Sophie

From:	William.Shearwater@btconnect.com
Sent:	24 May 2016
To:	Sophie.Daggert@yahoo.co.uk
Subject:	Re: What you need to know

Dear Sophie

Half-time is a mere ten minutes in rugby union. Footballers take fifteen. What better reason is there to choose round ball over oval ball? Talking of chasing eggs . . .

As I crept through the back door after our bus ride to Chelsham, guilt had already kicked in, having done little to trigger it. I had been living under the shadow of *Knowledge for the Growing Boy* by Sidney G. Hedges. Two years earlier my mother left this little red booklet lying around the house for me to pick up. Hedges' post-war mission was to protect newly adolescent boys from the terror of nocturnal emissions. 'Precious seminal fluid' shouldn't be wasted, argued Hedges, but absorbed into the bloodstream where it helps develop 'the many qualities which begin to show up in boys who grow straight and true'. Hedges, a contributor to

Boys' Own Paper, *Chums* and *Scout*, suggested wet dreams occur through 'too much supper, having too many clothes on the bed and sleeping on the back'. But how can a hapless teenage boy know he is sleeping on his back? By threading a piece of string through a cotton reel and tying it round his waist. If he rolls from his side it wakes him up. Over the following two years I absorbed so much 'precious seminal fluid' I could have stunt doubled for the Michelin Man.

Hedges persuaded me that sex had nothing but terrifying consequences. It didn't help when a classmate received a paternity summons. Though we were all in awe of his virility, I knew he was as good as damned for eternity. Even this, however, failed to dissuade me from bunking off school at lunchtime the next day. I furtively bought my first Rave shirt, with a swirly paisley design in rich reds, oranges and browns. I then went to a public lavatory to buy a packet of three condoms. This all happened years before AIDS made prophylactics socially acceptable and easily available at chemists. I felt grubby shovelling half-a-crown into the slot. I arrived home, telling Mum that games were cancelled, and tried on my shirt upstairs. It was ridiculously cool so I hid most of it under a dull, grey school jumper. I struggled to put on one of the condoms and couldn't imagine standing erect, in full view of Lucy, fiddling with slimy latex. Perhaps I could keep this one on and stay proud until the appointed time . . . but the minutes ticked away like hours. Finally, I splashed on some of my father's aftershave and sneaked round to Lucy's house like a criminal, convinced the curtain twitchers knew exactly where I was going and why.

I took off my grey jumper, opened the unlocked back door and spoke Lucy's name quietly. No reply. I crept into the hall and heard a familiar sound coming from upstairs: bump, squeak, bump, squeak, bump, squeak.

'Lucy?' I was at the foot of the stairs. Still no reply. I walked slowly up the stairs and, through a half-open door, saw Lucy, her back at least, on a rocking horse. It was my first encounter with Henry.

'Lucy, it's me,' I hissed.

She didn't turn round but waved and kept rocking gently, to and fro, to and fro. She was wearing her short red knitted skirt, white T-shirt and nothing on her feet. Did she know exactly what she was doing? At the time I was too naive to even consider the question. Many years later, I discovered 'the fantastic rocking horse' is regarded as a top ten sexual position. The man sits cross-legged and leans back supporting himself with both arms behind him. The woman kneels over his lap hugging him with her thighs and lowers herself . . . but this is surely too much information. Henry's smooth rhythm was hypnotic and mesmerizing, though at the time I had no real idea why.

'Hop on.' Lucy was still staring straight ahead.

'Where are we going?' I tried hard not to betray nervous exhilaration.

'All the way.'

I swear my heart almost burst out of my chest. 'What, to Chelsham Bus Garage?' She laughed and leaned forward so I could squeeze on behind. I didn't know what to do with my arms.

'Don't be so polite.' She pulled them round her breasts and set Henry rocking again. I buried my face in her sweet-smelling hair. She pulled back her hair and offered me her neck. I kissed it several times. She arched in pleasure and giggled. And again.

'What's so funny?' I said.

'You smell like my dad.' I was spared further embarrassment because at that point she noticed what I was wearing. 'Wow, nice shirt.' She guided my hands under her T-shirt. She wasn't wearing a bra. She also assured me it was the right time of the month and there was no need to take any precautions . . .

I will spare you the detail of what happened next. Suffice to say that it took a lot less than a rugby half-time. I could suck a quartered orange quicker. Grantland Rice, the American sportswriter, famously wrote: 'When the one great scorer comes to write against your name, he marks not that you won or lost, but how you laid the dame.' Well, that wasn't exactly what he wrote, but if he had I would have struggled to score one out of ten.

Lucy said her parents wouldn't be back for at least another hour but we were now in a foursome: fear and guilt had joined us in the room. I walked back to my house and sneaked upstairs to change my shirt before anyone could see it. I went down for tea and watched *Meet the Wife* on TV as if nothing had happened. I half expected my mother to notice that I had suddenly lost weight: after all, my days as a stunt double were over.

Billy

Chapter 37

Thursday 26 May 2016

Maybe it was just me. Or maybe it was the unrelenting gloom of deconstructing Graham Greene's *The Power and the Glory* which has seeped into me. While the book is a masterpiece, Greene's history of depression profoundly affected his writing. Bullied as a child at boarding school, he made several suicide attempts – including Russian roulette and taking aspirin before swimming in the school pool. You can feel it all going on between the lines.

At the end of today's last lesson, Lisa was waiting for me in the corridor.

'Miss, I'm worried about you,' she said. 'You haven't been yourself since . . . you know . . . is it me?'

'Of course not,' I said. 'I'm fine.'

'The whole class, we're worried about you.'

'I don't know what you mean.'

'You have the world on your shoulders, as if something is really bothering you.'

'That's modern teaching for you.' I began walking briskly along the corridor ahead of her and stopped outside the staff room. 'At this end of the term we're all ready to collapse.' I pointed inside at my colleagues.

'Miss, I know it's more than that but I don't want to cause you any more trouble. I just want you to know that I care and that I'll do anything to help. Or nothing, if that's best.'

'That's very sweet of you, Lisa,' I said. 'All I would say is that you should consider what has happened to me and think very carefully before embarking on a search for your birth parents.'

Lisa began walking away but then stopped dead in her tracks. 'You've found your father and he isn't what you expected.' She really is much too intuitive for her own good.

'I didn't say that.'

'What's he like?'

'Lisa, you are putting two and two together and making fifty-six.'

'Then why did you mention it?'

'I didn't.'

'Can I meet him? No, that's a silly thing to ask. Sorry, miss. I've said what I wanted say, anyway. I've got to learn to keep my mouth shut.' She sloped off home, leaving me determined that I must not tell her one more thing about my life and family.

Billy and I have been corresponding by email. After the initial shock, disgust and anger at his deceit, I found myself looking forward to the quack on the computer as his latest email drops into my inbox. Alongside my anticipation are feelings of guilt. My search has caused ructions in two families and led to the estrangement of my father from his wife. It wasn't supposed to be like this.

I always hoped there had been genuine passion in the union of my parents, whoever they were, but Billy writes with such intensity and attention to detail that you cannot help being swept up in it all. I have to keep reminding myself the events he describes actually happened and that I am the result of it all. Of course, when I was little I wanted the prince and princess myth to be true but the actual circumstances surrounding my conception are far more interesting and, dare I say, entertaining. Even if I hadn't been the product of the union, I would still want to know what happened next. And that's what I find so depressing. Billy has the power to lift me out of myself. Only one other person could do that before Canon William Shearwater.

Young David is right. I like him. I want a relationship with him but cannot have one that makes any sense. His being married was reason enough. But discovering he is my father is still making my stomach churn. I am angry, hurt, confused – and enchanted.

Chapter 38

Whoever designed the ground belonging to Much Sumner FC had the remarkable foresight to build a urinal wall so low that male spectators can watch the match while answering calls of nature. Exciting moments on the pitch may result in splashed shoes but true fans never complain, even when the urine isn't theirs. Much Sumner's facilities offer little else in which to rejoice. The main (and only) stand holds 180 spectators but its corrugated tin roof has also sprung a leak, for more than a decade. The walls of the changing rooms are so thin that earwigging the managers' half-time rants is a traditional part of the day's entertainment. The pitch slopes to one corner where water collects in pools. Playful dogs, let off their leads in the municipal park nearby, leap over a privet hedge and join in with games. But all who visit say the same thing: Much Sumner is a little club with a big heart and provides a great day out for all the family. Reaching round three of the Warmsley Bay Caravan Park Trophy in 1993 still inspires fans to believe better days are just around the corner.

The club's media facilities are non-existent but that is of little concern to Bishop Maureen and Canon Shearwater. Indeed, the whole point of holding a press conference at Much Sumner rather than Manchester United is to re-emphasize the nature of their campaign: to take football back to its roots in the local community. The only room big enough to cope with an influx of reporters and TV crews is the club's bar. Crammed in one corner, Billy looks appreciatively at the turnout from TV, radio, newspapers and online titles alike. With a bit of luck and a slow news day, *Our Goal: The Soul* may make the *Six O'Clock News*. He takes a deep breath. In spite of everything that has happened over the past few weeks, it is all coming together. At last. He nods at Bishop Maureen who taps the microphone in front of her.

'Ladies and gentlemen,' she says, 'welcome to Much Sumner FC. It is my first visit to this atmospheric ground and, yes, judging by several nods, that's true for many of you as well. We trust it won't be our last. One of the reasons we chose to hold a press conference here is our friendship with the club's chaplain, Father Vincent O'Donovan. Please stand, Father.' O'Donovan, eighty-something with arthritic hips, reluctantly gets to his feet and sits down again, slowly and carefully. 'Apart from praying for the souls of all who watch and play here, Father O'Donovan doubles up as bar and grounds-man. I'm told he is regularly to be seen on the pitch, dispelling not-so-holy water with a gardening fork.' There are murmurs of appreciation. Sitting behind Father O'Donovan, a reporter leans forward and asks him quietly for an interview after the conference.

'We are here because, for many years, one man has fought tirelessly to bring transparency to the heart of our national game. The simple values espoused by its Victorian founding fathers – honesty, integrity and fair play – have been tossed aside by corporate greed of biblical proportions. In fact, the Bible resounds with stories of similarly righteous men standing alone against the principalities and powers: Moses against Pharaoh, Elijah against the prophets of Baal, Jesus against Pilate. Not forgetting Jeremiah, Hosea, Isaiah and the rest, who protested against corruption and often paid the ultimate price.'

'A season ticket at the Arsenal,' quips a journalist at the back. Bishop Maureen acknowledges the joke and outlines the aims of *Our Goal: The Soul* once more but this time introduces a vital new factor: a grant from the Eutychus Trust.

'You can have a dream as big as you like but without the resources to make it happen it will remain just a dream. However, with the support of our friends at the trust . . .'

Billy doesn't hear the final words of Bishop Maureen's introduc-tion. A door has opened at the back of the bar and an Adam's apple has entered, a fraction of a second ahead of the human being from which it is still trying to escape. Father Nicholas Ledgard takes a seat alongside a reporter from the *Daily Telegraph*.

The blood drains from Billy's face. His heart races. Fight or flight? He begins to hyperventilate. Somewhere in the distance Bishop Maureen is talking about the role of fans' chaplains and the need to protect vulnerable young spectators. Briefly, he glances at Ledgard. He doesn't want to appear concerned. Ledgard looks smug but then he always does. How did he find out about the press conference? What has he got planned? He couldn't choose a better place to tell the world what he knows. He could stand up at any moment and fire a question like: 'Canon Shearwater, isn't it hypocritical to be calling on the football authorities to clean up their act when you fathered an illegitimate daughter about which even your wife knows nothing?' He might do so at any moment. At any moment.

'So, without further ado,' Bishop Maureen is saying, 'I'd like to hand over to Canon Shearwater who will outline what *Our Goal: The Soul* will do over the next three years.' She moves the microphone towards her colleague. He stares at it and says nothing. 'Billy?'

'Er, thank you.' Below the table and unseen by the journalists, Billy wipes sweat from his hands on to his trousers. He studies his notes then folds the paper neatly and puts it in his pocket. Nervously, he taps the table top with his fingers and takes a long, deep breath. 'Bishop Maureen, ladies and gentlemen, as many of you already know, I spend a lot of my professional life trying to ensure the media report fairly on people in my charge. At times I have gone to great lengths to be economical with the truth, to protect the good name of the institution and the people in it. Often my actions are justified; sometimes they are not. I have had to defend the indefensible on many an occasion.

'Sometimes, traumatic events from the past play their part in these incidents. They come back to haunt people at the most unlikely times. Indeed, there is someone in this room who went through a circumstance many years ago that has never come to light. He is still living with the consequences. Today I will name and shame him.' Billy glances at Ledgard. It is Ledgard's turn to shift uneasily in his seat. 'Key events shape all our lives. Fifty years ago Jimmy Greaves, arguably the most talented player of his generation, was left out of the England side playing West Germany in the nineteen-sixty-six World Cup Final. As Bobby Moore said later: "It broke his heart. That moment began his disenchantment with football." Greaves became an alcoholic; at times he is said to have put away pints galore of lager during the day and a bottle of vodka at night.

'Distressing events can change the course of our lives. You've probably watched ITV's *Long Lost Family*, in which broken-hearted mothers, suffering a lifetime's guilt and remorse, are reunited with sons and daughters they gave up for adoption as babies. The scenes of reunion are intensely emotional. And then there are their sons and daughters who, similarly, cannot rest until they know who gave them birth.

'Which brings me on to Mrs Sophie Daggert, who, as most of you will know, found mementos hidden by her birth mother in the saddle of a rocking horse.' Bemused nods from the conference. 'Well, it's not the story you came to Much Sumner for today but I can tell you that, although her mother is no longer with us, Mrs Daggert has found her natural father. His wife and family have no idea about her existence. How is it relevant to this press conference? I said I would name and shame someone in the room this morning. Bishop, ladies and gentlemen, you are looking at Sophie's father.'

Billy pauses. There are small bursts of embarrassed laughter.

'You're pulling our leg,' says one reporter.

'I couldn't be more serious.'

Bishop Maureen nudges Billy. He takes no notice.

'Andy Dobson, *Daily Telegraph*,' says Andy Dobson of the *Daily Telegraph*. 'Why are you telling us now?'

'Because it's the right thing to do.'

Again Bishop Maureen tries to gain Billy's attention but he doesn't respond. 'Until today only Sophie and one other person knew the truth. The relationship happened before I met Emma, my wife, but I have never had the courage to tell her.'

'Great story.' Andy Dobson shows not one ounce of sympathy but instead scribbles in his notepad. 'Who was Sophie's mother and where did you meet her?'

'We were both fifteen and lived in the same street.'

'What happened when she got pregnant?'

'Given the era in which it all took place, Sophie's adoption was inevitable, I'm sad to say.'

'Steve Darlington, *Daily Express*. The picture of those fans at the sixty-six World Cup Final, the one that appeared in our paper. Are you in it?'

Billy nods. 'As I said, traumatic events change lives.' He stares intently at Ledgard. 'I am not alone in making serious mistakes.'

'Well,' says Bishop Maureen. 'This has all come as a complete surprise. Canon Shearwater, I think we need to have a word before you carry on.'

'And I must apologize to you, Bishop,' says Billy. 'Now that all this is out in the open, I cannot, in good conscience, fight a campaign to clean up football. It is with regret that I am therefore stepping down immediately from *Our Goal: The Soul.*'

'Rock 'n' roll,' murmurs Steve Darlington. He grabs his mobile and sends a text to his news editor. Questions come thick and fast from the floor. The press conference eventually breaks up and it is only as the reporters leave to file their stories that Billy approaches his nemesis.

'I don't understand,' says Ledgard, quietly.

'I blinked first,' says Billy. 'Call it a pre-emptive strike. If you had asked me an awkward question, I would have come off even worse. As it is, I broached the subject, not you, and retained some credibility.'

'But I came here to extend an olive branch. What you said at the pub made sense.'

Billy looks sideways at Ledgard. 'I cannot believe you would come all the way here to bury the hatchet. You could have phoned me to do that. No, you had something planned.'

'For a minute or two I thought *you* were about to blow the whistle on *me.*'

'I still could, of course . . . but in a strange way I am relieved. I couldn't go on under this pressure. I don't want to admit it but you have done me a favour.'

'Nicholas, what are you doing here?' Bishop Maureen has wrestled herself clear from a reporter from the *Sun.*

'Ah, Bishop. Yes, I came to support William,' says Ledgard.

'There's nothing much left to support.' Her anger is palpable.

'William and I go back a long way.'

'Well, I think we've gone back far enough today. Billy, we'll talk about this mess in due course but, for now, I suggest you do something you really should have done already. Call your wife.'

*

'Oh, that's such a shame,' says Emma.

'A shame?' Mobile phone to his ear, Billy is standing next to a corner flag at Much Sumner FC.

'I had high hopes for you both.'

'I'm not with you.'

'Sophie is such a lovely woman and you get on so well. That was obvious from the moment I saw you together.'

'I don't understand.'

'You don't understand a lot of things, Billy.'

'I fathered an illegitimate child. I'm not sure that's gone in.'

'I've always said there was another side to you.'

'But – I expected you to be shocked and angry.'

'Shocked? Angry? No. I'm disappointed but probably not for the reason you think.'

'What do you mean?'

'You and Sophie make a great couple.'

'A great— what are you saying?'

'Billy, stop deluding yourself. We're over. It was just a question of when and who for both of us.'

'When and who . . . ? What are you on about?'

'I'm leaving you. I want a divorce. And this news confirms my decision.'

'But . . . don't be ridiculous. There must be someone else.'

'Roy.'

'The shelf stacker?'

'The chief librarian.'

'This has to be a joke.'

'He's a kind, sweet man who actually listens and cares about me.'

'What are you saying, that I *don't* care?'

'Billy, this isn't a sudden decision. While you've busied yourself with your great mission in life, I've had relationships you've never even noticed. None of them have come to anything much but Roy

248

is different. I hoped you and Sophie could find something similar but the fact that she is your daughter, well, it's spoiled everything ...'

*

It is later the same day. Billy has checked into a hotel, several miles from his home. The pages of tomorrow's newspapers are already appearing online.

TEARS FOR SHEARS

ANGUISH OF CANON CLEAN-UP'S SECRET LOVE CHILD

By Steve Darlington

Clean up football campaigner Canon William Shearwater yesterday confessed to being the father of English teacher Sophie Daggert.

Adopted as a baby, Sophie, 48, found mementos smuggled away in the saddle of a rocking horse by her natural mother. They included a photo of Shearwater at the 1966 World Cup Final, published for the first time in the *Express* a few days ago.

In light of the revelations, Shearwater, admitted he now lacks the credibility to lead a campaign that is calling on football's governing bodies to greater transparency. Speaking at non-league side Much Sumner FC, Shearwater explained how his relationship with Sophie's mother, the late Lucy Pitcher, took place when they were both 15.

'Sophie is a daughter to be proud of even though the circumstances of her early life were difficult,' said Shearwater. 'My relationship with Lucy happened some time before I met Emma, my wife. I regret not telling her and my family about it all. This has come as a complete shock to them and I can only apologize.'

Mrs Shearwater was unavailable for comment.

249

Billy calls Sophie and reads her the article.

'If only you had been straight with me from the start,' says Sophie. 'And yet, at the same time, I'm sorry for my part in it all.'

'It's not your fault,' he replies.

'Of course it is. Everything was working out for you until I came along.'

'Emms would disagree.'

Sophie sighs. 'I tried to tell you there were problems.'

'What "other relationships" is she talking about? I've never noticed anything or anybody.'

'Exactly. You were too busy to notice.'

'She never told me she was unhappy.'

'Maybe you just weren't listening.'

'You're saying I'm to blame.'

'No. It takes two to not tango.'

Billy smiles. 'Why do you have to be my daughter, Sophie?'

'Hah. Well . . . weird hardly covers it. Finding out who you really are has eased the tension. I don't have to worry whether you are attracted to me or not.'

'And that makes you even more attractive.'

Sophie frowns. 'I'm not Lucy, Billy. I never was and never can be. Have you any idea where Emms is?'

'With the shelf stacker, I imagine.'

'So, are you going home?'

'There were three reporters and a snapper outside my house a couple of hours ago, so I'm holing up at a small hotel until the heat dies down. In the words of Captain Oates, I may be some time.'

Chapter 39

From: William.Shearwater@btconnect.com
Sent: 27 May 2016
To: Sophie.Daggert@yahoo.co.uk
Subject: Home is where the hearth is

Dear Sophie

I tried to talk to Emms this morning but every call I made went straight to voicemail. So I'm holed up here, in this depressing little room, stomach churning with a cocktail of emotions about her and this 'chief librarian'.

Reading my last email back, I need to explain that when I think of Lucy I don't get wistful about our physical union. Instead I recall the conversation we had on the long walk back from Chelsham Bus Garage. Every word seems transfigured in my mind. What I'm trying to say is that everything changed after our brief moment of intimacy. No more crazy bus rides. Very little laughter. Thinking about it now, I may have brought some fall-out from the relationship with Lucy into my marriage: a sense of inevitable failure, a fear of abandoning myself to someone again. Several times over the following few weeks I turned up at the Plaza as the crowd came out. I walked Lucy home. She seemed moody and withdrawn. On two occasions she was sick before she reached Leehart Gardens, though I was too naive to suspect why.

The last time I saw her, and I mean *ever*, was one Tuesday evening. She got me a free ticket to watch *In the Heat of the Night* with Sidney Poitier and Rod Steiger, one of my all-time favourite films. Whenever it comes on TV I have to turn it off: too many painful memories.

'Let's get a coffee at the Colibri,' she said. The Colibri was a 1950s-style coffee bar over the road from the Plaza. I sensed she

251

was about to tell me something I didn't want to hear. I expected to be dumped.

'You know when we . . .' she said, stirring her coffee.

'The best moment of my life.'

'Yes, well . . . the thing is, I was wrong about the time of the month.' Her face was white. She couldn't look me in the eye.

'You're not—'

'I am.'

Pure panic. That's the only way I can describe it. The only other time I have ever felt so hysterical was when Ledgard walked into the press conference. 'Do your parents know?'

She shook her head. 'And I'm not telling them.'

'So . . . what are you going to do?'

'Someone I know has offered to pay for an abortion.'

'Who?'

'They've told me not to say. But I don't believe in abortions anyway so I'm running away to have the baby. Tomorrow.'

I was stunned. 'Tomorrow? Where to?'

'I can't say.'

'I don't believe this is happening.'

'You will tomorrow.'

I held her hand across the table. We both welled up, trying hard not to let anyone see. There were several people in the Colibri we knew. 'Is there anything I can do?'

She shook her head. 'I'm sorry. I didn't want to do this to you. It's been forced on me.'

'Well, we both had something to do with it.' I dug into my pocket and pulled out a small silver necklace, the one you found in Henry's saddle. It wasn't expensive but it was all I could afford. 'Here. I've been meaning to give you this for weeks but there's never been a right time. You've seemed too moody. Now I know why.'

The floodgates opened. Lucy ran out, sobbing. I eventually talked her round and we walked home, slowly.

'What are you going to tell your parents?' I said.

'I'm sneaking out early in the morning and leaving a note on my bed.'

252

'Saying what?'

'That I've met a second-hand car dealer and I'm going to live happily ever after with him.'

'Have you?'

'Of course not.'

'Will they believe you?'

She shrugged her shoulders. 'I'm not telling them about the baby.'

'Are you going to keep it?'

'If possible.'

'Can you afford to?'

'No.'

We walked on in silence. I felt useless and afraid. We kissed in an alley on a street parallel to ours but it was brief and almost formal. We were both too upset to be affectionate. The truth is, I didn't think she would go through with her plan but I hardly slept that night and kept looking out of my bedroom window, just in case. I finally dozed off about 4 a.m. She must have left soon after that.

Mr and Mrs Pitcher were at my house waiting for me when I got home from school that afternoon. In Mrs Pitcher's hand was Lucy's note. I'd never seen her hair so loose and untidy. Her make-up, usually immaculate, was smudged and desperate.

'Do you know anything about this?' She handed me the note.

'Now then, don't go for him, love,' said Mr Pitcher. 'He's been a good friend to our Lucy. All we need to know, Billy, is if you can tell us anything about this man she's supposed to be meeting.'

'Wow,' I said. 'You mean she's run away. Do you know where?'

'That's the problem – we've no idea where to, or who with.'

Mrs Pitcher started to sob. 'She's treated us so badly. We've sacrificed it all for that girl. She's had everything she's ever wanted.'

'I know, love,' said Mr Pitcher, 'but this isn't helping.'

'We've never given a thought for our own needs.' Mrs Pitcher rarely listened to her husband. 'We've struggled and struggled to make ends meet, so she could go to the best school and have the

253

good things of life which we never had. This is how she repays us. Smoking pot, hanging around with beatniks and going off with a man from the motor trade, of all things.' She ran out of the house, hysterical. Mum followed her and tried to comfort her in the garden.

'We've obviously done something very wrong,' said Mr Pitcher.

'I don't think you have,' I said. 'Lucy is very strong-willed.'

Mr Pitcher nodded. 'I wonder if sending her to boarding school was such a good idea. Billy, you don't know if she's . . . in trouble or anything?'

'What sort of trouble?'

'You know.' He pointed to his stomach.

'Oh, that. She hasn't said anything.' I was learning how to lie.

'Well, if you hear from her, you will let us know, won't you?'

'Of course.'

'We're going over to the Hendersons next. Mrs Pitcher still blames them for what's happened.'

I felt for Hendo that evening because all hell broke loose. Leehart Gardens had never heard anything like it and probably hasn't since. It was all too much for the Pitchers. Within a few weeks, their house was back on the market.

Writing all this has helped work it out of my system. I hope you will see that I really loved your mother, Sophie.

Billy

From:	Sophie.Daggert@yahoo.co.uk
Sent:	27 May 2016
To:	William.Shearwater@btconnect.com
Subject:	Re: Home is where the hearth is

Oh. My. God. Billy, how can such an intelligent man miss a giant redwood for a matchstick? You write eloquent prose about a doomed relationship, so detailed and affectionate it could have happened yesterday. And then you say: 'I may have brought fall-out from the relationship into my marriage.' Are you kidding? Do

I really have to spell it out? You have been secretly obsessed with my mother for almost fifty years!!

Emms is hurt and angry. There was always someone else in your head. She couldn't break the hold of a woman she wasn't even sure existed! Now the dam has burst, there's a chance for everyone to move on. Unless you do, your marriage is over, for good. The choice is yours. I'm sorry to be so blunt but there it is. It's what daughters are for.

Earlier today, and completely out of the blue, Emms phoned me. It was one of those calls where you indulge in small talk, waiting for the moment when the person on the other end says, 'Anyway, the reason why I phoned is . . .' But that never happened. So I am still not sure what the call was about. I think she feels protective towards me, what with everything that's going on. That's only part of it, though. In my opinion, no matter what she says, she is unsure of her 'relationship' with this librarian. Roy, is it? I can't explain why. It's more of an intuitive thing. I'm sure she's in a form of denial, as well. She is more shocked about discovering you had another daughter than she admits. Her cool response was a defence mechanism. Maybe this relationship is all part of that reaction and will blow itself out. I hope so.

Sophie

From: William.Shearwater@btconnect.com
Sent: 27 May 2016
To: Sophie.Daggert@yahoo.co.uk
Subject: Re: Home is where the hearth is

Dear Sophie

Well, that's me told! Disappointingly, I cannot disagree with what you've said. I need some time to take it all on board, though. In my defence, I didn't have a chance to go through the usual stages of a teenage relationship with Lucy: infatuation, exploration, union, doubt, disillusion, parting. I got as far as union, briefly. When I met you it was as if I could, at last, pick up where I'd left off. Only, I couldn't.

If I recall correctly, the moment the dam broke was one Saturday afternoon. Lucy had sent a couple of postcards to her parents, assuring them that when she and her 'boyfriend' were ready she would bring him home. Just to confuse matters, the postcards were posted from Hull and Sutton Coldfield. Mrs Pitcher presumed Lucy was moving around because of her boyfriend's job. My guess is that Lucy was getting an old school friend to post them for her. I never heard from her myself but I didn't expect to. That would have aroused suspicion.

The Pitchers sold their house quickly and began packing all their goods into boxes and crates. One day Mr Pitcher appeared at my doorstep. I was at home alone.

'Billy,' he said, 'I need to have a word with you, about a personal matter.' I could see he was a man under pressure. In his hands was a cardboard box. 'Are your parents around?' I'm certain he had waited until he saw them leave the house ten minutes before.

'No,' I said. 'Come in.'

He stood in the hall. 'I'll not stay, only . . .' Out of the box he pulled the necklace I bought Lucy, a booklet, *How to Know if You're Pregnant*, and my grey school jumper. In the rush to get out of Lucy's house on *that* afternoon, I left it there. My mother had sewn my name into it, the way she did with all my school clothes since my first day in the infants. Because I had a few similar jumpers, I had forgotten to collect it. 'All these were tucked away together in one of Lucy's drawers. I need you to be honest with me, Billy. Is Lucy pregnant?'

I stood there petrified. 'I don't know, Mr Pitcher. And I don't know how my jumper got there.'

'Now, Billy, I know you and Lucy were good friends but was it more than that? I won't get mad at you. I just really need to know.' He was on the edge of tears. To this day, I think he genuinely liked me and hoped I had nothing to do with her disappearance. It was suddenly too much to cope with. I burst into tears and told him what had happened. He put his arm round me, thanked me for telling him and wept like a baby himself. He was a kind man and I'll never forget that moment.

Of course, the balloon went up when Mrs Pitcher found out her beloved daughter was in the club and that I, of all people, had robbed her of her innocence. She marched round to my house and started shouting at my parents in the front garden. As for Mum and Dad, they were in a state of shock and spent the next week walking round muttering, 'I simply can't believe it,' every few minutes. All four of them met without me, before the Pitchers left Leehart Gardens for good. They agreed that no one, not even the closest family members on both sides, must know I was your father. Also, the baby would be adopted and Lucy and I would not be named on the birth certificate. That was how they did it in those days: close ranks, limit the damage. As a father, still less as a child father, I had no rights. My opinion was irrelevant.

No more than a week later, I watched the driver of the removal van lift and slam shut the vehicle's drop-down ramp, take one last drag on his cigarette, flick the butt into the gutter, climb up into the driver's seat and chug to the bottom of Leehart Gardens. He turned left on to the main road and took what was left of Lucy Pitcher out of my life for ever.

I presume the adoption agency told my parents you had been born and that you were a girl. That's all I knew. I wasn't allowed to see you or Lucy, or ask any questions. I was expected to get on with my life as if nothing had happened. I couldn't, of course. Precious seminal fluid no longer coursed round my bloodstream. Now it was guilt. I was tempted to lose the plot entirely and let the guilt turn into rage. But I went the other way. The rest of my life was to be a penance. Within the safe, sacred walls of the Church I could repent, perpetually, for my wrongdoing. A poor theology, I'll grant you but that discussion is for another day.

Thank you for encouraging me to relate the whole sorry tale. It has been a cathartic exercise, providing an unexpected measure of comfort and resolve.

Billy

From: Sophie.Daggert@yahoo.co.uk
Sent: 28 May 2016
To: William.Shearwater@btconnect.com
Subject: Re: Home is where the hearth is

Dear Billy

My own cathartic exercise has been keeping a diary, the one you saw on your first visit. I was getting through the denial, anger and bargaining stages of bereavement. Then I began to search for my birth parents. You talk about experiencing a cocktail of emotions. Try borrowing my head for half an hour. At least I now know the full story and cannot imagine how awful you must have felt when both sets of parents discovered the truth.

I can't write any more right now as I received an email earlier from NHS Blood and Transplant, asking me to give blood again. Stocks are dangerously low on O RhD negative. It's the least I can do, given the help they gave Daggert, especially towards the end.

Sophie

From: William.Shearwater@btconnect.com
Sent: 28 May 2016
To: Sophie.Daggert@yahoo.co.uk
Subject: Your blood group

Sophie, it is very, very important that you answer this email quickly and accurately. I am standing by for your reply, frozen to the spot.

In your email you say you are blood group O RhD negative. Please confirm the letter O. I am blood group AB rhesus positive. If you are O, according to what I know about blood groups, it means one simple thing. I cannot be your father.

Billy

Chapter 40

Here's the strange thing. After the initial shock and bewilderment, I had become quite comfortable with the fact that Billy and Lucy got jiggy with it under the watchful, dispassionate gaze of Henry. To my mind, the four of us were a sort of family unit: fractured in time and wildly dysfunctional, but a unit nonetheless. The latest twist in the tale has shattered all that.

I have just finished a telephone conversation with Billy that lasted the best part of two hours. He is convinced the argument between Hendo and Lucy before Bishopsgate occurred because Lucy told Hendo she was pregnant that very morning: and that's why Lucy tucked the event programme into Henry's saddle. Weeks later, Billy got the blame. After all he has been through over the past fifty years, you can hardly blame him for being incandescent with rage.

I rested easy with his original account of my conception because my greatest fear, that I was a lunchtime bonk behind the bike sheds, hadn't been realized. Rereading Billy's emails at regular intervals made me engage more with the tale every time. They persuaded me I was the result of a genuine love story, however brief and ultimately doomed.

This latest twist, however, has got me looking up Isetta bubble cars on the internet. It's hard to imagine Hendo and Lucy found a way to . . . I mean, bubble cars are so tiny and cramped . . . the bench seating can hardly take a couple sitting upright, never mind . . . the hinged steering wheel would swing in and make it a threesome . . . and the central gear lever, poking up from under the bench, could do serious damage to exposed and tender parts. There are those, however, who will have found a way round these obstacles, such is the overpowering passion of youth. Maybe Hendo and Lucy were two of them.

It is more likely that the first cells to divide and form the embryo that became the present writer did so in the back of a Munton Moffett fruit and veg van: with my mother sandwiched between two Vox AC-30 amps, a rogue turnip digging into the small of her back and the twin odours of cabbage and cauliflower penetrating her nostrils.

Hendo and Billy lost touch with each other soon after Lucy ran away from home to have me. Billy thinks the chances of tracing him now are slim. Whether he is my father or not, I have no desire to meet him, if that's what he could do to a 'friend'. My overriding emotion now is not one of disappointment but guilt. I should have been content to find out which woman in the world gave birth to me. Few people conceived to teenage parents in that era ever make contact with their father, it seems, even if they discover their identity. What possible good can come of it now? He may not say so but I fear the real object of Billy's anger is me, for my part in bringing it all to light. What a mess.

In the middle of writing this I received an email from a Clive Lacey from Saffron Walden. He's read about my search in the papers and, if I am interested, will tell me what happened to Lucy. The thing is, I have had similar emails from several people offering all sorts of information and they've all proved false. I'm tempted to follow this one up because he writes in an entertaining, intelligent way but I'm putting it in the pending file for now. I'm not even sure if I want to know what he has to say, even if it is true.

Chapter 41

Bishop Maureen paces round her study, arms folded. 'I'm shocked, bewildered, disappointed. You gave me no warning.'

'That's because—'

Maureen raises a hand. Billy is to remain silent. 'You left me looking a complete fool.'

'I didn't mean—'

'No.' Maureen shakes her head. 'Let me finish.' Billy bites his lip and studies the laces of his shoes. 'I have had to apologize to the Eutychus Trust for wasting their time. *Our Goal: The Soul* is over before a ball has been kicked and we've been made a laughing stock by the media. In the meantime you disappear without trace, leaving me to sweep up the mess. I am sorry for what has happened to you on a personal level, particularly the situation with Emma, but the way you handled this is entirely unacceptable. I trusted you implicitly, Billy. Sadly, this incident has changed all that.'

Her visitor slumps further into a high-backed chair. 'I was under stress but that is no excuse, Bishop.' His voice is low, his words measured. 'To add insult to injury, I have since discovered I am not Sophie's father after all.'

Maureen hovers over her desk. 'Which means . . .'

'Fifty years ago I was told a lie.'

'So, the obvious question . . .'

Billy shrugs his shoulders. 'I have no idea.'

Maureen sits at her desk. 'Why ever didn't you tell Emma you had a daughter from the start?'

Billy shrugs again. 'It was a different world back then. Having a child out of wedlock brought shame on the family. The Pitchers took the whole thing out of their daughter's hands. I wasn't allowed to see her when she was born. After a few months it was easier to pretend she didn't exist.'

Bishop Maureen stares out of her window, to a well-kept lawn being mown by a local gardener. 'I understand and I'm not unsympathetic,' she says, slowly. 'The difficulty is your deceit.'

'I was fifteen. It wasn't even my deceit. It was a family decision.'

'No matter. I've made big mistakes over the years but they're there for all to see. The diocese has suffered significant reputational damage over this matter.' Maureen looks long and hard at her guest. 'Reluctantly, I think it best if we terminate your services with immediate effect.'

'You're . . . *sacking* me?'

'Well, we can't sack you. We are simply not retaining you as a consultant from the end of this month.'

'But I fell on my sword at the press conference. Unloading me is entirely unnecessary.'

Bishop Maureen stands and walks to the door of her study. 'You have some fine skills and a great deal to offer, Billy. It just cannot be here any more.' She hovers by the door. 'I think we've gone as far as we can today.'

'Oh, we haven't even turned on the ignition.' The position of Billy's chair means he has his back to his host. 'You want to dispense with my services because I have become toxic. That's disappointing because I thought we had a good relationship.'

'You don't realize how angry and humiliated I feel.' Maureen's voice is taut and strained.

'You don't need to tell me about anger and humiliation, Bishop. Stir in fifty years of guilt and you have William Shearwater.'

'I could recommend a good counsellor.'

'Now that's just patronizing.'

'I'm sorry you see it that way.'

'What's disappointing is that I've worked with a number of cub bishops. Most don't cut the mustard but I have high hopes for you.'

'Now *that* is patronizing.'

'I think you'll go to the top.'

'Well, that is gratifying but it doesn't change anything.'

A difficult silence is punctuated only by the creak of chair springs as Billy reaches for his briefcase. 'Does Pettigrew know about your decision?'

'As diocesan secretary he has to know.'

'I'm surprised.'

'Why?'

'He knows how cautious you have to be in these situations. I doubt he suggested letting me go. I trust you are aware of its implications.' Billy springs open the two catches on his briefcase and pulls out a dossier. 'May I respectfully suggest we have an informed and considered conversation?' He nods in the direction of her desk.

'You are trying my patience, Billy.' Bishop Maureen reluctantly returns to her desk. 'This had better be significant.'

'Oh, it's significant all right.' Billy flicks through the pages of the dossier. 'As you will remember, Father Nicholas Ledgard was at the press conference.'

Bishop Maureen studies Billy, quizzically. 'I thought we had moved him on.'

Billy nods. 'To another diocese far, far away. And very aggrieved he was, too. So much so that he arrived uninvited at the press conference with one intention, to get his own back. He was going to inform the world's media I had an illegitimate daughter but I beat him to it.'

'I see, but your point being—'

'That the diocese has been less than transparent in dealing with Ledgard. And he is just one of a number of cases over the past fifty years. Victims of abuse have been hushed up by a succession of bishops. I hardly need remind you of Kingswood Marsh, our own Church of England children's home where I am reliably informed young residents were' – Billy reads from the dossier – 'drugged, straitjacketed, locked in isolation and physically, emotionally and sometimes sexually abused.'

'And you're reminding me of this because?'

Billy leans forward in his chair. 'Keeping all of this out of the papers has required someone who understands the dark arts. I've been a bloody good gamekeeper, Bishop.' He throws the dossier on to Maureen's desk. 'I could become an even better poacher.'

*

It is later the same day. Sophie stands on the pavement outside the Cloak and Dagger. On the other side of the door she hears intermittent bursts of male groaning. The C&D, as it's popularly known, is a sports bar and England are playing Iceland in the knock-out stages of the European Championships. The beer may be of good report but this is no place for a single woman. Billy has sent a text message informing her he is 'at the back of the lunge'. It is unlike Billy to spell any word incorrectly, even on a text.

Fearing the worst, she gathers herself then pushes open the pub door, reminding herself to walk confidently past clusters of male drinkers. In her haste she bumps into one of them. He is tall, overweight and sporting another of those dreadful Viking beards. Looking her up and down he says there's no need to apologize, she looks lost, can he help? She politely declines the offer (lunge bar sounds just about right) and looks round nervously for Billy. There is no sign until a crumpled figure, pressed up against a jukebox, catches her eye.

'My God,' she says, arms like teapot handles. 'What's going on?'

'Ah,' slurs Billy. 'A familiar voice.'

'How many?' Sophie points to the glasses in front of him.

'Nowhere near enough.'

'It's becoming a habit.'

'You sound like Mrs Shearwater.'

'So she's become Mrs Shearwater?'

'I'm using the title while I can.'

Sophie shakes her head and pulls up a stool. Billy looks at his companion through glassy eyes. 'You could say I'm channelling Roy Orbison.' He smiles and taps the jukebox. 'Sitting opposite a pretty woman, far too attractive to be my daughter. But as for my life . . . it's over.' To the backdrop of derisory boos and catcalls at England's desperate display in Nice, he relates his meeting with Bishop Maureen.

Sophie sighs. 'And the outcome?'

'She's talking it over with Pettigrew.'

'And if he agrees with her?'

'You don't want me to sing the song, surely. Here, let me get you a drink.'

'No, no. I'd rather you didn't leave me alone, even for two minutes.' Sophie rolls eyes at the pub's clientele. 'Billy, it's easy for me to say but alcohol solves nothing.'

'It numbs the anger.'

'With me?'

Billy smiles. 'Of course not.'

'The bishop?'

'Oh, her, she's just doing her job. No, my anger is reserved for Godfrey Henderson. Hendo must have dumped me in it all those years ago. I was played. In fact, they all played me. The Pitchers and my own parents presumed I was responsible and didn't argue. And they did it by never telling me the exact date of your birth.'

'Third of March nineteen-sixty-eight.'

Billy nods. 'It means Lucy must have been expecting before I found her on Henry.'

Sophie shakes her head. 'I'm sorry, Billy. If only I'd left well alone, none of this would have happened.'

'And I would have spent the rest of my life marinating in guilt. But now, just like Emms, guilt has dropped me. Anger is my new and constant companion.'

Sophie shifts uncomfortably on her stool. 'Be honest, Billy, since we found out you're not my father there is nothing to keep us in touch with each other.'

'Oh, I see.' Billy stares into an empty glass. 'My feelings for you haven't changed. In fact, I am relieved the "i" word no longer hovers over us, much as I was proud to think of you as my daughter.'

'Yes, well . . . our moment has come and gone. I am still in recovery.'

'I am still in our moment.' Billy reaches for Sophie's hand. She resists the advance.

'Your feelings are for my mother, not me,' she says.

Billy sighs. 'In my current state of mind, I won't convince you otherwise. Instead I would suggest that, for the first time, we have a common objective.'

'To find my father?'

Billy nods. He runs a finger round the rim of an empty glass. 'Of course, you may want to call it a day.'

All around them, profanities grow louder and more intense as the national side finally capitulates to Iceland. TV cameras focus on England's players lying on the grass, distraught in defeat. 'I imagine the first person we need to find is Hendo,' says Sophie, at last.

Billy shrugs. 'I don't even know if he's still alive.'

'We could make enquiries.'

'I've already made them and drawn a blank. So have the BBC. They're still keen to film a Bishopsgate reunion. When they first suggested the idea I wasn't interested. But events over the past few weeks lead me to think it may be our one and only chance of flushing him out.'

A few minutes later they file out of the pub, behind a bunch of disillusioned football fans.

'I've said I'll help you, Billy,' says Sophie, as they climb into a taxi, 'but there's one thing you must understand. You haven't got rid of your guilt, just exported it. I no longer have any desire to find my father. It can only bring more pain. But I brought this mess on you and Emma and everybody else. Now I have to find a way to rid myself of your old friend.'

Chapter 42

Next morning Billy wakes to find himself on a settee. His settee. At least, he thinks it is. Everything else about the room seems different. The cushions! All the cushions have gone except the one he bought featuring Mevagissey harbour. Emms never liked it but then she has never liked Cornwall. The framed picture of Venice has disappeared. Emms bought that, after a holiday there with her close friends fifteen years ago. It had been on the wall so long there are dirty marks where the frame rested. The paint underneath is a fresher shade. The whole wall will need repainting. She must have taken half the room away with her yesterday. A burglar would leave the place in better shape. He saw none of this last night. For that matter, he can't remember even turning on the light when he got back from the Cloak and Dagger.

He resists the temptation to kick the few pieces of furniture left. He brews some coffee in the kitchen. There is a note on the fridge door. 'Delighted to hear Sophie isn't yours. Now she can be. Emms.' He swears, screws up the paper, throws it in the bin. He turns on the radio. Roy Hodgson is no longer manager of England. He considers how he once cared. He takes a shower and reaches for the shampoo. It's not there. Most of the towels have gone as well. He swears again. Surprisingly, the razor blades are intact. The shelf stacker uses a different make, obviously. He puts on yesterday's shirt. All his others need washing. He throws three of them in the washing machine. Oh, she's been good enough to leave the powder.

He checks his emails: a couple of journalists want to do a follow-up story on the revelations at Much Sumner. As yet, they have no idea he isn't Sophie's father after all. He dumps himself on the sofa and thinks of calling Emms but does he really want to get into a slanging match? He is angry. Livid is a better word. But he is not sure of the object of his anger. Is it Emms? Or the shelf stacker? Hendo even? Or is this self-loathing? He could contact

Beth but she will tell him he had it coming. Daughters always side with their mothers. He is tempted to text Sophie but she will be at work. And it's too desperate. Maybe there's an old friend or two he could call. Maybe not. He's let too many lapse over the years. In any case, why should they listen to his woes?

The phone rings. It is a withheld number, probably a journalist. No message is left. It wasn't that important, then. The phone rings again. He decides he must get away. A long way away this time, not just a local hotel. Somewhere remote. A deserted cliff will do but not Beachy Head. He isn't ready to jump. Yet. The Gower peninsula, perhaps. Maybe further up. Sophie has turned him on to North Wales but the coast is too tourist friendly. It has to be somewhere deserted. Sophie sang the praises of Pennan but he has a softer spot for *Local Hero*'s other main location, popularly known as Ben's Beach, where the old beachcomber scuppers the plans of oil tycoon Felix Happer. Billy checks on the internet. The location's real name is Camusdarach and it's out on the west coast of Scotland, some ten hours' drive. Perfect.

He pulls his newly washed shirts out of the tumble dryer and throws them in a suitcase, unironed. He drives to a small hotel just north of Glasgow, leaving early the following morning. A website tells him that Camusdarach 'sits in one of the most scenic parts of the Scottish Highlands, between Arisaig and Mallaig with great views over Eigg, Rum and Skye'. It is early afternoon when he reaches his destination. Puffy clouds drift casually across a rich, Scottish-blue sky. Camusdarach's sand is as white as a bride's dress, the sea a clear and glorious turquoise, bleeding into brilliant blues and greens. He stands on a grassy dune and inhales the smell of damp seaweed on a warm breeze. Dear God, this place is intoxicating. Somewhere around here is where they must have built Ben's rickety wooden hut. At the far end of the beach he sees the holiday house transformed into a church for the film. He is alone, except for a boy, maybe thirteen or fourteen, skimming stones at the water's edge. The boy, with tousled brown hair, sports an unrecognizable football shirt, probably some tiny Scottish club's away kit. Billy is loath to be seen talking to a minor in an isolated location. He ducks away but the boy has already spotted him.

'Hey, mister.'

Billy waves politely. Now the boy beckons Billy to join him. Billy shakes his head and begins walking away.

'Hey, mister, I need your help.' The boy points to a plaster cast on his leg and a pair of crutches lying on the sand. Billy looks round for the boy's parents, resenting the need for such caution. He sees no one. The boy points to a small stone in his hand. 'Any more up there, mister? Flat ones if you can find 'em.'

Billy smiles back. The request evokes fond memories of his childhood. 'I'll take a look.' For several minutes he scours an outcrop of rock where small pools of water fill and empty with the tide.

'Here you are,' he says, approaching the boy. 'Five smoothies. Go find Goliath.'

The boy stares at the new stones in his hand. 'Wow, these are perfect. I could get ten skips with these. It's a scientific fact that you can't get more than that.' He looks up at Billy, hand shielding his eyes from the sun. 'Are you an angel or something?'

Billy smiles. 'Damn. This jacket was supposed to hide my wings.'

'The thing is, you appeared from nowhere.'

'That's what angels are supposed to do.'

The boy shrugs. 'No one usually bothers to help.'

'So you come here often.'

'Only when I'm sent.'

'Who sends you?'

'I come from over there.' The boy points to a distant range of mountains then glances down at the plaster cast. 'But I haven't got out much recently.'

'I can't place your accent.'

'I've lived all over.'

'That looks a nasty break.'

The boy nods. 'The player who tackled me was built like . . .' He smiles. 'Goliath.'

'Goliath was over nine feet tall.'

'Not in the film, he wasn't.'

'I was thinking of the book.'

'What book?'

269

'The Bible.'

'There, I knew you were an angel. My name's Charles. Some people call me Chuck but I prefer Charlie.'

'I'm Billy.' They shake hands. Charlie skims four of Billy's five stones, but with a leg in plaster is unable to bend low enough for the ideal trajectory. His fifth and final throw results in eight skips, the best of the day. He smiles contentedly.

'Talking of films . . .' says Billy.

'You've come to the right place. This is Ben's Beach.'

'An impoverished beachcomber takes on the might of a giant oil baron and saves people from themselves, from their own greed. That was David versus Goliath, too.'

At first Charlie doesn't reply. He is looking out to sea, towards the Isle of Skye. 'I can deal with Goliath. Feeling angry or hurt about people is much harder.'

Billy takes a sideways look at Charlie. 'That's very profound.'

'For a kid?'

'For anyone.'

Charlie looks down at the plaster cast. 'The collision was so bad I won't be able to play competitively again. My career was over in an incident that lasted seconds. Trying to forgive someone for smashing up your future . . . it might take years. But if I don't want to end up crippled by bitterness, it's my only hope.'

Billy falls silent. Two seagulls screech and squabble overhead. A fishing boat sails slowly across the horizon. 'I've no idea if you're interested,' he says at last, 'but I've written a couple of books on the history of football. I've got them in the car. I'd like you to have them.'

'I don't have any money,' says Charlie.

'They're a gift. And when I get back I'll take your email address, if I may. I'd like to stay in touch.' With that Billy strides up and over the dunes, to where his car is parked, some three hundred yards away. He collects the books and walks back, to find the beach deserted.

*

That night he stays at a small hotel in nearby Mallaigmore where, sitting alone at the bar, he strikes up a conversation with a middle-aged American lawyer tracing his Scottish roots. The man's wife mentions how Donald Trump's mother was from the Hebridean island of Lewis and that her husband is proud to share the heritage of 'setch a wunnerful ma-an'. Unprovoked, Billy lays into Trump's politics of polemic and appalling excuse for a theology. He finds himself ranting at the couple and realizes, too late, that he is transferring his anger and frustration on people who are perfectly respectable, if misguided.

He checks out early next morning, anxious to avoid the couple over breakfast, and heads to Skye. He spends the day walking along part of the great ridge at Trotternish that bristles with stacks and pinnacles. The weather is uncommonly good. He doesn't have the gear to camp overnight, unlike many fellow walkers. However, there is still time to bag some glorious views over Staffin Bay and the Quiraing before heading back to his car. But still he seethes. Charlie's comments were perceptive but he was too young to understand how deeply things can go. He rehearses what he will say to Emms and the shelf stacker when he next sees them; and Hendo, if he ever gets the chance to confront him. He drives to a local bed and breakfast for the night but wakes several times, his pillow soaked in sweat.

Leaving the island in the morning, he considers driving even further north but before doing so, pulls into a lay-by. Three days have passed since he last turned on his mobile phone. It has been several years since he was incommunicado for this long. He considers the power of the device in his hand – friends and family who use it to flounce, vent or fish for compliments with narcissistic selfies. Yet the same device can be used to bring down corrupt governments, empower developing world farmers and locate survivors in the rubble of an earthquake.

He hesitates. He has wandered through Scotland in fake freedom, on the dark side of the technological moon. He now fears what information awaits him on his return to earth. At some point he must find out. He sighs. It might as well be now.

'You have twelve new messages . . .' Eight of them are routine. They include a couple from his publisher suggesting ideas for new books and one from a national newspaper asking him to write an article on famous footballers who got ordained at the end of their playing days. More significantly, Sophie has called. 'I can't seem to get hold of you anywhere,' she says. 'Please let me know you are OK.' Daughter Beth is less polite. 'Where the bloody hell are you? The least you could do is phone us and put our minds at rest.' There is much about her mother in Beth. The use of the word 'us' suggests Emms may have wound her up. It is the final voicemail, left just minutes before, that makes Billy turn the car smartly and head back south. It is from the BBC researcher.

'Hi, Canon Shearwater,' says the recording. 'I thought you'd like to know we've tracked down the surviving members of Second to None, along with Garry Kite and, believe it or not, the bouncing bard who recently had a double hip operation. All of them are coming to our reunion at the 4000 Holes in Blackburn. I know you'll be especially pleased we've located Godfrey Henderson, in China! He recently retired after teaching English as a foreign language for most of his life. He says he can't wait to meet up with everyone again.'

Chapter 43

Even before vinyl spun back into our lives in the late noughties, Martin Riley's 4000 Holes was well established as the go-to shop for hard-to-find records. Riley's only musical claim to fame was deputizing for the regular drummer in the Scooby Doos, a short-lived Manchester band. He did this on just one occasion: when they played support to the equally obscure Chosen Blue at Clacton-on-Sea. But in the same way great football players rarely become great managers, Riley was more than a beat ahead in recognizing that CDs would never be as collectable as 12-inch vinyl. It's best summed up in an interview he gave to the *Independent*: 'For a child of the 1960s, purchasing, then playing a new LP was a moment of high ritual. On returning from the record shop and with grave solemnity, he was duty bound to unveil the host from its gatefold sleeve, reverential palms touching only the vinyl's rim, and elevate it to the watching room. "Sit, listen. This is my new album . . ." Surface crackle before the first track called the faithful to humble and holy worship, like a peal of Sunday bells.'

The reputation of Riley's store spread far and wide. In spite of its location in the unfashionable town of Blackburn, Lancashire, collectors travelled hundreds of miles to the 4000 Holes. Artist signing sessions followed and, inevitably, the demand for a live venue where they could perform once again to their fans, devoted if diminishing in number. In another shrewd move, Riley spotted a nearby pub in terminal decline and, under the same title, turned it into a mecca for pre-loved (his phrase) pop, rock and folk artists and, more recently, their tribute acts.

The 4000 Holes: A Complete History lies unopened, however, in Billy's suitcase. His mind is on more than the venue's redoubtable history as his train nears Blackburn station.

'So, how are you going to play it?' says Sophie.

'Play what?' says Billy.

'Godfrey Henderson.'

'Hendo? By ear. See what he has to say for himself.'

'He may not broach the subject.'

'You've got to be kidding. As soon as he sees you, he'll click. I want to see his face.'

'You're sure he doesn't know I'm coming?'

'Certain. The BBC didn't want to put him off.'

'Well, thank you . . .'

Billy smiles. 'You know what I mean. If he'd got wind of an ambush, he'd have stayed in China. This could be the day you've been waiting for.'

Sophie shakes her head. 'I've already told you. No good can come from this. I'm only here to support you and absolve myself. I just hope I'm doing the right thing.'

They get off the train and take a taxi to the venue.

'Aye, quite a party goin' in there, by t' looks,' says the driver, writing a receipt for the fare. 'Summat to do with that posh BBC Four what-'ave-you.'

They walk into the 4000 Holes, past a scale model of the Albert Hall, and gape at walls adorned in alternative 1960s memorabilia. In one glass case hang a pair of black flares with split crotch, allegedly belonging to P. J. Proby. Displayed on a velvet cushion is the fly button Mick Jagger lost on stage during the Rolling Stones' 1969 tour, Jagger famously saying to the crowd, 'You don't want my trousers to fall down, now do ya?' Next to that are the remains of a TV thrown from the twelfth floor of a US hotel room by The Who. Reputedly.

'Ah, Billy and Sophie,' says Adrian, the BBC producer. 'We meet at last.' He shakes hands, warmly. 'Come and meet some of your old friends, Billy.' They walk through to the Green Room. 'This is Neil Price of Second to None. You'll remember him from Bishopsgate.'

Billy shakes Neil's hand. 'I've told countless people I was once on the same bill as Second to None. They don't believe I was ever that cool.'

Price smiles and gestures towards the woman standing next to Billy.

'Forgive me,' says Billy. 'This is Sophie. Sophie Daggert.'

'Unofficial PA for the day,' she says, quickly.

Price shakes her hand. 'Very pleased to meet you.' His eyes linger a little too long on her face and neck.

'And someone we used to call plain Garry,' says Adrian.

'Mr K!' Billy bows. 'Or should I say Lord Kite.'

'You're greeting the luckiest man alive,' says Kite. 'I owe it all to Cecil Henderson. It's so sad he didn't live to see this day. Is there any news on Godfrey?'

'The plane has been delayed,' says Adrian.

'His father was a wonderful man, a visionary,' says Kite. 'Cecil not only saw an opportunity, he made it happen.' He turns to Billy's companion. 'So you're Sophie. I've been looking forward to meeting you.'

'I have to admit, I'm a bit star-struck,' says Sophie. 'I've referenced several of your films in my classes.'

'That's very gratifying. You're a teacher, then?'

'Of English literature. And a big movie fan.'

'Very good. I believe that father and daughter were eventually brought together by a rocking horse!'

'Not exactly.' Sophie glances at Billy. 'Brought together but not as father and daughter.'

'Oh,' says Kite. 'I thought I'd read—'

'You did,' says Billy. 'But incompatible blood groups rule that out, apparently.'

'All a bit of a shock,' says Sophie.

'Yes . . . yes, I can imagine. Quite a surprise.' Kite shakes his head. 'I was sad to read your mother had died so young, Sophie. She led us a merry old dance at Bishopsgate, as I recall.'

Billy smiles. 'But taking Godfrey's place in the band is something I've dined out on ever since, so I can't complain.' He glances at Sophie. 'Like you, we're particularly keen to see Godfrey again.'

Adrian returns and calls the room to attention. 'I'm sure there's loads more to catch up on, folks, but we really need to go through what we've planned.' A scaled-down version of a 1960s 'happening' is what Adrian has planned. Strewn across the floor in the venue's main function room are tyres and sawdust; on the stage, a trampette.

'We wanted to be entirely authentic and introduce a huge vulva but abandoned the idea,' he says. 'On a BBC budget, it had to be less than a metre high. All a bit Spinal Tap, I'm afraid.'

Of the surviving cast from Bishopsgate, only Second to None will perform. Garry Kite, now in his mid-seventies and mildly arthritic, will introduce a range of new performers, including flame throwers and another bouncing bard who performs poetry from a trampette. Young people, drawn from the locality and dressed in retrospective 1960s gear, will form the audience. The rest of the Big Top cast, like Billy, are lined up to comment on the show for the BBC4 documentary, discussing the cultural influence of Bishopsgate 1967 and the ensuing Summer of Love. Sophie offers the original programme to Adrian.

'Excellent,' he says. 'We can make great use of that.' As he is speaking, a traditional Indian music group arrives with sitar, tabla and flute. Filming gets under way, which for any TV show means a lot of stop, start, repeat, stop, start, repeat – and waiting around, endlessly. In between takes, Sophie offers to buy Garry Kite a drink at the bar.

He nods. 'But strictly fruit juice. Haven't touched a drop of alcohol in more than a decade.'

'Really? What prompted you to give it up?' Sophie glances sideways at Billy.

'I've seen too many friends get drinker's nose.' Kite points to the equipment dotted around the 4000 Holes. 'These ultra hi-def cameras show no mercy.'

'I can imagine.' Sophie studies Kite's profile. 'I have to say, I can't see one thread vein.'

'Well, thank you.'

'Of course, our ears and noses never stop growing.'

Kite nods. 'That's especially true in men, which is why some of my old colleagues' faces look out of proportion on TV these days. And we sag over the years, too.' They sit together at the bar. 'That old programme you have from Bishopsgate bears cruel testimony to the passage of time.'

Sophie studies the page featuring a young, ebullient trapeze artist. 'Nice pic. Your hair was very cool.'

Kite laughs. 'I was well behind the times. I didn't drop the pompadour until the early seventies.'

'So, a humble trapeze artist ends up a lord of the realm,' says Sophie. 'Topping the bill must be second nature to you.'

Kite smiles. 'I'd like to think it will inspire more young people to make a name for themselves. I remember Cecil saying that Billy could have made it as a musician. Where is he, by the way?'

'Over there,' says Sophie. Billy has positioned himself as near to the front door of the venue as possible. Kite beckons him to join them.

'Stay cool, Billy,' says Sophie, quietly.

Billy shrugs. 'I'm just hanging around, like everyone else.'

'But you look like a bouncer.'

Moments later, a portly man steps cautiously through the door in an ill-fitting dark blue blazer with white trim, university scarf, straw boater – and long, white sideburns.

'Hendo!'

'Billy? My God, you look just like your mum.'

'And you're a ringer for your old man.'

'Couldn't imagine being this ancient back then, could we? Wow. It's good to see you again. Seriously.' They shake hands vigorously. Over Billy's shoulder, Hendo catches sight of Sophie. 'Bloody hell! This just has to be . . . your daughter.'

Sophie smiles and shakes his hand. 'Lucy's daughter, yes. Billy's no.'

'You were . . . her second child, then.'

'First.'

'But I thought—'

'It's complicated.'

'Well, I can see I've got a lot of catching up to do.' He studies the venue. 'This place! These kids, all kitted out! The BBC weren't joking.'

'A pretty good copy of the Big Top, eh?' says Kite.

Hendo nods. 'Dad would be proud.'

'It's good to see you again, Godfrey.'

'You too, *Lord* Kite.' They shake hands.

'Come now, it's not that big a deal. I'm still the same old Garry who visited your house many times when you were a young boy.'

A production assistant introduces herself and takes Hendo and Kite to the Green Room. His overweight frame lists to the left as he walks.

'He played that well,' murmurs Billy.

'I don't see any resemblance,' says Sophie.

'You don't look like anyone except your mother. It's uncanny.'

But Sophie doesn't reply. She has picked up the Bishopsgate programme and is studying it intently.

*

Introduced by Garry Kite, a range of solo artists and bands revisit Bishopsgate in Blackburn, with Second to None topping the bill. The bouncing bard mark II reads her poetry, with attendants standing by the trampette: health and safety has come a long way since 1967. Without the benefit of joints and hallucinatory drugs, the audience is more baffled than blown away. But Adrian is happy. He has the pictures he was looking for. To camera, Billy gives his opinion of the 1960s and their legacy. Garry Kite reminisces about his long career. Neil Price compares the music scene, then and now. The two bouncing bards compare poems. Hendo eulogizes about his ground-breaking father. It's a wrap.

As the equipment is packed away, Neil Price strikes up a conversation with Sophie. Billy catches Hendo's eye and lifts an imaginary glass to his lips. Hendo nods and joins him at the bar. Garry Kite is already there, talking shop with Adrian. Billy and Hendo exchange histories, finding out what happened to friends and family. Inevitably, the subject turns to Lucy Pitcher.

'I never said how sorry I was you had to go through all that,' says Hendo.

Billy stares at him. 'I'm wondering why I had to go through it at all. I wasn't Sophie's father.'

'It must have been quite a shock to discover that, after all these years.'

'For me, yes, but not for you.'

Hendo frowns. 'What are you implying? You don't think I—'

'Well, someone took my school jumper, a book and a necklace and put them in Lucy's drawer. Stitched up like a kipper, I was.'

278

'But I didn't . . . I mean, it wasn't me, I promise you.'

'As DNA is your judge?'

'Here.' Hendo performs a mock cheek swab. 'Look, Billy, you need to know why Lucy and I had that huge row on the morning of Bishopsgate.' He pauses. 'She discovered me with someone else – Tony, the drummer.'

Billy looks at his old school friend in complete disbelief. 'You mean . . .'

Hendo nods. 'I liked Lucy a whole lot but I used her as cover. You had to be careful in those days. I wasn't careful enough. She caught us in the Munton Moffett van, *in flagrante delicto*.'

'Fuck me,' says Billy, under his breath.

Hendo smiles. 'If only.'

Billy finishes his brandy in two gulps. 'Well, if it wasn't you . . . Sophie and I are totally stumped.' He asks Sophie for the original Big Top programme. 'Lucy left this in Henry's saddle.'

Hendo thumbs through its pages. 'And you're thinking someone in here dumped you in it.'

'We've nothing much else to work with, except the painting of a child dangling a piece of string.' He points to Neil Price who is locked in conversation with Sophie. 'I have to say, he mentally undressed Sophie when he saw her earlier.'

Hendo shakes his head. 'Unlikely. Lucy never made it to the Big Top so I don't think she even met him. It has to be someone much closer to home.'

'Cecil Henderson.' Startled, Billy and Hendo turn to see Garry Kite, back to the bar, hands in pockets, staring thoughtfully into the distance. 'Your father was a lovely man, Godfrey, but he couldn't keep his hands off the young wannabes. They played along because he could make them stars.'

Hendo gapes at Kite. 'You're saying my father had . . . with . . . ? I can't believe that.'

'Remember those long hours he spent in his London office?'

'Yes, but . . . Dad and Lucy? It doesn't bear thinking about.'

'Rumours spread that he had got a fifteen-year-old into trouble,' says Kite. 'I seem to remember he offered to pay for an abortion but the young girl, Lucy I presume, insisted on having the baby, so he needed a scapegoat. It was a long time ago and I could be completely wrong but that's what I remember.'

Billy gazes silently at the floor. 'You're saying that she already knew she was expecting that afternoon. And I . . . I was naive enough to think—'

'That she loved you? She was under pressure from a very powerful man, Billy. I have no idea if Cecil forced himself on her, but even if he did the police wouldn't have believed her. Dozens of children tried to blow the whistle on Jimmy Savile. By the time anyone took any notice, he was dead. Presenters like Savile are the usual targets because they are well known. But there's a whole batch of people like Cecil, in the same circles but under the media radar, who got up to all sorts of tricks, too, and they will continue to get away with it because they aren't so famous.'

Billy shakes his head. 'For all these years the guilt has defined me. And I discover it was Mr Henderson, all along.'

Kite puts an arm round Billy. 'Cecil was very persuasive and charming but he could be ruthless, too. You didn't stand a chance, Billy. Don't be too hard on yourself.'

'I wish you'd told me before.'

'It only came back to me when I read about Sophie in the papers and I thought it best to let sleeping dogs lie. Overhearing your conversation, though, made me think it was time you knew the truth.'

Billy turns to Hendo who has sat down on a barstool. 'You've gone very pale,' he says.

Hendo's breathing is laboured. 'I think we both need another brandy.'

'Let me buy this round,' says Kite. 'It might be wise to tell Sophie her search is over.'

Billy beckons to Sophie who apologizes to Neil Price for breaking off their conversation. She joins Billy, Hendo and Kite at the bar.

'If you haven't had enough shocks already, prepare yourself for another.' Billy points to Hendo. 'Meet your half-brother.'

Sophie stares at Hendo, then Billy. 'Is this a joke?'

'They're being deadly serious,' says Kite. 'Tell me what you want to drink and I'll tell you what I know . . .'

*

An hour later, three people are left at the bar. Hendo, still in a state of intense shock, has taken a taxi to his hotel.

'Life hasn't treated him kindly,' says Billy. 'And this revelation isn't going to help.'

Sophie is holding the Bishopsgate programme tightly. 'I am struggling to get my head round all this. We're missing something, I'm sure. It doesn't make sense.'

Billy glances at his watch. 'Whatever the case, I suggest we call it a day and worry about it tomorrow. I'll phone for a cab.'

'No need,' says Kite, raising a hand. 'I drove up from London and we're in the same hotel.' They head out of the venue to Kite's 1961 Austin Healey 3000. Billy low whistles at the green-and-cream-coloured convertible.

'A little classic and a big indulgence,' grins Kite. It is parked in a reserved space, close to the pub's main entrance. Kite gets into the driver's seat. Billy, aware that the car is old enough not to require seat belts, climbs into the back of the car, next to Sophie. Kite fires the ignition and eases the car out of the car park on to the main road, then speeds out of town on a dual carriageway. Billy stares out of the car window at unfamiliar streets.

'I found Mr Henderson very friendly and encouraging,' he says. 'It's upsetting to discover his dark side.'

'After Lucy, you went into the Church, then?' says Kite.

Billy nods. 'It was my way of doing time for what I'd done.'

'Well, you need to stop beating yourself up. We all make mistakes.'

Billy shrugs. 'The one good thing that has come out of it all is Sophie.'

'You mean Lucy mark two?' Kite looks at her in his rear-view mirror.

'For me she's Sophie mark one,' says Billy. They both look for a reaction from Sophie. Oblivious to the conversation, she is staring intently at a photo in the Bishopsgate programme.

'Talking of the sixties, I'll never forget getting stranded three and a half miles off the coast, on one of those pirate radio ships,' says Kite. 'I arrived one weekend as a special guest. I was there to be interviewed as an up-and-coming film producer. However, that weekend the weather was so bad and the seas so rough, no one could travel from shore to ship. The station manager, who had been broadcasting live for more than six hours, was exhausted. He virtually threw the microphone at me and said, "You're a natural. Play what you like until the A team arrive." So, anyway . . .'

Surreptitiously, Sophie digs Billy in the ribs. She points to the photo of a young Garry Kite in the Bishopsgate programme, in particular the outline of his nose. She then gestures discreetly in the direction of her own nose. It is only small but Garry of 1967 has the same distinct ridge, in exactly the same place; a ridge no longer visible on Lord Kite.

Sophie looks at Billy. Billy looks back at Sophie.

'It was the first time I had ever received fan mail.' Kite is gathering speed on a dual carriageway. 'Me! Fan mail—'

'When did you have a nose job?' cuts in Sophie.

'When did I . . . well, I . . . why are you asking?'

'Just curious.'

Kite glances at himself in the rear-view mirror. 'No one else has ever noticed.'

'When did you have it done?'

'I can't remember exactly . . . nineteen-seventy-one, I think. I had chronic sinusitis. The doctor said the corrections would improve my breathing.'

'I don't believe you.'

'You don't *believe* me?' Kite fixes Sophie in the mirror. 'What's this all about?'

Sophie holds up the picture. 'You wanted to get rid of a little ridge. A ridge identical to this one here.' She points to her own nose. 'It wasn't good enough for the publicity pictures.'

'What is this . . . what are you implying?'

'You know full well. I've spent most of the evening wondering where I'd seen you before. It was in the fucking mirror.'

'You think I'm . . . ? Don't be ridiculous. It's been a long day.'

'And the picture of the sad little girl,' says Sophie. 'The one I found in Henry's saddle. She is trailing a piece of string along the ground with bunting on it.'

'Something on the end of the string has blown away and left her on her own to face the music.' Billy leans forward and says calmly:

'Lord Kite, at the risk of sounding like Jeremy Kyle, did you or did you not fuck Lucy Pitcher in nineteen-sixty-seven?'

'Of course I did.' The speed and smoothness of his reply is breathtaking. 'I am amazed it's taken you fifty years to work it out. And you can hardly blame me, can you? She was just like her daughter, bloody gorgeous.'

'Oh, my God,' says Sophie.

'And just a child,' says Billy.

'That didn't stop you either, did it, Canon Shearwater?' says Kite. 'But then it was good training for the priesthood. Anyway, people are obsessed with the age of consent. What were the sixties if they weren't about throwing away the Victorian rulebook?'

Billy's whole body simmers with rage. 'And you quietly got up to your tricks when you went out looking for Lucy that day, when she was at her most vulnerable.'

'Now that's the hopeless romantic in you.' Kite puts his foot hard on the accelerator. He is touching 70 in a 40 mph zone. 'You've spent your life with a distorted image of the perfect girl next door, Shearwater. Accept the truth. Lucy wasn't the sweet little virgin of your boy-next-door dreams. She wanted it. I wanted it.'

'But you didn't want me,' says Sophie, quietly. 'And you dumped the guilt on that boy next door.'

'Then blamed a so-called friend who cannot answer back,' says Billy. 'You're despicable.'

'I'm a survivor.' Kite is fast approaching a major road junction, a quarter of a mile from Merfield Court Hotel. He swerves to narrowly avoid a cyclist.

'And an evil bastard.'

'God knows,' says Sophie. 'The only place for you is jail.'

Billy nods. 'And I'd love to turn you in . . .'

Chapter 44

Discharged from hospital after two days, Sophie is back in the same building, sitting next to an unconscious Billy. It is four days since the accident in Blackburn and the death of Garry Kite. She sighs and picks up a dog-eared version of *Under Milk Wood*. The words are rich and hypnotic. As she reads she hears Richard Burton in her head. It is the second time she has begun at the beginning of the Dylan Thomas classic in the past twenty-four hours.

There were moments during the first reading when she thought she saw Billy's eyes flutter: a sign he may be recovering consciousness. Probably wishful thinking. She has done most of the things you should do when visiting someone in a coma: announce your name on arrival, tell the person about your day, sing the odd song, read a passage from a book. She has even held Billy's hand, though she hasn't taken up the suggestion of stroking his skin.

Many times she has explained to students how this 'play for voices' is a sort of Welsh *Groundhog Day*: one period of twenty-four hours, endlessly repeating itself. Parked in a basic hospital chair, she has never experienced so many uneventful minutes turning slowly into hours.

She has always found something transcendent and mesmerizing in the words of the Welshman. As one critic said: 'Thomas conscripts metaphors, rapes the dictionary and builds a verbal bawdy-house where words mate and couple on the wing, like swifts.' Maybe Billy will respond to it all on another level of consciousness. Halfway through the second rendition, Jack Staniscliffe calls her mobile.

'How is the patient?' he asks.

'No longer in intensive care but still out for the count.'

'Has his wife been to see him?'

'Of course. Why do you ask?'

'It's just . . . you don't need any more stress right now, what with the coroner ordering a post-mortem.'

'I've given the police a statement.'

'Do you have a solicitor?'

Sophie hesitates. 'Kite was travelling far too fast in a forty-mile zone. That's all there was to it. Billy and I, we're lucky to be alive.'

'And the police are happy with that?'

'Well, they've insinuated that one of us may have caused the accident.'

'Which is why you need a solicitor. You'll have to make a statement at the inquest and the results of the post-mortem will be critical.'

'Now you're just trying to scare me.'

'That isn't why . . . I'm not . . . I'm worried about you.'

'You needn't worry.'

'I do worry. You're obviously . . .'

'Obviously what?'

'In love with Billy.'

'I'm . . . *what?*'

'I sensed an attraction when he first came to the college.'

'Jack, how can you say that? For weeks I thought he was my father.'

'Not at first you didn't. And after the latest revelations, you're . . . well, you're at the hospital more often than his wife.'

'There's a reason for that.'

'You're in love with him.'

'No, you don't understand. And even if it was true, and it isn't, why does it concern you?' There is a brief silence. 'Wait a minute. Ginny.'

Jack hesitates momentarily. 'What about her?'

'Is she still . . . I mean . . . are you still . . . together?'

There is another short silence. Then: 'She's returned to Abidjan.'

'That explains it.'

'You think I'm jealous of Billy?'

'Only you can answer that.'

'I care about you.'

'Then you'll give me time to work this through.'

'I . . . don't want to lose you.'

'You can always find another teacher.'

'No, I mean lose you, out of my life.'

'I'm not in your life, Jack, not in that way, and anyway this isn't the time—'

'But it's never the time, is it?' Jack rings off, abruptly: another savage gear change. Shaken, Sophie switches off the phone and puts it on Billy's bedside cabinet. She buries her head in her hands.

'Oh God, oh God . . .' At first, she doesn't notice the door open slowly.

'Sophie, you're here again. What's wrong?'

'Emms.' Sophie gathers herself. 'It's nice to see you.'

Emms hugs Sophie. 'You've been through a nasty accident, love. You need to look after yourself. If you're not careful, you'll be back here, in a bed of your own. Let me get you a coffee.'

Emms returns and the two women swap medical notes.

'The consultant says he could be in a coma for weeks,' says Sophie. 'He might wake up gradually and be very agitated.'

'With me, but not you,' says Emms.

Sophie frowns. 'Why do you say that?'

'He adores you. You connected straight away.'

'He thinks you've been palming him off on me.'

'I haven't had to.'

'I'm not a marriage wrecker, Emms.'

'You can't wreck a wreck.'

'He still loves you.'

Emms shrugs. 'He's just stubborn. He doesn't like change. I'm a habit.'

'That's not true.'

'More importantly.' Emms looks long and hard at Sophie. 'Are you in love with him?'

Sophie looks away. 'Not you, too.'

'What do you mean? Who else . . . ?'

'I told you, I don't break up marriages. I'm here because I have brought all this on you both. I feel so guilty.'

'You haven't answered my first question.'

'It makes no difference.'

'It makes all the difference.'

'Only if you intend to act on it.'

286

They fall silent.

'Are you anywhere nearer finding your father?' says Emms, eventually.

Sophie rolls her eyes. 'You could say that's died a death. Billy was sure this Hendo friend of his was the culprit but he denies it. He's also gay. I don't think we'll ever know who was to blame.'

Emms holds her hand. 'You've no need to feel guilty, Sophie. Discovering the truth has liberated me and I'm grateful to you for that.'

'But you and Billy . . .'

Emms shrugs. 'He brought this on himself.'

'But he didn't. I was responsible.'

'Not for what happened fifty years ago.'

'He was fifteen.'

'He lied to me for decades.'

'You must understand why.'

Emms fixes Sophie with another long stare. 'You *are* in love with him.'

'I don't know what I think and how I feel any more. Here, it's your turn.' She sighs, stands and hands Emms her copy of *Under Milk Wood*. 'I'd got to the point where Lord Cut-Glass talks about his sixty-six clocks, one for each year of his life. I'll end up just as much of a loony if I sit here much longer.'

Chapter 45

When Jack phoned today I was tempted to disclose what really happened in Blackburn. I dare not tell him, though, or anyone else for that matter.

I thought the whole incident was as good as over after the police interview but Jack has unnerved me about needing a solicitor. It seems a cyclist saw someone lean towards Kite from the back seat of the Austin Healey, arms flailing, as if an argument was going on. When the police sergeant confronted me, I said I was trying to get Kite to slow down. But I was lying. It wasn't me at all. It was Billy who grabbed Kite, causing the accident. Kite's long-standing deceit was hard enough for Billy to take and the way he blamed Cecil Henderson was unforgivable. But Kite's casual, dismissive admission of having sex with Lucy really was more than Billy could bear. The red mist came down. He grabbed Kite: a foolish thing to do but you can hardly blame him. My 'confession' was a spur-of-the-moment thing. The police sergeant, I forget his name but it begins with 'P', wasn't entirely convinced by my account, I have to admit.

Of course, if Billy recovers consciousness and tells them the truth, we are both in trouble. That's why I have been at his bedside beyond the call of duty. I really need to be there before he spills the beans. I'm not sure why I said what I said to the police. I feel an overwhelming sense of guilt for causing all this and my admission was probably a form of self-absolution. As it stands, there is no obvious motive for Billy's attack. However, if the police find out that Kite was my father and that he stitched up Billy all those years ago, everything changes.

And if all this wasn't enough, within minutes of each other, two people probe me about my feelings for Billy and come to the same conclusion: I am in love with him. Am I? Am I really? Did I lie to the police because I am in love with him? It's true that I couldn't bear to see him go to prison for attacking the man who messed up his life. But in the split-second before he lashed out, I looked at him and he looked at me. We were thinking the same thing. I'm not sure it was love but in that moment we were united in our loathing of Lord Garry Kite. If Billy hadn't grabbed him round the neck I might have done the same. I wouldn't have wished Kite dead but feel nothing but contempt for him now, though I dare not tell anyone why.

My only regret is that because of his demise I never got to know any more about my mother. I hoped that my father might fill in the missing pieces of the Lucy Pitcher jigsaw. Perhaps Kite knew what happened to her. Perhaps he didn't know or care.

All of which reminds me that I've had another email from Clive Lacey from Saffron Walden.

Dear Mrs Daggert

I think you may have overlooked an email I sent you a few weeks ago. Being IT manager for a grown-up technical college they now call a university, I am used to being ignored until about 11 p.m., when I get calls asking me, 'Where the hell are you, the wretched thing won't boot up?' So I'm not offended. Close friends (you'll not be surprised to know I have only a few) tell me I define the term nerd. My acne, though not as virulent as in those long-lamented teenage years, still threatens to flare up during trying circumstances involving CRMs, meta tags and carrier aggregations. And I never disown the whiff of stale odour escaping from my armpit. It is proof positive I have the geeky skills to fix a crashed Apple or two.

Why am I writing again to you in this rambling and incoherent way? It's because I am at work and bored. And there's a limit to the number of *Star Trek* clips you can watch in between calls from students who have forgotten their passwords (again) and for whom getting their dissertations in by 4 p.m. is 'a matter of life and death . . . you're my only hope . . . pretty please . . . begging you!'

Where was I? Yes . . . I wrote to you originally, following several reports in the papers about your mother, believed to be Lucy Pitcher. My Uncle Roger knew Lucy in the late 1960s. Roger is no longer with us but I can tell you what I know, if you wish. I imagine you have been deluged with sightings of Lucy, from nutters drawn by photos of your good self in the newspapers. I can only hope that the tone of this particular missive persuades you that I, conversely, am entirely cogent and sane.

Sincerely

Clive Lacey
IT Manager
Ledchester University

After another trying day, this email made me laugh. It is so bizarre that I am going to have to ring this Clive Lacey tomorrow to make sure it is just a wind up.

Chapter 46

Sophie phones Clive Lacey. 'Your email, it was . . . creative.'

'I'm not paid to be creative.' Lacey is deadpan, matter-of-fact. 'I'm paid to develop and implement policies and procedures for electronic data processing and computer systems operations, ensuring all data complies with legal regulations. And you have beautiful eyes.'

Sophie laughs. 'I . . . you've never met me.'

'From the photograph in the paper.'

'Oh, well . . . thank you.'

'But I sense I've made them glaze over with my reply.'

'No . . . no. We all rely on IT though some of us struggle with machines that crash but never burn.'

'Very good. I like that line.'

'Anyway, you shouldn't be so down on yourself. I read somewhere about a Geek Pride Day.'

Lacey brightens. 'My niece bought me a pair of Chewbacca slippers in celebration. They emit two different Wookiee roars when you walk.'

'That sounds . . .'

'Sad.'

Sophie chuckles. 'I never quite got *Star Wars*. That was Daggert's bag.'

'Daggert?'

'My late husband. He was a big fan. He said a theme in one of the films was nature proving superior to technology.'

'When the Ewoks rise up against the empire on Endor?'

'I've no idea.'

'Despite the primitive nature of the Ewoks' weapons – sticks, stones, arrows and spears – they defeat the Imperial troopers. George Lucas was alluding to the Vietnam War, in which the less technologically advanced side was ultimately victorious.'

'Now that's interesting. I like films that reference political issues. I often use them in class.'

'Yes, the paper says you're a teacher.'

'Now *your* eyes will glaze over.'

'Teachers are a big part of my unimpressive life. One more won't harm.'

'Mr Lacey ...'

'It's Clive.'

'Clive, why are you so ... so *Eeyore*?'

Clive lowers and slows his voice to sombre. 'Gaiety. Song and dance. Here we go round the mulberry bush.'

Sophie wedges the handset in the crook of her neck and claps. 'A direct quote pulled from thin air! You're too well read to be unexciting.'

'You're not the first person to say that, I'll admit, but you want to know about Lucy, not Eeyore.'

'I'm all ears.'

'Like Eeyore,' they say in unison and laugh.

'As far as I know, Uncle Roger, surname Tyler, first met your mother in Hyde Park in July nineteen-sixty-nine,' says Clive. 'It was the night before the free Rolling Stones concert and Roger and his university friends bagged a spot on the grass near the stage. They knew it was going to be packed the next day so they got there very early.

'It grew darker and colder and they had no more than the summer clothes they stood up in, so they made a bonfire out of deck-chairs and broke branches off several trees to feed the flames. At some point, a young girl said she was cold and asked if she could join them round the fire. Being lads, they welcomed her into the group. Roger said his friends were quite straight but this young girl turned them on to some seriously freaky substances.'

'That sounds like my mother!'

'Yes, well, I seem to recall Roger saying he was spaced out next day, for the whole of what was an all-afternoon gig, I think. The last thing he remembered was Mick Jagger coming on in a white dress and seeing thousands of butterflies flying around. He couldn't recall anything after that. Roger told me he adored Lucy but there was something very lost and preoccupied about her. The following month they ended up at the Isle of Wight festival together.'

'The British Woodstock.'

'So they say. On the way there she told Roger she had given birth to a baby girl about eighteen months before. The baby had been taken away for adoption and she reckoned she would never get over it. She was very tearful. Roger was shocked because she was still so young. Lucy then spent a lot of the festival getting high.' Clive pauses. 'Have you ever taken LSD, Sophie? Sorry, maybe that's being a bit intrusive.'

Sophie laughs. 'I'm too much of a coward.'

'That's very sensible.'

'Boring, more like.'

'Seriously, don't do it.'

'Hmmm. I sense a wayward, indulgent side to the world's dullest IT manager.'

'Put it this way,' says Clive, hesitantly. 'I saw a castle in the sky that shone as it revolved. I conversed intelligently with an oak tree and when I went to the bathroom, the tiles melted in front of me. My clothes felt as if they were made of liquid sunshine. And it's a challenge working out a bus timetable when all you can see is a set of oscillating black blobs.'

'It sounds a lot of fun.'

'I was one of the lucky ones.'

Clive explains how his uncle took Lucy to the Isle of Wight specifically to hear Bob Dylan, her favourite artist. It was to be the singer's first live performance for more than three years. To play the festival, Dylan snubbed Woodstock, taking place in his own backyard in New York State. Some 150,000 people invaded the Isle of Wight, among them Roger and Lucy. Controversy surrounded Dylan's appearance. He came on two hours later than scheduled and played only for an hour or so, to the disappointment of many in the crowd. One person wasn't disappointed.

'Lucy was already in love with "Mr Tambourine Man" before the festival,' explains Clive. 'After the gig, Roger said she kept singing the words over and over again, like a mantra, all that stuff about being near the sea and dancing out of her head, beneath a sky of diamonds, like a mad thing.'

The next morning they went for a walk towards the Needles, a famous ridge of steeply dipping chalk.

'Apparently, it was a beautiful day,' says Clive, 'and though the holiday season was in full swing, hardly anyone was around. He had no idea Lucy had dropped more acid. If she had been on a bad trip, he would have taken her away from the cliffs overlooking Scratchell's Bay but she had shown no signs of it.

'He went in search of a place to have a coffee. Lucy didn't follow him. One minute she was singing about dancing beneath the diamond sky, the next minute she just wasn't there. Roger spent several minutes looking for her. He heard a commotion in the distance and eventually saw her body at the bottom of a cliff. He heaved up with shock. At first he thought she had slipped, then supposed it was suicide, given the fragile nature of her mind. However, the coroner found significant traces of LSD in her bloodstream as well as alcohol. It wasn't the first time some-body taking LSD had jumped from a great height, thinking they could fly. The verdict was accidental death from a fatal fall while under the influence of drugs. I have some press cuttings following the inquest and a few photos that Roger took of the two of them at the festival, if you would like to see them.'

'Yes . . . yes, I would.'

'The incident haunted Roger for the rest of his life. I'm so sorry to have to tell you such a sad tale.'

'That's . . . that's OK.'

'Are you all right?'

'Not really, but I'll get over it, as I have had to do with everything connected with my natural parents.' They fall silent. On a tree in Sophie's back garden a grey squirrel leaps effortlessly from branch to branch. It shows no fear of falling.

'If you like I'll send you all the information I have in the post,' says Clive, at last. 'Or I could give you the bits and pieces personally and have a look at that misbehaving computer of yours.'

Sophie brightens. 'Yes, come for a meal on Saturday. My grand-son is staying overnight but if you can put up with a highly energetic seven-year-old, already a *Star Wars* fan, you would be very welcome.'

'Does he play games on your computer? I could bring a couple of new ones for him.'

'He'll be on the computer all day, if I'm not careful.'

'Well now, I think there's a way to prevent that.'

'What's his name?'

'David.'

'Ha! Even better.'

*

Two hours later, after she receives a phone call that Billy is showing clear signs of recovering consciousness, Sophie heads to the hospital. She has several things to talk to him about: events leading up to the crash in Blackburn, the death of her mother and the fact that she is in love with Canon William Shearwater.

Chapter 47

It is moonless and starless in his bible-black, bandaged world. Drifting and dreaming, he lies as deathly dark as a domino. Only he can see Mrs Pitcher's severe bun, Nicholas Ledgard's Adam's apple, Lord Kite's reconditioned nose. Only he can hear the velvet voice of Kenneth Wolstenholme, the skim and swish of Charlie's stones, the screech and squeal of Austin Healey tyres. Only he can smell the fusion of Emms's Eau de Parfum and warm duplicator ink. Only he can touch her teenage skin, mesmerizing and marble smooth. Only he can cry 'Man overboard' and shipwreck in her thighs. Time passes. Time passes. Dawn inches up. Slowly he surfaces from a sleep that has lasted not five days but fifty years. He does not feel agitated. His body aches but his mind is focused. He is no longer confused. He is elated. William Shearwater has been born again.

Sophie sees Billy's eyes open for the first time. She marks a page in *Under Milk Wood* and rests the book on a bedside cabinet.

'Sophie?' Billy turns his head slowly, his voice a hoarse whisper.

'Thank God! You recognize me.'

Billy closes his eyes and appears to drift off to sleep again. It is two minutes before he says slowly: 'I know it's you . . . but . . . I keep seeing Richard Burton.'

Sophie laughs. 'Sorry, I can't do the accent.' She is about to ask him what he remembers of the crash when a nurse bustles in, suggesting firmly that her patient needs more time to recover before any sort of meaningful conversation can take place. Sophie withdraws, but before she does so kisses Billy on the cheek and squeezes his hand.

*

She returns the following evening, to find him propped up in bed. There are signs of activity on the bedside cabinet. A book. A newspaper.

'Sophie! At last.' His voice is still weak.

'I was here yesterday.'

'So it wasn't another dream.'

'You look so much better.'

'They tell me I am well on the road to recovery.'

While a male orderly pours a cup of tea at the end of the bed, Sophie tells Billy her version of events leading up to the accident.

Billy looks puzzled. 'You're sure that's what happened?'

'Absolutely.'

'As far as I recall—'

'You saw me lean forward, trying to get Kite to slow down.' Sophie squeezes Billy's hand firmly and stares at him.

'But—'

'No buts.' She rolls her eyes at the orderly.

'Yes, well, it was all very confusing.'

'Very.' The orderly rattles his trolley to the next bed. 'I told the police exactly what happened, too,' says Sophie, quietly. 'I was trying to prevent an accident.'

'The police?'

'Someone on a pushbike saw me move towards Kite just before the crash. There'll be an inquest.'

'Yes . . . yes, of course.' Billy leans towards her, wincing in pain. 'But it was me. Why are you doing this?'

'Because I . . .' Sophie hesitates, then says quietly: 'You've already served a fifty-year sentence for that bastard. Being sent down for manslaughter, it's not going to happen.'

'But it's a lie.'

Sophie nods. 'You would have been proud of me.'

Billy leans back. 'I can't let you take the blame.'

'You can and you must, or we are both in trouble. Have you told anyone else your version of events?'

'I began to tell Emms yesterday but I wasn't making much sense.'

'Good. Anyone else?'

'No.'

'And does she know Kite was my father?'

'She thought I was delirious.'

297

'And you were, because if they find out what happened all those years ago we would both have a motive to do away with him.'

'I didn't mean to do it,' Billy whispers. 'One minute we were talking away in the back seat of the car, the next minute I was here.'

'It was the same for Roger Tyler,' says Sophie. 'One moment Lucy was by his side, the next . . . I'd better begin at the beginning.'

*

Billy wells up as Sophie finishes recounting Lucy's demise.

'I'm sorry. It was insensitive of me to tell you at this time,' she says.

'I'm glad you did. Believe me, these are tears of relief.' He reaches out for Sophie's hand. 'I had some vivid dreams before I recovered consciousness. They say you see your life flash before you when you're drowning. It was like that, except Charlie, the young lad I met at Camusdarach, was my guide. He didn't say anything. He was just there, skimming stones. As I was waking up I remembered what he said on the beach: forgiving someone for smashing up your future – you have to do it if you don't want to end up crippled by bitterness.'

'It's time to move on.'

'Exactly.'

'For both of us.'

'Yes.'

Sophie squeezes Billy's hand again. 'I've been thinking about things, too and wanted to tell you—'

The door of the ward swings open. 'Billy, you're awake!' It is Pettigrew, the diocesan secretary, with news that, after discussion with Bishop Maureen, Billy is to be retained by the diocese. Sophie shakes his hand politely, curses him under her breath, excuses herself and finds a coffee machine along the corridor. She wanders around the hospital, wondering if she should go home or return to the ward. Maybe Pettigrew will have left. An elderly, unshaven man in a thin blue hospital gown shuffles past her in the corridor. The gown is ill-fitting and his back is bare to the elements. He looks distracted, confused. It is upsetting. She stands outside the entrance to A&E. An ambulance pulls in, sirens wailing, lights flashing. It has only been a few days since she arrived in the same way. It is unnerving. She wanders slowly back to the ward. Pettigrew is saying his goodbyes.

'I was afraid you had gone.' Billy gestures to the chair by the bed.

'I needed some fresh air and coffee.'

'Of course. These places are dehydrating. It's just that, well, there's something I need to say.'

'Me too, but you go first.'

'It's about Lucy.'

'Lucy. Yes . . . yes, of course.'

'She's gone.'

'I'm not sure . . .'

'Even before I recovered consciousness, she'd gone. All those feelings were locked inside because I never had the chance to grieve over losing her. I felt dumped and abandoned. I had to deny she ever existed.'

'And you imploded, emotionally.'

Billy nods. 'As I was coming to, all sorts of people were dancing around in my head, but the one person missing was the very person you'd expect to be there, Lucy. Did Clive tell you where she is buried?'

'No, but I can ask him.'

'Most of all, I would like to visit her grave with you.' Billy squeezes her hand. 'It's time to say goodbye in person.'

'I'd like that, too.' Sophie leans towards him and kisses him on the cheek. 'We've been on one mad journey, you and me.'

'From the moment I walked into your college!'

'We can make a fresh start, both of us.' Sophie squeezes his hand again.

Billy pauses and takes a long breath. 'While I was in the coma so many people and events swam around in my head but only one person dominated my thoughts. Sophie . . .' He holds Sophie's hand firmly. 'I'm going to try and win back Emms.'

'Emms? Oh . . . I thought . . . well, yes, of course.'

'I was in an emotional coma for five decades. I know it's going to be hard to convince her but I have to give it my best shot. I do love her, you know.'

'Yes . . . yes, of course. I know you do.'

'Like you said before the accident, Emms and I have something special. We've got to try and can find it again.'

'Yes,' says Sophie, distantly. 'Yes, I understand.'

'Anyway, all that's in the future. You said you had something to tell me.'

Sophie smiles thinly. 'It wasn't important. You've been through enough today. It's getting late. I'd better get home.'

'Do you have to go?'

'I'm afraid so. Take care, Billy.' She kisses him briefly on the cheek and leaves.

Chapter 48

'Dean can fly as well.'

'Who's Dean?'

'My friend. He flew off the garage roof.'

'That's not flying, though is it?'

David disagrees by nodding vigorously at Clive. 'He had a Spiderman costume on. Was Lucy wearing a costume?'

'I doubt it. And she didn't fly. She only thought she could fly.'

'What made her do that?'

'Drugs.'

'Paracetamol, you mean?'

'No, something much stronger than paracetamol.'

'Mummy has lots of pills in her bathroom cabinet. She says that if she takes enough of them, I might disappear.'

'But you never do.'

'No, but I'd like to be invisible. If no one could see me I'd . . .' David pauses to consider his options.

'He never shuts up.' Sophie gets a word in edgeways.

'Oh, I'm sure Lucy would have been very proud of him.'

'She looks very nice in the pictures,' says David.

'Uncle Roger thought the same. As you can see, he wrote some kind things about her on her gravestone.'

'Which reminds me,' says Sophie. 'Billy wants to visit the cemetery and so do I.'

Clive nods. 'I'll take you there. It's on the Isle of Wight.'

'Nan wrote some words about Lucy too, you know, in a poem,' says David.

'I'd like to read that.'

'No, you wouldn't,' says Sophie.

'It's all about her mummy coming for Christmas,' says David, 'only she never does.'

Before Sophie can stop him, David has sprinted upstairs to Sophie's bedroom. He returns and reads the poem out loud, substituting Milly with Lucy.

If Lucy comes for Christmas
I won't feel so alone
We'll sniff around the strawberry patch
Dig up that juicy bone
Other dogs, they know it's there
I growl and make them run
This bone is for a special dog
Who's lots and lots of fun

If Lucy comes for Christmas
She'll teach me not to bark
At scary shadows in the yard
She doesn't mind the dark
I'll let her doze all afternoon
Upon my snuggly bed
The floor is cold but I don't mind
If I sleep there instead

If Lucy comes for Christmas
I'll need no brand new toys
I'll go to bed on Christmas Eve
And never make a noise
When Santa comes a-calling
We'll wag our tails like mad
And tell him how the kids are good
Even if they're bad

She won't be here for Christmas
It happens every year
I wonder what she's doing
And why she can't be here
Lucy is my mummy
We've never met, you see

But somewhere, far across the world
I hope she thinks of me

The room falls silent.

'You have a wonderful grandmother,' says Clive, at last. 'My uncle would be very touched by those words.'

'Well . . . anyway.' Sophie walks to the kitchen and puts on the kettle. 'Clive kindly came to help me sort out my computer, David, as well as to tell us about your great-grandmother. You're not giving him a chance.'

'Have you got any new games?' says David.

'That's not why he's here!' calls Sophie from the kitchen.

'If your nan is agreeable, I do have a couple.'

'Please, Nan.'

'I thought you liked *World of Witchcraft*,' calls Sophie.

'It's *Warcraft*, Nan, and I've played it a thousand times.'

Sophie shrugs her shoulders.

'Well,' says Clive, 'I have *Stormfall: Age of War* with me.'

'Mark's got that. I love it.'

Sophie returns to the living room and sighs. 'How long will it take to set up?'

'Not long.'

'Enough time for me to make some lunch?'

Clive nods. David scampers up the steep stairs, slipping on the fifth and bruising his shin. He doesn't feel the pain. Clive follows him.

'This is Nan's computer. She needs a new one.'

'Not necessarily.'

'It's so slow.'

'She doesn't need it to be fast.'

Clive boots up Sophie's PC.

'Have you got any grandchildren?' says David.

'I don't even have any children.'

'Are you married?'

'Not any more.'

'Is that because you're a nerd?'

Clive smiles. 'Probably.'

'Nan said that's what you are.'

'She's right.'

'Grandagg died, you know. Nan is very lonely.'

'I would change the "n" to a "v".'

David thinks about it, then nods. 'Mark said he would, too.'

Clive smiles again.

*

Fifteen minutes later, Sophie calls them down for lunch. Clive descends to the living room. David promises to leave the computer screen any minute.

'He's a very determined young man,' says Sophie.

'And perceptive. He was aware of having a close encounter of the nerd kind.'

Sophie puts her hand to her mouth. 'That's my fault. But you're not really a nerd.'

'My former wife would disagree. She left me for someone who couldn't be less of a nerd.'

'I'm so sorry. Her new partner, he's not into dingles and terrabits and stuff like that, then?'

'She doesn't know one end of a memory stick from another.'

'Oh . . .' Sophie grimaces in sympathy.

'I would have coped better had it been another man. I felt humiliated and searched around for the reasons. Maybe I was too fat, too thin, too busy, too lazy. I thought this woman must be incredibly sexy or intelligent.'

'And?'

'She was. On both counts.'

'When did all this happen?'

'Five or six years ago.'

'And no one else has come along since?'

'Sort of, here and there, but I'm always thinking of Uncle Roger. He had a succession of broken relationships after Lucy, fathering a couple of children by different partners. The relationships ended and he never saw them grow up. I don't think he ever got over Lucy. I've always been afraid of making the same mistake.'

'This mother of mine was quite a lady! She left a trail of destruction.' Sophie pauses. 'When I lost Daggert, someone said the best thing I could do was to let the grief pour over me. Resisting it only prolongs the process of healing.'

'Maybe I'm still too angry to get over it.'

'And you feel guilty for being angry, making you more angry.'

'I hadn't looked at it like that.'

'Nerds are allowed a few feelings, too, you know.'

'Maybe. I meant to ask you. Did you ever find out the name of your father?'

Sophie pauses. 'I hardly know you, Clive, but I need to tell someone. Can I trust you?'

'Yes, of course.'

'Only, right now I am nothing short of terrified.'

'Of what?'

'That I am going to be sent to jail for his manslaughter.'

'Bloody hell.'

*

More than half an hour passes before David finally slopes downstairs.

'Now the computer's gone really slow.' He slumps into a chair. 'It started off fine but now, whenever I press a key, the game freezes and the computer starts saying crazy things to me.'

'Oh dear, there must be one of those virus thingies in it,' says Sophie, looking at Clive.

Clive shakes his head. There is the faintest of smiles on his face. 'Let's have a look at it.' They all troop upstairs. David hits the q key in frustration.

'I'm sorry, Dave. I'm afraid I can't do that,' says the voice.

'You see?' He hits the b key.

'Just what do you think you're doing, Dave?'

He hits several keys at once.

'Look, Dave, I can see you're really upset about this. I honestly think you ought to sit down calmly, take a stress pill, and think things over.' Now the voice, slurred and slow, starts singing. 'Dai . . . sy, Dai . . . sy.'

David turns to see his grandmother and Clive, both trying to conceal their laughter. Sophie looks at Clive. 'You're responsible, aren't you?'

'Well, the last thing we want young David to do is end up a nerd,' he says. 'I suggest we all stretch our legs, go for a walk, kick a football around maybe, chat some more. All very dull, I know, but by the time we get back, who knows? The computer might let the young man here start on the next level.'

Chapter 49

Billy tosses and turns, his body bathed in sweat. Since coming round from the coma, his sleep pattern has comprised a series of restless catnaps, wrecked by the rattle of medical equipment echoing down corridors and coughing fits from fellow patients. His blood pressure is dangerously high too, and while some of that can be accounted for by his physical condition, he knows most of it is mental. He is scared, so very scared. Little did he imagine, when he began his 'confessions' on Christmas Day, that he would end up confessing to the manslaughter of a member of the House of Lords: for that is what he is about to do. There is no way he can let Sophie take the blame for Kite's death.

And while he is lying in bed, he can do nothing to persuade Emms that they can still have a future together: a different kind of future. Death would have been so much easier. Emms could shack up with the shelf stacker, if that's what she really wants. Sophie would be free to love again, knowing the truth behind her conception at last. But he didn't die. He is still alive and kicking . . . which in turn reminds him of a previous time, a few lifetimes ago, when he cared passionately about the state of our beautiful game: all just a glorious distraction, taking him away from what really matters, the people in his life.

He glances at his watch. Detective Inspector Oliver Byrne will be here at any minute. Oli gave him the 'background' on Mrs Stonebridge. He will make a full and open confession to Oli over his part in Kite's demise. The last thing he wants is to be sent down for that deceitful bastard but, at all costs, Sophie must not suffer the same fate. With a little help from friends like Oli and a top lawyer, he might end up with a reduced sentence. The chances of rebuilding a marriage with Emms will be slim to negligible but he's got to give it his best shot.

Learning of Lucy's demise has helped him reach this point, as well. He got too close to someone mischievously out of control: whimsical and creative, fascinating and fallible, weak and manipulative. A child of the 1960s, she was a daydreamer who dumped him in a nightmare. But if the only way he can be absolved for what he has done is to take another punishment, so be it. Sophie deserves a future more than him.

It is during one of his catnaps, with these thoughts dancing around his tired head, that he hears a familiar voice.

'What have you been up to now, Shears?'

'Oli, it's good of you to come and see me.'

'Well, you aren't in any state to come and see me.' Oli pulls up a chair next to Billy. 'What's the damage?'

'Three fractured ribs, a broken leg and wrist, severe whiplash, bruises galore and concussion.'

'So . . . a couple of Anadin and you'll be out in the morning. Seriously, Billy, by all accounts you're lucky to be alive. No seat belts and travelling at seventy in a forty-mile zone.'

'That's what I wanted to talk to you about.'

'I believe a witness saw something going on in the car.'

'Yes.' Billy takes deep breath. 'You see—'

'Well, before you go on I think you'll be interested in the results of the post-mortem.'

'And?' Billy's heart races.

'It seems our lordship was pumped up on a cocktail of barbiturates, amphetamines and cocaine. In fact, he was sky high at the moment of collision. The woman with you . . .'

'Sophie. Mrs Sophie Daggert.'

'Yes, well, Mrs Daggert's attempts to stop the driver will be considered the only reasonable course of action given the speed Kite was travelling, especially under the influence. There are no marks on Kite's body to suggest an assault. From what I gather, Mrs Daggert had not met Kite before the evening in question.' Billy nods. 'So there couldn't have been a lovers' tiff or family argument as neither of you was related to the deceased. The inquest will need to go through the formalities but word is that she will have no case to answer.'

'I am so relieved . . . for Sophie.'

'It's another tragic accident brought on by the drugs those hippies sang about so happily in the sixties. Now, what did you want to see me about?'

'Yes, well . . . the post-mortem. I was going to ask you if you had heard anything. You've already answered my questions. You're right, Oli. I am lucky. I am very lucky and relieved to be alive.'

Chapter 50

'Batty' Betty Gibson is not upset about her epithet. In fact, she is proud of it. Now approaching her eightieth year, Betty's regular routine is well known in Beresford. Only the severest of storms will blow her off schedule. Unlike so many who have come to this small coastal town to retire, Betty has always lived on the Isle of Wight. In fact, she has never even been to the mainland. She is adamant that 'There's nothing over there that I haven't seen over here.' A spinster, Betty lives with two cats and a rescued Staffordshire bull terrier whose boisterous character earned him the temporary name of Asbo in the local dogs' home. It stuck. A renowned dog whisperer, Betty soon had Asbo under control and, with him padding obediently by her side, she picks up the usual bunch of flowers from the corner shop. She smiles at a young girl outside, maybe eight years old, waiting for her mother to finish shopping.

'Are you Batty Betty?' says the girl.

'So they say.'

'I've been told never to speak to you.'

'Well, you'd better stop, then.'

'Are you going up to the cemetery?'

'Yes.'

'We're doing that in maths soon. It scares me.'

Betty looks puzzled for a moment, then smiles. 'I think you'll find you're doing symmetry. And in any case, there's nothing to be scared of in a graveyard.'

'Why do you go there?'

'To pray for people.'

'But they're all dead.'

'Not the ones burying family and friends or visiting graves.'

'Is anyone being buried today?'

'I've no idea.'

'What if no one's there?'

'I clean the gravestones.'

'You must know them all by now.'

'I suppose I do.'

'What's your favourite?'

'That's an interesting question. Probably the grave of Edwin Richards, beloved husband of Agnes.'

'What words are on it?'

'Say not good night, but in some brighter clime, bid me good morning.'

'What's a clime?'

'A shortened word for . . .' She is unable to finish. The girl's mother comes out of the shop and snatches her daughter away with a long, threatening stare. Betty is not offended. It happens regularly. She never does anyone any harm. Besides, Beresford is where Betty has lived all her life and, as she says, 'Where I belong, I'm right.'

There are several thousand graves in Beresford Cemetery, some dating back to the mid-1800s. Betty knows most of them by location, name, date and epitaph. However, it is not this knowledge alone that has led to her acquiring such a nickname. In a bag she carries a scrubbing brush and cleaning fluids, for use on gravestones neglected over the decades. Curious bypassers often stop and ask her if she is related to those in the relevant grave. 'We're all one,' she replies. 'Besides, the dead deserve our respect.'

There are surprisingly few visitors in the cemetery today, even though the weather is pleasant enough, if breezy. Squirrels dash between gravestones without fear. Above her, in a tall birch tree, a crow squawks. Betty pauses by a newly reopened grave. Its only previous incumbent was Harold Drake, who died on 14 September 1995. She never knew Harold, but for many years has wondered how long it will be before his wife joins him. What name goes with Harold? Maybe Hilda or Hattie? When the memorial mason updates the stone she will finally find out. Further along the same row she tends the grave of Alice Howe (born 21 September 1889, died 4 August 1923, always loving, always loved). She is about to leave her posy of flowers in the small vase at the foot of the gravestone when she spots a party arrive at another plot some fifty yards away.

311

She is shocked. That's where they laid the teenager, young Lucy Pitcher, in 1969. The grave is dirty and Betty regularly cleans it. In all the years, no flowers have ever been left for the poor girl. She remembers reading about her death in the local paper: a very sad story. Now, out of the blue, three adults and a young boy have arrived to pay their respects. Why now? What has happened? She edges closer.

One of the men is taller than the other: he is older, more distinguished and walks with a limp. He is wearing a clerical collar. Maybe he is leading a small service. The woman looks younger and is dressed impeccably. The other man is younger again but seems relatively casual, a little detached from the others.

Encouraged by the woman, the young boy steps forward, opens up a piece of paper and begins reading. Betty edges close enough to overhear his poem.

Christmas Day in heaven
I wonder what it's like
It must go on and on because
In heaven there's no night

Bulging stockings three miles high
Gifts galore to open
Up there toys don't break at all
At least that's what I'm hoping

I'd like a T. Rex robot and
A plastic scuttling bug
A blast pad missile launcher
And a super hero mug

Remote-controlled tarantulas
To really frighten Mum
Giant whoopee cushions, hidden
Under Daddy's bum

Christmas Day in heaven
Grandagg will be there
Looking like he used to
They'll give him back his hair

But most of all I'd like to see
Up high above the throng
No longer made of lifeless wood
But now with sinews strong

A mighty snow-white stallion
Henry, born again
A girl who lived and died too young
Taking up his reins

Christmas Day in heaven
Just cannot be complete
Without a special moment when
At last two people meet

I'd give up all my presents
Yes, every single one
If I could see my nan with arms
Wrapped firmly round her mum

When the boy has finished, he steps back. The woman hugs him warmly. For a few moments there is silence. The priest tries to say something but is overcome with emotion. Tears stream down his face as he attaches an envelope to the gravestone. He can't be the usual hired-in dog collar, considers Betty. The woman is crying, too. Young Lucy Pitcher must have meant something to both of them. The other man is not crying but, head bowed, is still in some emotional distress. None of them seems to know what to do next. Only rarely does Betty intrude on personal grief. Today, however, the compulsion to do so is overwhelming.

'I never met Lucy but I know a little bit about her, from the newspaper,' she says, placing her posy in the graveside vase. 'I'm Betty, by the way. I'd like to say a few words, if I may.'

The priest nods.

Betty stands in the middle of the group. 'We remember Lucy. We rejoice at those memories, however long ago they were, however joyful, however painful. And now we do the hardest thing of all. We release her.' She looks up to see the priest weeping uncontrollably.

'Thank you, Betty,' he says, recovering his composure. 'That was perfect.'

'Yes, thank you,' says the woman. 'You came along at just the right time. We're going for a coffee. Please join us.'

'I don't want to interfere.'

'You're only interfering in the way an angel interferes.'

Betty smiles. 'You are very kind but my job is done. I really need to be getting home.'

A few minutes later she watches from a distance as the small party wends its way down to the car park.

'Well, that's a surprise,' she murmurs. She had presumed the priest and the woman were partners. But they aren't. The priest is walking ahead, talking to the small boy. The woman tucks her hand into the arm of the other man and leans her head on his shoulder.

When the party is safely out of sight, Betty returns to the grave. The envelope on the tombstone is not sealed and the words inside are haunting and beautiful. They talk of a time of confession, a 'dying voice' and, in a moment of fury, the planting of a seed watered by the writer's tears. The words echo a thousand psalms and hymns of ages past. There are biblical allusions, too, that Betty knows well. She glances at the foot of the page. To her surprise these are the lyrics of a song by Bob Dylan. Isn't he that one with the gravelly voice, a big attraction on the island all those years ago? She has never had much time for his music but there must be more to him than she thought. She will look up 'Every Grain of Sand' when she gets home.

'Come on, Asbo.' Betty returns the paper to the envelope. As usual, she had come to the cemetery to help anyone in need but it has been a morning of surprises. At an untended grave, a young boy has read a poem to a dead relative he has never met, laden with ironic wit and delivered with passion. A clergyman has been so overcome by emotion he has hardly been able to speak. And in her own mind the words and images of a song she has yet to hear have already moved her to tears. Yes, a morning of surprises. A morning of new beginnings.